the
condition

also by jennifer haigh

Mrs. Kimble
Baker Towers

the
condition

a novel

JENNIFER HAIGH

HARPER ● PERENNIAL

NEW YORK ● LONDON ● TORONTO ● SYDNEY ● NEW DELHI ● AUCKLAND

HarperCollins books may be purchased for educational, business, or sales promotional use. For information, please write: Special Markets Department, HarperCollins Publishers, 10 East 53rd Street, New York, NY 10022.

A portion of chapter 1 of this work was originally published, in a slightly different form, in *Ploughshares*.

FIRST INTERNATIONAL EDITION

Designed by William Ruoto

Library of Congress Cataloging-in-Publication Data is available upon request.

ISBN: 978-0-06-168591-0

08 09 10 11 12 ID/RRD 10 9 8 7 6 5 4 3 2 1

In nature, all is useful, all is beautiful.
—ralph waldo emerson, "Art"

To regret deeply is to live afresh.
—henry david thoreau, *Journals*

1976

the captain's house

Summer comes late to Massachusetts. The gray spring is frosty, unhurried: wet snow on the early plantings, a cold lesson for optimistic gardeners, for those who have not learned. Chimneys smoke until Memorial Day. Then, all at once, the ceiling lifts. The sun fires, scorching the muddy ground.

At Cape Cod the rhythm is eternal, unchanging. Icy tides smash the beaches. Then cold ones. Then cool. The bay lies warming in the long days. Blue-lipped children brave the surf.

They opened the house the third week in June, the summer of the bicentennial, and of Paulette's thirty-fifth birthday. She drove from Concord to the train station in Boston, where her sister was waiting, then happily surrendered the wheel. Martine was better in traffic. She'd been better in school, on the tennis court; for two years straight she'd been the top-ranked singles player at Wellesley. Now, at thirty-eight, Martine was a *career girl*, still a curiosity in those days, at least in her family. She worked for an advertising agency on Madison Avenue—doing what, precisely, Paulette was not certain. Her sister lived alone in New York City, a prospect she found terrifying. But Martine had always been fearless.

The station wagon was packed with Paulette's children and their belongings. Billy and Gwen, fourteen and twelve, rode in the backseat, a pile of beach towels between them. Scotty, nine and so excited about going to the Cape that he was nearly insufferable, had been banished to the rear.

"God, would you look at this?" Martine downshifted, shielding her eyes from the sun. The traffic had slowed to a crawl. The big American engines idled loudly, the stagnant air rich with fumes. The Sagamore Bridge was still half a mile away. "It gets worse every year. Too many goddamned cars."

A giggle from the backseat, Gwen probably. Paulette frowned. She disapproved of cursing, especially by women, especially in front of children.

"And how was the birthday?" Martine asked. "I can't believe *la petite* Paulette is thirty-five. Did you do anything special?"

Her tone was casual; she may not have known it was a tender subject. Like no birthday before, this one had unsettled Paulette. The number seemed somehow significant. She'd been married fifteen years, but only now did she feel like a matron.

"Frank took me into town. We had a lovely dinner." She didn't mention that he'd also reserved a room at the Ritz, a presumptuous gesture that irritated her. Like all Frank's presents, it was a gift less for her than for himself.

"Will he grace us with his presence this year?"

Paulette ignored the facetious tone. "Next weekend, maybe, if he can get away. If not, then definitely for the Fourth."

"He's teaching this summer?"

"No," Paulette said carefully. "He's in the lab." She always felt defensive discussing Frank's work with Martine, who refused to understand that he wasn't only a teacher but also a scientist. (*Molecular developmental biology*, Paulette said when anyone asked what he studied. This usually discouraged further questions.) Frank's lab worked year-round, seven days a week. Last summer, busy writing a grant proposal, he hadn't come to the Cape at all. Martine seemed to take this as a personal slight, though she'd never seemed to enjoy his company. *He's an academic*, she'd said testily. *He gets the summers off. Isn't that the whole point?* It was clear from the way she pronounced the word what she thought of *academics*. Martine saw in Frank the same flaws Paulette did: his obsession with his work, his smug delight in his own intellect. She simply didn't forgive him, as Paulette—as women generally—always had. Frank had maintained for years that

Martine hated him, a claim Paulette dismissed. *Don't be silly. She's very fond of you.* (Why tell such a lie? Because Martine was family, and she *ought* to be fond of Frank. Paulette had firm ideas, back then, of how things ought to be.)

In Truro the air was cooler. Finally the traffic thinned. Martine turned off the highway and onto the No Name Road, a narrow lane that had only recently been paved. Their father had taught the girls, as children, to recite the famous line from Thoreau: *Cape Cod is the bared and bended arm of Massachusetts. The shoulder is at Buzzard's Bay; the elbow at Cape Mallebarre; the wrist at Truro; and the sandy fist at Provincetown.*

Remembering this, Paulette felt a stab of tenderness for her father. Everett Drew had made his living as a patent attorney, and viewed ideas as property of the most precious kind. In his mind Thoreau was the property of New England, of Concord, Massachusetts, perhaps even particularly of the Drews.

"Is Daddy feeling better?" Paulette asked. "I've been worried about his back." Martine had just returned from Florida, where their parents had retired and Ev was now recovering from surgery. Paulette visited when she could, but this was no substitute for Sunday dinners at her parents' house, the gentle rhythm of family life, broken now, gone forever.

"He misses you," said Martine. "But he made do with me."

Paulette blinked. She was often blindsided by how acerbic her sister could be, how in the middle of a pleasant conversation Martine could deliver a zinger that stopped her cold: the backhanded compliment, the ripe apple with the razor inside. When they were children she'd often crept up behind Paulette and pulled her hair for no reason. It wasn't her adult life, alone in a big city, that had made Martine prickly. She had always been that way.

They turned off the No Name Road onto a rutted path. It being June, the lane was rugged, two deep tire tracks grown in between with grass. By the end of summer, it would be worn smooth. The Captain's House was set squarely at the end of it, three rambling stories covered in shingle. A deep porch wrapped around three sides.

As she had every summer of her life, Paulette sprang out of the car first, forgetting for a moment her children in the backseat, Scotty whiny and fidgeting in the rear. For a split second she was a girl again, taking inventory, checking that all was as she'd left it the year before. Each member of the family performed some version of this ritual. Her brother Roy rushed first to the boathouse, Martine to the sandy beach.

But it was the cottage itself that called to Paulette, the familiar stairs and hallways, the odd corners and closets and built-in cupboards where she'd hidden as a child—the tiniest of the Drew cousins, a little Houdini—in games of hide-and-seek. The Captain's House, the family called it, in memory of Clarence Hubbard Drew, Paulette's great-great-grandfather, a sailor and whaler. Clarence had hired a distinguished architect, a distant cousin of Ralph Waldo Emerson. The house had the graceful lines of the shingle style; it was built for comfort rather than grandeur. A house with wide doors and windows, a house meant to be flung open. On summer nights a cross breeze whipped through the first floor, a cool tunnel of ocean-smelling air.

Paulette stood a moment staring at the facade, the house's only architectural flourish: three diamond-shaped windows placed just above the front door. The windows were set in staggered fashion, rising on the diagonal like stairs, a fact Paulette, as a child, had found significant. She was the lowest window, Roy the highest. The middle window was Martine.

She noticed, then, a car parked in the sandy driveway that curved behind the house. Her brother's family had already arrived.

"Will you look at that?" said Martine, coming up behind her. "Anne has a new Mercedes."

Paulette, herself, would not have noticed. In such matters she deferred to her husband, who was partial to Saabs and Volvos.

Martine smirked. "Roy has come up in the world."

"Martine, hush." Paulette refused to let her sister spoil this moment, the exhilarating first minutes of summer, the joyful return.

They unloaded the car: brown paper bags from the grocery store in Orleans, the oblong case that held Gwen's telescope. Tied to the roof were suitcases and Billy's new ten-speed, an early birthday present. Martine stood on her toes to unfasten them.

"I'll do it," said Billy, untying the ropes easily, his fingers thick as a man's. He had sailed since he was a toddler and was a specialist at complicated knots. Not quite fourteen, he towered over his mother. He had been a beautiful child, and would be an exceptionally handsome man; but that summer Paulette found him difficult to look at. His new maturity was everywhere: his broad shoulders, his coarsening voice, the blond peach fuzz on his upper lip. Normal, natural, necessary changes—yet somehow shocking, embarrassing to them both.

They followed the gravel path, loaded down with groceries, and nudged open the screen door. A familiar scent greeted them, a smell Paulette's memory labeled *Summer*. It was the smell of her own childhood, complex and irreducible, though she could identify a few components: sea air; Murphy's oil soap; cedar closets that had stood closed the long winter, the aged wood macerating in its own resins, waiting for the family to return.

Paulette put down the groceries in the airless kitchen, wondering why her sister-in-law hadn't thought to open the windows. Billy carried the bags up the creaking stairs. The house had nine bedrooms, a few so small that only a child could sleep there without suffering claustrophobia. The third-floor rooms, stifling in summertime, were rarely used. The same was true of the tiny alcove off the kitchen, which had once been the cook's quarters. Since her marriage Paulette had slept in a sunny front bedroom—Fanny's Room, according to the homemade wooden placard hanging on the door. Fanny Porter had been a school chum of Paulette's grandmother; she'd been dead thirty years or more, but thanks to a long-ago Drew cousin, who'd made the signs as a rainy-day project at the behest of some governess, the room would forever be known as Fanny's.

The sleeping arrangements at the house were the same each year. Roy and Anne took the Captain's Quarters at the rear of the house, the biggest room, with the best view. Frank, if he came, would grouse about this, but Paulette didn't mind. *Someone* had to sleep in the Captain's Quarters, to take her father's place at the dinner table. That it was Roy, the eldest son, seemed correct, the natural order of things. Correct too that Gwen shared prime accommodations, with Roy's

two daughters, on the sleeping porch, where Martine and Paulette
and their Drew cousins had slept as girls. The porch was screened on
three sides; even on the hottest nights, ocean breezes swept through.
Across the hall was the Lilac Room, named for its sprigged wallpa-
per; and Martine's favorite, the Whistling Room, whose old windows
hummed like a teakettle when the wind came in from the west. Billy
and Scotty took the wood-paneled downstairs bedroom—the Bunk
House—where Roy and the boy cousins had once slept. It was this
sameness that Paulette treasured, the summer ritual unchanging, the
illusion of permanence.

THAT AFTERNOON they packed a picnic basket and piled into the
car. Their own bit of coastline—the family called it Mamie's Beach—
had been the natural choice when the children were small. Now that
the boys had discovered body-surfing, the rougher waters of the National Seashore held greater appeal. For this brief trip Paulette took the
wheel, with a confidence she never felt in Boston. She loved driving
the Cape roads, familiar, gently winding; she could have driven them
in her sleep. Scotty claimed the passenger seat after a tussle with his
brother. ("Billy, darling, just let him have it, will you?" she'd pleaded.)
After sitting in the car all morning, her youngest was wild as a cat. In
this state Paulette found him ungovernable and rather frightening.
Her only hope was to turn him loose outdoors, where he could run
and roar the whole afternoon.

   She sat on a blanket in the shade of an umbrella, *My Ántonia*
lying open in her lap. She'd brought *Lord of the Flies* for Billy, who
would read his daily chapter without complaint, and *Little Women* for
Gwen, who would not. Paulette believed firmly in summer reading,
and because she'd loved the Alcott books as a girl, she couldn't fathom
why Gwen did not. Seeing Orchard House had been the greatest thrill
of Paulette's twelve-year-old life. "That's where Louisa grew up, right
here in Concord," she'd told her daughter. This proved to be insuf-
ficient enticement. After a week of cajoling, Gwen still hadn't opened
the book.

Paulette shifted slightly, moving nearer the umbrella. Its positioning had been the subject of much discussion. Her sister-in-law, Anne, coated in baby oil, wanted as much sun as possible; Paulette needed complete shade. She'd been cautioned by visiting her parents in Palm Beach, a town populated by leathery retirees who lived their lives poolside, their bodies lined in places she'd never imagined could wrinkle.

Martine stood back from the discussion, laughing at them both. "You make quite a picture," she said. Paulette wore a large straw hat and, over her swimsuit, striped beach pajamas, their wide legs flapping like flags in the wind. Anne wore a white bikini more suited to a teenager. The bikini was made of triangles. Two inverted ones made up the bottom. Two smaller ones, attached by string, formed the top.

Paulette had known Anne most of her life. Roy had met her his final year at Harvard, when Paulette was fourteen, and she had fallen in love with Anne too. They were as close as sisters—closer, certainly, than Paulette and Martine. Paulette admired her sister, but couldn't confide in her. Martine seemed to find the world so easy. She had no patience for someone who did not.

Anne lit a cigarette. After giving birth to her second daughter, she'd taken up smoking to regain her figure. Charlotte was twelve now, and Anne, so thin her ribs showed, still smoked.

They watched as Martine joined the boys in the surf. In the ocean she was a daredevil. Paulette got nervous just watching her. Martine waiting for her moment, her slick head bobbing; Martine diving fearlessly into the waves.

"You can relax now," Anne said, chuckling. "Auntie Lifeguard is on duty."

"That's the problem. She'll get them all killed." Paulette shifted slightly, to avoid the streaming smoke. "When is Roy coming?"

"Friday morning. He's dying to put the boat in the water." Anne rolled onto her stomach, then untied her bikini top. "Can you grease my back?"

Paulette took the baby oil Anne offered and squirted it into her hands. Anne's skin felt hot and papery, dry to the touch.

"I don't know if Frank will make it this year," said Paulette. *I don't know if I want him to*, she nearly added. At home they coexisted peacefully, more or less, though Frank spent so much time at the lab that they rarely saw each other. At the Cape they'd have to spend long days together. *What will we talk about all day?* she wondered. *What on earth will we* do?

She knew what Frank would want to do. His sexual demands overwhelmed her. If he'd asked less often, she might have felt bad about refusing; but if Frank had his way, they would make love every night. After fifteen years of marriage, it seemed excessive. Paulette sometimes wondered whether other couples did it so often, but she had no one to ask. Anne didn't shrink from personal questions, but she was Roy's wife. Certain things, Paulette truly didn't want to know.

Married sex: the familiar circuit of words and caresses and sensations, shuffled perhaps, but in the end always the same. The repetition wore on her. Each night when Frank reached for her she felt a hot flicker of irritation, then tamped it down. She willed herself to welcome him, to forget every hurt and disappointment, to hold herself open to all he was and wasn't. The effort exhausted her.

Years later she would remember those marital nights with tenderness: for the brave young man Frank had been, and for her young self, the wounded and stubborn girl. She'd had a certain idea about lovemaking, gleaned from Hollywood or God knew where, that a man's desire should be specific to her, triggered by her unique face or voice or—better—some intangible quality of her spirit; and that of all the women in the world, only she should be able to arouse him. And there lay the problem. Frank's passion, persistent and inexhaustible, seemed to have little to do with her. He came home from work bursting with it, though they hadn't seen or spoken to each other in many hours. "I've been thinking about this all day," he sometimes whispered as he moved inside her.

This.

That one little word had the power to freeze her. Not, "I've been thinking about *you*." But, "I've been thinking about *this*."

It would seem comical later, how deeply this upset her. Like so many of her quarrels with Frank, it seemed ridiculous in hindsight. Once, early on, she had tried to explain it to Anne: *Frank loves sex. If he hadn't married me, he'd be having sex with someone else.*

So? Anne said.

For me it's different, Paulette insisted. *I love Frank. If I hadn't met him, I never would have had sex with anyone.*

It wasn't true, of course, but she wanted it to be. Her ideas were fixed, impossibly idealistic: Frank was the only man she could possibly have loved. Later this would seem a childish notion, but times had been different then. Paulette, her best friend, Tricia Boone, her closest girlfriends at Wellesley—all had thought, or pretended to think, this way.

Frank, meanwhile, did not share in this illusion. She knew that he looked at other women. A certain type attracted him, large breasted and voluptuous, a figure nothing like hers. When they went out together, to the symphony or the theater, Paulette found herself scanning the crowd, looking for the women he'd be drawn to. She was nearly always right; Frank proved it by ogling them right under her nose. He'd ruined her birthday dinner by flirting shamelessly with the waitress. That night, at home—she declined the hotel suite—he was surprised when she wouldn't let him touch her. *What's the matter?* he asked, genuinely mystified. *Didn't we have a good time?* She could have told him (but didn't) that he'd made her feel invisible. By then she didn't want to talk to him. She didn't want him anywhere near her.

They were apart twelve hours a day, six days a week. In that time, how many nubile young students did he imagine undressing? When, in a weak moment, she'd admitted her concerns, Frank had merely laughed. *Honey, there* are *no pretty girls. It's MIT.*

This was not the answer she'd hoped for.

Recently her worries had grown sharper. The department had hired a new secretary. Now, when Paulette called Frank at work, a young female voice answered the phone. Paulette had done research: the secretary, Betsy Baird, was blond and attractive. Was it her presence that fired Frank's libido?

I've been thinking about this all day.

"Here are the girls," Anne said. Gwen and her cousins, Mimi and Charlotte, had come in a separate car. Sixteen that spring, Mimi had insisted on driving, proud of her new license.

The three girls trekked down the beach, towels draping their shoulders. Mimi led the way—tall and coltish, with her father's dark eyes and patrician nose. Charlotte, blond and freckled, resembled her mother. Gwen brought up the rear, her little legs scrambling. She was the same age as Charlotte, but a head shorter. Next to her cousins she looked tiny as a doll.

Paulette watched them. "Charlotte certainly shot up this year," she observed.

"Yes, she did." Anne turned over onto her back. "It's done wonders for her tennis game. I think she takes after Aunt Martine."

The girls laid their towels high on the dunes, away from their mothers. The breeze carried their laughter as they stripped down to swimsuits. Mimi wore a triangle bikini similar to her mother's; but on her the effect was different. The rear triangle scarcely covered her rounded bottom. Her breasts, high and firm, peeked out the sides of the top.

"My daughter," Anne said, laughing, as though she'd read Paulette's mind. "Roy's going to have a heart attack when he sees that bikini. If he had it his way, he'd never let her out of the house."

Paulette watched her niece in wonderment. Mimi was the first infant she'd ever held. In college then, she was overwhelmed by a feeling she couldn't name. She'd loved everything about Mimi—her baby smell, the dense, rounded weight of her. Holding her, Paulette felt a knot low in her belly, an ache between her legs. The feeling was nearly sexual, shocking in its intensity: *I want this. I want one.*

She had adored her niece for sixteen years. Now she was reluctant to look at the girl. Mimi with everything ahead of her—love, discovery, every gift and possibility. Mimi's happiness lay in the future; Paulette's, in the past. She was stunned by her own meanness. *I love this child*, she reminded herself. How ungenerous, how unseemly and futile to long for what was past.

Anne lit another cigarette. "It's awful. I have this beautiful daughter, and my whole body is sagging by the minute. I feel like a shriveled old hag."

(Years later Paulette would marvel at the memory: how old they'd felt at thirty-five, how finished and depleted. *We were still young and beautiful*, she would realize far too late.)

"So don't I," she agreed. "I'm not ready. I don't want Gwen to grow up, not ever."

Anne chuckled. "I wouldn't start worrying yet. It looks like she has a long way to go."

They watched as Gwen charged into the surf. She wore a red tank suit with a pert ruffle around the hips. Her chest was perfectly flat, her belly rounded like a little girl's.

Anne frowned. "She's twelve, right? Same as Charlotte?"

"Older, actually. She'll be thirteen in September."

For a long time Anne was silent.

"Funny," she said finally, "how these things work."

THAT NIGHT they grilled hamburgers on the porch. Paulette squelched a wave of panic as Martine showed Billy how to light the charcoal. "Relax, will you?" said Martine. "He's a big boy. He'll do fine."

"You're right, of course. Frank is always telling me not to hover." Paulette said this lightly, hiding her irritation. How like Martine to instruct her on child rearing, an expert despite having no children of her own.

She spread a checkered cloth over the picnic table. This was her favorite part of the summer, these long, manless evenings. The children amused each other, leaving her free to drink wine with Anne and Martine. Had Frank and Roy been there—holding court on the patio, talking past each other, airing their opinions about nothing too interesting—the women would have retreated to the stuffy kitchen. They'd have turned the dinner into more work than was necessary, simply to have something to do.

That year Mimi had taken over the kitchen, mixing the salad, husking ears of corn. Watching her—fully dressed now—hand the platters to Billy, Paulette remembered the triangle bikini, the miserable wash of envy she'd felt. The feeling had dissipated completely. As if sensing this, Mimi flashed her a shy smile, filling her with tenderness.

"What a helpful daughter you have," she told Anne.

"Billy's a good influence. Trust me, she never does this at home."

In that moment, warmed by the wine, Paulette was proud of the children they'd raised. In the fall Billy would go away to Pearse; in a few years he would bring home girlfriends, pretty girls like Mimi. He would fall in love. Watching him, she was struck by all that was delightful about this. Falling in love with Frank was the most thrilling thing that had ever happened to her. It seemed tragic to experience this just once, at the age of nineteen, and never again. Raising her children would give her a second chance at living those best years. A second and third and fourth chance.

"It's all so exciting," she told Anne, so moved she could barely speak. "The children growing up. It's a wonderful time." For years the summers had blended into each other, each much like the last. But now every summer would bring new developments. Mimi, then Billy, starting college, getting married, having children of their own. Of course there was sadness, the depressing reality of aging. (Anne: *I feel like a shriveled old hag.*) But Paulette refused to feel as Anne did. She had been the pretty one in her family, a distinction she'd enjoyed her whole life. Now she would cede the title gracefully. Watching Mimi clear the table, she was proud of her own generosity.

Good for you, sweetheart, she thought. *It's your turn.*

Inside the house, the telephone rang, a shrill intrusion. The distant world seemed perfectly irrelevant. Everyone she needed was right here, close enough to touch.

"Paulette," Martine called through the open window. "Frank's on the phone."

"Daddy!" Scott cried. "I want to talk to Daddy!"

"In a minute," Paulette said, rising. "Let Mother talk to him first."

She hurried into the kitchen. The house's only telephone, a rotary model heavy as a bowling ball, sat on the counter. "Frank?" She drained the wine from her glass. "Is everything all right?"

"Hi." He sounded rushed, agitated. "Listen, I only have a minute, but I wanted to tell you. I think I can get down there this weekend." She heard the clack of a typewriter. Frank was always doing two things at once.

Are you there alone? she wanted to ask.

"What are you typing?" she said instead.

Mimi came into the kitchen then, loaded down with dishes. *Excuse me*, she mouthed. She placed the salad bowl in the sink.

"More revisions on the paper. Sorry. I need to get this thing out the door."

Mimi bent over to scrape the plates into the trash. Paulette stared at her suntanned legs. The denim shorts—she hadn't noticed, until then, quite how short they were—rode up dramatically, revealing the bottom crease of her buttocks. For a moment Paulette saw the girl as Frank would see her. She felt her throat tighten.

"Are you still there?" Frank asked. "I'll try to make it down there on Friday. It won't be easy, but I think I can swing it."

No. Paulette felt again the wave of sickness she'd felt watching Mimi at the beach, sour and corrosive, sharp as glass. Her family, summer at the Cape, her love for this dear girl: these were precious things, and fragile. Too delicate to be placed in Frank's careless hands.

"Dear, I know you're very busy. You don't have to come if it's too difficult. I shouldn't have pressured you."

"That's okay. I want to." He lowered his voice. "I'm not good at sleeping alone."

More typing, a bell sounding; he had reached the end of a line.

ENDLESS DAY. The blond expanse of the National Seashore: the sand fine as sugar; coarse tails of sea grass undulating in the wind. The days were cut along a template. Each morning sandwiches were made, a basket packed. Damp swimsuits were retrieved from the line. For the rest of her life, Paulette would remember these summers. Would long to return there, to the quiet richness of those days, the life of her family unfolding like a flower, ripening as it was meant to, all things in their proper time.

One morning, the car loaded, she noticed a child missing. "Gwen!" she called. "Where's Gwen?"

"Out back," Scotty said.

Paulette found her curled up on a chaise longue on the porch, still in her nightgown. Paulette hadn't seen her since breakfast. With three adults and five children in the house, Gwen had gotten lost in the shuffle.

"Gwen? Get dressed, darling. We're going to the beach."

"I'm not going." Her cheeks were red, her mouth set. Paulette had seen this look before, after an altercation with her brothers, an unfair reprimand. It was a look that meant trouble.

"Gwen, don't be silly. Everybody's waiting. Mimi, and Charlotte."

"I don't want to go."

"What's the matter?" She laid a hand on her daughter's forehead to check for a fever, only half joking. Gwen was crazy about the beach. At the end of the day, shivering, sunburned, she clamored for an extra half hour. Paulette often resorted to blackmail—strawberry ice cream at the general store in town—to get her to leave.

Gwen shrugged her mother's hand away. "I hate the beach. It's no fun anymore."

Paulette frowned. Gwen had a sunny disposition: more extroverted than Billy, who was prone to moody silences; less rambunctious than Scotty. She had always been the easy one.

"I hate Charlotte," she said vehemently. "She won't even go in the water."

"Well, you can swim with your brothers. And Aunt Martine."

"I hate my bathing suit," she said, her chin trembling.

Paulette sat next to her. "What happened? You liked it a week ago." They had shopped for the suit together, making a day of it, lunch and shopping at Filene's downtown. Charmed by the little ruffle, Gwen had chosen the suit herself.

"I hate the stupid ruffle," she said now. "I look like a big baby."

"Sweetheart." Paulette chose her words carefully. She'd known this conversation was coming; she just hadn't imagined it would happen so soon. "Are you upset because Charlotte looks so different all of a sudden?"

Gwen would not answer.

"It's strange for you," she said gently. "To see Charlotte growing up."

"But I'm *older*. Her birthday isn't until *December*." Gwen's face reddened. "It isn't fair."

"I know. It isn't." Paulette brushed the hair back from Gwen's forehead. "When I was your age, I was the smallest girl in my class. I came back to school in the fall and it seemed that all my friends were entirely different people. They were taller, and their figures were changing. And I hadn't changed at all. I was exactly the same."

Gwen stared up at her, her eyes rimmed with red.

"Back then they called it being a late bloomer. It took me a little longer, but it all happened eventually. And when it did I was very glad." Paulette drew her close and Gwen settled in. She was a cuddly child, more affectionate than her brothers. The difference, Paulette supposed, between boys and girls.

"I know what we can do. Let's get you a new bathing suit. A two-piece, like Charlotte's. We can drive into Provincetown tonight."

"Okay," Gwen said grudgingly.

Paulette stood and held out her hand. "Come on. Everybody's waiting." *Thank God that's over*, she thought.

For girls it was never simple. Later, riding in the car, shading her eyes against the morning glare, Paulette thought of her own puberty. All these years later, the memory still pained her: the interminable months of waiting, her failure so conspicuous, displayed for all to see. In her long, sunny childhood she'd never felt envy, but at puberty it filled her every waking hour. She envied ceaselessly, obsessively, the few classmates who, heaven knew why, seemed to transform overnight. She'd hated them blindly, indiscriminately; hated even Marjorie Tuttle, her dear good friend. Now, as a mother, she remembered those girls with compassion, knowing they'd faced their own difficulties: attention from older boys, grown men even; foolish adults like Frank who couldn't distinguish between a woman and a child. Once, twice, she'd caught him ogling girls barely out of grammar school. *I'm not a pervert*, he insisted when she brought this to his attention. *How am I supposed to know?* She had to admit, it was a fair question. The girls had adult-looking bodies, and dressed to show them: miniskirts, tight T-shirts, sometimes with nothing underneath. She'd been lucky—hadn't she?—to come of age in more modest times. She recalled how, at Wellesley, they'd worn raincoats over their whites as they crossed campus to the tennis court. Those rules had existed to keep girls safe and comfortable. And, it seemed to her, to make things more equitable. Proper clothing kept the buxom from feeling conspicuous, and preserved the vanity of the shapeless and the plump. How cruel to be a girl now, with no such safeguards in place. To be exposed to adult reactions no child was equipped to handle, the lust and ridicule and pity, the creeping shame.

God help Gwen, she thought. God help us all.

The ferry was crowded with people: the young in college sweat-shirts and denim cutoffs, showing suntanned legs; the old in windbreakers and clip-on sunglasses, comfortable shoes and Bermuda shorts. There were a few windblown men, like Frank McKotch, in business attire; but most wore chinos and golf shirts. They toted bicycles and fishing tackle, suitcases, duffel bags. A group of longhairs carried tents in backpacks. The whole crowd inhaled the ferry smell—a potent blend of fish and diesel—and shouted to be heard over the engines. On every face, in every voice, a palpable elation: *We're almost there! We're going to the Cape!*

Frank watched them in mute puzzlement. He witnessed the same phenomenon each summer in his wife and children, his decrepit in-laws. Even his sour sister-in-law displayed a brief burst of enthusiasm. The Drews considered Cape Cod their birthright. Summer after godblessed summer, they did not tire of strolling its beaches, sailing its shores, guzzling its chowder. For heaven's sake, what else was summer *for*?

He could think of a hundred answers to this question. To him the Cape meant crowds and traffic, glacial waters, unreliable weather that often as not left you marooned indoors with a crew of whiny, disappointed children and restless, irritable adults. What, exactly, was the attraction? For once, he was stumped.

It was a sensation he had seldom felt. Frank read widely in all the sciences, in English and in German; he followed the latest developments in theoretical physics, the emerging field of string theory, with rapt interest. He believed, fundamentally, that all things were knowable, that the world could be understood. But when it came to the Cape, he simply *didn't get it*. Summer after summer, he landed at Provincetown with the same deflated feeling: *Okay, now what?*

He supposed it came down to upbringing. Didn't everything? His wife had spent half her childhood on the water, or near it. She could swim, sail, dive like a porpoise. Frank was twenty before he caught his first glimpse of the ocean, on a road trip to Atlantic City with some buddies from Penn State. His recollections were vague, clouded by alcohol: White Castle hamburgers, girls in bathing suits, cans of beer smuggled onto the beach.

The ocean wasn't the point, Paulette reminded him each summer. What mattered was getting The Family together. But Frank had never gotten too excited about anybody's relatives, his own included. Since his marriage, he'd made exactly three trips back to the Pennsylvania town where his father still lived. The place paralyzed him with sadness. The company houses, the black smoke of the steel mills. His mother had died early and horribly, a metastatic breast cancer. Grief had turned his father stern and silent, or perhaps that was simply his nature. A dour old man, fatalistically pious, plodding through the years in mute patience, waiting for his life to be over. Frank couldn't imagine him any other way.

The family he'd married into seemed glamorous by comparison. They had attended the best schools, traveled widely; in youth they'd been cherished and guided and subsidized in ways Frank had not. He didn't resent these distinctions. On the contrary: he wanted to be absorbed by the Drews, to become like them. He was prepared to love Roy and Martine, old Everett and Mamie, the army of blue-eyed cousins converging in Truro every summer (Drew cousins only: no one invited or even spoke of Mamie's tribe, the ragtag Broussards). But Frank—from a part of the world where people pronounced their *r*'s—wasn't a Drew and never would be; if he'd had any illusions on that score, they'd been shattered long ago. Now Frank counted himself lucky to be free of the family neuroses, which seemed congenital: Paulette's prudery, Martine's bitterness, Roy's laziness and self-importance; their unconscious sense of entitlement and absurd reverence for the Drew name, which no longer meant a thing to the rest of the world, if it ever had. To Frank, who was smarter and more industrious, who'd busted his ass for every break he'd ever gotten, the success of a guy like Roy Drew was insulting.

The horn sounded. Dieseling loudly, the boat approached the dock. Frank rose and waited; there was no sense in fighting the disorderly mass of humanity scrambling to disembark. Finally he stepped onto the gangplank and spotted Paulette waving from the crowd.

"Frank! Over here!" She wore a navy blue dress that fit close at her waist. Her bare arms were white as milk. Several heads turned to look at her. This happened often, and still excited him. *My wife*, he thought proudly. *My wife.*

"Hi," he said, scooping her into his arms. She smelled of the outdoors, sea air and Coppertone. "Where are the offspring?"

"I told Martine we'd meet them at the beach."

"I have a better idea." Frank kissed her long on the mouth. "Let's go somewhere."

"Don't be silly." She stepped back, smoothing the dress over her hips. "Everybody's waiting for us. Scotty's out of his mind. Daddy, Daddy. It's all I've been hearing for days."

She handed him the keys to the wagon. Frank always drove when they were together; he hadn't been her passenger in years, not since the hair-raising spring when he'd taught her to drive. It was an arrangement they both preferred. Sitting in the passenger seat, he made Paulette nervous, and the feeling was mutual. Her style was to roar down the highway like an ambulance driver, slamming on the brakes at every yellow light. A year before, to his horror, she had totaled his brand-new Saab 97, a car Frank loved in a way he would never love another. He forgave her immediately, grateful she wasn't hurt; but the car's demise still haunted him. He would drive it occasionally for the rest of his life, in dreams.

On the road to Truro she filled him in on the week's events. Martine had taken the children fishing; next week, winds permitting, Roy had promised a sail to the Vineyard in the *Mamie Broussard*. There had been a few squabbles between Charlotte and Scotty, who'd been even more rambunctious than he was at home. It was a complaint Frank was tired of hearing. *What do you expect?* he wanted to say. *For God's sake, he's a boy.*

"What about his diet?" he asked instead. "Are you watching his sugar intake?"

They turned down the dusty lane that led to the Captain's House—an outstanding example of shingle-style architecture and, in Frank's mind, a monument to the financial ineptitude of his father-in-law. A century ago, the Drews had been one of the wealthiest families in America, thanks to one ancestor who'd amassed a whaling fortune. The old captain had helped build the railroad from Taunton to Providence and had owned property—waterfront acreage on Martha's Vineyard, a grand house on Beacon Hill—that was now worth millions. A small fortune for each of them, if his descendants had simply hung on to it; but Paulette's father, born into money, seemed constitutionally unable to earn any himself. Everett Drew had sold off the family assets one by one, pissing away the proceeds with a series of disastrous investments. Now that Ev had retired to Florida, his law firm was in the hands of Paulette's brother, Roy, a guy less principled than his father and, in Frank's opinion, even less competent. The house in Truro was the last significant Drew asset. Within a few years, Frank imagined, it would slip through Roy's fingers.

They got out of the car and climbed the stairs to the front porch, where Roy Drew sat smoking a cigarette. He was a tall, spindly fellow with a receding hairline and a long, aquiline nose. An aristocratic nose, Frank thought, suitable for looking down.

"Roy! You made it." Paulette embraced her brother. "We were starting to worry."

Roy offered Frank his hand. "You had the right idea taking the ferry, my friend. Traffic was murder. Welcome."

Frank smiled grimly. The *welcome* rankled. It was Roy's way of reminding him who would inherit the house in a few years. Paulette had always been her father's favorite, but Roy was the only son—and in the Drew family, tradition always trumped sentiment. Already Roy had benefited unfairly, making partner in the firm at the puppyish age of thirty. Since Ev's retirement, Roy had handled his parents' finances; their assets, Frank imagined, were being siphoned off at a discreet rate into Roy's personal bank account—to cover the new Mercedes, the endless maintenance on his boat. By the time the old man finally died, his will wouldn't much matter. Roy would already have socked away most of the take.

Roy offered him a cigarette. "No thanks," said Frank. *Better cut back on those things,* he thought. *Hang around long enough to enjoy my wife's inheritance.*

"How's the lawyering?" he asked briskly.

"What can I say? We're having a great year." Roy leaned back in his chair, stretching out his hairy legs. He wore runner's shorts, cut to the upper thigh. Nothing uglier than a man's legs, Frank thought.

"Glad to hear it," he said, clapping Roy's shoulder. "Good for you." His duty done, he followed Paulette into the kitchen, where Roy's skeletal wife was packing a picnic basket. "Hi, Anne," he said, kissing her cheek. Like her husband, she reeked of cigarette smoke. "Where are the kids?"

"Martine took them to the beach." Anne had wrapped half a dozen sandwiches in waxed paper. "I'm heading there right now."

"Where's Mimi?" Paulette asked.

"Oh, she met up with a girlfriend from school. Her parents have a place on the Vineyard." Anne returned the cold cuts to the fridge.

"Oh, that's too bad." Paulette turned to Frank, beaming. "Mimi is growing into a delightful young woman. I'm sorry you missed her."

"Me too," Frank said, though he hadn't seen Roy's kids in years, and in truth, had never been able to keep their names straight. He thought of the empty house, the quiet front bedroom: a rare opportunity to get his wife alone at the Cape.

"I'll go get my bathing suit," Paulette said.

Frank watched her climb the stairs. "We'll meet you over there," he told Anne. "No sense waiting around for us."

At the bedroom door he waited a moment. Hard years of marriage had taught him that timing was key. If he waited until she'd undressed, a yes was much more likely. He opened the door.

"Frank!" Paulette stood in the center of the room, naked as a newborn. She was about to step into her swimsuit. "Someone could be in the hallway. You really should knock."

"Nobody's there." He went to her and pulled her close, before she could cover herself. He felt the tension in her shoulders: a no was still possible.

"Anne and Roy are waiting downstairs."

"Don't worry. I said we'd meet them later."

She relaxed in his arms then, the signal he'd been waiting for. "I did miss you," she said in a small voice, as though it were an admission of guilt.

"Let me look at you." They always made love in the dark; it was a rare thing to see her naked in daylight: her tiny nipples, the lush dark hair.

He laid her down on the bed, a little roughly. "I thought about this all week."

FRANK FOLLOWED his wife an endless mile up the beach, loaded down with an Igloo cooler, an umbrella and two beach chairs. His feet sank into the soft sand. Tomorrow morning—he knew this from experience—he'd have a powerful backache.

"How about here?" he suggested, dropping the cooler in the sand.

Paulette shaded her eyes. "No. Over there." She pointed to a pink umbrella far in the distance. Like all the Drews, she had firm convictions about what constituted a suitable location for lounging on the beach. She'd make him tramp through the hot sand for fifteen or twenty minutes, then choose a spot that, to Frank's eye, was indistinguishable from any other.

They trudged onward. Sweat dripped down Frank's forehead and into his eyes. A small plane buzzed overhead, trailing a lettered banner: SULLY'S CLAM SHACK BEST CHOWDA ON THE CAPE.

"Here," Paulette said finally. "This is perfect."

Frank spiked the umbrella viciously into the sand. He despised the beach. The sun was unkind to his freckled skin; while the Drews basked, he reddened, perspired, longed for a drink. *Bring a book*, Paulette suggested. *Take a nap*. But reading in the sun made his head ache, and Frank hadn't napped since he was in diapers. Instead he sat for hours doing nothing. The inactivity caused him almost physical anguish. Why Paulette insisted on torturing him this way—what satisfaction she got out of keeping him trapped, idle and bored out of his mind—he would never understand.

He opened the beach chairs and settled them under the umbrella. His objections went beyond boredom. It was the ocean itself he hated, its droning eternality. *It puts everything in perspective*, Paulette sometimes said, and that was Frank's point precisely. He didn't want to be reminded of his own insignificance, the brevity of his life, the pettiness of his concerns. What kind of lunatic wanted to think about that?

He stretched out under the umbrella and shaded his eyes from the sun.

"Hey there!" a familiar voice called. "We're over here."

His sister-in-law Martine jogged toward them, her compact body fit and sexless in a no-nonsense blue suit. Frank rose to greet her. He couldn't think of another woman whose near nakedness affected him so little.

Paulette sat up on the blanket and waved to Scotty and Gwen, wet and blue lipped under a striped umbrella, wrapped in beach towels. She shaded her eyes. "Where's Billy?"

"He rode into Provincetown on his bike," said Martine. "That's okay, right?"

Paulette frowned. "There's quite a bit of traffic on that highway. Frank, do you think he'll be all right?"

"Don't be silly. The kid can handle himself."

"Daddy!" Gwen called, running toward him. Another, taller girl followed behind.

"Hi, baby!" he called. "How's the water?"

"Cold!" She grasped him around the waist. Her head was wet against his shirt front. "Do you like my new bathing suit?"

"I love it." He scooped her into his arms. On her the purple bikini was adorable, the top placed roughly where breasts would be. Half of it had gone slightly askew, revealing one pink nipple. He tugged it gingerly back into place.

"Darling, you're burning." Paulette reached into her bag for a tube of zinc oxide. "Put this on your nose."

"I could use some of that too," said Frank. The poor kid had inherited his complexion. He took the tube from Paulette's hand, put a dab on his own nose and rubbed it onto Gwen's. She giggled, delighted.

"Hi, Uncle Frank," said the other girl, who had joined them.

"Hi there." Frank bent to kiss her cheek. "I thought you went to the Vineyard."

"That was Mimi," said the girl. "Her and her stupid friend."

"Oh, *Charlotte*." The younger one, then; she was Gwen's age. He eyed the two standing side by side. Like Gwen, Charlotte wore a bikini, but she had small breasts to fill hers. Her shoulder was level with the top of Gwen's head.

"I'm freezing," said Gwen, her teeth chattering. "Daddy, we're going to lie down on our towel."

He watched them climb the dune, Gwen's sturdy legs pumping. "That's Charlotte?" he said to his wife, whose nose was buried in Willa Cather. "She's twelve? Like Gwen?"

"Charlotte's three months younger. She'll be thirteen in December." Paulette turned a page.

The wind shifted, a sudden chill. Frank knew, could never again unknow, that something was terribly wrong.

Traffic was brisk on the road to Provincetown. Billy rode carefully, keeping an eye on his rearview mirror. He was a responsible cyclist; he kept to the right and always signaled before he turned. Most drivers gave him wide berth, but there was the occasional hoser who roared up behind him and leaned on the horn or flashed the headlights. He was beginning to understand that life was full of such people—the aggressive, the crude. Once in a while they paid for their bad behavior, but usually not. Mostly they took over companies, dominated sport's teams, ran for president. Hosers basically owned the world.

It was the kind of thing his aunt Martine was always saying. *No good deed goes unpunished.* And: *The freaks shall inherit the earth.* He'd begun to see that it was true. The past soccer season had kicked the crap out of him. Coach Dick—his actual name—had humiliated him practice after practice. *He had a losing season, and you're his scapegoat,* Billy's father had told him, rather unhelpfully. *Never be a scapegoat.*

How do I do that? Billy had demanded.

You'll figure it out, his father said.

Billy hadn't figured it out. He had waited it out. As of June first, Pilgrims Country Day was officially behind him. In the fall he would go to boarding school in New Hampshire, where the coaches would not be hosers. He'd been promised this by his uncle Roy, who had gone to Pearse a hundred years ago and probably didn't know what he was talking about.

Billy turned off the highway and down the beach road, past a row of tiny cottages. Last night they had gone into Provincetown together, Billy, his mother, and Gwen. Scotty hadn't been allowed to come because, according to their mother, he'd behaved abominably all day. As far as Billy could tell, that meant picking at his dinner, making rude noises at the table, and teasing Charlotte, who, in Billy's opinion, deserved it. Charlotte had turned into a giant pain in the ass. He felt sorry for Scotty, but was glad to be away from him. This year Scotty had the top bunk, where he snored and thrashed and mumbled in his sleep, waking Billy ten times a night. Billy hated sharing a bedroom. And his brother was only nine, a little kid.

In Provincetown they'd had ice cream, Billy a chocolate cone with jimmies, Gwen a strawberry frappé. Then their mother led them into a shop called Outer Limits. In the windows were beach towels, T-shirts, bathing suits. A tie-dyed hammock hung from the ceiling.

We'll be a few minutes, his mother had told him. *You can look around. Just don't leave the store.*

Billy had walked around the shop. At the cash register, under glass, was an assortment of strange pipes, one of which cost twenty dollars. There were earrings, shell necklaces, rings that changed color depending on your mood. In the back he found racks of postcards. The National Seashore, the Provincetown lighthouse, whales, lobsters, girls in bikinis. An entire rack was devoted to pictures of men in uniform: policeman, fireman, soldier in camouflage. Billy took one of the cards and slipped it into his pocket.

He had stolen for a long time. Little things only—comic books, pocket knives, things he didn't really want. At the drugstore in Concord, he'd stolen four tubes of Crazy Glue. Why, he didn't exactly know.

He looked over his shoulder. To his horror, a clerk was coming toward him. He had never been caught before, and he wondered what the clerk would do. As always when he was nervous, he had an immediate urge to pee.

Hi, said the clerk. He reminded Billy of a pirate. His head was wrapped in a blue bandanna. He wore a tiny hoop earring in his right ear.

What are you doing here? The clerk's tone was friendly, not at all menacing. He didn't see me, Billy thought, confused.

My sister is getting a bathing suit.

The clerk perched on the corner of a low display case. *Are you staying in Ptown?*

Our house is in Truro, Billy said.

The clerk nodded toward a bicycle leaning against the display window. *Is that your bike? Or did you drive?*

My mom drove us. I'm only fourteen.

Oh. The clerk stood, glancing over his shoulder. *I thought you were older.*

Is there a bathroom here? Billy asked.

Not for customers. There's a public one on Commercial Street.

Okay. Billy glanced back at the changing rooms. *If a lady comes out, tell her I'll be right back.*

The bathroom was dark and smelled terrible, bleach and dampness and other things he didn't want to think about. Billy remembered his mother's advice to touch nothing but himself. He had read a great deal about microorganisms. The average toilet was home to billions of viruses, parasites, bacteria. To Billy they were like the dastardly supervillains Batman fought on TV. He imagined them masked, in flashy costumes. Evil Salmonella. Shit-loving Escherichia, the dirtiest organism imaginable: the very definition of filth.

He stood at the urinal and did his business. Zipping up, he heard a noise coming from one of the stalls.

The door of the stall was trembling, as if something were banging against it. Billy looked down at the floor. There were two pairs of boots in the stall, standing toe to toe. The door continued to shudder. When it stopped, Billy turned and fled.

He told nobody what he had seen. Who was there to tell? His cousin Mimi was older and knew more than he did; but when he saw her back at the house, sneaking a cigarette on the porch, he found himself unable to speak. For one thing, what exactly had he seen?

He had an idea about it, or maybe it was just a feeling. He kept his feeling to himself.

Now Billy parked his bike outside the shop and went inside. He looked for the pirate clerk but found a different one on duty, a suntanned girl in a halter top. He locked his bike to a lamppost and went down the street to the restroom, which smelled even worse during the day. The doors of the stalls were all closed. A pair of feet was visible beneath one of the doors: a man sitting down, his trousers around his ankles.

Billy washed his hands.

The man came out of the stall. He was old and fat, wearing red pants. Billy stepped aside to let him use the sink. When the man left, Billy examined his face in the mirror, thinking how the clerk had thought him older. Sixteen, old enough to drive.

Again he washed his hands.

He was drying them on his shirt when a man entered the restroom. He was wearing a policeman's blue uniform, and Billy thought of the postcard he had stolen from the store.

The man stood at the urinal and unzipped.

"What are you looking at?" he asked Billy.

"Nothing." In his nervousness, his voice had cracked. He felt his face warm.

The man finished and gave himself a shake. "Aren't you a little young to be hanging around here?"

"I'm sixteen," Billy said, his heart racing.

The man gave him a hard look. "I could get you into a lot of trouble. Now get out of here before I change my mind."

It was bedtime before Frank could get his wife alone. By then he had eaten dinner with the children, coated his sunburned shoulders with Solarcaine, and thrown a Frisbee to Scotty for what seemed an eternity. ("Tire him out," Paulette had instructed him. "For heaven's sake, Frank, the child *will not sleep.*") He had endured hours of his brother-in-law's conversation: sailing stories, fishing stories, tales of masculine adventure in which Roy Drew emerged, always, as the hero. Frank knocked back four gin and tonics and moved his chair periodically, to stay upwind of Roy's cigarette smoke. Finally he excused himself and climbed the stairs to the bedroom. Paulette was in her nightgown. She had just turned back the coverlet and was climbing into bed.

She gave him a wary look. *Once a day is plenty*, it seemed to say. *Don't think for a moment it's going to happen again.*

"I need to talk to you."

Her whole body relaxed, as though she'd been spared a punishment. Frank tried not to notice her relief. She listened closely as he spoke. Then, to his astonishment, simply shrugged.

"Oh, Frank. You know she's always been small for her age."

"It's more than that. Haven't you noticed? Seeing her with Roy's girl, I couldn't believe they're the same age."

"All Gwen's school friends are taller than she is." Paulette said this lightly; maybe she meant nothing by it. Maybe it was Frank who supplied the subtext. *You would have noticed that if you were a better father. If you were ever at home.*

"Doesn't that concern you?" he demanded.

"Not at all." She smiled tightly. "I was the same way, at her age. I'm still petite. Like my mother, and Martine. All the women in my family are small."

"She's almost thirteen. Shouldn't she be starting puberty by now? Breast development, pubic hair. Something."

"Can you please lower your voice?" Paulette's cheeks were scarlet, her voice a heated whisper. "Frank, I know a bit more about this than you do. I was a girl once. And it just so happens that I developed on the late side." She smiled grimly. "Maybe she'll end up like me. Wouldn't that be terrible?"

"What is that supposed to mean?"

"You prefer voluptuous women. I know that. I've always known that. But that doesn't mean there's anything wrong with the rest of us. Some men actually appreciate a slim figure. For heaven's sake, it's not a medical condition."

"Jesus, what's the matter with you?" He stared at her, dumbfounded. "I prefer *you*. I married you, didn't I?" As he said it, he knew it was hopeless. Hopeless to say he loved her, wanted her, had chosen her over numberless other girls. Hopeless to point out that *she* was the one who always said no, who regularly pushed him away.

He took a deep breath. "Listen. We're not talking about you. We're talking about Gwen. Something could be wrong. Medically." He waited a moment for this to sink in. "I think she should see a doctor. Just a checkup, to make sure everything is okay."

"She goes to the doctor every year. I've been taking her since she was a baby." Paulette's voice was perfectly even, a trick of hers: the further she pushed him, the calmer she became. "And Billy. And Scott. Frank, they are *perfectly healthy children*. And I am a good mother." She paused. "Lately, as it turns out, I am even a fairly good father."

"What is that supposed to mean?"

"Really, Frank. How many mothers have to teach their sons to shave?"

He colored. A few months back, Billy had found one of Frank's razors and cut himself, trying to remove the peach fuzz from his upper lip. Frank was out of town—the annual meeting at Cold Spring Harbor. Something he would never be allowed to forget.

"You know," she said thoughtfully. "I find this really interesting." She seemed to be waiting for a response.

"What?" he said wearily.

"The only time you've ever shown the slightest interest in our children's health, it concerns something sexual." She said the last word in a hoarse whisper. It would have been comical, he thought, if it weren't so sad.

"Who mentioned anything sexual?" *I could kill this woman*, he thought. He felt his heart accelerating, his arms and legs flooding with blood. *No: she will kill me. She is subtracting years from my life.*

"Frank, you've always been obsessed with sex."

It impressed him that she pronounced the word at a normal volume. He knew his wife, knew the effort that must have cost.

Exercising heroic self-control, he did not answer. He'd been taught never to hit a girl, and that applied also to the verbal. He didn't say what he'd been thinking on and off for years: *You are the most repressed woman I've known in all my life.*

The night is still, and the house sleeps fitfully. In the front bedroom, the couple lie close together in a too-small bed. Each resents the other body, its warm breathing, its radiant heat. The man considers slipping outdoors for a walk, but fears waking his sister-in-law, an ill-tempered sentry at the top of the stairs. His wife feigns sleep, perspires into her cotton nightgown. She is too angry to sleep unclothed.

Downstairs, in the deep part of the house, their younger son is snoring. He dreams of the surf, the flying Frisbee, the dog they will not let him have.

His older brother lies awake in the top bunk, remembering boots in a bathroom stall: worn cowboy boots with intricate stitching, the others black leather, shiny and new.

On the screened porch the girl cousins sleep the deep sleep of children. A cool breeze kisses their cheeks.

In a year the house will be sold. Frank and Paulette McKotch will communicate through lawyers. It is the last summer for this family. Nothing will ever be the same.

the condition

chapter 1

S now was falling fast in Cambridge, small dry flakes, oblique and furious. The first storm of the season, wholly unexpected. Frank McKotch's topcoat was still at the cleaner's. Rain had been forecast, and he had dressed accordingly. He crossed the street with a decisive step, swinging his useless umbrella, his trench coat flapping in the wind. The walk took twenty minutes, a significant expenditure of time; but Frank was convinced it enhanced his productivity. Quicken the respiration, he thought. Move the blood.

His route bisected the campus of the Massachusetts Institute of Technology, where he'd spent most of his career. Five years ago, lured by promises—funding, a lighter teaching load—he'd accepted an appointment at the Grohl Institute; but the campus proper, the hulking rectangular buildings arranged around a quadrangle, remained as familiar as his living room. Just beyond it lay the corporate headquarters of Protogenix, where Frank served on the scientific advisory board. He'd spent the entire morning in meetings in the low brick bunker, not removing his jacket. Now, on campus, there was a feeling of holiday in the air. The semester had ended and traffic was conspicuously light. Students loped along in down jackets, drinking tall coffees. Overgrown boys in parkas, yarmulkes, eyeglasses; scrawny kids hauling heavy backpacks. "Professor McKotch!" a boy called from across the street. Frank raised his hand in salute. A number of his old students were still on campus, as grad students or research assistants or postdoctoral fellows, the treadmill of study and academic appointments that a young scientist could run for years.

They were the finest young scientific minds in the world—from fifty states, a hundred countries; from planets known and not yet discovered, it often seemed to Frank. Over the years, he'd taught Saudi princes and teenage prodigies; the sons of Teamsters, four-star generals, diamond miners, Soviet dissidents. He enjoyed his students and basked in their achievements. At the same time, it exasperated him—struck him as totally unnecessary—that these brilliant young men were such lamentable physical specimens. Bad haircuts, poor musculature, acute cases of cystic acne. By nineteen, half were already paunchy; the rest looked downright starved. Athletes were rare; the hottest contest on campus was the annual Integration Bee, in which young geniuses went head to head, feverishly solving equations. Female students were few, and seemed fewer—plain Asian girls, quietly dressed, in unflattering clothes that nearly hid their gender. It was easy to forget that a couple of miles to the west, Harvard girls modeled sweaters, suntans, tall boots that hugged a bare leg like a leather sleeve. If, like Frank, you'd walked Kendall Square for thirty years, you could almost forget that women existed in the world.

He arrived at Grohl in eighteen minutes, a new record; he bypassed the elevator and climbed the three flights of stairs to his lab. It was a small discipline he'd maintained for years, part of his daily regimen for keeping fit. Push-ups and sit-ups, weekends on the bicycle. A chin-up bar hung in the doorway to his study. He was fifty-nine, and his waist had not thickened. No excess flesh hung over his belt.

From the landing he watched one of the secretaries, Betsy Baird, step out of the elevator, a grocery bag in her arms. She was a small, energetic woman with lacquered hair and a wide painted mouth.

"Booze," she explained. "It's Christmas, remember? Your team is thirsty."

He followed her through the reception area, which a few of the younger staff—there were five grad students and eight post-docs— had decorated with red lights and tinsel. In Frank's own office Margit Lindgren sat perched on the desk, beer bottle in hand. She was too tall to perch gracefully—six feet, the same as Frank. Margit ran her own lab on the first floor, but made frequent visits to the fourth.

"We started without you," she said. "Where have you been?"

He pulled up a chair. "Progen. Meeting with the board." In the distance a telephone rang. "Jesus, now what?"

"Poor Frank," Margit said. His foray into commercial science had provided them with hours of conversation. Based on all he'd told her, Margit viewed the management team at Protogenix as a band of marauding Huns, a conclusion with which he agreed. Her response to his tales—ardent sympathy and quiet horror—satisfied him deeply.

Betsy Baird stuck her head in the doorway. "It's Neil Windsor again."

"I'm still at Protogenix."

"He called over there. They told him you'd already left."

"Tell him I'm not back yet. You don't know where I am."

Betsy disappeared, and Margit took a pull on her beer. "Neil Windsor?"

"Old friend. Classmate, really. He's in town for a couple of days."

"You don't want to see him?"

Frank shrugged. "Theoretically I do. But Gwen is coming tomorrow. I have a lot to do." It was a thin excuse. His daughter's visits required no preparation. They ate their meals in restaurants. His seldom-used guest room was tidy as a laboratory.

"Windsor. That name sounds familiar."

"He's at Stanford," Frank said nonchalantly.

"Oh, *that* Windsor. You saw his paper in *Nature*?"

"Sure," said Frank. The new issue had arrived yesterday. The timing was obviously coincidental—the paper would have been submitted months ago—but seemed calculated to cause him maximum distress.

"And of course," said Margit, "the Academy."

Frank nodded grimly. That April, like every other, he'd waited eagerly for the National Academy of Sciences to announce its new members. They were the anointed few, the top guys in mathematics and engineering, astronomy and physics, biology and medicine. From its ranks, every few years, came another Nobelist. Frank had had his share of successes, been awarded and endowed and fellowed and fêted. At MIT his position was secure; but for some reason, the Academy had eluded him. The elections process was lengthy and cumbersome: scientists were nominated by their individual sections, then voted upon by class. Frank had been asked, a few years back, to supply a curriculum vitae and a list of publications; year after year, he imagined his name working its way up the list of nominees. He'd been certain that this would be his moment. Instead it had been Neil Windsor's. Margit, who knew all this, gave his arm a squeeze.

"When does Gwen arrive?" she asked.

"Gwen and Billy." He grinned, pleased at the change of subject. "He managed to tear himself away a day early. They land tomorrow afternoon, and I have them for the evening. They'll drive to their mother's on Wednesday." The visit was an annual tradition for Frank and his daughter. Billy hadn't joined them in years. Scott, Frank's younger son, had never come.

"Bring them by the lab," said Margit. "I'd love to see Gwen again."

"She'd like that." Frank hesitated. "She's the same, I guess. Nothing ever changes with her."

Margit shrugged. "Why should anything change? She loves her work. She likes her life."

"I worry that she's lonely."

Margit looked at him a long moment. "Being alone is not the same as being lonely. Billy is also single. Do you worry about him?"

Frank grinned. A good-looking kid, Billy had never wanted for girlfriends. At Princeton he'd dated a real thoroughbred, Lauren something or other, the kind of statuesque blonde you saw on magazine covers. Billy no longer brought women home—Paulette had seen to that—but a New York cardiologist with his looks would have his pick. "I doubt Billy's ever lonely," he said, a touch of pride in his voice.

"Silly man. I don't mean sex. I mean companionship." Margit drained her beer and set the bottle aside. "Billy is working all the time, just like Gwen. They are both doing what they love."

"I suppose," he said, though of course it *wasn't* the same. Billy saw patients five days a week; he had plenty of human contact, while Gwen was spending her young womanhood in the basement of a museum, cataloguing relics. What kind of life was that? Gwen had never been gregarious, and her work had made her even more antisocial. Strangers found her awkward. Even among family she was reserved and stubborn, prone to long silences. About her personal life she volunteered nothing. She maintained an air of strongly held opinions kept quiet; at times Frank sensed her studying him in a distinctly anthropological way. All in all, his daughter was not easy company; when she left Cambridge Wednesday afternoon, he would feel guilty relief. But Margit truly enjoyed Gwen, found her many eccentricities perfectly comprehensible. Frank only pretended to. And Gwen, who was not easily fooled, could tell the difference.

"You're right," Frank said. "Gwen is fine. Keep reminding me of that."

He took the bottle Margit offered, and they drank in companionable silence. They'd been close for years, since Margit's arrival at MIT. On the surface it was an unlikely friendship. Frank was a natural teacher, charming and extroverted in the classroom, beloved by the students, generous with his time. He kept in touch with dozens of former postdocs, wrote reference letters, dispensed advice. A few years back, his team had thrown a surprise party for his birthday, a sort of raucous celebrity roast highlighted by clever toasting, fond ribbing at Frank's expense. It was just the sort of gathering he liked. For the first time in years, he had felt like a father.

His enthusiasm for teaching mystified Margit. To her the classroom was a trial. The students' demands exhausted her. Even her postdocs had to jockey for her attention; she sneaked out of the lab each day like a star ducking the paparazzi—*the Garbo of Grohl*, Frank often joked. They were the same age; both divorced, with grown children. They favored the same movies, the same books. Half the volumes in Frank's study had Margit's name on the flyleaf. Each year they shared season tickets at the Huntingdon Theatre. Once, at a performance of *Miss Julie*, they'd run into a student Frank fancied, a pretty Indian girl he'd taught the semester before. She'd assumed Margit was his wife.

The two women had laughed at the mistake; but Frank was speechless. *My wife?* he'd marveled silently. *But she's so* old.

He'd heard it said—by Betsy Baird, or Ursula the lab tech—that Margit was *attractive*. Those who said this were always middle-aged women. They admired her leanness, her runner's legs; they didn't care— why would they?—that her behind was flat, her breasts nonexistent. Margit's gray hair was cut short as a man's; she wore distinctive eyeglasses, red or purple, with angular frames. At the theater she dressed dramatically, long skirts and silky shawls. Heads turned at the rustle of all that fabric; but Frank's was not among them. If pressed, he would describe her as handsome.

His ex-wife, Paulette, was not handsome. As a girl, a young woman, she'd been a fullfledged knockout. Back then, in the early sixties, she was often compared to Jacqueline Kennedy, another dark-eyed beauty who exuded elegance and privilege. In Paulette those qualities had become brittle with age. When he'd last seen her, three years ago, her skin looked fragile and crepey. Her face reminded him of a crushed flower. But her presence still had a sexual quality, something enervating and deeply feminine. At Billy's medical school graduation, Frank had watched their son introduce her to a few of his professors, and the old coots had come to life in her presence. Even past her prime, Paulette had that effect on men.

"Frank?"

He looked up too quickly. That lush voice, warm and throaty: his ear was trained to its frequency. Working late in his fourth-floor office, he'd swear he could hear her in the street.

"Do you have a minute?" Cristina Spiliotes, one of his postdocs, stood in the doorway holding a drink.

"Excuse me," Frank said to Margit. He rose and followed Cristina down the hall. Today she wore a thin blouse the color of eggplant, the top three buttons undone. Two buttons was her usual. She hadn't undone three buttons in months.

"What's up?" After months of practice it was second nature: he fixed his gaze on her nose, her shoulder—away from her lush mouth, the dusky skin of her chest.

"I have a draft of the paper," she said breezily, handing him a manila folder. "Can you take a look?"

"Whoa, whoa. Wait a minute. Don't you think you're jumping the gun?" He grinned affably, though he was taken aback by her nerve.

She waved away his objection. "Of course you're right. There is more work to do. I simply want to be prepared when the time comes." Again she offered the folder. "Please?"

Frank blinked. Ambitious postdocs were nothing new. In the course of his career, he'd hired dozens of them; many years ago he'd been one himself. But Cristina was different. Her ambition overlaid a bedrock of arrogance. Or so it seemed to Frank.

"I may have some time over the holiday," he said. "I'm not promising anything, but maybe I can take a look."

"I know it's early, but I'd love to hear your thoughts." She gave him the folder, her hand brushing his. "Thank you." Her fingers were startlingly warm, her eyes velvet brown like a deer's.

"I can't promise I'll get to it," he repeated.

"Of course," she agreed. "But, you know. Just in case."

She had worked in Frank's lab for just over a year, each day a torment. He had hired her on a whim, his judgment clouded by loneliness, doubt and despair. Deena Maddux, his girlfriend of six years, had left him for a tenure-track job at Berkeley. Twenty years younger, she was desperate for children; only a marriage proposal would keep her in Cambridge. When none came, she drove up in a moving van. The house and furniture were Frank's, but Deena had bought the rugs and curtains, the sheets and comforters, the decorative pillows. Now she took these with her. The rooms were stripped of everything soft.

The place echoed without her. "Take some time alone," Margit advised. "It will be good for you." But he slept poorly without Deena beside him. Female company was essential to him, like water or oxygen. He had never lived like a monk, and he was too old to start.

A few friends, all married, set him up on dates. The women were fiftyish, or a bit younger—at any rate, past the age of clamoring for what Frank wasn't prepared to give. There was the Harvard professor, the vegetarian chef, the third-world economist from the Kennedy School

of Government. Not one but two members of the clergy, a Method-
ist minister and a Reform rabbi. Accomplished women, sophisticated,
ridiculously well educated. He dated each one a few weeks or months.
He bought dinners, gave back massages, took a Tuscan cooking class
at the Cambridge School of Adult Education. He tried Rollerblades
and snow shoes, went candlepin bowling, browsed through street fairs
and, God help him, the Brimfield Antique Mart, where he'd narrowly
escaped an awkward encounter with his ex-wife. For six months, a
year, he had a great deal of middle-aged fun. Except for the vegetarian
chef, he liked all the women immensely. He kissed and cuddled them.
But, to his horror, he *did not desire* them.

His dick—up to now so hyperactive that it sometimes got him
into trouble—had gone inert and sulky. Like a moody teenager, it
wanted to be left alone. The women, naturally, did not understand. Attempts were made. After five sexless dates, Rabbi Kleinman proposed
a weekend at a bed-and-breakfast in New Hampshire. The room was
outfitted with a whirlpool tub and a complimentary bottle of domestic champagne. There was no television. Cornered, Frank pleasured the
rabbi twice a day; on a rainy weekend in rural New Hampshire, there
was little else to do. Twice, half hard, he managed to penetrate her. She
feigned satisfaction. They drove back to Cambridge singing Beatles
songs with the radio. Days passed. Finally she sent him an e-mail: she
was reconciling with her ex-husband. Mortified, he sent a message of
congratulations, grateful that he would not have to face her again.

If his dick was depressed, perhaps the rest of him was too. It was
not implausible. He was under pressure at work (though this was not
unusual; he'd been under pressure for thirty-five years). And Deena's
defection had wounded him more deeply than he'd realized. Depression could strike anyone: a teenager, a young buck of twenty. Age had
nothing to do with it. And, with the new serotonin drugs flooding the
market, his condition could be treated rationally, without the indigni-
ties he'd suffered years ago, in the final days of his marriage, when Paulette dragged him to a therapist. If *Time* magazine were to be believed,
every other person he passed in the street was swallowing Prozac. Any
GP could write him a scrip.

He made an appointment with his internist, a smart Harvard guy named Cheng. The word, *impotence*, proved impossible to pronounce. "My sex drive is off," he said instead, his heart pounding. "I'm just not interested."

Cheng cut him off with a wave of the hand. "Listen, Frank." He was a Chinese Texan who spoke with a twang. "The last thing you want is Prozac. It's a great drug, but that's the number one reason guys stop taking it. Inhibited sexual desire. Sometimes the whole deal stops working."

"The whole deal?" Frank repeated.

"I mean they can't get it up." Then, seeing his look: "Relax, will you? For every problem there is a solution. The Brits have a terrific impotence drug in the pipeline. Very promising. If it pans out, we'll all be popping wood into our nineties."

"You're joking," said Frank.

"Mark my words," said Cheng.

Frank swore off women. Shaken by the Kleinman debacle, he feared further humiliation. Someday, perhaps, a magic pill would save him; but in the meantime, a man in his condition was better off alone. He threw himself into his work: weekends in the lab, nights on his office couch. He'd gotten funding for an additional postdoc. A single posting yielded a hundred applicants; he had his pick of the brightest young scientists in his field. All were qualified; a half dozen were veritable stars. Frank settled on a prodigy named Kevin Cho, a twenty-something whiz kid with a newly minted PhD from Stanford. He was about to make Cho an offer when Betsy Baird handed him yet another CV and cover letter. "This came today. Squeaked in under the deadline."

He glanced at the letter, looking for, but not finding, the familiar names: Stanford, Harvard, MIT.

"Forget it," he said, handing it back. "I've got my man."

"You could at least meet her."

"What for?" he asked, genuinely puzzled. "Cho's the guy. Why waste everybody's time?"

"*Okay*," Betsy said, in the mock-patient tone he hated. It meant that she considered herself a step ahead of him, which was often the case. "I have the voluntary declaration forms." She paused significantly. "Should I send them upstairs?"

He recalled a recent flurry of memos about hiring practices from Steve Upstairs—Steve Zeichner, the director of the institute, who occupied a top-floor office with a striking view of the Charles. For reasons unknown to the staff, Steve Upstairs was suddenly vigilant about hiring, or at least interviewing, applicants from underrepresented groups. At Grohl—run by white and Asian men—that meant blacks and females. When the first applications rolled in, Frank had been surprised by how many—30 percent, it turned out—came from women. This was his first and last thought on the matter. Without Betsy's prodding, it would never have dawned on him that all six of his choices were male. That he hadn't interviewed a single woman.

"Oh, shit," he said.

"Light dawns over Marblehead." Betsy handed back the letter. "Take a look."

Frank skimmed the first paragraph. Cristina Spiliotes had done a PhD at Baylor under Alan Manning, whom Frank knew by reputation. Manning was a leader in the hot new field of apoptosis; he'd been an early proponent of the theory that, under specific conditions, cells committed suicide—and that when this mechanism went awry, disease followed. Too many cell suicides, and you had the damaged blood vessels of ischemic heart disease; too few, and defective cells multiplied uncontrollably into tumors. The field was only a few years old, but its potential seemed boundless. If scientists could learn to control the genes that triggered apoptosis, promising new therapies—for Parkinson's, cancer, heart disease—could result. To Frank, the possibilities were dazzling. He was a traditional oncogeneticist; he'd made his reputation by discovering a specific oncogene, XNR, and its role in tumor-cell signaling. He had no background in apoptosis, but devoured the literature on the subject. Instinct told him that this could be the next big thing. Of course, it was a young man's game, dominated by kids like Cristina Spiliotes, who'd spent the last few years at one of the hottest apoptosis labs in the country. If an old dinosaur like Frank wanted to break into the field, this could be his chance.

"Bring her in Friday," he told Betsy.

"You're booked all day."

"It won't take long. I'll meet her for lunch."

He wondered, in retrospect, if that had made the difference. Every other candidate, Kevin Cho included, had come to his office, shaken his hand across his cluttered desk. Cristina Spiliotes had suggested a restaurant he'd never heard of, a little Spanish place on a side street near Harvard Square. She was waiting when he arrived, her dark hair loose. She wore tiny pearl earrings and a silky white blouse. Her legs were hidden by a sweep of flowered tablecloth.

He'd been charmed by her warmth, her slight accent, her musical laugh. To his surprise she ordered a glass of wine. "The tapas here are really wonderful," she said. "Would you like to try them?" Small plates arrived: olives, garlicky mussels, fried things from the sea.

As they ate Frank questioned her about her science. For three years she had studied a specific gene—an X-linked inhibitor of apoptosis, or XIAP. She had already done the molecular biology, developed reagents to shut off the gene in vitro. Her next step was to breed a transgenic mouse, genetically altered so that XIAP was knocked out in all its cells. If, as Cristina hoped, switching off XIAP made the mouse resistant to tumors, the case was clear: this gene, *her* gene, played a role in cancer development.

Frank nodded, fascinated. His ex-wife had called him a poor listener, and he knew it was often true; but when a scientific question engaged him, his concentration was boundless. Cristina spoke rapidly, her lovely hands flying; she wore an armful of silver bangles, but no ring.

Her words captivated him; so did—why pretend?—her bare throat, her glossy hair, the astonishing suedelike texture of her skin. Like good science, feminine beauty always got his attention; but it was rare to find both in the same package. Listening, watching, he was aware of the muscles in his arms and legs, the blood warming his face, the simple pleasure of his beating heart.

When the paella arrived, the subject changed. They talked about politics, the price of real estate, a new photography exhibit at the

MFA. Cristina had interviewed that morning at Harvard, with Frank's old nemesis Otto Mueller; certain he'd make her an offer, she'd already begun looking at apartments. (At the time, Frank found this confidence appealing. Later it seemed evidence of her arrogance.) She'd seen a terrific place in Cambridgeport, but was concerned about the safety of the neighborhood. "I have to be careful," she explained, lowering her voice, "as a single woman."

Frank took note—he couldn't help it—of the word *single*.

She ordered a second glass of wine.

"Let's get a bottle," he suggested, which made sense: it was cheaper than ordering by the glass. Over his second glass, he found himself alluding to his breakup with Deena Maddux, and Cristina's eyes widened in sympathy. Her bra glowed beneath her blouse—a white bra, he guessed, much lighter than her olive skin. When the flan arrived she rose to excuse herself. Her skirt clung to her backside, round and cloven, like an apricot.

He was lost.

She started immediately; she would take time off later, they agreed, to settle into her new apartment. Frank felt invigorated. Cristina was a hit with the other postdocs; passing their shared office, Frank often heard her laughing with Martin or Guei. Her science was stimulating; so—he admitted it to himself—was her simple presence. Though his conduct with her was perfectly proper, he observed her discreetly, and made exhaustive mental notes. On certain days she wore her hair in a bun, exposing plump earlobes; often a dark curl escaped, trailing down her bare neck. She favored silky button-down shirts in deep colors; she left the first two buttons undone, and sometimes the first three. When summer came, he discovered another feature of these shirts: in an air-conditioned room, they did not hide her nipples. Without ever seeing or touching it, she had revived his limp appendage. What Rabbi Kleinman, with full use of hands and mouth, had barely achieved, Cristina unknowingly brought about several times a day. His condition was cured.

Frank McKotch was not finished. He was as virile as ever. The future stretched ahead of him—shorter than it used to be, but promising still. There would be other women. Another Deena, clasping him fiercely; another Paulette breathing his name.

For months this knowledge was enough for him. Of course it was! His worst fears had been banished, his manhood affirmed. Certainly he expected nothing more of Cristina. She was his postdoc; he was responsible for her professional development, a duty he did not take lightly. And she had already given him the greatest gift.

Filled with gratitude, he believed this. Believed it right up to the moment when, coming out of a coffee shop, he heard a motorcycle roar into Kendall Square. The driver was young and swarthy. A woman clasped him around the waist. She climbed off and removed her helmet, shaking loose her dark hair. Her round cloven backside could belong to none other. She bent to kiss the driver's mouth.

The bike squealed away, running a red light. Frank stepped into a doorway and waited for Cristina to pass. She hadn't seen him; he was certain. His chest ached; a cold sweat broke out on his forehead. His stomach churned.

He recognized the symptoms of myocardial infarction.

It was a preposterous notion: his blood pressure was low, his lipid profile exemplary. But he was not a young man. In those few moments he'd aged twenty years.

Cristina had a lover. Not surprising: she was a beautiful girl. That the lover was young and vital, a swarthy Greek on a motorcycle, likewise made perfect sense. It was a probable outcome, wholly predictable if he'd been paying attention. He had simply been looking at the wrong data. For months he'd fixated on apricots, earlobes, protruding nipples. Busy counting buttons, he'd ignored other crucial facts. One morning she'd come to work sullen and bleary, eyes swollen as if she'd been crying. The next day a bouquet of roses arrived at the lab; when Betsy Baird teased her, Cristina had blushed.

It was irrational, this feeling that she'd betrayed him. He recalled, obsessively, that first lunch together: *I have to be careful, as a single woman.* On some level he'd believed she was signaling him, letting him know that she was free.

The intensity of his anger astonished him. In the office, the lab, he could not meet her eyes. He saw the truth in all its ugliness: he had hired her because he wanted her. And believed, in some deluded way, that she wanted him too. In weak moments, self-pity overwhelmed him. He began to feel that she had taken advantage of *him*, his all-too-obvious fascination with her. Unfounded, of course; but the feeling dogged him. Their hour-long weekly meetings seemed interminable; he found excuses to cancel them, which seemed best for all concerned. The sight of her filled him with resentment, and such sentiments had no place in a lab.

Meanwhile Cristina toiled away on her transgenic mouse. The work proved more difficult than expected. XIAP was not cooperating; she'd had some difficulty turning off the gene in the mouse's stem cells. Such glitches were common in gene manipulation; but as the months passed, Frank grew nervous. He began to see apoptosis as a long shot, his interest in it a spell of temporary insanity. He'd made lousy hires before, but never for such a contemptible reason. An old dog's fascination with a beautiful young woman: was anything more pitiful? His motives would be obvious to anyone paying attention; the lab techs and postdocs, Betsy Baird and Margit, all must have seen him for the fool he was. Meanwhile, Kevin Cho had stayed on at Stanford. He'd been snapped up—didn't it figure?—by Frank's old buddy Neil Windsor. Cho was studying signaling proteins in the growth pathway—far less risky than Cristina's apoptosis work. Frank understood that he'd missed a rare opportunity. A blind man could see that Cho was destined for a hit. Cho was as close as Frank had ever come to a sure thing.

Then, at long last, Cristina's luck shifted. After months of manipulating stem cells, she succeeded in turning off the gene. She had the knockout! And twelve weeks later, her transgenic mice showed mammary tumors—a direct result, presumably, of deactivating XIAP.

And in a stroke his judgment was vindicated. Cho had been the safe choice; but Frank McKotch was not timid; Frank McKotch had never shied away from risk. Beneath Cristina's comely surface was a true scientist, and only he had seen it. The postdocs, the lab techs, even Steve Upstairs: all would be awed by his perspicacity, his uncanny prescience.

Frank sat in the bar of the Charles Hotel, waiting for Neil Windsor, staring out at the snow. A storm was moving in from the west. Gwen had phoned him from the Pittsburgh airport to tell him that her flight was delayed. A couple of hours only, but Frank resented the holdup. They'd have to drive directly to South Station to meet Billy's train, fighting rush-hour traffic, then go straight to dinner. Frank hadn't seen his daughter in a year, his son—was it possible?—in three. *At least we have tomorrow*, he thought. They would spend the morning and afternoon together before the kids left for their mother's house in Concord.

He glanced around the bar. He felt summoned here against his will. Grohl had closed early for the holiday, and Betsy Baird had left at noon. After he and Gwen hung up, the phone rang again immediately, and Frank answered without thinking. When he heard Neil's voice, he knew that he was trapped.

Now he sat nursing a martini, fortifying himself. He would make small talk with his old buddy: swap some gossip, ask about the wife and kid. A new round of massive DARPA grants had just been awarded; Neil would know who'd gotten the nod. There was plenty to talk about besides the academy, Kevin Cho, and the *Nature* paper, the bolus of resentments that sat inside his gullet, the betrayals of the past.

He startled when Neil clapped him on the shoulder.

"McKotch! Man, are you a hard guy to track down."

Frank rose. "Jesus, it's good to see you." To his surprise, he meant it. He was always startled by how familiar Neil looked, how much like his old self. Nearing sixty, he was as scrawny as ever; his crazy metabolism had not slowed. In grad school it had earned him a nickname, Tapeworm. Frank thought of the cold-cut sandwiches—slappers, they'd called them—Neil had made each morning. He'd carried them to the lab in a grocery sack, half a dozen slappers a day. His hair had been thinning even then. Now he was virtually bald, his shoulders beginning to stoop. Frank still had a full head of hair, to his great satisfaction: thick and wavy, with only a touch of gray.

Neil seemed to read his mind. "My God, look at you. Aging beatnik. Get a haircut, wouldya?"

"Envy's an ugly thing, Weisberg."

Neil grinned appreciatively. "Is that a martini?"

"Want one?"

"It's a little early for me. But hey, knock yourself out."

Thanks for your permission, Frank thought sourly. "So what brings you into town?"

"I gave a talk at Dana Farber." Neil poured his beer into a glass. "Then I met with your outfit this morning."

"Protogenix?" Frank stared at him, surprised.

"Yeah. They want me on the SAB."

"No kidding." Frank felt himself sweating. He'd been on the scientific advisory board for nearly three years; his agreement expired in a month. He groused about the management to anyone who'd listen, but that didn't mean he was ready to be replaced.

"I told them no. The money's incredible, but I've got too much on my plate." Neil reached down the bar for a bowl of peanuts. Tapeworm had always loved peanuts. "Seen Paulette lately?"

"Not in a few years." Frank speared his olive with a toothpick, a mortal blow. "When Scott moved back from California, she let me come for dinner so I could get a look at my grandkids." He said the word a little sheepishly.

Neil laughed. "Don't much like the sound of that, do you, old man?" He tossed a peanut into his mouth. "Where's Scotty these days? Vermont somewhere?"

"Connecticut."

"And why Connecticut?"

Here we go, Frank thought: Neil was never happier than when he was asking questions. In the old days it had driven Frank crazy. He hadn't minded the factual ones—*where did you take Paulette for dinner?* But those were just the warm-up. Neil wanted to know the reasons for things. *Why were you home so early? Why did she get mad at you? Why do you suppose she felt that way? Are you sure that's the reason?* At the time Frank had been flattered; he assumed that Tapeworm, with no girlfriend of his own, was living vicariously through him.

Later he saw those questions in a different light.

His friend's curiosity, the depth and dazzling breadth of it, was his primary strength as a scientist. Other investigators, including Frank, were driven to find the correct answer to a question—the single, uniquely perfect answer. Neil was interested in the whole range of possibilities; he truly enjoyed positing theories, playing out scenarios as far as imagination could take him. Unlike Frank, he didn't mind being wrong. *It's the only way you learn anything*, Neil often said, but Frank found the whole process tiresome. He didn't have the patience for mistakes.

"Teaching," he said, draining his glass. "At some prep school there."

"Choate?" Neil asked. "Taft? Pomfret?"

"One of those." Frank couldn't remember the last time he'd discussed his younger son with anybody. Scott the longhair, the college dropout, who'd gone west and married a girl the family had never met. Billy was the son Frank talked about. But Tapeworm, as always, went right to his weak spot.

"Billy's practice is thriving," Frank said.

"Good for Bill," Neil said. "And Gwen?"

"I'm seeing her tomorrow. She and Billy are coming for an early Christmas."

"Did she ever make contact with Doug Levin?"

Frank hesitated, a bit surprised. He'd forgotten that years ago, trying to track down an endocrinologist for Gwen, he'd asked Neil for a referral. "I think so."

"Levin's top-notch. He was in on that Turner study at the NIH." He poured his beer into a glass. "She's still taking the estrogen, I hope."

Frank felt a flash of anger. *None of your goddamn business*, he thought, draining his glass. It shamed him to admit he had no idea. Gwen was an intensely private person. For years now—her whole adult life—she'd spurned any conversation about her health. Questions were met with stony silence. And estrogen was more than a health question; it was a sex question. Frank was no prude. He'd always—well, until recently—enjoyed a healthy sex life. But he froze at the idea of discussing sexual matters with his daughter, who *was* a prude. She was possibly as uptight as her mother, a prude of world-class proportions.

"She won't discuss it," he said. "To be honest, I have no idea if she's taking it or not."

Neil frowned. "Frank, you know the arguments. Bone density. Early cardiovascular disease."

"It's her decision. She's not a kid anymore."

"All the more reason she should understand the ramifications."

"I'm sure she does," Frank said, a bit sharply. *She's short, not retarded*, he wanted to add. *She's an intelligent girl*.

"'Nuff said, then." Neil slurped at his glass. "How's your science, amigo?"

Frank signaled the bartender. Clearly another martini was in order. "Nothing to report just yet, but things are moving forward. Yourself?"

Neil grinned. "You saw the paper, right?"

"What paper?" Frank said smoothly.

"Oh, it's in a little journal called *Nature*. Ever heard of it?" Neil chuckled. "I can't take all the credit, of course. I've got a terrific post-doc. I believe you know him. Kevin Cho."

Frank's heart quickened. "Hmm. Can't say I do."

Instantly he realized his mistake. Neil stared at him with interest. "Oh, really? He says he interviewed with you a couple years ago. Smart Korean kid. Looks about twelve."

"Oh, *Cho*," Frank said miserably. "Sure. I remember Cho."

"Well, you did me a huge favor by not hiring him. I should thank you, my friend. He's turning out to be my secret weapon."

What's mine is yours, buddy, Frank thought. *Kevin Cho, Protogenix. Do I have anything else you might want?*

Neil made another dive for the peanuts. "How's your apoptosis girl working out? Any luck?" He chewed loudly. "I've heard rumblings that Radler is getting close."

Frank blinked. He knew, of course, that Cristina wasn't the only one studying XIAP. Her old lab at Baylor had the gene construct; so did Fritz Radler's team at the University of Chicago. Either group might beat them to the finish line, as Neil well knew.

"Oh, Cristina's a real go-getter." Frank lowered his voice. "I shouldn't be telling you this, but we're getting positive signals from *Science* about our paper."

"No kidding," said Neil. "Has it gone out for review?"

"Out and back." The lie burned in his throat like whiskey, part pleasure, part pain. "We're revising now, but the changes are minor. I can't imagine it won't go through."

"Frank, that's fantastic. Mazel tov, my friend."

"The girl has turned out to be quite a find. A force to be reckoned with."

A fresh martini was placed on the bar. Frank reached for it gladly.

"Of course, you've had a hell of a year yourself," he continued. "The Academy and all." Smiling had begun to hurt him. His jaw ached all the way back to his ears. "Congratulations on that too, by the way."

"Frank, you're a mensch. I don't mind telling you, if things were reversed, my guts would be in a knot." Neil grinned broadly. "That's the value of sports. Builds character. I've tried to get my kid into soccer, but no luck. He takes after his dad."

Frank guzzled his drink. Neil had married late, a vivacious Israeli woman ten years younger. He'd been fifty when his son was born. His wife, a paleontologist, had pulled some strings at the Stott Museum to get Gwen an internship. Ten years later, his daughter still worked there. It was the only job she'd ever had.

"How's Tova?" Frank asked, reaching for a new subject.

"Nuts," Neil said happily. "Did I tell you she's keeping us kosher? Since I got to Boston I've eaten three cheeseburgers. It feels like adultery." He reached for his wallet. "Seriously, she's great. The kid's great. Frank, I am a lucky man."

When they'd first met, in the fall of 1960, it seemed Frank would be the lucky one. Already luck had carried him further than anybody he knew. He'd left his father and stepsisters back in Bakerton, a tiny mining town in western Pennsylvania, in the company house where he was born. His father, and all Frank's boyhood friends, worked in the coal mines. A high school classmate had died there at the age of twenty, crushed in a mine collapse. Luck had given Frank size, speed, and strength, a quarterback's ability to think on his feet. Luck had also blown out his knee his second season at Penn State. The timing was auspicious. His athletic scholarship was replaced by an academic one, and Frank McKotch began his studies in earnest, at what he now understood to be a rare moment in history. The Salk vaccine had taught the world a critical lesson, that the lab was the battleground, the frontier where disease would be conquered. Polio, heart disease, even cancer: though he barely remembered her, Frank thought often of the condition that had killed his mother. No opponent was unbeatable—or so he believed then, the cocky athlete, young and careless and intoxicated by his own gifts.

Luck had prevented mishaps with his many girlfriends—Marla, Rita, Louise, Rosemarie. Pretty Pennsylvania girls spoiling for husbands; in that hope, they had all opened their legs for him. They were not easy girls, a phenotype readily distinguishable in the late fifties. They were all beautiful, all virgins. At least that's what they'd told him, as though it were a selling point. As though, to a randy young man like Frank, it made any difference.

Luck had put him in the lab of Kendrick Moore, whose brilliant scientific mind would succumb eventually to dementia but was then at the height of its power. It was Moore who'd seen his potential, who'd urged him on to graduate study at Harvard, where Neil Windsor was already sweating at the bench. Frank had lucked out too in choosing a course of study; he'd picked developmental biology at precisely the right time.

As graduate students he and Neil were roommates; the university housing department had assigned them to each other. At first glance Frank was unimpressed. He had the athlete's habit of sizing up another man in a single glance. On the playing field—in life too—it was a crucial skill. Neil clearly lacked size and strength. His speed too seemed dubious. The guy's shoes were forever untied. He could barely cross the street without falling over his feet.

McKotch, Neil repeated after Frank introduced himself. *Scotsman?*

Sure, Frank said easily. He got that all the time—his height, his reddish hair. He knew little about Scotland but liked the associations: golf, family tartans, expensive single malts. His actual background, Hungarian and Slovak, was less appealing and harder to explain.

Windsor, he said. *The royal family?*

The black sheep. Notice how they never mention me. Prince Neil.

Prince Neil had gone to Harvard as an undergrad, and knew his way around Cambridge. He pointed out the libraries, the labs and—not that he'd ever ventured there—the gym and athletic fields. Frank considered him an expert on all things Harvard. Their first weekend approaching, he asked the all-important question:

Buddy. Where are the girls?

At that Neil had simply shrugged. *Radcliffe, maybe? How would I know?*

Frank understood, then, that Neil's predicament was even more dire than it appeared, that the guy was still a virgin. And though Frank didn't know Cambridge—had never, but for a single trip to the Jersey shore, left the state of Pennsylvania—Neil's problem fell into his narrow purview. He knew what to do about that.

For the next week, he took the long way home from the lab, making a slow detour through Radcliffe Yard. There he met a pretty blonde named Janet Smart, sunning herself on a September afternoon. *She's a smart girl*, he said when he introduced her to Neil. And Janet, who'd probably heard that line a hundred times, giggled in delight.

That weekend Frank and Neil had their first Radcliffe dates;

Janet's roommate, Muriel Kline, had agreed to come along. They saw *Psycho* downtown, a perfect date movie: Janet clutched his hand and hid her face against his shoulder, and by the famous shower scene she was nearly sitting in his lap. When the lights came up, Janet suggested a drive down to Nantasket, a moonlit walk on the beach.

That September was Indian summer; they'd walked for five minutes under the low moon. Then Frank led Janet away, to where the beach was fringed with tall sea grass. They had stopped at the girls' dorm to pick up a blanket, a fact Frank had noted. He and Janet were clearly thinking the same thing.

They lay together a long time, though Janet stopped him in the end. This didn't discourage him: she would let him next time, or the time after. He never minded waiting a little. It gave him something to look forward to.

They found Neil and Muriel still walking the beach. *Where've you been?* Neil demanded. *It's freezing out here.*

They drove back to Cambridge in virtual silence, Janet leaning against Frank's shoulder, her hand high on his thigh. When Frank dropped the girls at their dorm, Neil stayed in the backseat.

What's the big idea? he demanded. *We were walking for over an hour. I felt like a sand crab.*

Frank stared at him in the rearview mirror. *You were* walking? *Jesus, Windsor. I get you a cute girl, I drive you to a beach. Do I have to kiss her for you too?*

I didn't want to kiss her.

A cold feeling settled in Frank's stomach. He had heard of guys like that, but had never encountered one. He was stumped for a response.

Muriel seemed nice, he said finally. *I'm surprised you didn't like her.* If you're queer, he thought, just tell me. I'll find another roommate. It's no big deal.

I liked her fine. Neil ran a hand through his hair, a tic Frank had come to recognize as a nervous habit. *But Frank, Muriel is Jewish.*

Frank shrugged. He was Catholic but had dated Lutherans, Episcopalians. *Yeah? So?*

Well, I'm Jewish too.

No kidding? He turned to look at Neil. The only Jews he'd ever known were merchants back in Bakerton: the Lippmans, who had a flower shop, the Friedmans, who owned the furniture store. *Windsor is Jewish?*

Our real name was Weisberg. My dad changed it when he was applying to grad school. He couldn't get into the Ivies as a Weisberg, so he changed his name to Windsor. Princeton took him right away.

No kidding, Frank said again. He was amazed at what Neil's father had done, and filled with envy. His own father had left Hungary as Anders Mikacs; a clerk at Ellis Island had misspelled his name. A government paper pusher had renamed him, and Frank's father had simply accepted it. Trained in Budapest as a dentist, he would mine coal for the rest of his life. Intimidated, speaking little English, he'd been passive as a lamb.

So you're a fraud, Frank said.

Absolutely.

Me too. Frank parked the car. *I'm from the royal family too. Royal losers. The American dream in reverse. I should go back to Hungary and pursue the Hungarian dream.*

The Scotsman, Neil said, laughing.

The Prince of Wales.

They got out of the car.

I don't get it, said Frank. *What's the problem with Jewish girls?*

It would be like kissing my sister.

Got it, Frank said.

What I want to know is, how'd you find me the only Jewish girl at Radcliffe? The odds of that must be astronomical.

Shut up, Weisberg, Frank said. Over the years he would say it a thousand times.

OUTSIDE, THE snow was still falling. Frank turned up the collar of his coat. Seeing Neil made him think of the past, in ways that tore at him. Made him think, achingly, of Paulette. Not his angry ex-wife, the bitter final days of their marriage, but an earlier iteration. The young Paulette. The girl he had loved.

Against all odds, it was Neil who'd introduced them. Paulette was the only girl he knew in greater Boston—possibly, with the exception of his three sisters, in the entire world. For two years, as an undergrad, Neil had tutored Paulette in math. As she would later explain to Frank, trigonometry mystified her as completely as it bored her. But she was about to apply to college, and even a legacy couldn't crack Wellesley with such lamentable board scores. Something had to be done.

Her father had hired Neil on the recommendation of an old friend, one of Neil's professors at Harvard. One look at the kid had undoubtedly clinched the deal. If you had a daughter as stunning as Paulette, Neil's awkwardness would have to be reassuring. Her virtue, surely, would be safe with him. After Paulette entered Wellesley, the tutoring stopped; but she and Neil kept in touch. When she invited Neil to a Wellesley Christmas mixer, Frank did something he'd never done before. He tagged along.

He was free then, and on the make. He'd tired quickly of Janet Smart; but when he tried dating other Radcliffe girls, they all seemed to know about him. Blackballed his first semester, he was forced to look elsewhere.

The Wellesley girls, by and large, did not impress him. They struck him as opinionated, even strident. Though beautifully dressed, they were nothing special in the looks department. He'd known prettier girls, loads of them, at Penn State. *Wellesley to wed, Wheaton to bed*, Frank thought, and wondered why they weren't at a Wheaton mixer instead.

He was dancing with an especially irritating girl, a willowy redhead, when Neil Windsor sailed past with a girl in his arms. A dark-haired girl with an exquisite face. Not merely pretty: a knockout. The most beautiful girl in the room.

Excusing himself, Frank disengaged from the redhead, crossed the dance floor, and tapped Neil's shoulder. And before they'd exchanged a single word, he had Paulette in his arms.

That girl you were dancing with is Edith Anderson, she said. *You were very rude to her. You left her stranded on the dance floor.*

I didn't like her, he said. *I liked you better.*

You could have waited.

I couldn't wait. He spotted the redhead across the room, dancing with a new partner. *Is Edith a friend of yours?*

Paulette giggled. *I can't stand her. She's a witch.*

I'm glad I ditched her, then. Frank pulled her closer. *Come on. Let's go dance next to her.*

They met in baggage claim, their usual arrangement. Frank stood next to the belt, waiting for his daughter's small purple suitcase. It was easier than finding Gwen in a crowd.

"Hi, Daddy," said a voice near his elbow, startling him. She'd always had a way of sneaking up on him.

Frank stooped to embrace her. His natural inclination was to lift her into his arms; but years ago a counselor had admonished him against this.

"How was the flight?" he asked. Her appearance hadn't changed in twenty years. Pale skin dotted with freckles; carrot red hair cut short and choppy, with a cowlick that couldn't be subdued. She wore jeans and a Pittsburgh Steelers sweatshirt, boys' size Large. Gwen was the only one of Frank's children who followed sports. Together they'd watched the Steelers win four Super Bowls. Two at home in Concord. Two more in a bare, drafty apartment on Mass Ave, where Frank had squatted after the divorce.

"Wait a minute," he said. "Where are your glasses?"

"No more glasses." She grinned. "I had the surgery."

"Radial keratotomy?" He stared at her, confounded. Gwen's childhood had left her with a lifelong horror of doctors. It was inconceivable to Frank that she'd let someone take a knife to her eyes. That she'd seen a doctor of any kind.

He kissed the top of her head. "What's gotten into you?"

"I'm taking a dive trip next month. I figure as long as I'm down there, I might as well see something." For years she'd complained about her prescription dive mask, heavy and, in warm waters, perennially fogged. Her vision was so poor that a regular mask was out of the question, and despite years of nagging by Paulette, she refused to consider contacts.

"That's wonderful, Gwen. Good for you." He spotted her suitcase and swung it easily from the belt. Gwen was a famously light packer. She'd learned long ago not to pack more than she could carry.

"Is that everything?" And then, with a twinkle: "No pocketbook?"

Gwen rolled her eyes, and they both laughed. Paulette was outraged at Gwen's refusal to carry a pocketbook. It was a dialogue Frank had witnessed many times—years ago, when his presence was tolerated at school functions and graduations.

But where do you keep your wallet? Paulette would demand.

In my pocket.

What about your lipstick?

I don't wear lipstick.

If you carried a pocketbook, Paulette insisted, *you could start.*

They headed for the car-rental counter. "Reservation for Gwen McKotch," Frank told the clerk, a bald Latino with a lobeful of earrings.

"Where's the driver?" he asked.

"Here," Gwen said.

The clerk looked down at her, and frowned. "Can I see a license?"

Gwen fished in her pocket and handed over her driver's license. He stared at it a long time, his eyes returning twice to her face, which had flushed a deep red. Frank understood that his daughter's life was full of such moments, the stares of strangers trying to figure out what she was. At thirty-four, Gwen was four feet eight, the height of an eleven-year-old child. Even her voice was childlike, clear and high pitched. In elementary school she'd been a regular soloist in the school choir, with a voice that astonished her teachers: more boyish than girlish, the joyful banshee cry of a young hooligan making mischief. A voice with perfect pitch, remarkable in its clarity and power.

The clerk handed back her license. "All right," he said uncertainly. "We got you in a Chrysler LeBaron. Or for an extra thirty bucks, you can get a Cadillac."

Frank knew without asking that Gwen had requested a tiny Ford Festiva, as she did every year.

"The LeBaron is a mid-size," he told the clerk. "The reservation was for a compact." He could hear the counselor's voice in his ear: *She's a grown woman. Let her fight her own battles.* But she shouldn't have to, he thought, glancing at Gwen's scarlet cheeks. She shouldn't have to fight at all.

"I didn't take the reservation, so I don't know what she asked for," the clerk said. "But don't worry. I ain't charging her for the upgrade."

Finally Gwen spoke. "That's not the point. I can't drive a mid-size."

The clerk's eyes widened. "I'm sorry. I didn't think."

"No problem," Gwen said, putting away her license. "It isn't your fault."

They retrieved Frank's Saab from the parking garage and began the slow rush-hour crawl toward downtown. The clerk had been unable to locate a compact. *Screw the counselor*, Frank thought, and stepped in to give the guy a dressing-down. His outburst hadn't changed a thing— Gwen still had no rental car—but Frank couldn't help himself.

"That jackass," he fumed. "A simple car rental. How difficult is that?"

"Dad, don't worry about it." Gwen fumbled under the passenger seat and found the lever to raise it.

"They can bring the Chrysler to the house tomorrow morning," Frank suggested. "Billy can drive it up to Concord."

"That won't work," Gwen said.

"Why not?"

"Bad news, Dad. Billy isn't coming."

Reflexively Frank slammed on the brake. "What do you mean, not coming?" He glanced over at his daughter. She sat strapped into her seat, staring straight ahead.

"He's on call tonight."

"When did that happen?" Disappointment pressed on his chest like a bully's hand, goading him into a fight. "I thought we had a plan."

"I don't know the details, Dad. Just that he's on call."

"Why didn't he tell me? Would it have killed him to pick up the phone?"

"He's pretty busy. Honestly, I hardly hear from him myself."

Frank eyed her suspiciously. When Gwen clammed up, there was no way to pry her open. Billy phoned him twice a year, on his birthday and Father's Day, and responded politely to his e-mails; but when Frank traveled to New York for the occasional conference, his son was never free for lunch. Frank had wondered lately if Billy were avoiding him. Always he pushed the thought away.

He changed lanes quickly, cutting off a Jeep Cherokee in the passing lane. The other driver leaned on the horn.

"I could have invited Scott," said Gwen. "I doubt he would have come, though. He's got his hands full with Penny and the kids."

"Sure." Frank couldn't remember the last time he and Scott had spoken. He wondered, now, if his son were like the young fathers he saw trekking along the Charles on Sunday afternoons, carrying babies in backpacks or slung across their chests. It was the sort of spectacle you never saw back in the sixties, when Frank's children were small. He was privately glad to have been spared the indignity of toting a baby in a sling, which struck him as unmanly. Was this why his kids didn't want to see him? he thought irritably. Because he'd never pushed them around town in a stroller?

He felt suddenly unmoored, unsure what to do next. Stop by the lab and see Margit? That, he thought despairingly, would kill some time. The evening, so promising a moment ago, stretched dismally before him. How strange it was, this annual tradition, how stripped down and hollow: father and daughter exchanging gifts in a restaurant, two days before Christmas. Billy's presence would have changed everything. For once it might have felt like a family gathering, something Frank hadn't experienced in years. Of course, the kids got plenty of that at their mother's house. Year after year, Paulette was hell-bent on reenacting the genteel New England Christmas of her childhood: formal dinner, midnight mass, opening presents around the Douglas fir; rituals in which, to his everlasting relief, he was no longer required to take part. Only Gwen continued to make time for her father. Only Gwen, perhaps, had nothing better to do.

He glanced over at his daughter. To anyone who knew Turners syndrome, her condition was obvious. She was short but not petite; her broad chest seemed to be sized for a much taller person. Her short legs were thick and muscular. She had the powerful build of an Olympic child gymnast: the narrow hips, the shield chest. Watching the games last summer, Frank found himself wondering if *all* the team were Turners. At their young ages—thirteen or fourteen—it was hard to tell.

Severe cases of Turner's, where a girl's second X chromosome was missing entirely, were easy to identify. Small stature plus certain telltale physical features—low-set ears, a low hairline, folds of excess skin at the sides of the neck—could have no other cause. But Gwen's second X chromosome wasn't missing, just partially deleted. This explained her asymptomatic childhood and probably, her good health as an adult: by Gwen's age, many Turners women developed serious ailments. Thirty percent had kidney abnormalities; a congenital bicuspid aortic valve was extremely common. But with most of her second X chromosome intact, Gwen had escaped these complications entirely.

Frank was still married to Paulette when he'd had Gwen karyotyped. From a medical standpoint, the news could hardly have been better; but Paulette refused to hear it; she was simply furious. Frank's explanations were wasted on her. To his amazement, she seemed determined to learn as little about Turner's as possible, as if ignorance would make Gwen's condition disappear. Any objective discussion of Turner's incensed her. What sort of man—sort of *person*—could think this way? she demanded. What sort of father could talk about *his own child* in such a cold and clinical way?

The truth was that Frank had been a scientist longer than he'd been a father. If he'd been trained to observe in a certain way, to describe his observations in precise terms, that did not imply a lack of feeling for the subject. Concern for the subject, deep concern; anger and protectiveness on her behalf. A powerful urge to kick the shit out of an Avis clerk who couldn't handle a simple car rental, to tear out all his hoop earrings and grind them savagely under his heel. Frank had never failed to love his daughter. He wanted simply to help her, to give her the best life possible. Presumably Paulette wanted the same. Yet how to do that was a subject on which they'd never managed to agree.

They climbed the stairs to the lab, Gwen leading the way, her sneakers squeaking on the steps. They reached the landing just as the elevator doors were opening.

"Frank?" Cristina Spiliotes stepped out of the elevator, smiling warmly. She wore a green velvet pullover with a deep V neckline. A diamond hung in the soft hollow at the base of her throat. She seemed dressed for somewhere more festive than the lab—a Christmas party, perhaps.

"How are you, Frank?" She touched his elbow. "Merry Christmas to you."

He smiled uncertainly, bewildered by her friendliness. Most days they exchanged a perfunctory hello, or nothing at all.

"Is this your little girl?" she asked.

A sick feeling in his stomach. *Jesus, no*, he thought. But Gwen's back was to Cristina; from the rear, she certainly looked like a child. It occurred to him that the two women were about the same age.

He laid a hand on Gwen's shoulder. "Gwen, this is Cristina Spiliotes, one of my postdoctoral fellows. My daughter, Gwen McKotch."

He willed her to step forward, to offer her hand in a confident way. But Gwen seemed to be hiding behind him. "Hi," she said, her voice small.

For the first time he could remember, Cristina seemed genuinely rattled. She looked from Gwen to Frank, and back again.

"I'm sorry," she stammered. "My mistake. Please forgive me."

"No problem," Gwen said for the second time in an hour. "It's not your fault."

The snow was falling, falling on the house in Concord, and this more than anything else—more than gifts or garlands, more than the familiar old carols or the insipid new ones playing in the bank and hair salon and grocery store that afternoon—made December twenty-fourth feel like a holiday. Her errands done, Paulette stood at the front door and stared out through the frosted glass. As a girl she'd loved the snow, its first appearance each year a thing to celebrate, Roy and Martine dragging their Flexible Flyers to the top of the hill behind their house, stopping periodically to wait for her, too little to keep up. Now her brother and sister lived in warmer climates—Martine in Taos, New Mexico; Roy and his new wife in Arizona—and only Paulette was left to witness the crystalline scratching at the windowpanes, the heavy blanket accruing on the front step.

The house, on a wide tree-lined street at the edge of town, had seen many winters; one hundred ninety-nine, according to the town clerk. It had been the boyhood home of Josiah Hobhouse, a Unitarian minister and ardent abolitionist. Paulette cherished this history as though it belonged to her, as though it were her very own ancestor who'd fought at Harpers Ferry alongside John Brown. Perhaps because of this, she couldn't imagine selling the place, as the men in her family—Billy, her brother, Roy—periodically urged her to do. In financial terms, the house was a disaster. Like all the elderly, it had begun to break down.

Walls, floors, nothing lasted forever. Paulette had not arrived at this insight on her own. For years she'd served on the local Patriots' Day committee, which planned the annual reenactment of the Battle of Concord; and last Patriots' Day, she'd met a young carpenter named Gilbert Pyle. He was a direct descendant of John Hawes Gilbert, a Concord Minuteman; each April, Pyle donned a tricorn and breeches and played the role of his ancestor in the skirmish at North Bridge. When not in costume, he specialized in historic restorations; in Concord his skills were much in demand. He had walked Paulette through the house, pointing out cracks in the foundation, the sagging porch, the ominous settling of the kitchen floor. Problems expensive to correct and—for a homeowner blinded by sentiment—all too easy to ignore. To Paulette the house was not a simple investment. The place was like a beloved grandfather, mute and broken, plagued by a host of hidden ailments, but still sentient. Still aware of this new winter descending, silently, on a clean wind from the north.

For Christmas she'd taken pains to make the house inviting. There were huge bouquets of white flowers in the foyer and dining room: orchids and lilies, a few roses; eucalyptus leaves for fragrance and green. She had a wonderful florist, accommodating and inventive. She disliked anything too seasonal—mistletoe, with all the silly business about kissing; poinsettias, available now in grocery stores, in vulgar shades of peach and pink.

Outside the wind was howling, a sound that thrilled her. She had prepared for a storm—firewood in the basement, boxes of candles in case the power failed. She longed secretly for this to happen, the family gathered around the fireplace, wrapped in blankets, looking out occasionally to monitor the snowfall.

The one problem with this fantasy, she realized, was her pottery. In an upstairs room were three hundred-odd urns and vases, plates and paperweights, shelved and cataloged by age and manufacturer. The room was drafty and faced north; if the power failed, the temperature would quickly drop below freezing, a frightening thought. Her oldest pieces were vulnerable to crazing, the tiny hairline cracks that appeared, weblike, in the porcelain's glaze. A sudden drop in temperature increased the risk. An antiques dealer had told her that fifty-five degrees was optimal, and Paulette tried to keep the house at that temperature. If that meant wearing a wool sweater eight months of the year, it seemed a small sacrifice to make.

She felt it her mission to protect these pieces, noble survivors from another age. Time was the enemy; with each passing year she became more aware of its momentum, the destruction it wrought. Her own face was a constant reminder: still beautiful, her son insisted, but Paulette was not fooled. Her skin was delicate, etched with tiny lines. She was so vigilant about her weight that her features were sharper than they used to be; her hair, if she were to stop coloring it, would be more gray than dark. Most shocking were her hands, knotted with ropy veins. How transparent her skin had grown! It struck her as faintly indecent, her inner workings, the circulation of her blood, so utterly exposed.

She climbed the stairs to the back bedroom and switched on the light. The glass and pottery were neatly arranged on floor-to-ceiling shelves. Against an inside wall were the most precious pieces, manufactured by the Mount Washington Glass Company a century before. They moved her in ways she could scarcely articulate, partly because they were beautiful and partly because they were manufactured in New Bedford, Massachusetts, a city Clarence Hubbard Drew had helped build. In his day it was the wealthiest city in America, flush with whaling money. Paulette's first pieces, a Mount Washington tea set and nosegay vase, had come down to her from her grandmother. Paulette had admired them all through her childhood, imagined them displayed at the original Drew house on County Street in New Bedford, which had been sold to the city and turned into a museum when her father was still a boy. The tea set and vase were the centerpieces of her collection, which now included Hull and Roseville pottery, Hall china, and two dozen ornamental glass paperweights.

These objects brought her pleasure; more than that, they filled a space inside her, the cavern created when Frank left, the children grew up, her own parents decamped for Florida and died within a year of each other, her sister-in-law, Anne, succumbed quickly and horribly to lung cancer, seven months after being diagnosed. For a time Paulette felt like the passenger who falls asleep on a train and wakes up disoriented, in a place she never intended to be. She understood, then, the fragility of a life built around other people, the connections of blood and marriage that seemed elemental but eventually proved fleeting—of archival interest only, like relics kept under glass.

The changes had happened over three or four years, a time Paulette now remembered with a certain remove, like chapters of a novel read in her youth. Her response had been instinctive: after the divorce, she drew closer to her children; when the children left, she reached out to the family of her birth. When her parents, and later Roy and Martine, moved to the far edges of the country, she was tempted to follow; but something in her—pride? sentiment?—had rebelled. The house in Concord was dear to her. The children had been babies here, had played soccer and badminton in the grassy backyard. Those years *were* her life, no matter how painfully they'd ended. Subtract those, and she had accomplished nothing, experienced nothing. Without them, she'd be no one at all.

For a time she'd imagined that the house had a future. Her children—married, with families of their own—would gather here for Sunday dinner, as she and Roy had done at their parents' in Newton. But that, like her own marriage, hadn't turned out as planned. Billy seemed determined to stay single forever. (Not to mention Gwen, poor Gwen.) And Scott had married hastily and disastrously. He had always been vague about the particulars; for all Paulette knew, he'd found Penny by the side of the road. She was a dim, pretty girl, unwilling or unable to carry on a polite conversation. Worse, she let her two children run wild. To her dismay, this was how Paulette thought of Sabrina and Ian: as *that woman's children*. By the time Scott and Penny moved back from California, the children were five and seven, and the sudden acquisition of a grandmother seemed to puzzle them. Their manners were atrocious, which was to say completely transparent. It wasn't that they disliked Paulette; they simply didn't understand what a grandmother was *for*. Though she sent gifts each year on their birthdays, she had never received a thank-you note, a habit she had drummed into her own children but which Scott had apparently abandoned.

He'd been a stubborn boy, resistant to correction. She had always suspected that her influence on his character would be minimal, and that had turned out to be true. He'd been ten years old when she and Frank divorced, and had witnessed more adult suffering than Paulette could bear to think about. Rambunctious from birth, he'd needed stability more than the others did, and had gotten less of it. Paulette had been an excellent mother to Billy, a good one, in spite of the attendant difficulties, to Gwen. But with Scott she had been distracted, so consumed with rage and heartbreak that she'd failed him in the crucial years. How relieved she'd been to send him off to Pearse, a passage that should have saddened her. He was only fourteen then, a little boy, but she'd been ready—no, eager—to let him go. Her own father and brother had gone to Pearse, and Billy had thrived there; but she ought to have seen that Scott wasn't ready to take his place in the world. She'd neglected Scott and hovered over Gwen, who now seemed to resent her for it. Paulette saw that she'd been wrong on both counts. That she'd done everything wrong.

Downstairs she put a log on the fire and opened a bottle of champagne. She seldom drank during the day, and never alone; but she allowed herself this annual exception. It was nervewracking, this waiting, not knowing who would arrive first. Each of her children demanded something different of her, and it would ease her mind tremendously—*tremendously*—to know which role she would be expected to play when the doorbell rang.

For Billy she had to be *well*, in all respects. To look well. To feel well. He would notice if she seemed tired, so she'd gone to bed early the night before. (That he noticed such things, she took as evidence of his sensitivity. He'd always been the least selfish of her children.) For Billy she'd had her hair done, and spent the money for a facial; she'd shopped for something special to wear and had spent extra time with the florist. But she was getting over a cold, a fact that would not escape him. If, heaven help her, she sneezed in his presence, he would send her to bed immediately, like an old crone a breath away from pneumonia and possible death.

The hairdo, the facial, would be wasted if Scott arrived first; he wouldn't notice if she answered the door in overalls. When Sabrina and Ian were younger, Paulette's Christmas outfit was often ruined; their sticky hands went everywhere—her blouse, the doors, the walls. Scott's wife never commented on the heirloom ornaments, the floral arrangements. Paulette could hack and sneeze to her heart's content; she'd have to pass out at Scott's feet before he'd sense anything amiss. She would be pressed into immediate service as a babysitter—or, in recent years, a security guard. Her grandson was a one-man wrecking crew. Without constant supervision, he was likely to tear the house apart.

Gwen made no demands at all, yet her arrival caused the greatest anxiety, for one reason: *she didn't talk.* Left to Gwen, the conversation would end at "Hello." She seemed not to understand that social interaction required the participation of two people, that polite adults asked open-ended questions—*Have you heard from Uncle Roy or Aunt Martine? Have you bought any more antiques?*—and feigned interest in the answers, whether they were interesting or not. On certain Christmas Eves, faced with Gwen's silence, she had chatted with herself for an hour or more until the others arrived. *Relax, Mother,* Billy advised, when she broke her own rule and confided her frustrations to him. (In principle she avoided discussing her children with each other, but lapses occurred.) *You don't have to talk every minute. What's wrong with a little silence?* Paulette considered this advice preposterous.

Gwen wasn't just quiet; she was also touchy. Odds were good that Paulette, forced to ask a hundred questions, would eventually say the wrong thing. Not that she ever asked anything too personal. She'd never asked, for example, whether Gwen went on dates, the one thing she truly wanted to know. The only safe topic seemed to be Gwen's job. For years she had worked in the anthropology wing of the Stott Museum in Pittsburgh, though what precisely she did there, Paulette had no idea. At one Christmas dinner, stumped for conversation, she'd asked what Gwen wore to work. Her daughter's response had confounded her. She had simply laughed. The laugh lasted so long that Paulette grew nervous. It was, she felt, an unbalanced person's laugh.

"It doesn't matter," Gwen said when she'd caught her breath. "You won't believe this, Mother, but nobody cares what I wear."

Paulette had excused herself from the table, insulted and hurt. Only later did it dawn on her: maybe nobody cared what Gwen wore because nobody ever looked at her, this small, odd girl who'd possibly never been asked on a date. She'd felt terrible then, and tried to apologize: *I'm sorry, dear. I didn't mean to make you feel bad.* She'd hoped for a hug, but her daughter was not a hugger.

You didn't make me feel bad, she said simply. *I feel perfectly fine.*

And that, Paulette supposed, was the long and short of it. Gwen didn't hate her, didn't nurse secret resentments against her or anyone else. She was simply wired differently. That was how Frank had phrased it, a few years ago, when she'd telephoned him in tears over something Gwen had said. Or, more likely, hadn't said.

Fascinating, he said when she'd finished. *It could be related to the nonverbal learning issues.*

You mean it's caused by the—by her Turner's? The word felt strange in her mouth. She hadn't spoken of Gwen's condition in years.

It's certainly consistent with the literature. The research is sketchy, but there's some suggestion that Turner girls don't pick up on nonverbal social cues, or respond to them appropriately. He paused. *It's not you, Paulette. It's just the way she is.*

To her surprise it had comforted her, his precise way of explaining things. At one time she would have been angry. The phrase "Turner girls" would have incensed her. *This isn't a clinical trial,* she would have told him. *She's not a research subject. She's our daughter.*

For a brief time, not long after the divorce, they had stopped speaking entirely; but in her heart Paulette continued to argue with him. Day after day, they had vicious quarrels in her head. Making tea, or driving to Brimfield, she'd catch herself talking to Frank, still haunted by all the things she should have said, the brilliant arguments that would stun him into silence. That would force him to admit, finally, how wrong he'd been.

But in recent years, something had shifted. The quarrels had simply stopped. Now, when she thought of Frank at all, she remembered the days of their courtship, the handsome boy he'd been, how attentive, how dear. Lately she wondered how he fared with Gwen. Did their daughter *talk* to him when she visited Cambridge? Did he enjoy these visits? Did they ever discuss Paulette?

She finished her champagne and took her empty flute to the kitchen. The Christmas tree, a huge Douglas fir, stood in the foyer, waiting for the children to arrive. I ought to plug in the lights, she thought wearily, but she hadn't the heart. She was fifty-six years old; she had lived through more Christmases than seemed necessary. A Christmas every few years would suffice. Every four years, like leap year or the Olympics. Surely that would be enough.

As always, her tree was beautifully decorated. Grandmother Drew's glass bells and wooden soldiers; Grandmother Broussard's angel at the top. Piles of gifts ringed the tree. Most were for Scott's family: good sheets and towels, books for the children, the sorts of things she imagined they needed. It was hard to know where to begin; it had seemed to her, the one time she'd visited them in Gatwick—a town named for an airport!—that they needed *everything*. The house, a cramped ranch with low ceilings and small windows, was oppressively cluttered—newspapers and catalogs, the children's toys. Yet if you looked closely, it was apparent that Scott and Penny owned almost nothing. The walls were bare, the windows shaded with the metal blinds that had come with the place. They ate their meals from plastic dishes. There wasn't a single book, not even a dictionary, in the house.

Shopping for Billy posed the opposite problem: he already had the things he liked, and what he didn't have, he simply did not want. His apartment in New York was decorated in a style he called "minimalist": bare floors and invisible lighting, modern furniture in soft leather, everything in shades of beige. Paulette found it all very handsome, if a bit stark. Once a year he invited her for a weekend visit. He had a sunny guest room with a wonderfully firm mattress. It delighted her, after the theater and an excellent dinner, to fall asleep on her son's beige linen sheets. She wished he would invite her to New York more often. She was not the kind of mother who would invite herself.

For Christmas she'd bought him books, two cashmere sweaters, an exquisite leather belt. For Gwen, clothes were out of the question: misses sizes had never fit her, and the styles in the girls' department were inappropriate for an adult. Paulette had settled on a necklace and clip earrings (Gwen would not have her ears pierced), a cashmere hat and scarf. Good perfume. A Chanel lipstick in pale pink, the shade discreet enough that Gwen might be willing to try it. She'd searched everywhere for a small leather pocketbook. Shoulder bags were out of the question. The straps were always too long.

She had tried for years to help Gwen feminize her appearance. Her height confused people; that couldn't be helped. But why make matters worse by dressing like a boy? Makeup and a flattering hairstyle would signal to the world that Gwen was a grown woman; and then, perhaps, she would be treated accordingly. Each year at Christmas, Paulette prepared similar speeches in her head. But like her arguments with Frank, they were never articulated. One look at Gwen's small, stubborn face, the grim set of her mouth, and Paulette lost the heart to criticize. Gwen was still her baby. She was doing the best she could.

She was standing in the kitchen when the doorbell rang. *Be Billy*, she thought.

(Yes, she did have a preference. Mothers did.)

She hurried to the foyer and glanced out the window. An unfamiliar car was parked in the driveway: Gwen's rental, then. She took a deep breath and opened the door. Gwen stood on the doorstep in a ghastly purple ski jacket, hands jammed into her pockets.

"Darling!" Paulette embraced her. "Merry Christmas."

"You too. Mother, just so you know—"

Paulette released her abruptly, stunned to see Frank coming down the sidewalk.

"Paulette," he boomed, the false heartiness she hated. "Look what the cat dragged in." He wore dungarees and an MIT sweatshirt and carried Gwen's suitcase.

They stood there a moment, staring at each other. The snow was still flying; at first glance Frank's head seemed dusted with it, as though he'd hiked all the way from Cambridge. How curious, what aging did to redheads. Sprinkled with silver strands, his hair looked slightly pink.

"Hello, Frank," she said lightly, as though she'd run into him at a party. "Goodness. What are you doing here?"

"Don't mind me," he said. "I'm just the taxi service."

Next door the Marshes' porch light came on. Well, naturally: Barbara Marsh was a shameless gossip, and Frank's voice was loud enough to be heard in Lexington.

"Please come in," she said—quietly, hoping he would take the cue.

Inside he stamped his shoes vigorously, though they looked perfectly clean. "Sorry to barge in on you, Paulette. Avis muffed up Gwen's reservation, so I figured I'd give her a lift."

Gwen looked anxiously from one parent to the other, as though expecting the worst.

Frank eyed Paulette from top to bottom. She'd forgotten the way he looked at her—looked at every woman, in fact, who crossed his path. "You look good," he said.

Paulette flushed. "You too." Then corrected herself: "You're looking well." In fact he looked exhausted, his skin drooping around the eyes, as though he'd been sleeping poorly. Or maybe he—like herself, like everybody—had simply aged.

"Where is everybody?" he barked. (Was he hard of hearing? Was that the problem?) "No Billy yet?"

"I expect him at any moment," Paulette said.

There was an awkward silence. Frank looked around the room, at the Christmas tree in the parlor, the crackling fire, the champagne flutes waiting on the sideboard.

"Well, thanks for bringing Gwen," she said.

"None needed."

Do you have plans for dinner? she nearly asked, but Frank spoke first.

"I should get back on the road, I guess. I'm meeting someone downtown."

Of course: he had a woman waiting. Didn't he always? "All right, then," she said briskly. She opened the front door. In the distance she heard a crackling noise, tires on gravel. The roads had just been cindered.

"That must be Billy now," Paulette said.

Frank turned to look. A car was approaching, a silver Mercedes with New York plates. At the entrance to the driveway, it slowed and signaled. Then it accelerated suddenly and roared down the street.

"What the hell is he doing?" said Frank.

"It isn't Billy," said Gwen, who'd followed them outside. "It can't be. Somebody had the wrong house." At the corner, the red taillights turned and were gone.

THEY SAT at the kitchen table, the wind howling at the window-panes. Paulette had drained her second glass of champagne. Gwen had barely touched her tea.

Paulette glanced at the clock. She hadn't seen her daughter in a year; now, after a tense twenty minutes, she had resorted to bab-bling about the neighbors. Did Gwen remember Phillip Marsh, War-ren Marsh's younger brother? She didn't? He may have been younger, Scott's age. He was engaged to be married in the spring. Paulette had read the announcement in the *Globe*. Listening to herself, watching the expression—or lack of expression—on her daughter's face, she felt herself sink into despair. *Heavens, this is dreadful.*

She set down her glass. "I'm sorry to go on and on. There's no reason you should care about any of this. Tell me about you, darling. Have you—" She was just tipsy enough to say it. "Is there anyone special in your life?"

The change in Gwen was astonishing. Her face flushed. She squirmed uncomfortably in her chair. "Mother, I—" she began haltingly.

Just then, the doorbell rang.

"I'll get that," Gwen said, springing from her chair.

Paulette rose, half disappointed, half relieved. Had Gwen been ready to confide in her? Or—and this was far more likely—to storm out of the room in a fit of pique, casting a tense mood over the entire holiday?

She followed Gwen to the front door. "For heaven's sake, what is that noise?"

The sound tore through the foyer like a very loud lawn mower. Gwen opened the door. Scott stood on the sidewalk in a ratty old sweater, no hat or coat. The van idled loudly in the driveway.

"Good heavens," said Paulette. "What on earth happened?"

"We're dragging a *something*," Scott said, with a sheepish smile.

"Oh, dear." Paulette didn't catch what the *something* was; she was looking at her son. He had always favored the McKotch side, not the Drews; his features weren't as fine as Billy's, but somehow this made him more attractive. He had the kind of blunt, masculine good looks Frank had, minus the luxuriant hair. In recent years she'd noticed Scott's hairline receding, which saddened her. Perhaps to hide his bald spot, he'd grown his hair long and shaggy. She guessed he hadn't had a haircut in months.

"It happened back on the pike. We're lucky we made it." He bent to kiss her cheek. A stiff wind blew through the open doorway.

"Oh dear," she said again, eyeing the flowers on the hall table. The icy wind could be devastating to her orchids. "That's unfortunate. But, darling, you need to close the door."

"Just a sec. Guys, are you coming?" he shouted out to the van. "Grandma wants to close the door." He turned to his mother. "Where's Bill?"

Paulette and Gwen exchanged glances.

"Your brother's running late," said Paulette. She was certain it had been Billy's car they'd spotted. Why on earth had he run away?

PAULETTE BROUGHT out platters of oysters and laid them on the table. At the center of the table was the steaming soup tureen and the pink poinsettia (its plastic pot covered in *purple* foil) that Scott's wife had brought. Paulette had accepted it graciously, moving aside the nineteenth-century Scroddleware pitcher and bowl that usually occupied its place.

The family assembled around the table: Billy at the head and Paulette at the foot, the children and Gwen on one side and Scott and Penny on the other. "Heavens, you look chilly," Paulette said to her daughter-in-law, who invariably showed up in a summer blouse; after three years in Connecticut, the girl still didn't own a sweater.

Billy rose to fill their glasses with a lovely pinot gris he'd picked up at the wine shop in town. *So that's where you ran off to*, Paulette said when he explained. *Your father was so disappointed.*

Sorry I missed him, said Billy. *Maybe next time.*

"This is delicious, Mother," he said, and everyone agreed. Sabrina, uncommonly helpful, cleared the soup bowls while Paulette brought in the goose she'd stuffed that morning. She did not explain that the rest of the meal—the gingered carrot soup, roasted vegetables, a nice crusty bread—had come from a gourmet shop in town. Years ago such cheating would have been unimaginable. Paulette was an excellent cook, and during her marriage she'd entertained a great deal. Her grandmother's table seated eight comfortably—ten if Frank, amid much cursing, put in the extra leaf. Now, cooking for a crowd was out of the question. Scott's children were picky eaters, and Gwen, as always, ate like a bird. Both her sons loved her cooking, but could polish off a meal—an entire day's work—in ten minutes. Altogether it seemed more trouble than it was worth.

"You'll never guess whom I saw at the symphony," she told Billy as he cut into the Yule log. "Your old friend Lauren McGregor."

Billy handed Scott a slice of cake. "No kidding. She's in Boston?" He blinked twice, rapidly, but his face was impassive. Billy never lost his composure, but Paulette knew her son.

"Andover, I believe. Her husband works downtown. He's a banker of some kind."

"I didn't know she was married."

Paulette eyed him intently, surprised by the shift in his voice. "Oh, yes. And they have two children."

"No kidding," Billy said again.

"I wish you could have seen her," Paulette added impulsively. "Really, she hasn't aged a day. She was always a beautiful girl." Why was it so easy, now, to say this? Because it was all in the past, the girl safely married to someone else?

"She was hot," Scott agreed. "You blew that one, Bill."

"I suppose I did," Billy said mildly, unflappable to the end. "Well, good for Lauren." He nodded across the table to Gwen. "What happened to your glasses?"

"Your sister had her vision corrected," Paulette said. "Doesn't she look wonderful?"

"Wow," Billy said. "What prompted that?"

"I'm taking a trip," Gwen said. "To Saint Raphael."

Paulette looked at her, flabbergasted. "Gwen, that's *marvelous*. Why didn't you tell me?"

"Mother, I just got here." Gwen turned her attention to her plate, picking at her cake.

Paulette chose to ignore her surly tone. It was just like Gwen to bore them with talk about work when something truly interesting was about to happen. She couldn't decide whether Gwen did this on purpose, or simply couldn't help it. Maybe she truly didn't know what was interesting and what was not. It made Paulette wonder what else Gwen wasn't telling.

"There's great scuba diving down there," said Scott, his mouth full. Since marrying Penny, his table manners had degenerated gravely. Paulette couldn't understand it, particularly since Penny's, surprisingly, weren't all that bad.

"That's why I'm going," said Gwen.

Paulette frowned. Gwen's interest in scuba diving had always alarmed her. She blamed it entirely on Frank, who for Gwen's eighteenth birthday had paid for scuba classes at the YMCA. *She loves the water*, he'd told Paulette, by way of justification. *Jesus Christ, Paulette. It's the only thing she loves.*

"You're diving without me?" said Billy.

"What am I supposed to do, wait until you retire?"

For several years Gwen and Billy had taken an annual dive trip together, giving Paulette nightmares. She'd been relieved when Billy, busy with his practice, discontinued the tradition. If God had meant her children to breathe underwater, he'd have given them gills.

"Goodness, how adventurous," she said lightly. "And you'll be traveling with . . . ?"

"Nobody," Gwen said. "I'm going alone."

Paulette set down her fork. "Do you think that's wise?"

Gwen shrugged. "I have a week of vacation coming. Use it or lose it. It expires March first."

"But, dear." Paulette forced herself to smile. "Wouldn't it be more fun to take a girlfriend along?"

Gwen seemed to consider this seriously. "I don't think so," she said finally. "I think I'd have a better time by myself."

"Well, I just don't think it's *safe*," said Paulette. "Scuba diving alone!"

"I wouldn't be *alone*." Gwen spoke extra slowly, as though Paulette were a cretin. "There's a whole group, and a dive master."

"What in heaven's name is that?"

"An instructor, Mom. Geez. You act like I'm going up on the space shuttle."

Her grandson laughed. Dishes were passed.

The scene at the table seemed eternal: each in his usual chair, Grandmother Drew's silver and china. The wineglasses had been a wedding present. Like the platters, the soup tureen, they'd outlasted the marriage they were meant to commemorate. As they raised their glasses to toast the season, it struck Paulette that she had been divorced for twenty years.

The thought returned to her later as she rinsed the glasses at the sink. A strange feeling gripped her. Her heart raced; for just a moment the lights seemed to dim. She thought of her own life slipping away, her family dissolving and disappearing; little Gwen carried off, swallowed up; the sharks and octopi surrounding her, humans who resembled them waiting on shore.

Paulette closed her eyes. She'd experienced such spells before. Her doctor called them panic attacks, though Paulette wasn't so sure. The night before her father died, she'd felt a premonition not unlike this one; she'd known with a deep certainty that the end was near. Her father had been old and sickly, and there was nothing to be done; but this case, surely, was different. She ought to take action. She ought to call someone. She thought, irrationally, of the carpenter Gil Pyle, whose business was fixing things. Perhaps he would know what to do.

It's Christmas Eve, she told herself. Reasonable people were occupied with their families. Besides, what on earth would she say?

Gwen is going to the Caribbean all by herself. Something terrible is going to happen.

Breathing deeply seemed to help, and in a few minutes the feeling passed. When it did, she dialed Frank's number. Gwen had always—well, sometimes—listened to her father. Predictably, there was no answer. She supposed he was spending the night elsewhere. Or entertaining a woman at home, too busy to pick up the phone.

GIL PYLE could fix things.

Of the Battle Road reenactors—the lawyers and schoolteachers and history buffs—Pyle alone looked convincing in his costume. He was a lean, wiry man, with a scruffy blond beard and work-scarred hands. In his breeches and rough coat, he seemed battered by the long Colonial winters, but determined to endure. *He's a miracle worker*, said Barbara Marsh next door, who'd hired him to redo her clapboards. The Marshes' house was even older than Paulette's; without Pyle's repeated interventions, Barbara claimed, it would long ago have crumbled to the ground.

Paulette had hired him to save her kitchen, the floor that listed alarmingly downward; more and more, she felt as though she were cooking in the galley of a boat. The job would take a few weeks, Pyle told her, a month at the outside. The prospect alarmed her. She dreaded the disruption, the inevitable noise and dust. The presence of a stranger in her house.

Pyle's truck had arrived each morning at dawn. Paulette dragged herself out of bed, muzzy and disoriented, to open the back door—her hair disheveled, her unmoisturized face puffy from sleep. She would marvel, later, that she'd allowed him to see her in this condition, but at the time she'd been too groggy to care. She went back to bed, but Pyle's boots were loud, his radio audible through the floorboards. When she appeared later, dressed and groomed, he called her into the kitchen often, handed her a tape measure or instructed her to hold a board in place. *My helper quit on me*, he explained. *I need an extra pair of hands.*

She stood there awkwardly, watching Pyle heft and hammer. His plaid shirts were frayed at the cuffs and spattered with paint. She remembered how, as a teenager, her son Scott had bought brand-new dungarees with designer holes in the knees, a look she deplored. But Gil Pyle's clothing was battered by work, and this made its condition honorable. Made it, even, attractive.

As he worked, Pyle asked questions. How long had she lived in the house? From whom had she bought it? Did she know what year it was built? Paulette did know, naturally; she told him about Josiah Hobhouse, the Concord abolitionists, the Hobhouse descendants who'd inhabited the place ever since. *You know your stuff*, Pyle said, and asked more questions. She found herself talking about her childhood home in Newton, the long-lost Drew properties in Truro and New Bedford. Talking, for some reason, about the Mount Washington Glass Company, the exquisite urns and pitchers she'd purchased; the elusive other pieces—the Scroddleware and Hall—she coveted but had yet to find.

Let's see them, Pyle said, a request that astonished her. *Not now, but when I'm done.* And at four o'clock, when he'd finished for the day, they sat on the floor of the back bedroom as Paulette took vases and pitchers from their boxes.

You could use some shelves in here, Pyle said. *I could line the floor with cork, in case you drop something. To cushion the fall.*

I never drop anything, she said seriously. She hadn't meant to be coquettish, but Pyle broke into a grin.

I'll bet you don't, he said.

His concern for her treasures touched her profoundly. She wouldn't have expected a man like Pyle to care about antiques. In this way they were startlingly similar: they saw value in the past, in what had come before. Pyle spoke lovingly of the houses he'd restored, the vast cottages in Newport, the summer places on the Vineyard and the Cape. He'd spent years in the Army and had traveled widely in Germany, Belgium, France especially. *To see the churches*, he said. *I like the way they're built.*

Then it was Paulette's turn to ask questions. She learned that Pyle had backpacked through Vietnam and Thailand, slept on Turkish beaches, driven a dilapidated Jeep around the horn of Africa. It dawned on her then, how much of the world she would never see, how many places were off-limits to a solitary woman. The thought filled her with sadness. *Not necessarily*, Pyle said when she expressed this. *You just need someone to travel with.*

He worked at her house through the summer: the kitchen, the cork flooring, the shelves. His tools and scrap lumber took up residence in her backyard, terminally covered with a layer of sawdust. Then, in September, he told her he'd be leaving in two weeks: he spent winters in Florida, he explained, to be near his children. The boys' mother was a woman he'd never married, a woman he described fondly: *Sharon's terrific. We're still close.*

The name—*Sharon*—affected Paulette strangely. She took offense. Suddenly Gil Pyle's past seemed crowded with women, the ex-wives and girlfriends he mentioned casually, frequently, as though Paulette were an army pal or a drinking buddy. Wrinkled, sexless, all but irrelevant. A former woman, neutered by age.

"What's the matter?" Pyle asked, sensing her upset. And to her surprise, he took her hands in his.

In that moment a door opened, and Paulette glimpsed what lay behind it. She might have said anything, done anything; she might easily have walked through. Instead reason overcame her. Gil Pyle was a drifter, rootless, nearly homeless; he lived outdoors, in his truck, on other people's floors and couches. And he was only a few years older than her son Billy. Gil Pyle was *young*.

"Not a thing," she said briskly, meeting his eyes. "I appreciate the notice. I assume you'll finish building the shelves before you go?"

"Sure." Pyle frowned, blinked, released her hands. Abruptly the door closed.

Now months had passed, with no word from him. She had no reason to expect otherwise. Yet when panic squeezed her heart and choked her throat, it was Gil Pyle's hands she remembered. Why this should be, Paulette did not know.

In Cambridge, snow blanketed the sidewalk. Frank drove in second gear. Whether because of the snow or the holiday, the streets were nearly empty. A single car passed his, its headlights bright. Judging by the sky, it could have been midnight, or three in the morning. His watch said 5:15.

At certain times in his life, he had loved the early dark. When he and Paulette were newlyweds, it had simply meant more nighttime; when he came home from the lab they went directly to bed. More recently, he'd come home to find the windows bright, music blasting, Deena Maddux barefoot in the kitchen, singing and cooking dinner. Without her he found the dark evenings depressing, his few entertainments—TV, reading, booze—inadequate distractions. Most nights he fled the house to meet Margit for a movie. But he had seen everything playing at the Kendall. And Margit was on a plane to Stockholm, to spend Christmas with her children.

He drove slowly through Harvard Square. He considered ducking into the Harvard Book Store to warm himself, spend half an hour browsing through the used books downstairs. But the store, when he passed it, was closed, security lights glowing in the windows. Out of Town News was shuttered, its corrugated doors pulled shut. The Harvard Coop was dark; so were the cafés, the trendy clothing stores with unisex mannequins in the windows. A feeling of panic washed over him. For the next thirty-six hours, all his usual haunts would be closed. There was nowhere to go but home.

He parked on the street opposite his house, eyeing the dark windows, the front steps buried in snow. Last winter, he'd been fined twice by the city of Cambridge for failing to clear the sidewalk. He climbed the stairs and turned his key in the lock. Since Deena's departure, the living room had become an extension of his office. Books overflowed the shelves; he'd begun stacking them on end tables, the floor, the stairs. There were piles of scientific journals, notebooks, and manuscript pages; a year's worth of *Time* and *Newsweek*, and the dull, edifying magazines—*The Economist, Atlantic Monthly*—he subscribed to but did not read.

He flicked on a lamp and moved a pile of journals from his favorite chair. On top, a battered copy of *Endocrinology*—he'd subscribed for years, ever since Gwen was diagnosed. Oh, hell: He'd meant to find out—delicately, of course—whether she was seeing a doctor, taking the all-important estrogen. Neil Windsor was right. Estrogen was crucial for preserving bone density, for heart health. Not to mention the unmentionables: to keep vaginal tissue healthy, elastic and lubricated. Was this a part of her body Gwen even thought about? His daughter was thirty-four years old, yet to his knowledge, she'd never had a boyfriend.

Was it possible that she was still a virgin?

Was it possible that she was not?

Both scenarios were hard to imagine—in fact, equally so. Yet one of them, necessarily, was true.

For a time, when Gwen was in her teens, he'd been closely involved in her treatment. He'd had her enrolled in a clinical trial of oxandrolone, an anabolic steroid they hoped would stimulate growth. When that proved unsuccessful, he got her started on estrogen. They'd waited until she was sixteen—the eleventh hour—to give the oxandrolone time to work; once a girl started estrogen, gains in height were impossible. They had gambled and lost. The steroid had had no effect.

The decision haunted him. He had kept up with the literature; he knew that the protocols had changed. Now estrogen was started earlier, at twelve or thirteen. This helped build bone density in the early teens, a crucial moment in skeletal development. Had they done

Gwen a disservice by waiting so long? Had they endangered her tiny bones? He imagined his daughter many years hence, hunched and fragile from osteoporosis. Had his decision put her in jeopardy? It was too terrible to contemplate. And Frank would by dead by then. He would never know.

He set aside the *Endocrinology* and tossed another stack of magazines into the recycling bin—since Deena's departure, it had taken up residence in the middle of the living room. Early estrogen had other benefits. It improved social maturation, which had clearly been delayed in Gwen's case. She'd been a child at sixteen: unnaturally attached to her mother, afraid of the entire world. Paulette had aggravated the problem by treating Gwen according to her size, not her age, a common mistake. The estrogen hadn't changed her much physically, not in any visible way. It was her attitude that changed. Frank had never seen a more cogent illustration of the power of endocrinology. Not immediately, but slowly, Gwen seemed to take charge of her life: changing schools, moving far away from Concord, demanding that Frank teach her to drive.

What a transformation, the estrogenization of the brain.

In the kitchen he opened a bottle of wine—a cheap red, not bad for the money. A wine rack in the corner held the good Cabernet he saved for company. He'd discovered the Cab at a wine tasting with Rabbi Kleinman, and had bought the case to impress her. Now, with a lonely Christmas looming, he was glad he had.

Screw it, he thought, recorking the cheap stuff. *It's Christmas Eve.*

He opened a bottle of the Cab.

In the living room he flipped through a wire bin of DVDs, looking for something to watch. Many were gifts from Deena or Margit, who shared his taste for Bergman. What about *Hour of the Wolf*? He read the helpful summary on the back of its case. *Troubled artist Johan (Max von Sydow) is haunted by past memories.*

Er, perhaps not.

Autumn Sonata? *Wild Strawberries*? *Scenes from a Marriage*?

Dear God, no.

In the end he settled in with the television. It sat on a low table in the corner, where, if a family lived there, a Christmas tree would likely go. The thought did not depress him. He'd never had much use for Christmas. Maybe at first, when the kids were small. But as they grew older, Paulette's insistence on tradition irritated him: the cloying carols, the Drew family ornaments, most of them ugly, all more trouble than they were worth. When Christmas was over, it was Frank who had to take down the tree, while Paulette wrapped the goddamn things in layer upon layer of newspaper. One year, when she was pregnant with Scott, he'd had to put away the ornaments himself. Hanging over his shoulder, she had instructed him endlessly: so persnickety, so picayune, that he had lost his temper. What would she do if the house caught fire? he demanded. Save the goddamn ornaments? Then maybe, if she had a chance, come back for Billy and Gwen?

He drained his glass, came back from the kitchen with the rest of the bottle. He hadn't eaten, and wine always hit him on an empty stomach. He felt a little drunk, and he intended to get drunker still.

Seeing Paulette had unnerved him. She looked younger, somehow, than the last time he'd seen her, while he had aged dramatically. Back then—three years ago?—he'd been with Deena, and felt full of youthful vigor. When Paulette invited him to Concord to welcome Scott back from California, he had brought Deena along. It wasn't Frank's idea. Deena had been clamoring for years to meet his family, and he'd run out of excuses. Predictably, the evening went badly. Deena pouted for days afterward. And Paulette hadn't spoken to him since.

He'd believed at first that divorce would end his marriage. Later he understood that it wasn't so simple. For twenty years he and Paulette had lived a few towns apart, their lives running on separate tracks that had, when the kids were younger, occasionally intersected. At holidays and birthdays and graduations, Frank's presence was sometimes required, sometimes forbidden, seemingly at Paulette's whim. Over the years he'd fallen in and out of her good graces, for reasons he couldn't always discern. Not always, but often, he was banished after acquiring a girlfriend. The prettier the woman, the more protracted the ban.

Now, of course, he ought to be in the clear: he was completely, perhaps permanently alone. And Paulette? Was she alone too? He had no idea. For a time she'd *kept company*—the phrase she would use—with a wealthy antiques dealer. To Frank it sounded about right: a rich man who loved shopping for expensive junk. When the old boy keeled over, he'd left Paulette some dough, according to Gwen. Did Paulette miss him? Were women so different in that way? After all these years, all the women he'd known long and intimately, Frank hadn't a clue.

Maybe she was perfectly happy living alone in the drafty old house, where the drama of their marriage—comedy, then tragedy—had unfolded. He had a clear memory of the first time they'd seen it. He'd had doubts about buying such an old place, but Paulette had loved it immediately, enchanted by its history. She had a sentimental attachment to Concord, where her Drew grandparents had lived. In the end Frank left the decision to her, and not merely because her father had supplied the down payment. Frank's mind was elsewhere, on his troubled PhD thesis; he couldn't afford the distraction of an argument. Pregnant with Gwen, Paulette was moody, strangely volatile; flushed and plump and swollen. He'd known by touching her that she was pregnant. As she'd been with Billy: warm, always, to the touch.

Jesus: Billy. Frank thought of the Mercedes idling at the driveway, the driver's hesitation before slamming on the gas. Surely Gwen was right; the car was not Billy's. The alternative—that his son had fled at the sight of him—was unthinkable.

They'd always been close, in Frank's judgment, despite the divorce and the inevitable complications it caused. Away at Pearse, Billy had been spared both his mother's theatrics and the awkward weekend visits with his father. Frank had dragged Gwen and Scott to museums and zoos and ball games, suddenly conscious of the need to *entertain* his children, something his own parents had never dreamed of doing, something Frank himself had never done. Sunday nights, exhausted by the effort, he drove them back to Concord, careful to avoid Paulette and her strained silence, her baleful stare. Later, at home, he phoned Billy for an update on his classes, his soccer season, his plans for the future. The kid seemed well adjusted, serious and studious, too busy succeeding in his teenage life to miss tramping around a smelly zoo with his father. Frank had assumed, then, that Billy felt as he did, that family relationships ought to happen naturally, without contrivance, father and son each going about his business in mutual affection and regard.

He shook his head to clear it. Unsteadily he got to his feet, kicking over the empty bottle. The Cab had ignited a pleasant fire in his stomach. *A fire*, he thought. On a snowy Christmas Eve, it seemed the very thing. He examined the ashy hearth, the bricks white with creosote. He opened the damper and stared up doubtfully. The flue hadn't been swept in years, since before Deena left.

He went down to the basement, searching for firewood. He found a Duraflame log still in its wrapper. Deena had loved to screw by the fire, and they'd bought Duraflames by the half dozen. The fake logs didn't smoke or throw off sparks. They burned just long enough for what Deena called *one coital event*.

He brought the log upstairs, along with his snow shovel. At some point—after another glass of wine—he would clear the walk. He took matches from the mantelpiece and lit both ends of the log. The Duraflame ignited promptly, its chief virtue. In a moment the flame spread from end to end.

Frank sat back in his chair and watched it critically. No smoke, maybe, but neither was it much of a fire. He wished he'd thought to pick up firewood. Then a thought occurred to him: his whole house was full of kindling. He could—he really *should*—undertake an early spring cleaning.

He reached for the *Newsweek*s piled behind the sofa. One had a cover story on the new Mrs. JFK Jr. Another trumpeted the headline "The Mystery of Prayer." He tore into them vigorously, ink staining his fingers. Briefly the fire flared.

He swept a pile of paper from the hall table. He was drowning in junk mail. *Have Your Carpets Professionally Cleaned. The Penny Saver. Have You Seen This Child?* Gleefully he tossed them onto the fire.

He reached for another magazine, then realized what he was holding. The new issue of *Nature*. He'd flagged with a yellow Post-it note the article Neil Windsor had written. Neil and Kevin Cho.

He clutched the journal in his hand. It would give him enormous satisfaction, really, to toss it into the fire. To incinerate his envy, his ancient rancors, his own failure to produce. He would torch the last few limp, underachieving years of his life. He recapped, briefly, the grave mistakes he'd made in those years.

Not marrying Deena.

Not getting Gwen to the doctor.

Not hiring Kevin Cho.

He flung the journal into the fire. The flame responded with enthusiasm, filling the room with light.

Frank settled back into his chair. His open briefcase sat on the coffee table, overflowing with paper. On top of the pile was a thin sheaf of manuscript pages, neatly stapled. Cristina's paper, nowhere near completion. Publication—if it happened at all—was many months, perhaps a full year away.

His lie at the bar came back to him in a rush. *We're getting positive signals from* Science *about our paper. I can't imagine it won't go through.*

Shame filled him. Under normal circumstances, he was close-mouthed about ongoing projects. The field was competitive, wildly so: scientists borrowed, appropriated, stole outright. Grohl had invested heavily in Cristina's work, years and precious research dollars. Now that she was finally producing, Frank lived in fear that they'd be scooped.

Goddamnit: with the best minds in the world grinding away, racing to map the human genome, oncogenetics was set to explode. *We'll be picking cancer genes out of our teeth*, he thought. Scientists Frank's age were quickly becoming dinosaurs; his colleagues, more and more, looked like kids. Some, like Kevin Cho, really *were* kids, and they were the ones making the biggest finds. Frank—why deny it?—was nearing the end of his productive years. He wanted more than anything in the world to do what Neil Windsor was doing: to knock the field on its ear. A few times he'd come close; but the big discovery had somehow eluded him. And that—it was suddenly clear as day—*was his own goddamn fault.*

Again and again, he had focused on the wrong data. For years he'd felt superior to Neil, for reasons that now seemed foolish: charm, masculinity, athletic ability, sexual prowess. The first three counted for nothing, and the last had deserted him forever. He saw, now, a deeper disparity between himself and Neil, a single, powerful determinant—the real reason his own career had stagnated while Neil was welcomed into the Academy.

It all came down to character—forged, no doubt, in those formative years Neil had spent sweating at Harvard instead of pickling and fornicating at Penn State. All along he'd known what was important, and had acted accordingly. Neil had hired Kevin Cho, his secret weapon. And Frank had hired his midlife crisis.

He sank into his chair, Cristina's paper still in his hands. He glanced at the title page. "XIAP deficiency inhibits tumorigenesis in mice." Cristina's name led the list of authors; Frank's came last, the power spot. Well, it was the way of the world: Frank had lost count of the old lions—Charlie Stoddard at Harvard, Harry Drucker at MIT—who'd built their own careers and reputations on his hard labor. As a postdoc he'd been as ambitious as Cristina; he'd paid into the system for years. He felt no guilt, none whatsoever, about reaping the rewards.

He drained his glass and began to read.

THE PAPER was terrific.

Frank read it straight through, stopping once to stagger into the kitchen for a second bottle of wine. He spotted the cheap red, already opened, and took it back to the living room. The results were all there, laid out before him: in all three animal cohorts, knocking out XIAP had led to a sharp decrease in tumor growth.

Frank put down the paper and drained his glass. It always astonished him, the way good reporting could bring the science to life on the page. Cristina was a lively writer, so sharp and persuasive that it would be easy to miss the small holes in her science. To verify that she'd knocked out XIAP, she'd done a Southern blot of cells from the mouse's tail: the DNA strands were cut into fragments, then transferred onto a gel and probed, to show which fragments contained the altered sequence. So far, so good, except that the diagram in Cristina's paper showed only a portion of the results, the 3 prime end of the gene. Common practice, nowadays, but Frank was of the generation that disdained shortcuts. *WHAT ABOUT 5'? SHOW BOTH BANDS!!* he noted in the margin, his handwriting wavy on the page. If Cristina was more stylish than precise, Frank was sympathetic: he'd had the same tendency as a kid, until Charlie Stoddard, his mentor at Harvard, shamed him into thoroughness. Cristina was bright and ambitious; Frank owed her the same rigorous training he himself had received. He saw, now, that he'd denied her the time and attention he gave the other postdocs, that his attraction to her had incapacitated him. He had failed to deliver; but with this paper Cristina would redeem them both. With his guidance, who knew what she might accomplish?

Relief flooded him. He hadn't lied to Neil Windsor after all; he'd merely fudged the timeline. True, *Science* hadn't accepted Cristina's paper yet, but might very soon. If Neil pressed him, Frank could blame the editor, the slow-reading reviewers. *It's in the pipeline, buddy. It's on the way.*

He found, stuck to the refrigerator, a list Betsy Baird had typed, home phone numbers of each member of his team. He dialed. A recording asked him to leave a message—Cristina's voice, but deeper, weirdly distorted. *Jesus,* Frank thought. *Time to get a new tape.*

"Cristina, Frank McKotch here. It's Wednesday night"—he squinted at the clock—"kind of late, and, listen, I read this paper and I have to tell you, it's very strong. The discussion section is dynamite." He allowed himself an avuncular chuckle. "Of course, you *did* cut a few corners up front. What happened to the five prime end of the tail blot, for God's sake?"

He poured another glass of wine.

"We need to straighten out those diagrams first thing tomorrow morning." The lab director's *we,* which invariably meant *you.* "Oh, right: Christmas. Well, Friday then." He drank deeply. "No reason to drag our feet. Let's get this baby out the door."

chapter 2

T hree days before Christmas, Scott McKotch saw the billboard.
It loomed at the junction of Highways 8 and 61, fourteen feet
high and forty-eight across, the size of four garage doors laid side by
side. Scott squatted in the breakdown lane, just behind the guardrail,
and stared up at it. His own face, enlarged to the diameter of a bicycle tire, stared back. It was the sort of moment that comes blessedly
seldom in most lives, a moment of reckoning. He had grown adept
at fleeing such occasions, but this time he'd had no warning. The evidence had ambushed him on his way to work, leaped into his field
of vision across eight lanes of highway traffic. There was no ignoring
such evidence. No denying what he had become.

The photo had been taken three years ago at soccer practice.
In the grassy foreground, in navy-and-white Ruxton jerseys, were
two teenage boys jogging across the field. Behind them stood Scott
in shorts and a navy windbreaker, his hair windblown, his square jaw
handsomely set. The photographer had caught his hands in midclap. In
his first and final year of coaching Ruxton soccer, clapping was the one
skill Scott had mastered. With palms cupped for maximum resonance,
he clapped when his team took the field and when they left it, when
goals were scored and, especially, when they weren't, at which point
he would shout in his deepest voice, "Good effort!" Coach McKotch
clapped his palms raw. Coach was a clapping fool.

He took a step back from the guardrail. A cold rain had soaked
his shirt collar. Rush hour traffic whizzed past him, crashing through

puddles, spraying filthy water over his chinos. The two boys, he recalled, were brothers, now graduated. The older had been accepted at Brown, the kind of school to which Ruxton students were encouraged to apply. The younger was at Ohio State, the kind to which they usually went. Both kids were tall and lanky, with the blond and pink-cheeked look of English princes. Next to them Scott looked broad shouldered and powerful, his legs impressively muscled. Above the three heads was a caption in gorilla capitals: RUXTON ACADEMY. And then, crossing the boys' shins in bold italics: *Where Success Is the Goal.*

Scott got into his car, a twelve-year-old Volkswagen Golf with one windshield wiper and no hubcaps, and weighed the likelihood that anyone he knew, while speeding along Highway 61, might recognize the clapping dolt in soccer shorts, a pathetic pitchman for a third-rate prep school.

The likelihood was pretty freaking high.

Each day between seven and eight thirty, Route 61 was backed up for miles, the whole population of Gatwick on its morning run southward sucking coffee out of travel mugs, listening to inane radio chatter or improving books on tape. In the last twenty-four hours, every one of his neighbors and coworkers had already seen the billboard. There was no question in his mind.

"Okay," he said aloud. "Okay. So what?"

His neighbors and coworkers didn't matter. Anyone who lived in Gatwick existed at the sad margins of civilization, living a life as doomed and irrelevant as his own. These people were neither movers nor shakers. Their opinions counted for shit. But what if somewhere in the sea of cars, some graduate of Pearse Upper School (class of 1985 and the overlapping ones, '82 through '88) happened to pass through town? Driving northward from New York City, perhaps for the annual Christmas visit, one of his old classmates might glance out the passenger window and recognize the guy voted Class Clown and Rebel Without a Clue, known in the middle grades by the nickname Biter, come to this sorry end. (Alumni of Stirling College, which Scott had briefly attended, might also drive through Gatwick; but he was probably safe there. He hadn't been at Stirling long enough for anyone to remember his face.)

He ran a hand through his wet hair, checking his reflection in the rearview mirror. He raked the hair back from his forehead and glanced again at the billboard. Three years later, the difference was astonishing.

On top of every other indignity in his life, he was losing his freaking hair.

GATWICK, CONNECTICUT, was a town of forty thousand, built on what had been dairyland. When Scott and Penny moved there three years ago, Main Street was newly paved; a rich, bovine smell still hovered over the fields. Now Gatwick had matured into a sprawling bedroom community of cheap land and easy access to strip malls, its wide central artery lined with a small but spreading cluster of fast-food franchises and electronics emporia and video stores, their bright signage recognizable even to small children, the Big American Brands. Gatwick's adult citizens commuted, in equal proportions, to Hartford, Providence, and New Haven; a smaller share drove two hours each way to Boston. Gatwick was an exurb without an urb, a diffuse nowhere that looked, increasingly, like everywhere, a thought that filled Scott with despair.

When he accepted the job at Ruxton Academy, he'd pictured himself living in nearby Dumfries, a quaint Revolutionary War town twelve miles to the south. Built along the Quinebaug River, Dumfries had made its name in textiles; for exactly one year, 1818, it had the largest cotton mill in Connecticut. In the 1920s, the firm of Lipscomb and Blore opened four shirt factories within its limits, and Dumfries became known as Shirttown U.S.A. Those factories had long since closed, leaving Dumfries with no industry to speak of, only monuments to its former wealth: handsome Greek Revival architecture, a white Congregational church. The U.S. Post Office, a former blacksmith shop, had been a stop on the Underground Railroad; it, town hall and the old Lipscomb mansion had been designated historic landmarks. The local Heritage Society mowed and watered the town green. To Scott's eyes, accustomed to the barren newness of inland California, Dumfries looked enough like Concord to prompt an aching nostalgia, a feeling that he'd finally come home.

Accompanied by the only realtor in town, a brisk Yankee named Tom Harwich, Scott and Penny had toured every available house in Dumfries: a few creaky Victorians, some cramped Capes. Scott had a small inheritance from his grandfather Drew, most of which they'd piddled away on rent and utility bills, minimum payments on their maxed-out credit cards, the dreary monthly expenses of a couple with two children. What remained would cover a skimpy down payment; but these houses were at the upper end of their price range. Worse, all cried out for costly remodeling or, in Penny's view, a kiss from a wrecking ball. They'd nearly given up when Tom Harwich showed them a stone gamekeeper's cottage at the edge of town. "A little snug for a family," he admitted, "but the price is right." The house was tiny but graceful, with French doors opening into a walled garden. Charmed by the phrase "gamekeeper's cottage," with its literary and lascivious associations, Scott lobbied hard. He pointed out the random-width pine floors, the heirloom roses in the sunny garden. Penny was not impressed. The ceiling showed water damage. The appliances looked fifty years old. The place had no air-conditioning and only one bathroom. Oblivious to the stiff presence of Tom Harwich, she wondered aloud how people could live this way.

Scott started to explain that air-conditioning was unnecessary, that New England summers were nothing like the six-month human barbecue they endured in San Bernardino. He noticed in midsentence the sweat running down his forehead, his shirt plastered wetly to his back.

"Window units," he said, changing tactics. "We'll put one in each bedroom."

Penny sighed. Her sigh told him that arguing was futile. For all its decrepitude, the cottage was nearly as expensive as the much larger Victorians. Making it livable would require not just carpentry skills—which Scott had—but long months and vast sums of money, which he had not. There was no getting around it: the cheapest property in Dumfries cost more than they could afford.

Crushed, he settled into one of the black funks that had haunted his childhood, a rich, satisfying blend of outrage and self-pity that, once unleashed, overtook him completely—for hours or sometimes days, until somebody noticed and wheedled him out of it. Back then, his mother had wooed him with gifts or candy. Penny usually offered sex or ganja, but this time she was in no mood. He watched miserably as, disgusted by his wallowing, she took over the house search. She scanned the newspaper. She picked a new realtor out of the yellow pages, one with offices in nearby Gatwick. The agent, a perfumed blonde named Misty Sanderson, took them on a tour of the town, which at that time resembled a vast construction site.

From the backseat of Misty's Ford Taurus, Scott stared out at backhoes and forklifts, real men in blue jeans and work boots. He felt effete and infantilized, riding in the backseat like a child while Penny sat up front next to Misty. From behind they were as alike as sisters, their voices identically pitched, their hair streaked the same shade of blond. He tried, idly, to imagine them naked together, a fantasy that should have inflamed him: one writhing beneath him, one dangling above. But nothing. His pulse was slow, his blood sluggish. His misery was like a tourniquet strangling his groin.

"It's hard to picture right now, but trust me," Misty said brightly. "In six months you won't recognize the place." The car bounced along a stretch of unpaved road. Heavy equipment roared in the distance.

"Welcome to Loch Lomond Acres," said Misty. "The best address in town."

"What town?" Scott mumbled, and Penny shot him an angry look. Though less than a year old, Misty explained, the development was sold nearly to capacity. People were buying the houses faster than the Wood Corporation could build them. Only two lots remained.

"Oh, but we need a place right away," said Penny. "Scott starts work in September."

Misty flashed a dazzling smile. Her teeth were preternaturally white. "Don't worry. We can sell you the model, if you like it. We have exclusive rights."

This roused Scott from his torpor. "No," he said, rubbing his eyes. "No housing developments. No planned communities. Not for us."

Both women turned around to look at him, as if they'd forgotten he was there.

"They're fabulous houses," Misty protested. "One look and you'll change your mind."

"Come on, honey," Penny said. "We have to at least look."

"We most certainly do not."

Misty eyed him nervously. "Why don't I give you two a minute?" she said, stepping out of the car.

The door closed with a thud.

"What's your problem?" Penny demanded. "What's wrong with taking a look?"

"Listen to me," he said evenly. "You will become a widow in Loch Lomond Acres. One week here and I will blow my brains out."

"You're so dramatic."

"Nevertheless." He sat back, shading his eyes.

"Scotty, we have to buy something. Or rent something. You can't just *not like anything*."

"The cottage," he said. "I liked the cottage."

"Oh, get real. The kids are too old to share a bedroom. Where do you suggest we put Ian? Tie him up in the backyard?"

"We can add a room onto the kitchen."

Penny sighed. "You know we can't buy some falling-down piece of shit. We need a house we can move into in September."

He stared out at the muddy flats. Somewhere a truck was backing up. Its beep-beep-beep seemed aimed at him personally, a jeering assault at his brain.

"We should at least look at this." Penny's voice had gone tight and thin. "We should look at *something*, for God's sake. We can't live in a motel forever."

For the first time he noticed the deepening crease between her eyebrows. She was not yet thirty. Life with him had aged her.

"Fine." He stretched out on the seat and closed his eyes. "Get that Stepford wife back in here and have her take us to a house. A house not in a development. With two bathrooms. And I don't give a flying fuck what it looks like, we're buying it."

•••

Ruxton Academy sat at the northern edge of Gatwick, on a parcel of land first inhabited by the Quinebaug. The tribe had sold it to Dutchmen, and for two centuries it was the largest family-owned dairy farm in the state. Then, in the early nineties, the land was bought by a group of private investors known as the Merit Corporation, which had made a small fortune taking over the management of failed public schools. Paid with tax dollars by the school districts themselves, Merit swooped in, fired most of the teachers, and replaced them with bright, tireless college grads, willing to work cheap and embrace the Merit Method. Designed by Ruxton's headmaster, Rick O'Kane, the method emphasized rote learning and intensive preparation for standardized tests, the results of which bore out Merit's company motto: We Turn Schools Around. Ruxton was Merit's first foray into private schooling, which its directors had identified as a growth segment of the education market. (*There's an education market?* Scott had marveled in his job interview with O'Kane. He had since learned to keep such questions to himself.)

He'd taught at the school for three years. This qualified him as a veteran at Ruxton, from which teachers fled at a feverish rate: the youngest and brightest, for jobs at legitimate prep schools; the middle-aged and cynical, lured by pensions and decent health insurance, to Gatwick High. Either move was a step up. Ruxton offered its teachers the huge class size and mediocre students of a public school with the paltry salaries of the privates. Glossy marketing materials sold the school as an alternative to the top-shelf prep schools, to the wealthy but gullible inhabitants of places like Loch Lomond Acres. Rick O'Kane had a doctorate in educational administration from the University of Connecticut but was, constitutionally, a salesman: he'd sold cars, then insurance, before forming Merit with a group of college buddies. He'd outlined the company strategy for Scott in that first interview. *Ruxton parents,* he said with a gummy smile, *are used to paying for things.* They accepted that, in the way that bottled water was superior to tap, a private school education had to be better than what the local school district handed out for free. And because Ruxton was a day school, they were happy to pay its exorbitant tuition, comforted by the knowledge that they were saving big bucks on room and board. *It's like two percent milk*, O'Kane said, without a trace of embarrassment. *A compromise solution.*

Sitting in O'Kane's office, in the good suit he hadn't worn since his wedding, Scott found himself torn. O'Kane was a con man, that much was clear; but Scott was in no position to quibble. He was desperate to escape San Bernardino, his dire financial straits, the mean concrete bungalow where he and Penny were held hostage by their two hyperactive children. He had sent résumés to every private school in New England. Only Ruxton had offered him an interview.

And there was this: against his will, against all reason, he felt O'Kane's sales pitch working on him. Scott felt sized up by this man, his sterling qualities appreciated and understood. Of all the other applicants for the job—over a hundred, O'Kane assured him—only three had been offered interviews.

He was hired on a year's contract, to teach English and coach soccer. The coaching was a condition of his employment—every Ruxton teacher had to advise an extracurricular activity, at no additional pay. He'd explained to O'Kane that he'd never coached anything in his life, that he hadn't set foot on a soccer field since Pearse. In that moment O'Kane's face brightened, with the sort of beatific smile worn by saints in Renaissance paintings, and Scott knew he'd said the magic word. He understood, then, that his prep school education was the only reason he'd been granted an interview in the first place. This surprised him more than it should have. He had a General Studies degree from Cal State; for two years he'd taught remedial grammar at an inner-city vo-tech. Even for a fake prep school, he wasn't much of a catch.

THE FACULTY lot was full. Scott circled it twice, then headed for the student lot. Ruxton students disdained the school bus; each morning they or their parents wheeled up in a cortege of expensive automobiles. Scott found a narrow space in the first row and sat a long moment before cutting the engine. To his left was a black BMW convertible, brand new, with dealer plates; to his right a white Lexus sedan. Both had clearly been purchased by somebody's father. It was not lost on Scott that (a) with a blue book value of nine hundred dollars, his Golf was worth 4 percent of the cars on either side of it, and (b) he too was somebody's father. He reached into the backseat for the battered leather briefcase that had belonged to his grandfather Drew. He continued to use it in preference to the slick new one Penny had bought him last Christmas.

The rain quickened. As always, he had forgotten an umbrella. He would have to make a break for it. He threw open the car door and heard a metallic scraping sound.

"Shit," he said aloud.

He stepped out, rain pelting his head. His door had hit the Beamer's front quarter panel, leaving a two-inch gash. Some spoiled Ruxton kid was going to have a fit.

Quality, he thought. *McKotch, that was a quality maneuver.*

He knelt to examine the scrape, flecked with yellow paint from his own car door. He thought of a time, years ago, when his father had banged bumpers with a red convertible in a parking lot, the manful way each driver had stepped from his car, the sober exchange of phone numbers and insurance information. The other driver was only a kid, a few years older than Scott, and was clearly at fault. Alarmed and delighted, knowing his father's temper, Scott had watched from the passenger window, expecting an explosion; but Frank spoke to the kid in a low voice, nodded calmly, and in the end shook his hand. He had treated the little punk like a man, an equal. Seeing this, Scott had felt a stab of jealousy. Was that what it took to win the old guy's respect—slamming his car in a parking lot? Wasn't it enough just to be his son?

He rummaged in his pocket for a scrap of paper. The car's owner was nowhere in sight; a note on the windshield would have to suffice. He was standing there fumbling when a car horn sounded behind him. He turned to see Rick O'Kane's Mercedes backing into a space opposite his.

O'Kane lowered his window. "Can you believe this? Some little puke had the brass to steal my space." He stepped out of the car, under cover of a huge green-and-white golf umbrella. He looked freshly barbered, fit and healthy with his year-round tan.

"Jesus, what happened to you? You look like a drowned rat. Come on." He held the umbrella in Scott's direction. Seeing no way out, Scott fell in step next to him.

"Actually," he said, "I stopped to look at the billboard."

O'Kane beamed. "Pretty good, huh? It cost us a bundle, but if it brings in two new students, it pays for itself."

Scott nodded energetically. "That's good. Advertising is good. I just wasn't expecting—" he paused. "It's awfully big, isn't it?"

O'Kane laughed, an airy, horsy sound. "That's the idea, McKotch. We want them to see it from the highway."

Scott nodded. "But, well, it's kind of misleading. I don't coach soccer anymore. So, you know, why me?"

"Who else am I going to put up there? Mary Fahey?"

Scott laughed weakly. Mary taught first-year biology, a big, homely girl who'd led the women's field hockey team at Bryn Mawr. After his dismal 1–9 season, the team had been put into her meaty hands, making Ruxton the only boys' team in the conference with a female coach. When Scott pointed this out to O'Kane, he had merely laughed. *Relax, will you? Female is a relative term.*

Scott tried a different tack. "Where did that photo come from, anyway? I don't remember anybody taking pictures at practice."

"Great shot, huh? The candids are always the best."

Scott blinked. Arguing with O'Kane was impossible. He'd lost count of the times he'd shown up at the guy's office with a complaint and left with a smile on his face.

"Actually," he said, "it's a little embarrassing."

"Oh, come on." O'Kane thumped his shoulder, like a jockey gentling a horse. "It's aspirational advertising, McKotch. We're selling these parents a dream. And you're the dream."

Scott was stumped for a response.

"You know, of course, that your likeness can be used for publicity purposes," O'Kane added smoothly. "You *did* sign a release."

He charged forward, leaving Scott standing in the rain.

Wetly he made his way to his office, a cramped cubicle he shared with Jordan Funk, who taught history and civics and advised the drama club. By a cruel trick of destiny, Jordan was the least *funky* person Scott had ever known, a skinny kid in round John Lennon glasses—cool ten years ago—and a cardigan sweater that hung from his shoulders like a bathrobe. He had a tendency to stutter when excited; that and his puppylike enthusiasm made him seem younger than the students, who radiated boredom and cynicism. Fresh out of Bennington, Jordan was still plagued with teenage acne. The blemishes came and went in cyclical fashion, like constellations appearing in the heavens.

"Hey, man," said Jordan. A new zit had appeared on the bridge of his nose, red and shiny. "You look rough. What happened to you?"

Scott glanced down at his sodden trouser legs. "I stopped to look at the billboard. Jesus Christ."

Jordan glared into the distance, squared his jaw, and clapped loudly. "Good effort!" he grunted.

In spite of himself, Scott was impressed—by Jordan's effrontery, his skillful mimicry, the fact that his skinny chest could produce such a manly voice.

"Smart-ass." Scott scooped up a shrink-wrapped stack of blue books from a box on the floor.

"Are you serious?" Jordan said in his normal, sophomore-cheerleader voice. "You're giving a test?"

"Apparently I am."

"It's pretty c-close to Christmas. The k-kids are going to freak out."

"It's Tuesday," Scott said. "Christmas is Thursday. What's the problem?"

"It's Christmas week."

"Christmas *week*?" Scott repeated. "What's next: no tests in December because it's *Christmas month*? Which comes right after, oops, *Thanksgiving month*?" Irritation washed over him. In spite of its pretensions, Ruxton stuck to the standard public school schedule—short afternoons, no Saturdays. Instead of Greek and Latin, it offered test-prep classes: Vocab Builder (for freshmen and sophomores), Math and Verbal

Intensive (for juniors), and Senior Refresher (last chance, kids, before we give up and send you to a good trade school).

"Relax," said Jordan.

"What, I'm supposed to wait until January? And make *sure* they've forgotten everything I've said this quarter?"

"I'm having lunch with O'K-Kane," Jordan said abruptly. This was either a boast or a confession; Scott couldn't tell which.

"Oh yeah?"

"He wants to talk about the spring musical." Last year the drama club had mounted a lavish production of *Camelot*, which Scott remembered as the longest three hours of his life. Sitting in the darkened auditorium next to Penny, he'd felt nothing but sympathy for Jordan, who'd done his best with a tone-deaf Guenevere and a fifteen-year-old Arthur, hunched and mortified in his gray beard and baby-powdered hair. But to Scott's astonishment, the play had been a hit. The Parents' Association loved it, and Jordan was O'Kane's new favorite. Jordan! A sniveling kid whose desk was littered with toys: a plastic Slinky, Silly Putty, nostalgic reissues of items Scott had actually played with as a child. Half a dozen comic-book heroes, rendered in plastic, were arranged along the perimeter. Early on, to be friendly, Scott had feigned interest: *Is that Aquaman?*

Aquaman? Jordan repeated. *How old are you, anyway? Nah, those are the Transmatics.*

Sure, the Transmatics, Scott mumbled, feeling like an idiot even though *he* wasn't the one playing with dolls.

Now he wondered if it was this, his very childishness, that made Jordan so popular with the students—who, Scott imagined, knew all the Transmatics, had watched them every Saturday morning while eating their Cocoa Puffs, or some hipper, more current sugary cereal he was too middle-aged to know about. Every lunch period, and again after the final bell, students lined up in the hallway outside their office, waiting to see Mr. Funk. No one ever came to see Mr. McKotch. It was perverse for Scott to feel rejected, since the mere sight of his students irked him beyond reason. At the same time, he knew that Rick O'Kane noticed which teachers had developed a rapport ("made the connection") with students.

Scott's own desk was awash in papers. He pushed some aside and sat. Office hours were his only chance to check e-mail; at home, Penny was camped out at the computer all evening—doing what, he couldn't imagine.

His in-box was clogged with spam (Drugs from Canada! Young Danish girls show you everything!), a message from O'Kane—"Holiday Bulletin," undoubtedly bullshit—and a typically brief one from his sister.

```
Hi, Scotty, I'm leaving tomorrow, landing in
Boston in the afternoon. Wish me luck with
Dad. Holly Jolly safe travels! See you at
Mom's. xoxo Gwen.
```

He was always taken aback by the breezy, affectionate tone of her e-mails. When he saw her at his mother's on Christmas Eve, there would be no *x*, and definitely no *o*; he wouldn't even get a handshake. Only their mother was allowed to hug Gwen, an uncomfortable spectacle: his sister rigid and blushing, as though it pained her to be touched.

Jesus, his family. In twenty-four hours he'd be on the road to Concord, knocking off the miles in Penny's wood-paneled minivan, the humiliating vehicle of his premature middle age. Immediately upon arrival, he would be reminded of his own indecency. Last Christmas, as they'd crossed the threshold of his childhood home, Scott had noticed, too late, the pink wad of Juicy Bubble in Penny's mouth. He had never in his life seen his mother chew gum.

This year, like every year, Paulette would be waiting—nervous as a cat, ready to follow the kids around the house with a whisk broom, reminding them what not to touch. His brother would already have arrived, his silver Mercedes—the same model Rick O'Kane drove— parked in the driveway. It was the cleanest car Scott had ever ridden in, free of floor debris and mysterious, aging-food odors. Conclusive proof that neither the car nor Billy himself—calm, affable, impeccably dressed—ever came within ten feet of a child.

In the parlor a fire would be lit; his mother would open a bottle of champagne. For most of the evening Gwen would be silent, her eyes meeting Billy's in irritation or amusement. At least once—mysteriously, inappropriately—they would fall out laughing, for reasons they never bothered to explain. It had been this way for as long as Scott could remember, his brother and sister a united front against their parents. They treated Scott as an afterthought. Little had changed since the neighborhood ball games of their childhood. He remembered a particular summer, Gwen ten and scrappy, Billy a year older, already a star athlete. Himself a seven-year-old nuisance, allowed to bat under the condition that his outs and runs didn't count. And that was the way Scott still felt around his family: his efforts simply didn't register. His presence was tolerated, an obligation of blood; but ultimately he did not count. This would be his third Christmas in New England, yet he'd never been invited to join Gwen at their father's house in Cambridge. *You have school*, Penny reminded him. *The kids too. We wouldn't be able to make it anyway.* But to Scott this was beside the point.

"When do you leave for the holiday?" Jordan asked. He zipped open the backpack he used instead of a briefcase. It was the same pack the students carried.

"Tomorrow afternoon. I'll be with all the other assholes idling on the Mass Pike. You?"

"Driving into the city X-mas morning, while all the kiddies are home opening their presents. Alex's cokehead roommate is having a party." Alex was a production assistant at Fox television and, supposedly, Jordan's girlfriend, though the gender-neutral name made Scott suspicious.

"Cool," Scott said casually, as if he wouldn't have killed to be at a party with somebody's cokehead roommate instead of freezing in Concord with his wife and kids; no matter how many times he asked, his mother refused to turn up the heat. He'd hear about it all the way back to Gatwick: Penny complaining that the kids caught colds every Christmas, that she herself felt a sore throat coming on. *The house isn't that cold*, Scott would argue, feeling compelled to defend his mother, her Yankee parsimony. Though they'd be halfway back to Gatwick before feeling returned to his feet.

He glanced at the computer screen. A new message had appeared in his in-box: HAPPY XMAS, read the Subject line, YOU SON OF A BITCH. Even without looking Scott knew the return address: crook@lelandbrothers.com. Scott's very own cokehead roommate: for a lifethreatening year and a half, he and Carter Rook had cohabited—shared habits—at Stirling College, first in the dorms, later in an odorous basement suite at the Kappa Sigma fraternity house. Their friendship had survived pledge week, hell week, finals week, and all manner of chemical excess. Now they stayed in touch with occasional phone calls and vulgar e-mails, forwarded jokes, and links to porn sites. Carter lived in Princeton with his wife, Beth—the girl he'd dated all through Stirling—and their two children. He worked in the city as a trader and spent half his life sitting on the train. A year ago Scott had driven down to Princeton for a visit. He was awed by Carter's massive house, the silky sheets on the king-size guest bed, the Beamer and Range Rover parked in the three-car garage. *I could get used to this,* he thought. Beth had remained beautiful, her blond hair in the same silvery page boy she'd worn in college, her body long and slender in a printed sundress. She'd greeted him warmly and, he thought, normally, as though she didn't remember (maybe she didn't) their one drunken grope in the Kap Sig basement. "Come back again," she'd told him as he was leaving. "Bring your wife and kids."

"They don't travel well," he'd answered, not really joking; but Beth had dissolved into giggles, a flush spreading over her cheeks, her throat, her freckled chest. *That's nice,* Scott thought, watching her. *I could get used to that too.* The feeling haunted him all the way back to Gatwick. He hadn't visited Princeton since.

He opened the e-mail.

```
Merry Xmas, shithead! Another year gone by.
When can you come down for a visit?
Beth found this little tidbit online. Thought
it might interest you. Cheers! Carter
```

Scott clicked on the link and found himself directed to a Web site.

SUNDANCE FILM FESTIVAL ANNOUNCES WINNERS—
The jury and audience award winners were announced tonight at the
closing ceremonies of the festival in Park City, Utah.

Scott frowned. He'd expected jokes or political satire—Carter
was a cheerful fascist—or at least porn. Scott had nothing against independent filmmaking; he simply never thought about it. It seemed
extremely unlikely that Carter Rook did either.

Scott read on. Prizes had been given to feature films, short subjects, animated shorts. The Grand Jury Prize in the documentary com-
petition was given to *The Women of Kosovo*, directed and produced by
Jane Frayne.

Scott stopped reading. In the distance the bell rang.

"McKotch?" Jordan stood over his desk. "You all right, man?"

"Fine," said Scott, blinking.

"That was, um, the bell for first period?"

"Oh. Right." Scott glanced again at his screen, the plain first
name, the rhyming surname. He gathered up an armload of blue books
and headed out the door.

JANE FRAYNE had been his first love, though he'd understood this
only later. This was, he saw now, a hallmark of his character: the failure
to see what anything meant until it was gone forever. Other people
knew when they were in love, and behaved accordingly. Carter Rook
had told him freshman year that Beth was the girl he would marry. At
the time Scott had found this outrageous. *How can you possibly know?*
he'd demanded, laughing. Inwardly, though, he'd felt a strange panic.

Dude, said Carter. *I just know.*

At the time—and even now—Scott found such certitude unimaginable. Beth had been a pretty girl, one of the prettiest. But pretty
enough to keep Carter interested forever? Enough to compensate for
the incalculable *truckloads* of prettiness—hundreds of girls, thousands—
he'd be swearing off for good?

These were his thoughts in the winter of 1986, when he first met

Jane Frayne. It was his second semester at Stirling, his safety school; in his entire time there, he never thought of it any other way. The Ivies had rejected him summarily. He doubted anyone had read his application essays, "What I Bring to the Harvard (Yale, Dartmouth) Community," and "My Dinner with Hunter S. Thompson," the historical figure he'd most wanted to meet. *You do know that Thompson is still alive,* his college adviser, Mr. Woodruff, said dryly, barely glancing at the essay. *Why should that matter?* Scott countered, cocky to the end. But results suggested that Woodruff had been right. He was rejected despite the letters of recommendation from his dad's MIT colleagues (though with Scott's C's in calculus, chemistry, and physics, who could take those seriously?). From his safety school came months of silence. To be expected, according to Woodruff. Colleges mailed the first round of acceptances early, but most of those students ended up going elsewhere, leaving plenty of empty slots. Stirling awarded financial aid in March, which cost the endowment a bundle. By April they'd be eager for a few paying customers like Scott.

Knowing this, he'd arrived at Stirling with an attitude. The school was small—two thousand students—the campus postcard perfect, a movie director's idea of what a college should look like: gray limestone buildings arranged around a quadrangle, grassy lawns bordered by flagstone pathways, the tallest trees Scott had ever seen. (The trees figured strongly in his memory of the place. Beech? Chestnut? It shamed him to realize he didn't know. Back then he hadn't paid attention to such things.)

He scoped out the campus. To his surprise, the upper classes contained a good number of Pearse grads, fellow losers who'd also, apparently, picked Stirling as their safety. The Pearse guys were clustered on certain sports teams—soccer, lacrosse—and in a particular fraternity, Kappa Sigma. Dimly he recognized their faces, though more likely it came down to clothes and haircuts, ways of speaking, the posters hanging in dorm rooms. Details that hadn't been so obvious at Pearse, where everybody was more or less the same.

The Stirling students were a different crowd: small-town kids from Pennsylvania and Ohio and Maryland, louder, tougher ones from New Jersey and Long Island. Scott gravitated to the Kap Sig house, to play beer pong or smoke weed—he'd brought a sizable bag from home—with guys who seemed familiar, like cousins he saw once a year. Finally free of his family, he felt an intoxicating sense of possibility. His whole life he'd been the least interesting McKotch, the least important; but here nobody had heard of his freakish sister; his genius father; his handsome, overachieving brother. Strutting across campus with Carter Rook, he felt that all of Stirling noticed him. The 1986 yearbook ran a candid photo of Scott in his long coat and RayBans and Chuck Taylor Cons, his curly hair shaggy and tied back with a bandanna. *What a dipshit*, he would think later, staring at the photo, but at the time he'd walked with a swagger, proud of his style. And it worked: the Stirling girls couldn't get enough of him. He could have a different one every weekend, if he wanted. And he nearly always wanted.

He met Jane Frayne in a class called Shakespeare on Film, which she'd chosen because she was interested in screenwriting and Scott had chosen for the reading list (how could there be one, if all the Shakespeare was on film?). They were the only freshmen in the class, which—officially, anyway—had several prerequisites. Jane had written to the department chair requesting an exemption. Scott had simply shown up. He lurked outside the English building before the first class, waiting for the professor to arrive. *Hey*, he said when he spotted the guy. *Is this class full?*

The professor, an aging hippie named Dennis Gilligan, opened the folder he carried and glanced at a list. "Nope," he said. "You're in." (Years later—as a night student at Cal State, where every class seemed to fill in the first hour of registration—Scott appreciated how remarkable this was.)

He sat in the back of the room, next to a Kap Sig named Darrell Reed. Reed was an English major, odd for a fraternity guy, and captain of the swim team. His clothes, like his room back at the house, smelled of chlorine and feet. The class met Monday evenings. Night classes were unusual at Stirling, Gilligan explained, but it was sacrilegious to watch movies before dark. This prompted a murmur of female laughter from up front, which Scott found vaguely irritating.

"Faggot," Darrell Reed muttered, echoing his thoughts.

Gilligan was good looking, and every girl in the class seemed to hang on his words. One in particular, a dark-haired girl with very black eyebrows, sat directly in front of Gilligan's desk, where the guy perched with cloying casualness. She arrived early for class and was always the first to leave, charging out the door as if the building were on fire. Scott had noticed her the first day—because of the eyebrows, which made her look angry, and because she never shut up. Her questions—musing, discursive—could take up half the class, and by the time she finished speaking, she had usually answered them herself. This provoked whispering among the girls and rude comments from the boys, though Scott didn't understand what all the fuss was about. At Pearse everyone had spoken in class, even those, like Scott, who rarely did the reading assignment. He'd learned early that enthusiastic participation was a better defense than silence, even if he didn't know what he was talking about.

But this girl *did* know what she was talking about. She could have taught Shakespeare on Film herself. Once, after they'd suffered through Orson Welles's adaptation of *Othello*, she'd delivered a manic soliloquy on the camera work: was there a contextual purpose to Welles's use of chiaroscuro? Or was he simply showing off?

In his notebook, Scott wrote the word *chiaroscuro*.

"What are you writing?" said Darrell Reed, glancing at Scott's notebook. "She's not the teacher. She's a fucking freshman."

"She's hot," said Scott.

He angled his desk to see the girl better. She had a compelling profile: straight nose, sharp chin. Everything about her seemed smart and precise. He resolved to chat her up later, but the moment class ended, she bolted for the door. She tore down the hall and out of the building at a speed he found comical. Jesus, he thought. Where's the fire?

He spotted her again a day later, crossing the quad at the same blistering speed. "Wait up," he called, jogging behind her. She seemed not to hear. "You. Shakespeare on Film."

Finally she turned.

"Jesus, where's the fire?" He fell into step beside her. "You always walk this fast?"

"Pretty much." A smile flashed across her face. The smile had a furtive quality, as though she were surprised to find herself amused.

"You're in Shakespeare on Film?" she said. "Why don't I recognize you?"

"I sit in the back," he said.

"Oh. You're one of those." Again the smile. "Dennis is great, isn't he?"

Dennis. Gilligan's face lit up whenever Jane spoke in class; the guy fell all over himself to agree with her: *That's an astute observation, Jane. Jane makes an excellent point.*

"He's a dickweed," Scott said. "Why are you so into Shakespeare?"

"I like the tragedies. The comedies I could take or leave." She explained how, at the age of ten, she had portrayed the son of Macduff in an off-Broadway production, died violently on stage each night in a Prince Valiant haircut. *"He has killed me, Mother,"* she deadpanned, raising one black eyebrow.

"You were in a play?"

"My parents are actors. I didn't have a choice."

"No kidding," Scott said smoothly, as though he found this unremarkable. "TV or movies? Anything I might have seen?"

"Ever watch *The Magic Factory* when you were a kid?"

"Sure." It was one of the few television shows his mother had sanctioned, because it was educational and free of commercials.

"My dad was Larry."

"No way." He stared at her. The Larry character had appeared in a variety of sketches, most involving puppets. Scott remembered, now, that he'd had the same intense dark eyebrows as his daughter.

"He's classically trained, you know? At night he'd play Jason in *Medea*. Then spend all day with those asinine puppets. Plus it was public TV, so the resids are next to nothing." Larry traveled for much of the year, she explained, teaching and directing, acting in summer productions. Jane and her mother, a soap opera actress, lived in New York.

"Wow," said Scott, impressed. He was also a little winded—Jane hadn't slowed her pace, and he was out of shape from a semester of heavy pot smoking. "I love the city. My brother goes to Columbia." He rarely spoke of Billy, but at that moment couldn't think of anything else to say.

"I'm from Brooklyn," she said. "It's different."

"Sure," said Scott, as though he knew anything about it.

"Well, this is my stop." They were approaching Lathrop Hall, a women-only dorm known as The Nunnery. They had crossed the campus in two minutes. Jane flashed her furtive smile. "It was nice meeting you—" She hesitated.

"Scott," he said.

She stood facing him, her eyes level with his mouth. He could have kissed her eyelids, her fierce brow.

"Scott. I'll see you in class. Try sitting up front sometime."

He watched her go inside. Through the entryway windows he saw her sprint up to the second-floor landing. A moment later a light came on in a corner window. Standing there, a strange feeling washed over him. As though he himself were the dark room waiting. As though with the flip of a switch she had filled him with light.

"TIME," SAID Mr. McKotch. "Pens down, and pass them in."

Thirty heads lifted; thirty pairs of eyes met his. Usually he gave a minute's warning to let them wrap things up, but today there was nothing to wrap. Most of the kids had stopped writing ten minutes ago. A few seemed never to have started.

There was a general commotion as the blue books were passed to the front. Backpacks opened and closed. Thirty pairs of shoes headed for the door.

"Have a good break," Scott called after them. And then, feeling foolish: "Happy holidays."

Nobody responded. Scott arranged the exam booklets into a neat stack. He waited for the students to file out, then fought his way through the crowded corridor. The halls had been decked with religiously inclusive holiday decorations, long strands of tinsel in silver and red and blue. The effect was part patriotic, part aquatic, as if colonies of shiny algae had attached themselves to the walls. The students were more boisterous than usual, walking three or four abreast. Scott squeezed past them hastily. He was so intent on making his way through the crowd that he didn't notice Rick O'Kane following him.

"McKotch," said O'Kane, clapping his shoulder. "What have you got there?"

"Exams. The AP juniors."

O'Kane sighed, a long-suffering sigh. "Don't you read your e-mail? No exams during Christmas week. School-wide policy."

Scott remembered then: "Holiday Bulletin." "I must have missed it," he said lamely. Another quality response.

"Think, will you? How many students are traveling this week? Skiing, family vacations, whatever. The Parents' Association requested specifically that we not schedule exams, and I told them it wouldn't be a problem. I'm never going to hear the end of this."

"My mistake," said Scott. "I'll take the heat from the parents. Tell them it was my fault."

"Trust me," said O'Kane. "I will."

Scott made his way to the front door. The parking lot was mayhem: dismiss them two hours early, and the kids went crazy. As Scott approached his Golf, he remembered the Beamer convertible he'd scraped with his door. *Goddamnit.* Damaging a student's car was bad enough, but he'd been so flustered by seeing O'Kane that he hadn't left a note.

He quickened his pace. The student lot was already half empty; a long line of cars idled at the edge of the parking lot.

From a distance he spotted his Golf. The spaces on either side were empty. As he approached, he saw a sheet of paper tucked under his windshield wiper. He recognized the childish handwriting, the green ballpoint pen wielded with such force that it nearly tore through the paper. These were the scratchings of Aaron Savitz, son of a local car dealer who'd given Rick O'Kane a deal on his Mercedes. Perhaps as a result, O'Kane had dismissed Scott's complaints about the kid, a pudgy loudmouth who spewed sarcasm from the back row of his second-period juniors English. Early in the term, Aaron had aimed his ridicule at the few students who dared to raise their hands. Now the whole class had been shamed into silence.

The note was a single sentence, scrawled on lined notebook paper.

McKOTCH—YOUR CAR IS A PIECE OF SHIT.
YOU OWE MY DAD 500 BUCKS.

S c o t t   c o u l d think of nothing more dispiriting, more deflating to the soul, than pulling into his driveway in the middle of the afternoon. The house—a low ranch with attached garage—faced west, and in the morning, gently lit from behind, it had a certain dignity. But with the afternoon sun nearly overhead, there was no ignoring the shoddiness of the construction, the cheap windows, the textured vinyl siding that tried to pass itself off, pathetically, as wood. Penny's van was gone—where, he had no idea. The kids left for school at seven thirty, and returned home at three. What she did between those hours was a mystery to him.

He parked and gathered a stack of manila folders from the passenger seat. The prospect of an empty house—an hour of blessed solitude—gladdened him ridiculously. He couldn't remember the last time he'd had the place to himself.

But as he approached the front door, he could hear the television blaring. Penny was indeed at home; she had parked in the garage. Resentment prickled his skin. He braced the tower of folders against his sternum, then fumbled with the door. It opened directly into the living room, which meant that any visitor—any Jehovah's Witness or deliveryman or Girl Scout selling cookies—was immediately confronted with the chaos of their lives. Toys littered the carpet. There were piles of magazines, children's shoes, a basket of laundry waiting to be sorted. All this was usual. Unusually, a tripod was set up in the middle of the room.

"Penny?" he called, looking for a place to set his folders. Finding none, he piled them on the floor.

His wife came from the kitchen, the cordless phone at her ear, Jackie O., their aging Jack Russell terrier, yapping at her heels. Penny was barefoot, in shorts and a tank top; through the long Connecticut winter she kept the thermostat at seventy-eight degrees. *Phone*, she mouthed. Then pointed to the dog. Scott wondered how she could hear the other end of the conversation, between the barking and the television going full blast. He spotted the remote on the couch and hit the MUTE button.

"DADDY!" His son came running down the hallway, head down like a billy goat's. His head hit Scott square in the solar plexus.

"Hey, buddy." Scott took a step back to catch his breath. "What are you doing home from school?"

"Miss Lister sent me home." Ian leered up at Scott, his mouth sticky and unnaturally red.

"What are you eating?"

"Sucker." He chewed loudly, the painful breaking sound of teeth crushing candy. At his last checkup he'd had four cavities, yet to be filled. At the follow-up appointment, he'd refused to open his mouth.

Penny placed a hand over the receiver. "What happened to the TV?"

"Why so loud?" Scott asked. "I couldn't stand it."

"I was vacuuming."

He glanced at the carpet, the sofa surrounded by potato chip crumbs like a persistent dandruff.

Ian circled his arms tightly around Scott's hips. "I bet I can lift you," he said, putting his weight into it.

"Hush, buddy." Scott disengaged himself. "They sent him home? What happened?"

"More of the same." Penny leaned over the couch, searching for the remote. The backs of her thighs were taut as a teenager's. "This is getting out of hand. That Miss Lister needs to lighten up."

"I knocked over a desk," Ian said proudly. "But it was an accident." He placed his feet over Scott's and grabbed his father's hands.

"Buddy, can you go play in your room for a minute? I need to talk to your mom."

Ian tugged at Scott's arms, then placed his high-top sneakers on his father's shins and leaned backward. "I'm going to climb you." It was a game he'd loved as a little boy, but was getting too big for. Scott feared pitching forward on his face, crushing his son beneath him.

"Ian, get off me. I mean it."

The boy looked up at him, startled by the edge in his voice. Penny too looked surprised.

"Go play in your room," he said evenly. "I'll be there in a minute, as soon as I'm done talking to your mom."

Ian stomped down the hall. In a moment they heard his bedroom door slam.

"He was only playing," Penny said. "He hasn't seen you all day." Said it, as always, as though Scott had failed her—by ever, even for purposes of earning a living, spending a moment away from her and the kids.

"Half a day," he said calmly. "Five hours. Penny, what the hell happened?"

"I had to go pick him up, and now I have to make another trip back there to get Sabrina from practice. And somebody needs to take this dog out."

"In a minute. Did you *talk* to Miss Lister?"

"Barely. She was in class when I got there. And she wouldn't go into it over the phone."

"She didn't tell you anything?"

"Something about being disruptive. At least he didn't bite anyone this time." Penny found the remote and hit the VOLUME button. It was an ongoing struggle in their marriage: left to her own devices, she would turn on the television the moment she woke in the morning. Scott knew that while he was at work, three of their four television sets—in the bedroom, living room, and kitchen—played constantly, at considerable volume. Coming home in the evening was like walking into an appliance store. When he complained, Penny simply shrugged. *I need to know what's going on in the world*, she insisted, though her taste ran toward talk shows and a program called *Love Hollywood Style*, which focused on the marital difficulties of celebrities he didn't recognize.

"Can you please turn that off?"

"Just a second." Penny stared at the screen.

Scott took the remote from her hand and hit the OFF button. "Seriously, Pen. He knocked over a *desk*? How does that happen, exactly? He just stood up in the middle of class and knocked over a desk?"

"I know: right? I'm not buying it either." Penny settled on the couch. "Honey, not to be a nag, but in exactly one minute this dog is going to piss on the carpet."

HE MADE a slow circle around the cul-de-sac, idiotically named Canterbury Lane, the dead end where life had dropped him. Jackie O. tugged at her leash. The sky was low and heavy, promising snow. Somewhere under this same sky Jane Frayne was living furiously, effectively, each day a productive flurry of Frayneish pursuits. Scott imagined her filming, editing, stalking the downtrodden women of Kosovo and plying them with sensitive, insightful questions. He saw her fight her way through an airport in an occupied city—a grim Soviet-era airport, guarded by soldiers with machine guns. Jane would be oblivious to their leers and catcalls. She would move through the airport fierce and undeterred, all speed and grace.

He'd been a second-semester sophomore when things fell apart, a breathtakingly fast denouement to what had started so promisingly a year before. By then he and Jane were dating, which at Stirling meant sex most nights, coffee and doughnuts the next morning in the cafeteria. There was a certain tension to this arrangement, with Jane harping periodically that they never *did* anything.

What is there to do? Scott wondered. His days were genuinely full. He slept late, attended a class here and there, lingered after meals at the Kap Sig table, watching the girls at the salad bar. Occasionally, in the evening, he went to the library, where the Kap Sigs controlled several tables in the basement study room. If an exam were impending, he made halfhearted attempts at studying, borrowing the notes of some anal-retentive classmate who'd attended the lectures. Most nights he played pong or pool, smoked weed, and drank beer. He liked the taste of beer, the metallic tang. He could drink beer all night.

Each weekend Kappa Sigma threw a party, which meant more people and different music, the kind that made girls get up and dance. At first Scott had enjoyed these gatherings, the wall-to-wall bodies, the certainty of hooking up with a girl he'd had his eye on—if not his first choice, then his second. But recently parties had come to depress him: the bathrooms redolent of beer-induced puking, the feverish pursuit happening all around him, of which he, shackled to a girlfriend, could no longer partake. Once, twice, when Jane was tied up in rehearsal, he'd succumbed to temptation. He hadn't gone looking; in both cases, the girls had pursued him. He had simply taken what they offered.

Afterward, dread consumed him. He weighed the odds that Jane would find out, and rehearsed what he'd say if she did. *I was drunk. I barely remember it.* This fear was not unlike the buried panic that sometimes woke him at night, a humming anxiety that mounted as the semester progressed. He'd ended his freshman year on academic probation and spent the summer eating shit from his father, who threatened him with the army if he didn't get his act together. He got some play out of that story—the Kap Sig brothers found it hilarious—but Scott understood that a crisis was brewing. (It was a feeling that would dog him for the rest of his life, in dreams. Even as an old man he would sometimes return to Stirling during a late-afternoon nap, again a delinquent sophomore, a drunken Kap Sig with an econ paper due.)

He started his sophomore year with lofty intentions: to attend classes, to smoke less pot. To focus his full attention on Jane, whose discipline and academic success—last semester she'd brought down a perfect 4.0—would surely be contagious.

It struck him, now, as one of the great mysteries of the natural world that she had tolerated him at all. Beautiful Jane, her drive and intellect; Jane with enough energy to power a small city. What did she see in that inebriated joker with his struts and feints and loud opinions? He had loved her; more than that, he'd wanted to *be* her. (Still a dude, though.) To be the male version of Jane, humming with plans that would actually amount to something, alive and hopeful and destined for great things.

In the end the worst had happened: back early from rehearsal, Jane had stopped by the Kap Sig house and found him in a corner of the social floor, feeling up a drunken freshman. In retrospect, he saw that it could have been worse. He and the girl were still standing. In another ten minutes he would have taken her down to the basement. Then Jane would have had something to scream about.

Scott stopped periodically as Jackie O. nosed at drainage ditches, mailboxes, looking for a place to crap. In her old age she'd become particular about where she'd loose her bowels, evaluating each potential site against a mysterious checklist in her tiny brain. She seemed to prefer defecating at Loch Lomond Acres, an impulse Scott could understand. Its massive houses offended him, mainly because he felt invisible pressure to covet them: they were thirty years newer than his and Penny's little bunker, and three times the size. Each was built on an eighth of an acre, leaving a backyard the size of a pool table. The low-end model—it had doubled in price since Misty Sanderson tried to sell it to them—had five bedrooms and four baths, a cathedral ceiling in the entryway and a showy spiral staircase. If you had money to burn, you could add Jacuzzi tubs, extra fireplaces, a stained-glass window in the entryway. The builders would pile on as many gewgaws as you could pay for. No design principles, or questions of taste, seemed to apply. The owners of one house had actually added a widow's walk, high enough to offer a view of downtown Gatwick, with its glowing miles of chain restaurants and strip malls.

Scott had been inside a Loch Lomond house only once, for a barbecue hosted by Penny's friend Noelle Moss, who'd won the place in her divorce settlement. When he closed the front door with medium force, he felt the whole house shudder. Scott had worked, for a time, on union construction sites in La Jolla and Sacramento; he knew plenty about the shortcuts builders took. Walking home, fueled by gin, he found himself disparaging the house to Penny, and learned that it was impossible to explain why something was vulgar. You either saw it or you didn't. Penny loved the oversize bathtub with its gold-plated fixtures, the cavernous sitting room, fatuously called a Great Room, with the hollow acoustics of a squash court. "You could get lost in there," she said delightedly. "There's so much *space.*"

"The rooms are big," he allowed. "I'll grant you that." Their own house was a close fit; and as the kids got older the problem worsened. That year, with the whole family at home for the endless midyear break, Scott had nearly lost his mind. But there were ways—there had to be—to create a feeling of space without ostentation, without excess.

Scott knew what a well-built house felt like. His childhood home in Concord was two hundred years old, still solid and handsome. Scott knew without anyone ever having explained it to him why plaster walls were superior to drywall, carved moldings to the cheap mass-produced stuff sold at Builder's Depot. But Penny's childhood had been spent in various sorts of Californian substandard housing: the shoddy duplex, the long series of apartment complexes. From ages fourteen to fifteen she'd actually lived in a roadside motel in Pasadena, where the second of her stepfathers worked as a night manager. For a brief time, early in their history, these facts had struck Scott as exotic, even romantic. Against this gritty western landscape, he imagined Penny as a little girl, a nubile teenager, never suspecting that somewhere in her future, Scott was waiting to rescue her. Years would pass before he met any of her scattered family, visited their grim habitats. Her crazy sister lived in a halfway house in Portland. For six months of the year, her mother and current stepfather rented a campsite in Nowhere, Arizona. The rest of the time, they crisscrossed the country in an enormous Winnebago.

Understandable, then, that Penny could be impressed by a vinyl-sided tract house with paper walls and heated towel racks in the bathrooms. She simply didn't know any better. In the spirit of a field trip, Scott walked her through his mother's house in Concord, pointing out the high ceilings, the original oak floors; he wanted—and truly needed—her to see the difference. She agreed that the house was lovely, but when Scott went a step further and compared it to the monstrosities of Loch Lomond Acres, Penny simply smiled.

"I know you don't like them," she said, as though it were merely a matter of preference, as neutral as liking blue over green.

"It's not a question of *liking*," he said with deliberate calm. He couldn't seem to make her understand that the houses—from their grotesque proportions all the way down to their reproduction light fixtures ("Reproductions of what? There was no electricity at Versailles! None at all!")—were simply *wrong*.

At such moments he felt as though they were separated by a language barrier. Years ago, in med school, his brother had befriended a stunning Italian classmate named Lucia Bari. The *friendship* (Billy's word) had provided him with years of comic material: Billy's efforts to explain American social behavior, Lucia's amusing attempts at American slang. To Scott, visiting New York on a weekend trip with Jane Frayne, such misunderstandings had seemed trivial. When they met Billy and his *friend* for dinner, Scott was hypnotized by Lucia's heavy breasts, her succulent mouth. Who cared what that mouth was saying? Now he saw how those differences might have mattered. Penny, in her way, was as foreign as Lucia. There were things his wife would simply never understand.

WHEN SCOTT returned to the house, his daughter was in the living room with her friend Paige Moss. The girls wore tights and leotards. They lay sprawled on the dirty carpet, staring at the television. Penny was in the kitchen with Paige's mother, Noelle, who lived in Loch Lomond Acres but spent, by his calculations, two-thirds of her waking hours at his house. In that time she had never consumed anything but black coffee with Equal. She was a hungry-looking woman, a platinum blonde, excessively fond of the tanning booth; she reminded Scott dimly of his aunt Anne.

"Noelle brought her video camera," Penny informed him. "We're going to tape the girls doing their dance. Want to watch?"

Scott hesitated. His daughter's dance routines caused him paroxysms of discomfort. Last spring, during the annual recital, he'd been forced to watch her cavort around the stage with a handful of friends, dressed and gyrating like ten-year-old strippers. He had nearly swallowed his tongue.

"I have papers to grade," he said.

"That's okay, Dad," Sabrina said helpfully. "You can watch the tape later."

Scott picked up his stack of manila folders and headed downstairs to his *study*. He used the term ironically. Penny referred to it the same way, but without the irony, and this made him cringe. Shortly after they bought the place, he'd come back from Builder's Depot with a hatchback full of two-by-fours, and squared off a corner of what the realtor had called (ironically too, it turned out) the finished basement. The prior owner had hid the wiring with a suspended ceiling, covered the walls with paneling and the cement floor with thin carpet, but had done nothing to address the persistent dampness that bled through the foundation. Even with two dehumidifiers running, the room smelled of mushrooms, old socks, the dank imported cheeses Scott loved but Penny called revolting. They had arranged their old furniture there, a plaid armchair and stained sofa, in an approximation of what was called a family room; but even the huge new television—number four!—wasn't enough to lure Ian and Sabrina downstairs. The house had eighteen hundred square feet of living space, but it might as well have been a one-room hut in Calcutta. Penny and the kids lived their entire lives in the kitchen.

Scott stepped into his *study*. The room was eight by ten, with one high window that looked out on a corrugated tin window well and let in a thin slice of light. He dumped the manila folders on the desk—a hefty stack, one for each of the hundred and twenty juniors whose literacy he was to further that semester. Inside were sheets of loose-leaf notebook paper, blue books and—shamefully—weekly quizzes, to which he had recently resorted. The quizzes had seemed to him a capitulation, but he'd found no other way to coerce the students into reading the assigned number of pages from *Great Expectations*. He spent an unspeakable number of hours composing these quizzes. He

found himself looking forward to quiz making, the Sunday-night ritual of sipping a glass of wine while reading Cliff's Notes and scouring
the Internet for pirated study guides, the same strategies his students
used. He sometimes stayed up half the night devising questions that
couldn't be answered by these illicit means. It became a game to him,
the imagined battle of wits with his students, the satisfaction of ferret-
ing out the malingerers. It was the most rewarding aspect of his job.

As he booted up the computer he heard music overhead, the sort
of cloying dance tune his daughter favored. The flimsy ceiling groaned,
shaken by the romping of two little girls who weighed maybe sixty
pounds apiece.

He turned his attention to the computer screen, called up the
Lycos search page and typed *Jane Frayne.*

He had always planned to see her again, to finish what was un-
finished between them. He felt certain that Jane knew this, expected
it even, that she had known it all along. And recent technology had
made the world smaller. She could easily be found.

They were adults now, wiser, sophisticated. They would laugh at
the mishap that had divided them.

I overreacted, Jane would say. *I couldn't help it. I was crazy about you.*

I was an idiot, he would protest. *I made a terrible mistake.*

He imagined her still in New York, a couple hours' drive away.
He could easily slip away to see her. On weekends Penny scheduled
his every waking moment, but a weeknight would be easy. He could
leave straight from school. When Penny asked, he could invoke Parents' Night, a quarterly ordeal that lasted late into the evening.

He had never cheated on Penny, though he'd had chances: flirty
barmaids, a coworker in a video store in La Jolla, the addled college
girls and lonely single moms who'd bought his pot in San Berdoo. He
was flattered by their interest, but something had always stopped him.
There was the memory of his father, the hell of his parents' divorce.
Mostly, though, he hadn't seen the point. Chronic exhaustion had
tamed his libido. And the women who wanted him were lost souls,
floundering in their own lives, unlikely to fix what was broken in his.
Jane Frayne was different. Loving her might actually save him.

It seemed worth a try.

He waited. The computer was old and slow, the dial-up connection unreliable. He heard a scratching at the door. The dog had followed him downstairs. She approached him, tail wagging, and allowed her ears to be scratched.

"What's the matter?" he asked. "Are you lonely?"

Jackie O. whimpered. She was a social creature, spoiled in puppyhood. Penny had acquired her from a neighbor the summer they'd met, and lavished her with so much attention that the dog became slightly neurotic. *Our baby*, Penny called her—not knowing, then, that a real baby was already in the works, that a cluster of cells soon to be known as Sabrina was multiplying and dividing, the early arithmetic ticking away like a stock counter, marking off the last minutes of their youth.

THEY'D MET on a camping trip the spring Scott dropped out of Stirling. He had fled the campus under cover of night, having spent his tuition money on an aging Pontiac Sunbird and a large quantity of marijuana, which his townie friend Magic Dave had packed loosely into a Wonder Bread wrapper and double-bagged for freshness. For three days Scott drove in a straight line westward, that wonderful bag, that bag of Double Wonder, stashed beneath the passenger seat. He slept a night in Buffalo, Wyoming, then drove the last forty miles to Yellowstone, where he planned to meet up with some buddies on spring break. He never found them. The park was as wide as New Hampshire. Scott had spent his whole life in New England; nature was Cape Cod, its cottages and clam shacks; Walden Pond, an oasis in the suburbs. The high empty plains spooked him. The landscape seemed haunted and mournful. He felt, and was, a thousand miles away from the mess he'd left at school—the dean who had it in for him, the irate phone calls from his father, the weepy disappointment of Jane Frayne who, unmoved by his crapulous groveling, vowed never to see him again.

In March the park was virtually deserted. He hiked a day and a half before he saw the smoke of a campfire. By then his feet were blistered, his water supply nearly exhausted. He'd shivered all night in his summer-weight sleeping bag.

He approached the campsite, two dilapidated tents pitched at the top of a hill. A girl crouched before the fire. "Hello!" he called in a friendly tone; alone in the wilderness, she would be scared of strangers. "Can I borrow your fire?"

The girl stood. She wore blue jeans and a bikini top. Her head was wrapped in a blue bandanna; two yellow braids trailed down her back. Mixed in with the fire smell he caught a whiff of marijuana. "Sure," she said. "Come on up."

He scrambled up the hill, his blistered feet burning. The girl sat on her haunches poking at the fire, the nub of a joint pinched between her fingers. Scott squatted next to her and watched her exhale. In a moment he understood why she wore so little: the fire gave off a blistering heat. He took his own joint from his pocket and they passed it between them, drawing heroic breaths.

What did they talk about that night? For the life of him, he couldn't recall. He remembered only how slowly she spoke, how relaxed and reflective and content she seemed. How unlike Jane Frayne, who spoke in whole paragraphs and slept five hours a night, yet refused to temper her manic energy by chemical means. Pot made her paranoid, she said, and beer was a waste of calories. To Scott, who got high once or twice a day, this seemed an irreparable defect in their relationship, her unwillingness to follow him into the place where he was most completely himself. That night, staring into the fire next to Penny Cherry, he saw this with utter clarity, and decided he'd been right to leave. There was no turning back.

They squatted by the fire until his thighs ached. He noticed, but did not care, that sweat was running down his back, soaking his cotton turtleneck. Penny noticed too. "Take off your shirt," she told him, and he did, a little self-consciously. Three and a half semesters of beer and college food had padded his torso. This girl was lean as a deer, a wild creature. Men's jeans (whose? he wondered) hung low on her hips.

It was full dark when the others arrived. They brought fresh trout for the night's supper—caught out of season, pounds of slippery contraband. Scott watched them in hushed awe, like wildlife glimpsed through his binoculars. They were tanned, handsome people in boots and battered jeans. The females were wide eyed, long haired, unadorned. The largest male had a web of paisley tattoos snaking down his forearms; the others lacked distinctive markings, but appeared fast and strong. Scott looked for mated pairs, but the arithmetic eluded him: three girls, including Penny, and four guys. They assembled the dinner in cooperative fashion, with affectionate touching all around. A squat Mexican kissed each girl's mouth. Scott kept his eyes on Penny, to determine whose she might be. Anybody's, he decided. But after the fish was eaten, a bottle of whiskey and then another joint passed, it was Scott's hand she'd taken, Scott she had led, silently, deep into the woods.

She was a California girl, born in North Hollywood—a dump back then, she said, but an easy drive to Burbank, where her father, Whizzer Dooley, worked as a TV stuntman. He appeared mainly in a detective series called *Vegas Jack*, but he had done movies too. (Penny rattled off a list of titles: *Death Rangers, Rage on Wheels, The San Antonio Outlaws*—but only one, *The French Connection*, was familiar to Scott.) Whizzer had doubled for Robert Wagner, James Garner, and once— famously—for Steve McQueen, whom people said he resembled. Penny's mother, a former Miss Fresno County, had been Whizzer's high school sweetheart. They'd come to Hollywood in the late sixties, when Penny's older sister was just a baby—to the scorn of both their families, who called Whizzer a dreamer and a deadbeat and his wife a ninny who was throwing her life away with both hands. Whizzer proved them wrong by finding work immediately, on the set of *Vegas Jack*. The director loved Whizzer, who was not merely fearless but young and good looking. His resemblance to the show's star made shooting a breeze. Whizzer enhanced the effect by bleaching his hair and growing a handlebar mustache. "Vegas Jack!" a little boy once cried, pointing to him in the street.

Penny was seven when Whizzer left, for what she called "the usual reasons": somebody had screwed somebody, or was thought to have done so. She was the last in the family to see him alive. She was walking home from the school bus stop when she saw his lemon-yellow Chevelle pull out of the driveway. The windows were down, AM radio blasting. Whizzer seemed not to see her as he threw the car into gear. "Hi, Daddy!" she called, holding aloft her lunch box in a clumsy wave.

The car rolled past her—then, abruptly, squealed to a stop. Whizzer stepped out and ambled toward her, his hair wild, his face red. He wore a pink plaid shirt that was Penny's favorite, with pearly snaps down the front. These details she would remember forever. They were hers and hers alone, like the velvet-lined box of rhinestone jewelry she kept under her bed, a plastic ballerina twirling inside.

"Hey, baby," he said, a little breathless, and scooped her into his arms. He had not shaved; his rough neck was warm and tangy, the beery smell she loved. Over his shoulder she saw the car packed full with boxes, his guitar case, and what looked like (but couldn't be, oh no) the family Ping-Pong table folded in half. The gaping trunk was secured with rope.

Where are you going? she didn't ask.

I'm leaving you forever, he did not answer. *I will call you once, next year on Christmas, and give your mother a phone number that will soon be disconnected. I will race cars and live with a dancer in Nevada who, after I drive into a wall at a hundred twenty miles an hour, will send you a box of worthless crap that will tell you nothing about why I left, nothing at all.*

"You're so pretty," he said instead. "Never cut your hair."

She watched him get into the car. The door didn't close the first time; he reopened it and slammed it harder. Driving away, he stretched his left arm out the open window, as if he meant to pull her along behind him. He turned at the corner and was gone.

There were stepfathers. Henry Cherry was a widower with five blond sons. He had come to town on business; Penny's mother met him at the steak house where she'd been hired for her looks. Soon they moved into Cherry's sprawling ranch house on the outskirts of Boise, a lowslung place on six flat acres of grass. Penny and her sister had their own bedrooms; the five blond boys slept in bunk beds in a single large room down the hall. (Years later, Penny's mother told her the reason: to prevent them from touching themselves. A boy with his own room would have his hands down there all the time.)

In Idaho they heard services, and did chores. Penny picked vegetables from the garden, fed chickens, and gathered eggs. In North Hollywood her mother had been a casual housekeeper: toast crumbs on the counter, blue toothpaste misfires in the sink. Now, at Relief Society meetings, she learned pickling and preserving. Cherry's first wife had amassed a large collection of canning equipment, Ball jars boiled dull and smooth.

To Penny, who had recently eaten crackers for dinner, the transformation was alarming. She retreated to the hills behind the Cherry house with Benji, the youngest of her blond stepbrothers, a boy who scarcely spoke but could climb like a goat. Benji had been left back in school and was called slow, but he knew the names of trees and flowers, the scat of deer, antelope, and moose. Benji could identify bear tracks, start a fire without matches. He saw the shapes of constellations, the warriors and goddesses hidden in the stars.

Benji? The name reminded Scott of a movie he'd seen as a child, the misadventures of a scruffy little dog.

Penny was not amused. *He saved me,* she swore with surprising vehemence. It was Benji who'd kept her company until her mother's marriage collapsed—for reasons Penny didn't know, but could guess.

She told Scott this—all this!—in their first night together. At the time it had fascinated him, the twists and turns of the story, its exotic locales. Soon, though, there was a burden in so much knowing. This strange girl confiding her heartbreaks, her childhood terrors, believing him the first man who would not fail her.

He was nineteen years old.

That summer they rented an apartment at the beach in La Jolla, where Penny found a job in a surf shop. They bought a VCR and rented a copy of *The French Connection,* a film she had never seen. Together they watched the credits scroll past, the names of stuntmen long retired or, like her father, violently killed. Twice, three times Penny rewound the tape, but no Whizzer Dooley was listed in the credits.

About that, about everything, her father had lied.

• • •

SCOTT STARED at his computer screen. Lycos had returned half a dozen hits for Jane Frayne, including the Web site of her production company, Plain Jane Films, located in Brooklyn, New York.

What was a production company, exactly? He wasn't entirely sure. Still, he was impressed.

At that moment he heard a sudden commotion overhead: a rumble of footfalls, a sudden thud. *Mom, Ian's in the way!* His own chaotic life asserting itself.

"Scott!" Penny called. "Can you get up here? I only have two hands."

After eleven years he could still be amazed by his wife's voice, which cut like a buzz saw through the flimsy walls and floors. He got up wearily from his chair.

You got one chance in this life, he reflected, one precious chance. He had blown his years ago, on the tree-shaded campus of Stirling College, too dense to understand that every door in life was open to him.

He had made his choices. Now he was thirty years old, and all the doors were closed.

chapter 3

Tom and Richard served sushi for dinner. The delicate bundles of rice and fish were stacked in pyramids on lacquered trays. The dinner was served buffet style in the large living room; the men filled their square plates and repaired to the dining room, where calligraphed place cards were set. Billy McKotch examined his closely, impressed by its delicacy. He knew Tom's usual handwriting, the cramped block printing typical of architects. That these graceful letters had come from the same hand seemed a small miracle.

"Aren't they precious? Tom was feeling *Oriental*," Richard drawled. He'd come to New York from Alabama thirty years ago, and had become more Southern with each passing year. His partner Tom Kim had taken a sushi-making class at the New School; he'd spent the afternoon chopping cucumbers into matchstick-size pieces, rolling dried seaweed on bamboo mats. Richard had shopped for the sake, the jasmine-scented tea, the coconut sorbet for dessert.

Among Billy's friends, Tom and Richard entertained most often. They lived on Park Avenue in a classic four/five owned by Richard's old boyfriend Harry, who'd died back in the eighties. Harry had inherited the place from his stepmother, a friend of Brooke Astor; he'd sold it to Richard on his deathbed for the price of fifty dollars—a matter of convenience, simpler than making a will.

The men arranged themselves around the antique table, also from Harry's estate. (*Welcome to Tom, Dick, and Harry's*, Richard sang when opening the door to guests.) Billy wondered how Tom could stand it, his life furnished with his predecessor's treasures. *It would make me crazy*, he confided to Srikanth. To which Sri responded: *Tom is an architect. He appreciates beautiful things.*

Of the four couples, three lived on the Upper East Side. The fourth, Oscar and Eddie, had a loft in the west thirties, a cavernous space that doubled as Oscar's photography studio. The composition of the group had changed over the years, as the men coupled and uncoupled. Before Eddie, Oscar had lived with a cartoonist named Raj, known to Srikanth by some mysterious Dosco connection. It was Raj who'd brought Sri and Billy into the group. Raj had since moved to San Francisco, but Sri and Billy remained regulars at the dinner parties. To Billy these men were closer than family. They were his dearest friends.

"That's all you're eating?" Nathan asked, eyeing Billy's plate of sushi. "Didn't you run fifty miles today?"

"Nope," Billy said. "I don't start training for Boston until January. I've been sleeping late and eating like a pig." He'd finished the New York Marathon in three hours and two minutes, a personal best. Except for easy jogs through Battery Park at lunchtime, he hadn't run since the race.

Nathan's eyes narrowed. "Do I believe you?"

Billy grinned. He knew that Nathan and Jeremy considered his training schedule compulsive. *Don't take it personally*, Sri would tell him later. *They're just practicing their profession.*

"I'm fine, Nathan," said Billy. "Hey, take it easy on that coconut. Full of saturated fat." When Sri chastised him later, he would protest: *I was only practicing mine.*

"This is so civilized," Eddie said, sipping his tea. "God, I wish *we* had a dining room."

Billy glanced across the table at Sri, who wore a sly smile. They would laugh about it later, how their friends talked of nothing but apartments. For a long time Billy had found these conversations fascinating, the myriad ways people—gay people—lived in the city. Tonight, though, the conversation depressed him: rent control, condo fees, the impossibility of finding an honest contractor. The dialogue unchanging, year after year. His friends were not vacuous people. They were well read and well traveled; they did interesting work. Richard was a literary agent, Nathan and Jeremy psychotherapists, Eddie a classics professor at Hunter. Yet when the group convened, they spoke mainly of real estate, as though the rooms they lived in mattered as much as—perhaps more than—what transpired inside them.

It was Srikanth who'd opened this world to Billy, with his vast network of friends and acquaintances and, Billy suspected, past lovers. He didn't ask whether this was true, and Sri never volunteered the information; such revelations didn't suit his oblique style. As Sri's boyfriend, Billy was invited to gay brunches and housewarmings, seders and Easter buffets. He saw the insides of gay brownstones, medicine chests with his-and-his razors, the elegant bedrooms where men slept side by side. He was touched, profoundly, by the everydayness, the intimate banality of these shared lives. At the same time he sensed unspoken reproach. Of all their friends, he and Sri were the only couple who did not cohabit. Though he spent every night at Billy's, Sri had kept his apartment on Riverside Drive. A matter of convenience, Billy told anyone who asked. To which Sri, the presumptive beneficiary of this convenience—Sri who each morning schlepped ninety-eight blocks across town to Columbia, who spent twenty grand a year renting an apartment he never used—simply smiled.

That smile was an invitation to discussion, one Billy chose to decline. There were certain conversations he didn't wish to have. These included, but were not limited to, religion, past sexual partners, and the price of anything. (He'd been raised to consider such discussions crude.) And, of course, his family. Above all, he disliked talking about the future. He had only just gotten comfortable in the present.

"Billy?" Tom was speaking, smiling quizzically, and Billy realized he'd been asked a question.

"Tom invited us for Christmas Eve," Sri murmured.

"Oh. Sorry." Billy colored. "That sounds great, but I'll be at my mother's in Boston."

A sudden silence.

"Well, I'm free," said Srikanth. "I'd love to come."

Glances were exchanged around the table, or maybe they weren't; Billy was aware of his tendency toward paranoia. He knew that he and Sri, their separate holidays and apartments, were a topic of much speculation; that his friends considered him *closeted*, a term he found silly, antiquated, and, in this case, wholly inaccurate. In the past week, he and Sri had attended a wedding and two holiday parties; to their friends and colleagues they were a very public couple. When it came to family, Billy simply opted for privacy. That he'd never met Sri's parents—his mother was dead, his father aged and senile and in a nursing home in London—provided additional justification: the relationship was perfectly symmetrical. Billy suspected that many couples, given the choice, would prefer a life without in-laws. In this way he and Sri were luckier than most.

He had developed, over the years, a way of managing his family, a protocol he thought of, privately, as the System. He phoned his mother twice a week. For Christmas, Thanksgiving, and Mother's Day he traveled to Concord; each October Paulette spent a weekend with him in New York. The System prevented surprises, which Billy detested; it kept Paulette's expectations—and his own guilt—in check. The rest of his family demanded less attention. He spoke with Gwen every other weekend; Scott, approximately never. For years his brother had been unreachable, with California addresses that changed every few months, phone numbers disconnected faster than Billy could write them down. Thus his System had evolved without taking Scott into account.

For most of Billy's life, his father had required no management whatsoever; Frank had spent Billy's childhood and adolescence sequestered in the lab. But lately the old man had made friendly overtures—phone calls, invitations to lunch—which Billy found distressing. Unlike Paulette, Frank didn't shrink from asking personal questions. More conversations Billy didn't wish to have.

Of his family, only Gwen knew about Srikanth. Billy had not told her; she'd found out due to circumstances beyond his control. Two years ago, driving back to New York from a Pearse class reunion, he'd fallen asleep at the wheel and totaled his car on I-95, a week before the Boston Marathon (this fact was more devastating than his broken ribs). A card in his wallet had listed Gwen's name and phone number; she'd flown in immediately from Pittsburgh to make sure he was okay. He'd been asleep, zonked on painkillers, when she rushed to his hospital room and found Sri at his bedside. Billy wondered, often, what the two had said to each other. He'd never worked up the nerve to ask.

Now, sitting around the dinner table with his friends, he sensed, and resented, the unspoken censure. He was a failure as a gay man, a traitor to the tribe. He could redeem himself only by surrendering his dignity in grand fashion, confiding the most intimate details of his life to all who knew him, whether or not they cared. A vulgar confessional, cheesy and narcissistic; such a display, Billy felt, would be demeaning to all concerned. Self-revelation was not the Drew way. It was a lesson he'd absorbed from his maiden aunt Martine, about whom he'd always harbored suspicions. Martine shared a house in Taos with two other aspiring Georgia O'Keefes, yet felt no need to explain herself. Billy had never met anyone more self-involved than his father and Scott, more uptight than his mother and Gwen. He saw no reason to burden them with information they certainly didn't want to hear.

That summer, at a birthday party, he'd been tag-teamed by Nathan and Jeremy, the two psychotherapists, who'd suggested a few sessions of family counseling for Billy and his parents. His first response was laughter—the mental image tickled him. A moment later he was furious. Nathan had chalked this up to arrogance—*Typical physician! You refuse to think beyond the medical model.* But Billy's objections ran deeper. Heterosexuals were allowed their privacy: if he'd had a girlfriend, no one would care whether he introduced her to his parents. But because Billy was gay, Nathan's arguments had a moralistic tone, as though simple discretion were a betrayal of homosexuals everywhere. Billy found this idea ludicrous. *Thousands of gay men have come out to their families*, he told Nathan, *and it hasn't done a thing for me.*

I see, Nathan said dryly. *So it's every fag for himself.*

Exactly, Billy said. He'd spent his childhood in a state of unease, forced to play on sports teams; the experience had taught him that he wasn't a joiner. He had registered to vote as an Independent (another fact his friends found shocking). He didn't feel, or want to feel, solidarity with anyone.

GWEN PHONED the week before Christmas—a Sunday morning at eleven thirty, her usual time to call. They'd settled into this habit long ago, before Billy's car accident had outed him to his sister. He'd been unattached then, his social life more complicated, and late morning was a discreet hour: it allowed them both to avoid asking, or answering, indelicate questions about what each had done, or not done, the night before.

Billy imagined Gwen in her sunny kitchen, the windows so crowded with plants that from the street, the apartment resembled a greenhouse. The one time he'd visited her—four years ago? five?—he'd found all those plants a little creepy, their broad leaves pressed against the glass like splayed hands, pleading for rescue. He could picture her now, drinking her tea in striped pajamas that looked, and perhaps were, made for a little boy. Billy himself lay sprawled on the sofa, the Sunday *Times* spread out before him, the remains of breakfast—flaky croissants from a new bakery Srikanth had discovered—littering the coffee table.

"I'm flying out Wednesday," Gwen explained. "Dad's meeting me at the airport."

"I thought you were renting a car." Billy moved to clear the table—he hated a mess—but Sri beat him to it. He brushed the crumbs onto a tray and carried the jam-sticky plates to the kitchen.

"I am," Gwen said. "But there's all that road construction in Boston. The Big Dig."

"It's not finished?"

"Next year, I guess. Anyway, Dad wants me to follow him back to Cambridge. He's afraid I'll get lost again." The year before, mystified by endless detours, Gwen had spent two hours circling the city. Finally, in desperation, she'd called Frank from a rest area on the Mass Pike. When Billy heard of her misadventure, he'd been livid. It was just like their father to let Gwen wander a labyrinthine city—reduced now to a massive construction site—at rush hour, among the most aggressive drivers in the world. In Billy's view, New York cabbies were courtly by comparison.

"That's not a bad idea," Billy said grudgingly. For once the old man was thinking of someone besides himself.

"Hey, why don't you meet me there?" Gwen said this with elaborate casualness, as though the idea had just occurred to her. More likely she'd pondered it for weeks. "Dad's dying to see you."

"I doubt that," he said sourly, though he knew she was right. Their father had always favored him. It was one of many failings Billy held against him.

"Oh, come on. Just for a day. A day and a night. Then we can drive to Mom's."

"I don't think so."

"I already told him you were coming," said Gwen.

"You did what?"

Sri returned from the kitchen, fished the crossword from the pile of newspaper. Billy made room for him on the couch.

"Billy, he wants to see you. And he's lonely. He hasn't been himself since Deena left."

"I can't believe you said I was coming."

"Why are you being so stubborn?" said Gwen, the most stubborn creature on earth.

"I'm not stubborn."

"Billy." Her voice was very small; she had gone into wheedling mode. "Please?"

"Seriously, I can't. I'm on call Wednesday."

Sri looked up from his puzzle, his lips twisted in amusement.

"Oh," said Gwen. "Well, why didn't you say so?"

"I forgot."

Sri rolled his eyes.

Gwen sighed. "Then I guess I'll see you at Mom's. Can you come early, at least? Don't leave me alone with her." Gwen paused. "And tell Srikanth I said hello."

"Will do," said Billy, and hung up the phone.

"You are the worst liar in the world." Sri scratched idly at the crossword with a ballpoint pen. In ten minutes the boxes would be filled.

"Me? You have no idea what you're writing there. They're just random letters. You're lucky I can't read your Hindi handwriting."

"I'm just trying to impress you," said Sri.

"I'm already impressed."

Sri smiled. He was stunningly handsome when he smiled; knowing this, he deployed the smile sparingly. It was as if he'd spent his life surrounded by mirrors, so accurately did he gauge the effects of his good looks.

"What's happening Wednesday?" he asked.

"Gwen's going to Boston. To see my dad."

"Ah." Sri waited for Billy to continue. Then, when he didn't: "You don't want to go."

"Jesus, why would I? One day at my mother's is punishment enough," said Billy. "You know all this."

"I do?" *I'm listening*, his tone said—but it was an invitation, not a demand. Billy loved this about Sri: his coolness, his subtlety. There were no scenes with him, none of the high opera Tom and Richard sometimes engaged in, or the confusing emotional tango Billy had stumbled through, years ago, with Lauren McGregor.

"I saw him a few years ago," Billy said. "I didn't particularly enjoy it."

This was a gross understatement. That dinner in Concord—the first time in a decade his parents had suffered each other's company—had been excruciating for all concerned. All but Billy's brother, Scott, whose return to New England had occasioned the debacle. When Scott arrived with his noisy tribe, he was already bleary-eyed; he disappeared periodically into the guest room to fire up a joint. While the rest of the family bled, Scott had wandered through the day in a fog. (Typical! Years ago Billy had given his brother a nickname: *Scott Free*.) Their father, for some unknowable reason—sadism? childish spite?—had brought his then-girlfriend Deena. Paulette, unprepared for this bombshell, was icily polite; Deena made the best of a bad situation by drinking an entire bottle of Sancerre before dinner. She'd spent the evening sleeping it off in the guest room while Frank and Paulette glared at each other across the table.

"You never mentioned it," said Sri.

"It was before I met you," Billy lied.

"That's a long time."

"I guess so. I haven't noticed. I have nothing to say to him."

"Maybe he has something to say to you."

Undoubtedly this was true. Given half a chance, Frank would talk Billy into a coma, a hazard of thirty years in the classroom: a compulsion to lecture, an unnatural ease in one-sided conversations. Utter obliviousness to the listener's boredom, irritation, or outright rage.

"He only talks about his research," said Billy.

"Which is."

"Oncodevelopmental biology."

Sri raised his eyebrows. "This is a remarkable fact to keep quiet for so long."

Billy shrugged, rose to refill their mugs.

"It's fascinating, how gene-expression patterns that are normal in the embryo drive malignancy in the adult. Similar, really, to the dysregulated genes in heart disease. Too much Mef-two and whammo!" Sri broke off. "Why didn't you tell me? I'd love to know more about his research. We would have a great deal to talk about."

That's why, Billy thought.

HE'D MET Sri at a conference in Toronto—nearly four years ago, before Billy joined his group practice, when life was simpler and they both had time to attend such things. Billy had registered at the last minute; he'd planned to spend that Monday running the Boston Marathon, but had been sidelined by an injury, a painful groin pull. He and Sri would laugh about this later, how they owed their meeting to Billy's groin.

Sri was an MD fellow at Columbia, giving a talk on myocardial transcription factors, a hot topic in the early nineties. Listening to him speak—the crisp British inflection, the public school accent—Billy had felt something move inside him. Sri's beauty would have been striking anywhere; but in a conference room full of decrepit old men, it seemed, truly, obscene.

Is he? Billy wondered.

At the time—and even still—he had little instinct for such things.

The paper was received with enthusiasm; the team leader, a venerable professor at Columbia, was mobbed with questions. Sri stood off to the side, alone; Billy had a clear shot. *How do I do this?* he wondered. He had never approached a man before. The others—what few there'd been—had always come to him.

Sri's eyes, up close, were the color of coffee. His mouth looked firm and juicy, like a ripe plum. Billy's question, involving MyoD—the mother of all muscle-gene regulators—could have been answered in two minutes; but Billy surprised himself by suggesting a drink at the hotel bar.

They took a corner table, slightly secluded, two handsome young men in very good suits: Billy in Armani, Sri in a sand-colored linen Billy was dying to touch. He glanced around, feeling conspicuous. To his relief the bar was full of men sitting together, colleagues and coinvestigators winding down from the day.

Later, when they stepped into the elevator, Billy pressed the button for the fourth floor. "You're mistaken," Sri said softly. "I'm on five."

And just that easily, it was settled between them. Billy had never had to ask. Back in New York, they saw each other occasionally, then weekly, then every day. Their monogamy was spontaneous, accidental. Neither had expected it, or insisted upon it. At the outset Sri had another lover, and Billy saw an old Pearse classmate he'd slept with sporadically since college. Matthew worked for the State Department in Barcelona; once a year Billy vacationed there, and spent the better part of a week in Matthew's bed. Since meeting Sri he'd visited Barcelona only once. Sri hadn't pressed for details about this friend, this Matthew, but his sly smile suggested that he knew all. Once, at a dinner party,

Tom and Richard had raved about their own vacation to Barcelona. *Oh, Billy has intimate knowledge of Barcelona,* Sri had remarked. *He's crazy about Barcelona. He can't seem to get enough.*

But that was years ago. Now Billy couldn't remember any skin but Srikanth's, any mouth, any smell. *I don't want anyone else,* he'd once told Sri.

Of course you don't, Sri replied. *People irritate you. And you're terrified of change.*

Even now, if Billy were to fall into bed with someone—a stranger from a bar or bookstore, the cute blond barista who flirted with him at Starbucks—it somehow wouldn't matter. Sri would know instantly, and tease him mercilessly; but nothing would change between them. Billy knew this as surely as he knew his own name, and the knowledge comforted him deeply. He couldn't imagine his life any other way.

Different on the surface, they were alike in the ways that mattered. Both eldest sons of successful fathers (Sri's had been a close adviser to Sanjay Gandhi); both sent away to demanding schools (Billy to Pearse, Sri to Doon). With Sri, Billy was not merely happy. He was *understood.* When he thought of their lives together, he felt a deep relief. Sri was his solution to a particularly nettlesome problem: how a man like him was to live.

For years this was the phrase he used. As a teenager he viewed his sexuality as a medical condition, invisible to the naked eye, but requiring management. Watching other boys in class, on the playing field, he wondered: *Is he like me?* Some were, had to be. The most obvious case was a boy named Willie Neeland, who'd arrived at Pearse halfway through Billy's second year. From his first day on campus, Willie attracted attention; with his looks, he didn't have a choice. He was tiny, with a mop of blond curls and a comical gait. He didn't walk across a room, he *bounced.* And when Willie bounced into Pearse, Billy held his breath, expecting the worst. Willie was a sight gag: his loud shirts, his tiny hands and feet, his high-pitched voice so patently ridiculous that teasing him was nearly redundant. Willie was dead meat.

But for reasons Billy didn't understand, Willie Neeland was spared. More than that: he was so outrageous that he became something of a celebrity. He was talented, smart in all the ways Billy wasn't. He could draw anything, anyone, with astonishing accuracy. Most famously, he was an uncanny mimic. His face and body seemed made of plastic; he could become Mick Jagger or Richard Nixon or Muhammad Ali with a tilt of the head, a trick of voice. Soon his repertoire included every teacher at Pearse. The other boys applauded wildly, and left Willie in peace.

At first Billy was relieved. Then, strangely, annoyed. Willie's impersonations began to irk him. Even the name, *Willie*, was irritating: the girlish spelling, the phallic connotations. Most distressingly, it was far too close to *Billy*. They were both Williams, after all; but there the similarity ended. They were nothing alike. Billy had no interest in the Willie Neelands of the world. It was the athletes who inflamed him, his teammates in soccer and lacrosse, the bigger, tougher guys who played rugby and football. Guys who, if they suspected, would beat the shit out of him. Knowing this, he watched them furtively, shamefully, his desire inflamed by fear. (Years later he would grasp the perversity of this. But at the time, no. At the time he was inflamed.)

He would have forgotten Willie Neeland altogether if not for a conversation that happened at the end of his third year. Like every other May, Frank McKotch drove up to Pearse to empty out Billy's dorm room, to transport him and his junk back to Concord for the summer. They were packing boxes into the Volvo when Willie Neeland bounced past in one of his famous shirts, red gingham like a tablecloth, a sketch pad under his arm. Billy and Willie wished each other a good summer. In the Pearse way, they shook hands and shoved each other's shoulder. When Billy got into the car, his father spoke.

Interesting little fellow. Kind of flaky, isn't he?

Nah, Billy said, blushing mightily. *Willie's cool.*

(Did he imagine it, or did his father shoot him a sidelong glance? A warning look, heavy with meaning. Billy had replayed it so many times that the memory was tattered, distorted probably. It was impossible to say.)

Then Frank launched into a story that was meant to be comic, about a time he'd driven to the beach with his buddy Neil Windsor and a couple of Radcliffe girls. Frank had taken his date into the sea grass—*for a little privacy*, he told Billy, with an arched eyebrow. Billy felt his cheeks heat; he was sixteen and alarmed by such confidences, which his father offered with troubling frequency. *Neil didn't lay a hand on his girl*, Frank said, laughing. *I couldn't believe it. I thought for sure he was queer.*

The whole conversation lasted maybe five minutes, but Billy would remember it always. At the time—and still—he couldn't shake the feeling that his father had been signaling him: *I know what you are, and you'd better not be. Not you. Not my son.*

He couldn't, for a long time, think of himself as *gay*, a term he associated with the Provincetown queens who paraded down Commercial Street every Fourth of July, that titillating and frightening and haunting spectacle of his youth. He had been a sober, sensitive boy, and this remained his basic nature. Yet his condition was associated with costumes and dancing, Mardi Gras and drag shows, the kind of contrived merriment that had always grated on him. It was a troubling discovery. Even as a child, he'd hated Halloween.

He needed a man; he'd come to accept that. Yet he was often repulsed by men who were gay. Self-hatred, Matthew had called it, when Billy confessed it in a late-night phone call to Barcelona. Billy disputed the charge. It was in his temperament to be specific, and he knew precisely what he wanted. A serious man, a masculine man. Someone more or less like himself.

Reaching this conclusion—his basic nature, immutable, eternal—had taken years. Before that, halfheartedly, he had tried. In college he'd fallen in love—a kind of love—with Lauren McGregor, and it was Lauren who'd made everything clear.

He'd known her since Pearse, where she'd been his lab partner in first-year biology, the luck of alphabetical order. She was a plain, quiet girl with shaggy bangs she peered through cautiously, as though she feared what lay beyond. Tall, Billy's height, and so thin her skirts seemed empty—no curve of hip or ass, nothing at all. Lauren was the shyest girl in the class, and the smartest; she adored Billy with an intensity so obvious that he was constantly teased about it.

Quality, his classmates joked. *That girl is quality*. It was the ultimate Pearse word, in that it meant just the opposite of what it said. Failing a test was quality. Missing an easy shot was quality. A girl with shaggy hair, no tits, and no ass: that was the ultimate in quality.

Ichabod, the boys called Lauren McGregor. *Your girlfriend, Ichabod.*

At Princeton Billy forgot all about poor Lauren. Forgot about girls in general; between lacrosse and O-chem there was plenty else to fill his time. But buried beneath his busyness was a pulsating anxiety: at nineteen, at twenty, his virginity weighed on him. For that was the way he thought of himself, despite what had transpired in his dorm room his sophomore year at Pearse, with his roommate Matthew Stone. He'd awakened one night to the sound of Matthew's breathing, and had known immediately what his friend was doing in the next bed. Half asleep, and not knowing why, at first, Billy had done the same thing himself.

For a long time they didn't touch each other. They merely touched themselves in each other's presence. They did this a lot. But because this was something Billy did anyway, with or without Matthew, he decided it didn't count. It was only after Matthew climbed into Billy's bed one night, after they fell asleep naked and twisted together, a warm and sticky helix of boy, that Billy spun into a panic. That spring, without telling Matthew, he entered the housing lottery with a buddy from the lacrosse team. *I'm sick of you anyway*, Matthew joked when he discovered this, but Billy could see the betrayal had hurt him. They remained friendly, but were not friends. They wouldn't be friends again for a long time.

At Pearse, and later at Princeton, girls pursued him. Pretty girls, though not the prettiest; those would have required some effort on his part. His approach was passive: he would wait, and the thing would happen. Opportunities came and went; but for one reason or another he let them pass. And the longer he waited, the more daunting the prospect became.

The problem, he decided, was that girls he met at campus parties meant nothing to him; it wasn't as if he actually *knew* them. He was too fastidious to touch a stranger, or to want to do so. Sex would have to be with someone he knew. And from sports, from school—Pearse had been nominally coed, but the students were mostly male—he knew only boys. Could he ever know a girl as completely as he'd known Matthew Stone?

Such was his predicament his final year at Princeton—which, desperate to escape his parents, he'd chosen over the local options. This decision distressed his mother and confounded his father, who'd expected to steer him through the biology program at MIT. Billy's uncle Roy, freakishly loyal to Harvard, was even more outraged. A few years later, at his daughters' weddings (two for Mimi, one for Charlotte) Roy greeted Billy coolly, like a stranger he vaguely remembered instead of the nephew he'd sailed with summer after summer. *Princeton?* he mumbled, half in the bag at Mimi's first wedding. It was a circuslike extravaganza at Newport to which half the alumni of Pearse had been invited—including, to Billy's surprise, Lauren McGregor.

He didn't recognize her at first, so completely had she changed. Her hair was lighter, long, and teased into one of those eighties creations that would later seem embarrassing but at the time, somehow, had looked terrific. She stood at the bar with men on either side, sipping from a short glass. Her slinky dress clung to her long thighs. Until he saw it, Billy would have been unable to imagine her beautiful. The transformation was astonishing.

He'd had a few drinks and was feeling sentimental—for his mother, sitting alone at a table tapping her foot to the music, as though wishing someone would ask her to dance; for Mimi, the romantic heroine of his childhood, who'd made him swear, at age six, that since cousins couldn't, he would never marry. He'd agreed to this readily. If he couldn't marry Mimi, why would he want anyone at all?

It was in this condition that he'd first glimpsed Lauren at the bar. He touched her shoulder and was gratified by the way her face lit at the sight of him. On the dance floor she felt solid and correct in his arms, a discovery that seemed significant. He'd always been uncomfortable with the smallness of girls; but Lauren, in high heels, was exactly his height.

Flush with gin, he flirted, a thing he had never done. That it was

Lauren in his arms, not a stranger, made this possible; Lauren's shoulder and back, her hip and ass beneath his hand. Exhilaration filled him, and with it a sense of accomplishment. It was as though he'd solved a differential equation that had once mystified him, a complex problem that had bedeviled him for years.

The McGregors had booked a block of rooms at a hotel in Newport. Lauren, the last unmarried sister, had the room next to her parents'. Billy was mindful of this fact as he turned the key in the lock. He'd sent his own mother back to Concord with his aunt Martine, ignoring her stunned look, the reproach in her eyes. *A bunch of Pearse kids are staying overnight,* he told her. *I'll be home in time for breakfast.*

His mother had glanced pointedly at Lauren, who was waiting for Billy at the bar. *Is she staying?* his mother asked, but Billy only shrugged. He'd sensed her disapproval when he brought Lauren over to the table. *For her?* his mother's eyes said. *You're leaving me for her?*

What happened in that hotel room—if you considered the whole universe of sex, the dizzying variety of acts people performed on each other's bodies—was utterly usual; but to Billy it was rife with small discoveries. That a girl's body, despite its odd softness, was not so different from a boy's. Both had weight and warmth and texture, mouths that breathed and murmured and tasted. That the chain of sensations, the heat and pressure and friction, was remarkably similar. That in the end—could it really be so simple?—plain contact was the thing that mattered, skin on skin, mouth on mouth, the brief suspension of aloneness. The other heart beating in the room.

And just that easily Lauren became his girlfriend. She phoned him nightly from her dorm room at Yale, spent every other weekend curled around him in bed. She appeared and was beautiful at his fraternity formal; she impressed his friends with her intellect and wit. At those moments Billy was weirdly proud of her, like a parent who'd watched an awkward child blossom. He remembered Lauren at fourteen—awkward Ichabod, peering at the world from behind her curtain of hair—and found himself *rooting for her.* It was not the way other guys loved their girlfriends, but it was a kind of love nonetheless.

At Thanksgiving he took Lauren home to Concord. He would

wonder, later, what had possessed him, but at the time it seemed a reasonable idea. Lauren's parents had invited them both to Paris— her father ran the European branch of a company that made office equipment—but Thanksgiving break was only five days long, too brief for a trip overseas. His buddy Topher Craig spent holidays with his girlfriend's family, so Billy assumed this was normal behavior. Having finally secured a girlfriend, he took pleasure in doing things correctly. He was proud of Lauren, of himself for loving her. And because they'd always been, he assumed his family would be proud of him too.

His parents still tried, in those days, to spend holidays together, mainly for the benefit of Scott, who was still in high school. In ret- rospect, it seemed laughable. Considering how obviously Frank and Paulette hated each other, the benefits of this arrangement, to Scott or anybody, were questionable. (Were nonexistent, probably, considering the way his brother had turned out.)

Even before Billy and Lauren arrived, the day was humming with tension. When they landed at the house Thanksgiving morning, his mother was in a fit of preparation. "Oh, there you are," she said, barely looking up from whatever she was chopping. This was in sharp contrast to the way she usually greeted Billy, with a clingy effusiveness that made him squirm.

"Your room is ready," she said, like a surly innkeeper. "You can put her in the guest room." As though Lauren were an extra cot, some out-of-season item that required storage. Billy stared at his mother in amazement. He'd seen her weep in grief or loneliness or frustra- tion—outbursts caused, invariably, by his father. But never had the Drew manners failed her. He had never in his life seen her be rude.

They ate dinner at midday, the Drew Thanksgiving tradition. Paulette seated Lauren at the far end of the table and never once met her eyes. Scott, uncombed and sullen, stared at Lauren hungrily; for a seventeen-year-old punk he had a surprisingly heavy beard. Gwen picked silently at her dinner. Frank, ever genial, rushed in to fill the gap, asking Lauren a million questions. He seemed delighted that she was applying to medical school. Did she plan to specialize? Had she any field in mind?

For this Billy was truly grateful. For the first time in years, he was glad for his father's presence. But Frank's attention to Lauren only made Paulette angrier. Billy, so attuned to his mother's emotions, noticed her deliberate chewing, the slow, deep breaths she took, as though exercising heroic patience.

After dinner Billy suggested a walk. Normally he'd have helped clear the table, but subjecting Lauren to any more of his mother's company seemed cruel to them both. He and Lauren bundled into scarves and sweaters; they hiked across town to Sleepy Hollow Cemetery, their breath visible in the creeping dusk. *I'm sorry*, he said. *I don't know why she was like that.*

It's okay, Lauren said. *I didn't mind.*

A light snow was falling as they followed the path to Author's Ridge. Billy showed Lauren the Thoreau and Alcott plots, the two families buried twenty feet apart. He pointed to a rectangular stone no bigger than a dictionary, simply marked *Henry*. Small offerings decorated the grave site: a miniature pumpkin, a heap of colorful gourds.

They hiked the path to the higher ground where, chained off from the surrounding graves, the Emerson clan was buried. The plot was studded with modest headstones. At the center, a jagged boulder marked the spot where Ralph Waldo lay.

I love this, Lauren said, a little breathless. *This is how I want to be buried, next to my husband and kids. The whole family together. Don't you?*

I want a big rock, Billy said. *Like Ralph.*

Fine, Lauren said. *We'll put you in the middle. Between me and your mother.*

Standing at Emerson's grave, they had both laughed until they ached, the tense misery of the day evaporated. It was a moment Billy would remember for the rest of his life, himself and Lauren McGregor breathless in the snowy graveyard, laughing like fools.

Only later did an anxious truth strike him: Lauren had imagined them married.

When they returned to the house he shunted her quickly upstairs, shamed by the argument unfolding in the kitchen. *The way you flirted with that girl was disgraceful. Are you proud of yourself?* Those words stayed with Billy a long time. His father hadn't flirted with Lauren; he'd simply shown polite interest. For years Billy had listened to his mother's litany of grievances against Frank, and taken her side unquestioningly. Now he wondered whether any of it were true; whether his mother could be trusted or, when it came to his father, had simply lost her mind.

Back at Princeton, Billy couldn't forget what Lauren had said in the cemetery. With exams looming, he found himself inventing excuses to avoid trips to New Haven. *Don't you miss me?* she sometimes asked, her voice husky with hurt. *Of course I do,* he insisted, though it wasn't exactly true. How could he miss her when he already had her? Lauren thinking of him, caring what happened to him, his lacrosse practice, his biochem exam, the boring details of his undergraduate life.

What he didn't miss, in fact, was sex. He couldn't seem to conjure up the desire, the plain animal lust that made normal college couples wild to see each other, the real reason Topher Craig put five hundred miles on his car each weekend to visit his girlfriend at Cornell. *I don't know how you do it, man,* Topher sometimes said, as he packed his duffel on a Thursday night. *After a week I'm ready to explode.*

To this Billy had no answer. The real answer—that he did explode, nightly, alone in his room—was unspeakable and pathetic. Unspeakable too what he thought of as he pumped himself. He was not thinking of Lauren.

When she visited Princeton they saw movies, ate diner breakfasts, watched basketball games. Saturday afternoons they ran. Lauren was on the cross-country team at Yale—a dedicated runner, ambitious in her training, a perfect match for Billy's long stride. In the evening, tired but high on endorphins (and dehydrated; Billy would shudder later to think of it), they drank. At parties on campus, or at bars with Topher and his girlfriend, they pounded beer and cocktails—so many, often, that sex later was out of the question. Was that, in fact, Billy's intention? At the time he wasn't sure.

They might have gone on like this forever if he hadn't traveled, that February, to Maryland, for a lacrosse scrimmage against Towson. Instead of riding the team bus, he'd driven his own car; he planned to stay an extra day for a med school interview at Georgetown—and to look up an old friend, a student at Johns Hopkins. He arrived early and found the number in the Baltimore phone book: his old Pearse roommate Matthew Stone.

"Sure," Matthew said when Billy invited him to the game. Billy picked him out immediately in the stands. He was thinner than Billy remembered, with a different haircut. He wore a diamond stud in his right ear. Maybe because of the earring, Matthew now looked *gay*. And on Matthew, gay looked very good.

They greeted each other warmly, clumsily—the pumping hand-shake, the shoulder thump—Billy wondering all the while what his teammates were thinking, how he and Matthew looked. *We were at Pearse together*, he explained to no one in particular, as though an explanation were required.

They went back to Matthew's place, in a neighborhood where Billy hesitated to park his car. Matthew's building looked ready for demolition, but his apartment was spacious and interestingly furnished—a curving, asymmetrical sofa, an Eames chair. Matthew tossed him a beer from the refrigerator, and before he had a chance to open it they were in Matthew's bedroom.

What happened there was nothing like sex with Lauren, which, at its best, had been a tense experiment. With Matthew there was no effort involved, no concentration, no calculation. Matthew knew exactly what to do, how and where to touch. His body was intensely familiar—from the long-ago nights at Pearse and the many times since, when he had visited Billy's imagination, Billy alone in his room.

"That was incredible," Billy said afterward, breathing heavily.

"I've practiced," said Matthew, and Billy felt a stab of jealousy. Crazy of course, to hope that Matthew had waited for him. "What, you haven't practiced?"

Billy thought his guilt would choke him. Until that moment, he'd forgotten there was a Lauren.

The next weekend he drove to New Haven in a downpour. He had begged off the party at her sorority. *Let's go somewhere, just the two of us. It's important. I need to talk to you.*

He picked her up at her dorm. The rain fell in icy sheets. He had parked a block away; by the time they reached his car, Lauren's coat was soaked. She'd made a dinner reservation at the Rose Room, the sort of place Yale students took their parents at graduation or homecoming. The food was good—expensive, a little fussy—the drinks exceptionally strong. Billy drank two martinis before the salads arrived.

"I've been thinking," he began, the speech he'd rehearsed on his drive from Princeton. He was drunk enough to get through it, as long as Lauren didn't cry. "Things are getting crazy, what with med school decisions. We won't have a lot of time to see each other."

Lauren frowned. "It's almost summer. We can go to the Cape with my parents. We can see each other every day, if we want."

"Sure," said Billy. "The Cape would be great. Only—" Oh Jesus, how did people do this? He thought fleetingly of his parents, who'd dissolved a fifteen-year marriage over the course of a few months. How did anyone have the courage? How did you even begin?

The waiter arrived with their dinners. Billy looked down at the plates, his stomach clenching like a fist. There was no way he could eat a bite.

He looked over at Lauren, shivering in a sleeveless dress. It was pale green and silky, a dress he didn't recognize. Pearls at her throat, her blond hair dark from the rain.

"You look beautiful," he said with feeling.

She tucked a strand of hair behind her ear, revealing a pearl earring. Billy thought of Matthew, the diamond stud in his right ear.

"I'm going to be sick," he said.

In the men's room he leaned over the toilet. The gin washed up from his stomach in a sour wave. *Quality*, he thought. Running away from the table to hurl: that was quality behavior. When he returned to the dining room, Lauren was staring out the window, her dinner untouched.

"I'm sorry," he said. "I drank too much."

"This isn't how I thought it would be."

"What do you mean?" He stared at her, genuinely mystified.

"I thought there was something you wanted to ask me."

And finally he understood: the new dress, the Rose Room. "Oh, Lauren."

Her face looked ready to crumble, crushed with disappointment. It was almost more than he could bear, Billy who'd never disappointed anybody in his life.

"I don't understand," she said, her voice vibrating, and he saw there was no avoiding it: she was clearly, inevitably, about to cry. "Is it—just tell me. Is there someone else?"

The question hung in the air. Lifetimes passed. Their wedding at the church in Concord, Lauren in his grandmother's wedding gown; summers in Truro, their children playing in the surf. Billy and Lauren growing old and tender, the way his parents hadn't.

She got up quickly from the table, grabbed her handbag, and rushed for the door.

"Lauren, wait!" He reached for his wallet and laid bills on the table, fifty, a hundred, more. He felt the plastic tag in his jacket pocket. She had forgotten her coat.

He found her in the parking lot, sodden and crying. "Here," he said gently, wrapping her in her coat. They drove back to campus in silence, Billy sober finally, and shivering in the cold. He thought of the long wet drive back to Princeton, the long arid years of a life without her.

AND FOR a long time, love, the possibility of it, seemed lost to him. It was the cold reality of his condition. He could want another man, he could touch and be touched, fuck and be fucked; but this was not love. Was, rather, a terrible parody of it, somehow comical, somehow grotesque. Love was the movies of his adolescence, John Travolta strutting and preening, twirling the girl in the Lycra dress. Billy couldn't name the actress, couldn't even recall her face; but still he'd absorbed the lesson: it wasn't love unless someone was wearing a dress.

Sex, now: sex could be had. When he started med school that fall, he sensed its presence in the streets, in the dance clubs where he occasionally ventured, New Order playing so loud he couldn't hear a thing, only feel it in his chest. *How does it feel to treat me like you do?* Boys in boots, in peg-legged jeans, eyed him brazenly from across the room. The night-owl complexions, the hollow cheeks: to Billy, who'd spent his adolescence crushing on Bowie and Mick Jagger, they could hardly have been more seductive. But in the fall of 1984, they were also suspect. The virus had been identified, a name assigned. Still, the obituaries in the *Times* were full of code words: *of pneumonia, after a long illness.* Suddenly nobody looked healthy, and suddenly this mattered a great deal. For the average gay man, getting laid was a scary business. For Billy McKotch—coming off a tough first semester at Columbia, knowing more than he wanted to about virology and epidemiology—it was simply impossible.

So to hell with women; to hell with men. He would live like his sister Gwen, outside that dizzying and treacherous game. Med school consumed him; he studied, went to lectures, slept when time allowed. And when he wasn't sleeping or studying, he ran. Each day, awake before dawn, he passed the same lean strangers in the park, a ghostly fraternity darting through the half light. They exchanged glances, the curt runner's nod, and Billy thought of the other ghosts who still inhabited the city, the young men evaporated by *a long illness*, felled by a chronic condition. The men who were like him.

He finished the New York Marathon in three hours and sixteen minutes—six minutes too slow to qualify for Boston, but next year that would come. Crossing the finish line, he thought of Lauren McGregor, who'd made him faster and better. Afterward, his hands shaking from adrenaline and fear, he called her number in Connecticut. A machine answered: *I'm not here now. You know what to do.*

He called again and again, saying nothing, just to hear her voice.

1998

the cure

G wen packed her gear carefully. The duffel bag was narrow and lightweight, just large enough to hold her mask and fins and snorkel, her regulator and buoyancy compensator vest. As always, she worried that the airline would lose her luggage. Snorkels and regulators were easily replaced, but the BC had been custom-made to fit her perfectly. No dive shop in St. Raphael—in the entire Caribbean— would have one in her size.

Which was short and square. Sort of, but not exactly, small.

She has never explained herself to anybody. She has been asked, but not in a way that required a response.

What's your problem, Bitsy? Why are you such a freak?

Or:

Describe any way(s) in which your Turner's syndrome has affected your psychosocial development.

The second question is worse, being unanswerable. She has never been anyone else, anyone normal. Beyond the obvious—the breasts, etc.—she has no clue how they develop. And of course psychosocial isn't about breasts.

I am not a psycho, she'd written on the questionnaire as she was waiting to see the doctor, *nor am I very social*. The doctor, if he actually read this, would take it as a symptom of something. Her whole life was considered a symptom of something.

Unanswerable.

It wasn't as if something had happened to her, an accident or injury, an illness that struck overnight—she is thinking of tuberculosis or the other one, the spinal one—and left her crippled, a clear case of cause and effect. No. She'd been a child, normal, healthy. Then.

Then nothing, not a single thing, had happened.

Instead things had *failed to happen*. And how do you explain what has failed to happen? Gwen did not change. Other girls did. She can't know what they are like inside, their internal weather. What they are that she is not.

In her teens she devoured science fiction novels, full of alien invaders, the more fantastic the better. And it was to these creatures, visitors from another galaxy, that she imagined explaining herself.

I am small, she would tell them. *This is why I am small.*

They would have noticed her size, of course, in relation to her fellows; but to them, large headed and possibly without working lungs, it would seem a minor point. She would describe the metamorphosis humans typically went through—the sudden increase in size, the subtle changes in shape. The visitors would listen incredulously, the whole process as foreign to them, as bizarre and random sounding, as it had always seemed to Gwen.

Yet everyone experienced it: rich and poor, genius and cretin, millions of Africans and Asians speaking languages she would never understand. Years ago, as an undergraduate, she'd become fascinated with puberty rituals: the Sunrise Dance of the Apache, the Nigerian girls sequestered in fattening rooms, the bar mitzvahs and confirmations, the conferring of adult names. The local Algonkian tribe had performed the Ceremony of the Maide to initiate young girls into womanhood—a ritual deplored, and quickly outlawed, by Concord's Puritan settlers. It occurred to Gwen—nineteen then, holed up in the Wellesley library writing an exam for Cultural Anthro—that puberty was the one universal human experience. Not just for the billions of people now living, but the billions who'd preceded them. Everyone had gone through this passage. The realization shook her. She had never felt so alone.

• • •

SHE'D BEEN a girl like any other: small for her age, but not remarkably so. She liked being small, the attention it brought her. She'd been a showoff then, a singer and a dancer. The lead in every school play. The fastest runner in her grade.

She was competitive. Coming in second had made her wild. At Pilgrims Country Day she was branded a crier, but only because she hated losing. She'd tried to explain this to her mother: *I'm not sad. I'm just mad.* Emotional immaturity, her teachers called it. For this reason, Gwen was held back a year. *She's so little*, the principal told her mother. *She needs time to catch up.*

Gwen saw, in retrospect, that flunking was a blessing. It delayed the inevitable. It bought her an extra year of innocence. In the seventh grade she noticed girls changing. Not all of them, not yet; but more and more she spotted the square yoke of bra straps beneath her friends' white blouses. That summer at the Cape her cousin Charlotte had betrayed her; in the space of a year she'd become a different person, someone Gwen didn't recognize. At school she kept a mental tally: how many, like herself, still wore undershirts or nothing. As long as there were others, she didn't care. As long as she wasn't the only one.

Phys Ed, predictably, was a source of agony. Three times a week she stripped down quickly in the locker room. Naturally she didn't want to be seen. But just as urgently, she didn't want to see. She wrapped herself in a towel and headed to the shower, timing it carefully. If she moved fast, she could finish before most of the others had started. This worked, but never completely. Always she saw a pair of breasts or two.

There was no escaping it. Breasts were everywhere. Like a horny teenage boy, Gwen perused the lingerie pages of the Sears catalog. Breasts squeezed into sweaters, peeking out the sides of tank tops, curving under T-shirts, like the pillows of a neatly made bed. When she was finally diagnosed, the other facts of her Turner's were murky abstractions—the talk of ovaries, which until recently she wasn't aware of having; the old-person worries about bones and heart disease. But her flat chest tormented her. Breasts were what she wanted, symbols of all she would never have.

Behind closed doors her parents argued—in urgent whispers, in low voices. In the end they shouted, not caring if Gwen heard. The substance of these arguments was always the same. Her father wanted tests, doctors, X rays, hormones. Her mother wanted none of these things. Unless they were medical, Frank ignored her problems. Paulette treated her like a baby. At the Cape she refused to let Gwen bike in the dunes, insisting she take one of her brothers along. *Keep an eye on your sister*, she'd tell Scotty. *Don't let her get lost.* Never mind that Gwen was three and a half months older and had a reasonable sense of direction, while Scott couldn't find his way out of a parking lot.

Let her go, her father would have said, if he'd ever been around at such moments. *Gwen will be fine.* Of course, he knew everything about Turner's. Nothing made him happier than telling her all the things that could be wrong with her, but weren't. A few years back, he'd phoned her sputtering with excitement: a scientist at Berkeley had identified a gene responsible for early breast cancer, the disease that killed Frank's mother. Mutations in the gene were inherited—but Gwen, thank God, had little cause for concern.

It took her a moment to understand his delight. He was giving her another reason to be grateful. *Thank God for what?* she wondered. *That I don't have breasts?*

He'd spent her adolescence talking to doctors, *keeping up with the literature.* Billy, their father's actual favorite, often joked that Gwen was. She had an unfair advantage, he claimed: there was no literature on Billy or Scott.

I t w a s her father who first put a name to it, who took her for the blood test at Mass General. It was snowing that morning, the first day of Christmas vacation. Her parents had been fighting for several months. When the test results came back, it was Frank who explained what they meant. He talked for more than an hour using words Gwen didn't recognize, long words that obscured the important points. Which were:

1. She would be short forever.
2. She wouldn't have periods, or
3. babies, or
4. breasts.

She had two chromosomes, like everyone did, but one of hers was partly missing. And these other things would be missing as a result.

Suddenly everything about her had an explanation: her size, her shape; her dramatic entry into the world, the tiny preemie in an incubator. The time she'd gotten lost in Star Market was no longer just a story; it was evidence of her *spatial difficulties*, her *nonverbal learning impairment*. Even her lousy math scores had an explanation: apparently all Turners sucked at math. That Gwen rarely did her homework, that she doodled or daydreamed or wrote letters to Shaun Cassidy instead of copying the sample problems into her notebook, did not matter. She was no longer castigated for being lazy; she was simply taken out of Algebra and put into General Math.

Her parents argued.

After each argument her father dragged her to another doctor—an endocrinologist, a pediatric cardiologist. Blood was taken, an ultrasound image of her kidneys; X rays to see the bones of her hand. The shots would make her grow several inches if she was lucky. Of course, being Gwen, she wasn't lucky. A year later, she'd grown less than an inch.

Gwen had Turner's.

Her parents argued.

Her father left.

LONG AFTER he'd moved out of the house, Frank continued to explain things. He was endlessly interested in Turner's; it was as if they'd discovered a new hobby together, like stamp collecting or golf. Yet he never told her anything she truly needed to know.

She remembered a Saturday evening in the dead of winter, the radiators hissing. They were eating take-out pizza on the floor of his apartment in Cambridge. Frank explained. Gwen listened.

Q. Daddy, why did I get Turner's?
A. You didn't get it. You've always had it. Your second X chromosome was damaged in utero, perhaps since conception. (Then, seeing her frown) Since before you were born.

Q. So it runs in our family?
A. No, because Turner females are nulliparous. (seeing her frown) That is to say, they do not have children, and so do not pass on their damaged genetic material. Once a family produces one Turner, that line is in effect extinguished. If one of your brothers were to have a daughter, she'd be no more likely to have a damaged chromosome than any other girl.

Her questions were always simple, his answers always complicated. The more he talked, the less she understood.

SHE CHOSE Sacred Heart for high school instead of Pearse. She did this partly to please her mother and partly to spare herself. More and more, school was a torment. An evil new nickname, Bitsy, followed her through the halls. At Pearse there would be no escape from such misery: in the evenings, on weekends, you were always at school.

The hormones came next, with more promises. Her shape would change—"modestly," the doctor was quick to caution. She would have periods—not real ones, he added hastily; but for a few days each month she would bleed. *How is that different from a real one?* Gwen wondered. But by then she'd learned not to ask.

When she remembered that time, Gwen thought mainly of her mother. After Frank left, she and Paulette were inseparable. Her mother took her to the theater and the ballet, on picnics and nature walks, to concerts at Tanglewood and exhibits at the MFA. *He would never do this with me*, her mother often said. Of course Gwen understood who "he" was.

Her mother needed her. When Frank appeared on Fridays to take Gwen and Scotty for the weekend, Gwen claimed headaches and stomachaches. Her mother allowed this, even encouraged it. With Billy away at Pearse, Paulette was lonely. She wanted Gwen all to herself.

And Gwen wanted to make her happy. She allowed herself to be taken shopping, a chore she despised: the humiliation of department-store changing rooms, the perplexed saleswomen who eyed her up and down and asked what size she *usually* wore. When her mother suggested—with embarrassing optimism—that they buy Gwen a training bra, she did not resist. She monitored her chest daily, waiting for the hormones to kick in. No kicking had occurred. Still, a little training couldn't hurt.

Most shockingly (to her adult self, the person she would later become) she acceded to an urgent demand of her mother's. It was important—essential—that Gwen attend her winter formal.

She'd listened incredulously to this request. It was as if her mother had asked her to break into flight.

"Um, okay," said little Gwen, tentatively flapping her wings.

"Don't worry about a thing," said the mother bird. "I have it all figured out. You leave everything to me."

Paulette's old friend Tricia James, it developed, had a son Gwen's age. Patrick James was a senior at the Friends School in Philadelphia and had recently applied to Harvard; he was in the process, now, of scheduling his college visits. After the glowing letter of recommendation he'd received from Frank McKotch, Patrick owed the family a favor. He could schedule his Harvard interview for the week of the formal, and enjoy a fun evening with Gwen.

The preparations began two months in advance. After a long fruitless day of shopping, Paulette gave up and took Gwen to a dress-maker. Together they looked at fabric samples, silk and satin and tulle. No purple, which her mother insisted was vulgar. Gwen meekly agreed. She stood in her underwear as measurements were taken. In a few weeks a dress appeared. The style was simple—a deep neckline and fitted bodice, cut to accommodate the padded bra Paulette had bought her. The narrow skirt, floor length, would hide Gwen's shiny black Mary Janes, the only dress shoes available in her size.

She hadn't seen Patrick James in years and wouldn't have recognized him anywhere but her own living room, where he appeared that afternoon, two hours before the dance. Her father had driven him over from Harvard. *Gwen*, her mother had whispered, knocking at her bedroom door. *Come down and say hello.*

Patrick was sitting on the divan when Gwen came downstairs. His face was round and ruddy, his teeth straightened by years of orthodontia. He had curly blond hair of the sort found on baby dolls. He wasn't good looking, exactly, but he bore a passing resemblance to boys who were. Gwen smiled tentatively. The girls at the dance—Martha Hixbridge and the others who ignored her at school—would have to be impressed.

Paulette came into the room with a plate of scones. "Gwen, darling, you remember Patrick."

"Hey," Patrick said. Then, seeing an adult was present, he stood.

Gwen gulped in a way that may have been audible. He was tall. Not tall like her six-foot brother and father, which would have been bad enough. Patrick—a star forward, she later discovered, on the Friends School basketball team—stood *six feet five inches tall*. Her eyes were level with his sternum.

"Patrick was telling me about his day at Harvard," said Paulette. "He had a marvelous interview."

"Great." Gwen could feel her mother's gaze. "What are you going to study?" she asked dutifully.

"Pre-law," said Patrick. "I guess."

Paulette patted Gwen's shoulder. "Sit down, dear. Have a scone."

Gwen sat, sorry to see her go. Paulette's too-bright smile was unnerving, but at least she had *spoken*. Alone, Gwen and Patrick sat in silence.

"You're a junior?" he said finally. "I thought we were the same age."

I got left back a year, she could have said. *They flunked me for being short.*

"My birthday is in September," she said instead—the explanation her mother always gave. "I missed the cutoff date." She had known Patrick two minutes and already she was lying. This seemed a bad sign.

Her mother returned, then, and shooed her upstairs. "No sense waiting until the last minute. I'll come up later to help with your hair."

Gwen showered and dressed. She'd grumbled about the tedious fittings, the time and money spent on something she'd wear just a few hours; yet in spite of all this she loved the dress. It was the first garment in years that had fit her correctly, with shoulder seams that actually aligned with her shoulders. The fabric was grayish-blue, to match her eyes. Not the pastel blue of children's clothing, but a subtle shade, sophisticated and adult. *This is nice,* she thought. *I look nice.*

There was a discreet knock at the door, Paulette loaded down with a case of electric rollers, a makeup kit, the brushes and combs and hairspray Gwen had agreed to have used upon her. She had refused to spend the afternoon in a salon.

"Darling, look at you!" Paulette dropped everything on the bed and pulled Gwen into her arms. "You look beautiful."

Gwen squirmed, not unhappily. Usually when her mother said such things, she couldn't decide whether to be irritated or depressed. This time the words touched her. In the new dress she could almost believe.

In this hopeful state she submitted to the hot curlers, the paints and powders applied to her face. The results were good, if disorienting. She looked like a different person. Which, she supposed, was the whole point.

Her mother beamed, eyes filling. "This is for you," she said, handing Gwen a small box. "Your father gave me these as an engagement present."

Inside was a strand of pearls.

"I don't wear them anymore," Paulette added, showing unusual
restraint.

THE DANCE was held downtown, at a hotel in Copley Square.
"Your mother tells me you're an excellent driver," said Paulette, handing Patrick her car keys, oblivious to his glassy stare, his gaping grin.
Gwen had found him in Scotty's room, in a white shirt and tuxedo
pants; the two boys sitting cross-legged on the floor passing an immense water pipe. *Hang on*, he'd told Gwen, taking the pipe from
Scott. *I need one more hit.*

In the car Patrick was suddenly talkative. "Your brother's cool,"
he said. "That was killer weed."

Gwen smiled, recalling the way Scotty had looked at her in her
dress, his eyes wide and serious. *You look awesome*, he'd whispered as she
and Patrick were leaving. From a stoned fourteen-year-old it was the
highest praise.

They surrendered the car to a parking attendant and went into
the hotel. In keeping with the dance's theme—A Night in Paradise—
the Minuteman Ballroom reeked of lilies. The decorating committee
had been working all day, stringing lights and filling fountains, decking
the perimeter with potted palms. Gwen and Patrick walked through
an archway laden with flowers. They were photographed beneath a
bamboo pergola, also laden with flowers. A blonde freshman ushered
them to their seats, at a round table at the back of the room. The popular girls had chosen their tables weeks ago, and packed them with their
closest friends. Because Gwen hadn't turned in the seat-assignment
form, she and Patrick had been placed at this table of strangers. Behind
them, on a makeshift stage, the band was setting up.

Dinner was served, a rubbery breast of chicken. Patrick swallowed his in three bites, then entertained himself by laughing uproari-
ously with the boy next to him, trading lines from a Richard Pryor
standup routine. He seemed to have forgotten she was there.

After dinner the lights dimmed; the band played at a volume that
made conversation impossible. Gwen was grateful for the noise. At

each slow song, she watched the couples take the floor. She glanced furtively at Patrick. Of course, they would look cartoonish dancing together. The moment he stood in her mother's parlor, this had been her first thought.

At that moment Patrick rose.

"I'll be back in a minute," he said.

For nearly an hour she sat alone, watching the couples on the floor. Finally Patrick returned, his bow tie undone. He looked disheveled and slightly drunk.

"Where did you go?"

"There's a party upstairs. Somebody got a room. Come on." He offered his hand. "Let's get out of here."

Gwen hesitated a moment, then took his hand. Except for the shoves and slaps and head knuckling of her brothers, this was the first time a boy had touched her. She imagined her classmates watching her leave, Gwen McKotch hand in hand with an almost-handsome boy.

They bypassed the crowded elevator and headed for the stairs. Patrick took the steps two at a time. Gwen scrambled to keep up.

"Who's having the party?" she asked, her voice echoing in the stairwell.

"Who cares? They have a keg."

Gwen stopped at the landing. The reality of her predicament struck her. She was about to walk into a roomful of the classmates whose teasing haunted her nightmares. She had walked out of Winter Formals without dancing even once.

"What's the matter?" said Patrick. He stood two steps above her. Her eyes were now level with his belt.

"Let's go back to the dance."

"You're kidding me." Patrick looked pained. "You want to sit there all night listening to that shitty band?"

Gwen felt her cheeks warm. "We could dance."

"You want to dance?" Patrick grinned. "Sure."

He reached out and pulled her close.

It was terrible. Her face was squashed against his belly, his shirt buttons pressed into her cheek. He swayed slightly—whether from drunkenness or a lame attempt at dancing, Gwen couldn't tell. His hot hands rested on her shoulders. They were, she noticed, bigger than her feet.

"Nice," he breathed.

Gwen squirmed. His hands were moist and very heavy. They seemed to be pressing her shoulders downward.

"Lower," he said.

She wriggled away from him. "What are you doing?"

"While you're down there, you could do me a favor."

She shoved him with all her strength. He lost his balance and stumbled backward, catching himself on the railing. Her face had left a makeup stain on his shirt front.

"What the *fuck?*" he said.

"Get me out of here," said Gwen. "I want to go home."

IN HER SENIOR YEAR, at her mother's insistence, she applied to Wellesley. Her grades were good, except for math, but her test scores were mediocre; in Gwen's view it was a waste of a stamp. She was lucky even to be wait-listed; but when this happened Paulette was bullshit. Wellesley *had* to take her: Gwen's aunt Martine, her grandmother, and several great-aunts were all graduates. (That Paulette hadn't graduated—that she'd dropped out of school to get married—was yet another mistake she blamed on Frank.)

When Wellesley finally said yes, her mother was thrilled. Her father was less than ecstatic. "Why stick so close to home?" he demanded. "Why not strike out on your own?"

He often asked such questions. Gwen was usually stumped for a response, though in this case she had one: she hadn't applied anywhere else, something her father might have noticed if he didn't spend every spare moment with his new girlfriend. Last fall, just as college applications came due, he'd introduced Gwen and Scott to Traci, who worked in the registrar's office at Harvard. She was in her thirties but acted younger—she used teenage slang and teased Frank about his age, trying, Gwen supposed, to ingratiate herself with his kids. Gwen knew better than to mention Traci to her mother, but Scott couldn't keep his mouth shut. Of course Paulette had gone completely mental, banning Frank from Thanksgiving and Christmas, a ruling that would stand for several years. She made such a stink about their weekend visits that Gwen found herself making excuses not to see him. It wasn't worth upsetting her mother.

She was nineteen the fall she started at Wellesley. The campus was fifteen miles from Concord, so close that Gwen rarely slept in her dorm room. Her bed at home was far more comfortable, and her mother was happy to drive her to class, as she'd done for four years to Sacred Heart. Frank had offered repeatedly to teach Gwen to drive, but always she demurred. Her mother hadn't forbidden it, exactly, but the prospect made Paulette nervous: driving was dangerous to begin with, and Gwen's *difficulties* (the word Paulette used) made it even more so.

So each morning she dropped Gwen on campus, and after Gwen's last class the old Volvo would reappear. For a time Gwen had insisted on meeting her mother a block away from campus. Later she felt differently. Halfway through her freshman year, as she was leaving Physical Anthropology, she'd fallen into conversation with a classmate, a thing that rarely happened. The girl, Cynthia Denny, was from Tennessee horse country, which explained it. Gwen had noticed a difference—an ease, an indiscriminate chattiness—in girls from the South.

They talked about the day's class, a guest lecture by a scholar visiting for the semester. The professor, Andreas Swingard, had recently published an oral history of a little-known tribe of Amazonian Indians.

"You're ruining the curve," Cynthia complained. "You know just as much as he does."

"I read his book. It's interesting stuff."

"Can I ask you a question?" Cynthia said, with a sly smile that seemed nearly flirtatious. "How old are you?"

Gwen understood, then, that there was a point to the conversation. That Cynthia wasn't simply being friendly.

"Nineteen," she said warily.

"I know it's none of my business," Cynthia stammered. "We just thought you were younger. You know, some kind of prodigy. I saw your mom drop you off the other day." Again the smile. "No offense, I hope."

At the time Gwen had been horrified. Her classmates—the mysterious *we*—had taken her for a child. But the more she thought about it, the more she liked this vision of herself, which, if not exactly flattering, was preferable to the truth: it was better to be a genius than a mutant. After that she let her mother drop her off at the Hazard Quad, where all of Wellesley could see.

(Years later, looking back at this time, Gwen barely recognizes herself: how terrified, how passive, how crippled by shame.)

It was her grandmother, ultimately, who made her understand the gravity of her situation. Early in Gwen's sophomore year, Mamie suffered a debilitating stroke that left her right side paralyzed, her speech confused. Gwen and Paulette made frequent trips to Florida to visit. They took turns sitting with Mamie on the sunny lanai, overlooking a garden of fig and mango trees, bougainvillea and azaleas in constant bloom.

On one of these afternoons, alert and surprisingly lucid, Mamie had grasped Gwen's hand. *Dear heart, have you ever considered it? There is such a shortage of vocations. Everything happens for a reason, my love. God has a plan for each of us.*

It took Gwen a moment to make sense of this. Mamie had always been religious; she took Communion daily and had sent Paulette and Martine to Sacred Heart, scandalizing the Protestant Drews. Now she hoped—had hoped for years, she said—that Gwen would consider the convent. *It may be the best life, dear, for a girl like you.*

I'll think about it, Mamie, Gwen said, because what else did you say to a failing grandmother—devout, kindly—who worried about your future?

I'm so glad, said Mamie. *Thank you, dear.*

She died a week later, of a second, massive stroke; and true to her promise, Gwen continued to think about what her grandmother had said. (For years the thought returned to her unbidden, whenever misfortune arose: *There's always the convent.* This never failed to make her laugh.)

But the conversation had another, more immediate effect. Gwen realized, suddenly and powerfully, the need for a change. That fall, without telling anyone, she applied for transfer to the University of Pittsburgh, where Andreas Swingard had been hired as the new chair of anthropology. She chose it for its large student body, where she could be perfectly anonymous, and its undemanding admissions profile: according to Barron's they'd be perfectly happy with her B average, the undistinguished board scores that had wait-listed her at Wellesley.

When the acceptance arrived in the mail, Gwen told her father first.

"Pittsburgh?" Frank paused a moment, gathering his thoughts. Gwen could see a lecture taking shape in his head. "I have some experience with that part of the world," he said tentatively. "It's quite different from here, in many respects."

Gwen nodded, waiting. It was strange to see her father at a loss for words.

The University of Pittsburgh, while a fine school, was not Wellesley. Gwen understood that, didn't she?

"Yeah, Dad," she said. "That's kind of the point."

She explained, then, about Andreas Swingard and cultural anthropology. Pitt's department was larger than Wellesley's, and more specialized. And of course, Pitt offered the PhD.

Frank brightened visibly. Gwen knew her father, knew what pleased him. Shamelessly she invoked the Steelers, the Pirates, the Penguins. She could see that she had him. There was no need to mention that Pitt, unlike Wellesley, was coed.

She had no intention of taking the veil.

That spring Frank became her hero. She would go to Pittsburgh, he promised; her mother would be convinced. Gwen stood back while her parents battled. In the end, her father prevailed.

All that summer Paulette raged. *I can't believe you're leaving*, she said again and again—alternately angry and weepy, in a way Gwen hadn't seen since the divorce.

Gwen's response was always the same: *Mother, it's time.*

To her father's amazement, she requested driving lessons. Together they cruised the back roads between Lincoln and Lexington, practiced three-point turns in parking lots. Frank called it *a fascinating experiment*: most Turners had difficulty in judging space and distance, he explained, and Gwen was no exception. In spite of this she was a better student than Scott, whose lessons nearly killed Frank and had, in fact, finished off his transmission. After Scott passed his test, Frank had unloaded the old sedan, and Gwen learned to drive on his new Saab 900.

Her brother Billy, who ridiculed Frank's love of all things Swedish, called the new car *Dad's Nobel Prize.*

Before she left for Pittsburgh, her father gave her another gift. Gwen learned to scuba dive. The certification class, an early birthday present, was held twice a week in a high school swimming pool two towns over. This gift would be important later, in ways Gwen couldn't yet imagine.

The Stott Museum sat north of the Allegheny, just over the Seventh Street Bridge, in a cavernous brick building that had served as the original Stott brewery. The place had been gutted in the early 1980s, a renovation financed through the generosity of Juliet Stott, the old-maid heir to the Stott brewing fortune. Miss Stott had poured millions into the project, imagining her museum a centerpiece of Pittsburgh's renaissance, the city's transformation from dying steel town to gleaming technology center, from Rust Belt dinosaur to American Florence, a center of intellectual and cultural life.

Or something like that.

The Stott's collection was vast but eclectic (some said *incoherent*), its acquisitions guided largely by the whim of Miss Stott—who, accompanied by her cook, maid, and driver, had tagged along on a few archaeological digs back in the 1940s. Miss Stott had a great respect for the indigenous art of Oceana. The Minoans interested her. She was fascinated by all things Egyptian. The atrium of the Stott displayed a painstakingly reconstructed Maori meeting house. Yet the collection was light on the Cretaceous period; and when it came to the Jurassic and Triassic, virtually nonexistent. "No dinosaurs," the grande dame had decreed early on, and though the staff had bent this rule with small tetrapod fossils, they had never broken it. Now eighty-nine years old, Miss Stott still visited the museum occasionally, prompting a flurry of activity among the development staff. Buffets were laid, fresh fruit and pastry from an outside bakery. (The rest of the time, the staff bought weak coffee and thawed bagels at the dank basement cafeteria.) Miss Stott, despite her generosity on certain fronts (folk arts, Egyptiana) could be tightfisted when it came to what development called *added value* and what Miss Stott called *frills.* Development had lobbied for years to get funding for an IMAX theater which, they claimed, would increase traffic by 30 percent in the first year. In the second year, it would wipe the Buhl Planetarium off the tourist map.

(That Miss Stott had no interest in effacing the Buhl, that she had, in younger days, sat on the Buhl's board of directors, came as an embarrassing surprise.)

"A movie theater?" the old lady repeated. "Who wants to look at movies when you've got all this?"

The development staff exchanged glances, unsure how to explain that pottery and artifacts held little appeal for pampered suburban children who spent half their lives glued to high-resolution video screens.

The Stott was a nonprofit, it was true, but in recent years had become so nonprofitable that its very existence was in jeopardy. Attendance was off, impairing the staff's grant-writing efforts. Unlike its peers—Field in Chicago, Natural History at the Smithsonian—the Stott lacked big exhibits (e.g., dinosaurs) that grabbed headlines. And the building itself, while handsome, lacked profit-generating amenities. Its gift shop was minimal, its cafeteria in need of renovation. Development envisioned a full-service food court, with world cuisines thematically tied to the Stott's exhibits. Led by a dynamic new hire named Lois Kraft, development conducted factfinding interviews with certain of the collections staff:

These . . . indigenous tribes of Australia. The aborigines. What do they eat?

Their diet has changed in the twentieth century, said Gwen. *Now it's not so different from ours.*

Lois Kraft looked disappointed. *What about before?*

Roots and grubs, said Gwen.

Grubs? Lois repeated.

Worms, she said.

Such was the tenor of Gwen's interactions with senior staff. In
her own department she was, if not precisely liked, then valued and
respected. After seven years in collections she was considered a veteran,
an in-house authority on Stott history, policy, and procedures. With
her master's degree she was overqualified for the job, yet without the
intercession of Tova Windsor, Gwen wouldn't have been hired at all.
Tova—wife of her father's old friend Neil Windsor—knew the director, and had gotten her an interview for an assistant curator's job.
Face-to-face with Bennett Whitley, the suave man of forty who would
be her supervisor, Gwen found herself answering in monosyllables.
He said you were too introverted, Tova told Gwen afterward. *Honey, you
need to relax a little. Learn to open up.* She made a second call to the director and landed Gwen another interview. *It's a behind-the-scenes job,*
Tova explained. *Not much interaction with the public.* This time Gwen
met with the human resources rep charged with hiring underlings, a
bored-looking paper pusher who glanced frequently at his watch.

"This job is physically demanding," he said. "You'd be on your
feet a lot, and you must be able to lift forty pounds without assis-
tance."

Gwen tried to take offense at this remark, and found it impossible. The man scarcely looked at her, and she'd been sitting when he
arrived. It was possible he hadn't even noticed her size.

"No problem," she said.

He made a mark on the open folder in front of him "We've
never had a collections assistant with a Master's degree," he observed
mildly.

"That's okay," said Gwen. "I don't mind."

And she didn't. She enjoyed the research, the physical effort of
building the exhibits. "Wow, you're pretty strong," said her supervisor,
Roger Day, after watching her load an unwieldy plywood frame onto
a dolly. For some reason, this pleased her immensely. She loved surprising people with what she could do.

That was seven years ago. In that time her adult life had taken shape
in the same gradual, quiet way the estrogen had shaped her body. (*Modestly,*
as Dr. Chapin had said. She now wore, with some irony, a regular bra, in

the hard-to-find size of 38AA.) She'd kept her modest Volkswagen, ten years old but still reliable; her modest grad student apartment in Oakland, an easy bus ride from the Stott. Her modest salary kept pace with inflation (though her modest inheritance from her grandfather Drew had, after a few years' investing in an unprecedented boom market, nearly tripled.) Her modest circle of friends included her landlady, Mrs. Uncapher, and her master's thesis adviser Andreas Swingard (she had never finished the PhD). There was also Sister Felicia Pooley, a friendly nun who visited the Stott with her fifth-graders. (*Keeping my options open, Mamie*, Gwen sometimes thought.) Yet friends her own age eluded her. Her peers were busy marrying and having children, a way of life that seemed all consuming and that Gwen could not imagine for herself.

In her interests and attitudes, her daily routines, she had more in common with a sixty-year-old nun.

Her coworkers were not friends. Most were just passing through. In seven years the staff had turned over several times. Collections assistant was an entry-level job, filled, except for Gwen, with recent college grads. She called them, privately, the Toddlers. They arrived in early summer; in a year most would leave for graduate school. The current crop—Colin, Connor, and Meghan—seemed like teenagers. Meghan wore a tiny hoop earring in her left eyebrow; Connor's loose blue jeans pooled around his ankles and flashed the waistband of his boxer shorts. All day long they played music at a pulsating volume: rap, hip-hop, a frantic kind of dance music they called ska. The throbbing bass line gave Gwen a headache. She began wearing earplugs to work, but the noise wasn't really the problem. The Toddlers themselves troubled her, their youth and exuberance, their unconscious high hopes for the future. They treated Gwen with quiet deference, which depressed her. She was too young to feel so old.

Finally she'd complained to her supervisor. *I can't work this way. I need my own space.* But instead of moving the Toddlers, Roger had installed Gwen in the only available office, a windowless corner of the basement. Reasonable, of course: there were three Toddlers, and only one Gwen. They'll be gone in six months, she reminded herself, and settled in to her dank solitary confinement. Then Roger crammed a second desk into her office and hired Heidi Kozak.

Gwen disliked her on sight.

"Gwen's the expert," said Roger, by way of introduction. "She's been here forever. She'll show you the ropes."

Heidi smiled broadly, showing large teeth. Her smile was oddly familiar. *Where do I know her from?* Gwen wondered. She was a tall, bosomy woman with long hair the color of broom straw. Her fingernails extended half an inch past her fingertips.

"Welcome," Gwen said, relieved. The intrusion would be temporary. With those fingernails, Heidi Kozak wouldn't last.

But Heidi did last. She appeared for work each morning freshly bathed, it seemed, in floral cologne. Like her fragrance, she was impossible to ignore. Her first day on the job, she told Gwen her life story. She was a local girl, a steelworker's daughter, raised in a South Side row house with five brothers and one bathroom. (*Eight assholes, one toilet*, she told Gwen.) She'd dropped out of Pitt to marry her high school sweetheart, and had kept busy as a volunteer tour guide at the Stott. Recently divorced *(don't even ask)*, she now needed a paycheck.

All of which explained why Heidi looked familiar. Gwen saw the tour guides only in the cafeteria—the women in dresses, the men in ties. (The collections staff wore flannel shirts and blue jeans.) Never, in Gwen's memory, had a tour guide come over to the collections side.

Her résumé made Heidi unusual. Even stranger was her reaction to Gwen. Day after day, Heidi invited her to lunch, morning coffee, happy hour cocktails at the bar down the street. *She likes me*, Gwen realized, irritated and perplexed. Instinctively she refused these overtures. She wasn't sure why. Her *no*, immediate and reflexive, seemed to come from deep within her. Her impulse, always, was to protect her solitude—a way of life she clung to and protected fiercely, yet didn't especially like.

But Heidi kept asking, and Gwen finally relented, haunted by her own creeping loneliness. Her social calendar was empty, her other coworkers pleasant but distant. Only Heidi seemed to notice she was there.

They made an odd pair; walking down the street together, they invariably turned heads. Gwen had been watched by strangers her whole adult life, but in Heidi's company the attention was different. Heidi wasn't beautiful, but that didn't matter if you were blond and buxom and wore tight sweaters and short skirts. In her teetering heels Heidi was six feet tall; she dressed more like a teenager than a woman of forty. Gwen's mother would have raised an eyebrow at the bright colors and trendy styles. Any woman's best color, she often said, was beige.

But Gwen loved Heidi's warmth and brightness, her vibrant plumage. She loved Heidi's indiscreet laugh, her bottomless thirst for margaritas, the bawdy stories she told. Her aggressive driving, her willingness to flip the bird in traffic, her unselfconscious way of being in the world. Early on, over margaritas, she'd asked Gwen bluntly: *So what's your story? Are you married, single, what?*

I haven't had a boyfriend since grad school, Gwen said, her heart hammering. *Eric is married now. I haven't seen him in ages.*

She hadn't spoken of Eric Farmer in years, and was surprised by how it affected her. Confiding was a pleasure she'd always denied herself. It occurred to her that except for Eric, Heidi was the only friend she'd made since childhood, since becoming a Turner; and that she badly needed a friend.

SHE'D MET Eric Farmer her first semester at Pitt. He was the graduate assistant who taught her Physical Anthropology class—a minister's son from rural Indiana with a sweet, choir-trained voice that vibrated with excitement when he talked about primate evolution. His enthusiasm evoked snickers from the bored sophomores who'd expected an easy elective; but to Gwen his passion was inspiring. The lecture hall was enormous, twice the size of the classrooms at Wellesley, but Eric commanded it confidently despite his size. Showing a slide of Pygmy tribesmen in Africa, he had joked about his own height—five feet five, by Gwen's best guess. Her *spatial difficulties* notwithstanding, she could estimate a stranger's height with remarkable accuracy. She had been practicing for years.

They met again a few years later when, a grad student herself, Gwen spent a summer working as a research assistant to Andreas Swin-

gard. She'd refused her mother's entreaties to come back to Concord
for the summer. Paulette's loneliness frightened her. Scott was MIA in
California, and they'd scarcely seen Billy since he started med school.
We could rent a place in Truro, her mother suggested. *Just the two of us.*
Gwen imagined it: the family disbanded; the Captain's House, sold
years ago, now inhabited by strangers; herself and Paulette in a rented
cottage on the Cape. The most pathetic figure would be Gwen herself,
her defensiveness, her petulance. In her adult life she was sharp and
competent, reserved but unfailingly pleasant. In her mother's presence
she regressed to a moody teenager. Her own behavior sickened her.
Paulette, whatever her faults, had been a loving mother; she didn't
deserve such treatment. Gwen knew when she was being insufferable.
She simply didn't know how to stop.

All things considered, it seemed wiser to spend the summer in a
cluttered little office in the cavernous Forbes Quadrangle—built on
the site of the old Forbes Field, where her beloved Pirates had once
played, where Babe Ruth had hit his final home runs. In June the
campus was dead, the army of undergrads discharged for the summer;
only Swingard's PhD students stopped by the office. Gwen spent the
day transcribing tapes from Swingard's fieldwork, hundreds of hours of
interviews with his Amazonians. At lunchtime she walked in Schenley
Park. One morning she was sitting under headphones, rewinding for
the umpteenth time, when a familiar, resonant voice penetrated the
white noise.

"Hey, I know you."

She looked up, startled. Eric Farmer stood in the doorway.

"You were in my 201 class a couple years ago," he said. "Gwen,
right?"

"Good memory," she said, blushing. "There must have been a
hundred students in that class."

"And exactly one interested one." He sat on the edge of her desk.
"You're in the grad program now?"

Gwen nodded.

"Swingard's my adviser," said Eric. "You must be pretty good if
he's letting you near his tapes."

Gwen laughed. Swingard's protectiveness of the tapes bordered on neurosis. Her first day he'd spent half an hour instructing her in the operation of a cassette player, as though it were some sophisticated piece of equipment only a career anthropologist would know how to use.

Eric came by the office several times a week, to meet with Swingard or drop an envelope in his mail slot; and each time he stopped to chat with Gwen. Late one Friday afternoon, after Swingard had left for the day, Eric stuck his head inside the office door. "Happy weekend," he said. "Let's drink beer."

They spent two hours on the outdoor patio of a pub near campus, eating greasy things from plastic baskets and drinking Stott Golden Ale. After that, Friday-night beer became a weekly ritual, one Gwen looked forward to for days beforehand. She loved hearing about Eric's boyhood in Indiana, the omnipresence of the church, the strict father he was desperate to escape. He was an only son, the only Farmer male in four generations to refuse the ministry. When he admitted to believing in evolution, his father had tried to call forth his demons.

"I'm impressed," Gwen said.

Eric ordered a second pitcher, and Gwen found herself telling him things she'd never confided to anyone. She talked about her parents' divorce: her mother's neediness; her own paralysis. How disorienting, how lonely, the defection of her two brothers: one superachieving, one delinquent, but both so checked out that Gwen felt like an only child, swatted between her feuding parents like a red-haired tennis ball.

"A red-haired tennis ball," Eric repeated, grinning broadly.

A moment later they both dissolved into laughter, the kind of sickening, belly-aching laughter Gwen had shared, in childhood, with Billy or her cousin Charlotte. When the laughter subsided, one of them had only to repeat the phrase "red-haired tennis ball," and they were off again.

"They're going to throw us out of here," Eric said finally, wiping a tear from his eye. He glanced at the check and took a bill from his wallet.

Because he had not done this before—in grad-student fashion

they'd always split the check—Gwen felt momentary alarm. Was this dating? Were she and Eric on a date?

She stood, slightly wobbly. She was drunker than she'd imagined. Except for a man sitting alone in a corner, they were the only ones left on the patio.

"You okay?" said Eric.

He seemed tall to her, but not distressingly so. She was twenty-three and last kissed in childhood, by some reluctant Drew cousin in a game of spin the bottle. She leaned in and kissed him on the mouth.

"Let's get out of here," Eric said.

His car was an ancient Pontiac Ventura riddled with rust. Cruising down Schenley Avenue Gwen felt a heady vertigo, not unpleasant, that reminded her of sailing—her uncle's boat, the *Mamie Broussard*, riding a salty wind.

Eric parked on the street in front of her house. Dark windows in the first-floor apartment; it was after midnight, and Mrs. Uncapher was long asleep. They stumbled up the stairs.

She had rehearsed in her mind the way to undress for a man. It was less difficult than she'd imagined. Darkness helped. Drunkenness helped. The heat of his body startled her, the wetness of his beery mouth.

It hurt a great deal. Her doctor, scolding her again to take her medication, had explained that this was likely. But Gwen hated the pills, which gave her stomach-curdling headaches. She'd stopped taking them long ago.

Is this okay? Eric whispered, stabbing at her.

She had learned early in life that certain pains were necessary. Vaccinations hurt, and bone setting and cavity filling; but these were all to the good. That night on her lumpy futon, panties looped around one ankle, Gwen McKotch surrendered herself to the ancient procedure—salutary, she firmly believed, possibly lifesaving. She allowed Eric Farmer to save her.

Yes, she said. *Good.*

She woke in the dark a few hours later, parched and sweating. Eric was putting on his clothes.

"I have to go," he whispered. "I'll call you, okay?"

She watched from the window as the Pontiac Ventura disappeared around the corner. In the morning she drove to the pharmacy and refilled her prescription.

A day passed, then two. Was this normal? Gwen had no idea. She considered asking her brother Billy for advice, but quickly came to her senses. Such a conversation would be mortifying to them both.

The week dragged on, the days endless. Finally, on Friday morning—a full week later!—Eric appeared at Swingard's office.

"We should talk," he said, hovering near her desk. "Friday night, that was great. But I just don't, I can't really—" He stopped, blushed, tried again. "I'm up to my neck in this thesis, and I don't have room in my life for a girlfriend. What I'm trying to say is that I really like you. And I think we're better off as friends."

Fall came. Gwen was offered a teaching assistantship, but the thought of standing in front of a classroom horrified her; instead she continued as Swingard's assistant. She saw Eric occasionally around the quadrangle. A few times he stopped by Swingard's office to chat. But never again did he appear on a Friday afternoon to invite her out for beer.

Then, one morning just before Christmas, she saw Eric cross the campus with a girl.

A pretty girl, petite and dark haired. She appeared to be no more than five feet tall. At most a few inches taller than Gwen.

At most!

Later, when she ran into Eric at the anthropology office, he seemed in a hurry. "I've got to run," he said, glancing at his watch. "I'm heading out to the airport."

"Do you have visitors coming?" Gwen asked, avoiding his eyes.

"Going, actually." He hesitated. "My fiancée came out for a visit."

Gwen stared at him, speechless. Four months ago he'd been too busy for a girlfriend. Now he had a fiancée.

Jill had been his high school sweetheart, he explained, but in college they'd gone their separate ways. A few months ago she'd gotten back in touch.

A few months, Gwen thought. *Before August, or after?* "Wow," she said stupidly. "I mean, congratulations. I had no idea."

"Me neither. It just, you know, happened."

They stood a long moment looking at each other. Gwen felt her heart working inside her. For once she couldn't keep silent.

"Why didn't you tell me?" she blurted out. "You never even mentioned her."

"I didn't think you'd want to hear."

Gwen flushed miserably. He knew, then: how incessantly she thought of him, what that one night had meant to her.

"Don't be silly," she said quickly. "Of course I'm thrilled for you. When's the big day?"

"Next month. Over winter break." Then, seeing her shock: "We've been apart so long already. And Jill—both of us, actually—wants to start a family."

Family. The word hit Gwen like a slap. She'd given little thought to children, her inability to have them. What did that matter when she couldn't even find a date? That the two things might be related had never occurred to her. Had Eric Farmer guessed she couldn't have children? Was this something men—young men, her own age—even thought about?

To her relief he didn't invite her to the wedding. He took a tenure-track job at a college in Minnesota and kept in touch through annual Christmas cards. In later years the cards would be replaced by photos, printed with a generic holiday greeting:

> *Blessed Christmas to our friends and family.*
> *Love, Eric, Jill, Joshua, Hannah, and Michael.*

That she never saw him again was a fact that still astonished her. She had allowed few people to enter her life, and none before had left it. It was a lesson most people learned much earlier: that even deep friendships could have an undisclosed shelf life. That loyalty and affection, so consuming and powerful, could dissipate like fog.

She left Pittsburgh in the aftermath of a snowstorm. As the jet rose from the tarmac she could see the flashing yellow lights of the snowplows, scraping the empty expanse of I-90. *Where am I going?* she thought. And then: *Away, away.*

The trip had come about completely by accident. Heidi Kozak had booked it the summer before, but now her father, debilitated by Parkinson's, was moving into a nursing home; it was a bad time to leave town. The deposit was nonrefundable, she explained, only transferable. "You can buy me out," she said. "And PS, I really need the cash."

They were eating lunch in the museum cafeteria. "Saint Raphael is a little slice of heaven," she promised. "You'll have a blast."

"It sounds great," Gwen said, "but I can't."

Heidi understood that this no was automatic, a formality to be gotten through. She was not discouraged. She simply waited.

Gwen groped for an excuse, but none came to mind. Nothing, not the smallest thing, was keeping her in town. The Pittsburgh winter had arrived early and ferociously: a lake-effect storm had dumped a foot of snow on the city the day after Halloween. Work was slow; no one but Heidi would even notice her absence. The Toddlers continued to drive her crazy. Her unused vacation days beckoned.

Heidi knew all of this.

The silence opened between them. Normally it was Gwen's secret weapon, a tool she wielded with surgical precision. Other people feared it; faced with a lapse in the conversation they blinked, stammered, babbled incoherently. Her parents hated it. The Toddlers were particularly vulnerable. Faced with Gwen's silence they blushed and fidgeted, then scrambled to fill it, like lemmings leaping to their death. Only Heidi seemed to understand that Gwen didn't enjoy silence either. That sooner or later it would unnerve her, and she would be the one to speak.

"What are those dates again?" Gwen asked.

Heidi clapped delightedly. "You'll love it, I promise. You might never come back."

GWEN WRESTLED her bags through customs in Miami, boarded the small propeller plane, and landed on the island at noon. The blazing sun shocked her body, as though she'd been defibrillated. Her blue jeans clung unpleasantly to her sweaty legs. She peeled off her Steelers sweatshirt and tied the sleeves around her waist.

The Pleasures courtesy van was waiting outside the baggage claim, crammed already with guests and their luggage. Gwen climbed aboard and took a seat at the rear. The passengers were mostly women, chattering in pairs or threes.

"My sister came two years ago," said the woman to Gwen's left. "She met her husband here."

The driver, an elderly black man in a parrot green uniform, took a quick head count. "Welcome to beautiful St. Raphael," he said, his English thick and heavily accented.

He started the engine. They drove into Pointe Mathilde, the island's capital city. The narrow streets were clogged with traffic; on either side were jewelry stores and tiki bars, T-shirt shops and barbecue joints. Brightly painted signs advertised SAILBOARD RENTAL, DUTY-FREE CIGARETTES, LIVE TOPLESS GIRLS.

The van climbed a steep hill, its engine roaring. Gwen stared into the distance at the rocky cliffs, the turquoise-colored water down below, bordered by a thin strip of white sand. She counted the many long winters she'd spent in Pittsburgh, in the dim basement of the Stott, and thought: *This has been here all along.*

"We getting close," said the driver. "Pleasures is just ahead."

Now the road was lined with a tall hedge, dense and bursting with orange flowers. They passed through an ornamental iron gate. The long driveway—lined with palm trees and elaborate flower plantings—led to a white stucco building, its entrance shaded by a green awning. The van paused in the circular driveway. Gwen climbed out of the van and hefted her pack to one shoulder, her bag of diving gear to the other.

"Hey, little woman," the driver called. "You need help with dose tings?"

Gwen grinned. Was it his accent that made *little woman* sound charming, not insulting? Or just the fact that he'd *said* it, joyfully and unapologetically, out loud?

The driver took her dive gear and handed it off to a porter. She walked into a sun-filled lobby, redolent of lilies. Huge potted palms marked the perimeter; at the center, under a high skylight, a tree bloomed with yellow flowers. She took her place in line at the front desk and dropped her bags to the floor.

She felt drunk on warmth and color, the blossomy fragrance. The gray Pittsburgh winter seemed far, far away.

"Gwen?"

She turned to see a woman her own age, deeply tanned, a square, solid woman with straight black hair hanging down her back. "I'm Miracle Zamora," she said, kissing Gwen's cheek. "Heidi described you perfectly. I'd know you anywhere."

Gwen smiled hesitantly. The unexpected touch—and the idea of being described *perfectly*—made her cheeks flush.

"I'll wait while you check in," said Miracle. "You're lucky I got here first. It took me all morning to find our room."

"Next," called the ebullient girl behind the desk. Gwen stepped up to the counter. "Welcome to Pleasures!" the girl said brightly, in a voice strikingly similar to that of the Allegheny Savings ATM back home. She looked down at Gwen, and confusion briefly clouded her face. She recovered admirably. "Welcome to our island paradise! Welcome reception, three o'clock in the Breezes lounge. Come alone, leave with a new friend!"

"Great," said Gwen, collecting her room keys and minibar card, her schedule of activities and map of the resort. "But I'm really here to scuba dive."

"Activities coordinator, extension 300. You can book dive excursions by phone."

Gwen followed Miracle across the courtyard, down a path lined with flower beds. She could feel her nose and cheeks already burning; her sunscreen was buried somewhere in her backpack.

They climbed an outdoor stairway. Their room was brightly decorated in pink and yellow, with a mirrored ceiling and two queen-size beds. Miracle had already unpacked. Colorful sundresses hung in the closet. A dozen pairs of shoes were lined against one wall.

"That's all you brought?" Miracle marveled, eyeing Gwen's backpack.

"The porter is bringing my dive gear," said Gwen. "I try not to pack more than I carry."

"God, that's so smart. I almost killed myself going through customs. That thing weighs a ton." Miracle pointed to a half-empty suitcase lying open on the floor. It was the size of a coffee table.

"You brought all that for a week?"

"Shoes," Miracle explained. "Hurry up and change. There's that welcome thing at three."

Gwen hesitated. "I'm kind of wiped out from the flight. Maybe I'll stay here and unpack."

"Absolutely not," said Miracle. "This is where you meet everybody. If you miss it, you're screwed for the rest of the week. Besides, there's free champagne."

"HELLO EVERYBODY, and welcome to Pleasures! I'm Trina, your cruise director"—the girl gave a little curtsy—"and this is Fall in Love Week!" Trina's enthusiasm was palpable; she seemed ready to faint from excitement. With her muscled calves and brief outfit—a white circle skirt that barely covered her bottom, like a summer figure-skating costume—she reminded Gwen of the hyperactive tennis instructors she'd suffered, years ago, at camp.

"This just might be the most important moment of the week," said Trina. "Our speed meet and greet! We know you've had it with the dating merry-go-round, so the love experts here at Pleasures have devised this superquick, superfun way to connect with the guy or girl of your dreams."

There was a polite smattering of applause, which Trina seemed to take as encouragement.

"Okay, here's how it works. We've got the girls against this wall." She gestured toward the banquette, where Gwen and Miracle and a couple dozen other women sat at small round tables, drinking complimentary champagne from plastic flutes. "And over at the bar, getting a head start on the festivities, we have the boys."

The girls were fortyish, a few younger. Most of the boys were bald. Gwen glanced around the room to see if anyone else found the terms ridiculous. No one looked amused.

"When you came in just now, our cupid-in-residence, Jamie"—Trina pointed to a plump young man in the parrot green Pleasures uniform—"gave you a scorecard." She held up a sheet of paper. "Here you'll find all the girls listed by letter, and all the guys listed by number.

"Now when I give the signal, the guys are going to come into the atrium and pick a girl to sit with. You'll have exactly three minutes to get acquainted. Then Jamie will blow the whistle and you'll move on to the next lady in line."

God, no, Gwen thought.

"Now, some of you guys might feel like staying a little longer with a certain lady," Trina continued, winking, "but remember, you've got to keep it moving, because the next guy in line is going to want his chance. Besides, there might be someone you like even better just around the corner.

"So after each introduction we'll give you a second to mark your scorecard: 'hot' or 'cold.' And when you come to dinner tonight, you'll find one of these"—Trina held up a parrot green envelope—"tucked under your plate. Whoops!" The envelope dropped from her fingers to the floor. She bent to pick it up. "Phone numbers, room numbers, everything you need to make a love connection with one of your hot prospects. How cool is that?"

Applause and wolf whistles from the bar. These may have had less to do with the green envelope than with the view as Trina bent to retrieve it in her tiny skirt.

"And here's the best part," she continued. "You'll already know that *every single* guy or girl on your list is already hot for you. Jamie and I will spend the afternoon going over every single scorecard, matching your hot list and their hot list. This way there's no rejection! No guesswork! You can cut right to the fun part."

Gwen scanned the room for an easy exit. Despite its name, the Breezes Lounge was shut tight as a crucible. The only way out seemed to be the French doors directly behind Trina, in full view of the crowd. Wasn't that some kind of fire-code violation? *They do this on purpose*, she thought.

Trina removed her watch and held it up to show the crowd. "Here we go! Gentlemen, start your engines."

A general commotion as the men charged across the room, holding short glasses or frosty mugs of beer. A few grinned sheepishly. Others clapped loudly, flushed and enthusiastic. It was a scene much like junior high gym class, the dreaded ballroom-dancing lesson: boys and girls compelled, for the first time, to touch.

Gwen drained her champagne as a man sat down opposite her.

"I'm Gwen," she said. "Can you believe we're doing this?"

"Bobby." He looked to be in his early fifties, bald on top, his remaining hair gathered into a dark ponytail. His sweatpants were loose and patterned, the sort pro wrestlers wore.

"I think it's great," he said flatly. "No game playing, no manipulation. Two hours of bullshit, as opposed to two months or two years."

Gwen nodded politely.

"I'm recently divorced," he said. "My wife lives in Denyle."

Where is that? Gwen almost asked. Then thought: *Oh, right: denial.*

"She has issues with depression, inhibited sexual desire, past sexual abuse. That's what I'm coming out of, you know? That's what I'm trying to avoid." He took a long drink from his mug. "I like this forum because I can come right out and ask. Are you being treated for depression? Any sexual abuse in your past?"

"No," Gwen said. "And no."

"See, that was easy. As opposed to fourteen years of prevarication and denial and passive-aggressive shit. Get it all out of the way in the beginning. It's a huge time saver."

"TIME!" Jamie called from the back of the room. "Okay, time to move on. Everyone take a moment and mark your scorecards. Then you gentlemen are on to the next lovely lady."

Bobby rose, glancing at his scorecard. "What did you say your name was?"

"Heidi Kozak," said Gwen.

FOR TWO nights in a row she ate dinner alone on her balcony. Balmy air brushed her bare arms and shoulders, lingering like a human touch. The second night the moon was full. Gwen imagined it hanging low, casting silver light over the gentle surf. She would take a walk shortly to verify this. Heidi and Miracle had booked a poolside room rather than a more expensive ocean-view suite. You could see the ocean *anywhere*, Miracle had explained. She was more interested in the human scenery, the bare pulchritude of the suntanned bodies cavorting in the pool.

It was Miracle's fourth trip to Pleasures. She and Heidi had met there a few years ago, vacationing with their husbands. Now that they were both single, they met each January for a week of sun and mischief. "It gets me through the winter," Miracle said. "My mom takes the boys, and I'm like a kid again." She was an X-ray technician from West Texas. Divorced, with two children, she came to Pleasures to recharge her suntan, drink umbrella drinks, and, she admitted, to meet men: "I'm forty, and I live in a small town. There's no one left to date."

To these revelations Gwen had no answer. Her own social life was too bleak to discuss.

Now music floated up from the flagstone patio, steel guitars, the tinkle of a keyboard. The musicians, in dark vests and white shirts, looked bizarrely formal among the near-naked drinkers and bathers. In the golden light of the tiki torches, the guests appeared sunburned or inebriated or both. Their exposed flesh looked sweet and meaty, like baking ham. The scene seemed appropriate to tonight's dinner, the Lovers' Luau, served poolside. The pool was kidney shaped, its tiled bottom displaying the Pleasures logo: a nude couple, their bodies curved like the yin and yang characters, swimming in a tight circle together for all eternity.

Gwen stood, looking over the balcony. Dinner was winding down. Aproned black busboys were breaking down the serving stations, loading the leftover pig carcass onto wheeled carts. The air smelled of chlorine, citronella, roasting pork. The smiling drummer tapped gamely at his trap set. The singer warbled a familiar tune. Since landing at Pleasures, Gwen had heard it a dozen times. *When I dance they call me Macarena.* A woman in a flowered bikini stood at the edge of the pool, keeping time with her hips, going through the motions: palms down, palms up, hands on hips, roll the pelvis. *Wait*, she squealed, *I forgot!* The Jacuzzis were bubbling. The swim-up bar was open for business. In an hour Gwen would turn out the lights and blast the central air, as she'd done the night before. Its fan made a gentle white noise to screen out the laughing and shouting below.

She glanced at the bedroom clock. It was early still, a Sunday night. She took the cordless phone from the bedside table and punched in a number. She never called her brother in the evening, but she was desperate to hear a familiar voice.

"Billy, it's me," she said. "Sorry to bother you. Sounds like you have company."

"Sort of." Voices in the background, a chorus of male laughter. "You landed okay? How's it going down there?"

"I did two dives today. Stingrays everywhere, like we saw in Grand Cayman."

"I'm a loser," Billy said. "I should have come with you. Next year, I promise."

"How's the training?"

"Great. I did thirteen today, at race pace. My knee was fine."

"Wow, good." She hesitated. "I should let you get back to your guests."

"Call when you get back," he said.

"Okay." Gwen hung up the phone. Usually his voice comforted her. This time it made her even lonelier. Years had passed since she'd visited Billy in New York, but she still had a clear mental picture of his apartment. The memory was so vivid that she doubted it was accurate; it might be a chic urban apartment she'd seen in a movie. She remembered that the place was exceedingly handsome—like Billy and Srikanth, like the many friends, all male, who'd come to visit Billy in the hospital. Meeting all those beautiful men had affected her strangely. Not the fact that her brother was gay, or that he'd concealed this from her; neither, knowing Billy, was surprising. What struck her was that Billy was the most handsome man she knew. He could have had any girl he wanted, any of the exquisite creatures Gwen had envied her whole life but could never be. That Billy disdained these swans filled her with tenderness and gratitude. It seemed to her a grand gesture of loyalty, the ultimate kindness of a brother to a sister.

She replaced the phone in its cradle between the beds. Miracle's was piled high with sundresses, colorful pareos, a pink straw hat. *Borrow anything you like,* she'd offered, though except for the hat, none of it was likely to fit. Gwen rarely paid attention to what she was wearing, but sitting in the Breezes Lounge she'd felt sweaty and disheveled in her jeans and T-shirt. It was her all-purpose uniform, worn to work, happy hour with Heidi, Pirates games, weddings, funerals, church. When her jeans began to look grubby, she made a quick trip to the boys' department at Sears. Brushing her teeth took longer. Beyond this routine errand, she hadn't shopped for clothes in years.

Once, while waiting for a flight home to Boston, she had glimpsed another small woman in the Pittsburgh airport. *A Turner,* Gwen thought, her heart racing. Why was she so surprised? The condition wasn't all that uncommon; there must have been Turners all over Pittsburgh, dozens, hundreds, who knew? Yet despite this, Gwen had never known one personally. Long ago, a doctor had told her parents about a support group in Boston. Her father had been enthusiastic, her mother apprehensive; but for once they'd agreed that it was Gwen's decision. And Gwen had refused to go.

The woman in the airport was her size exactly, and dressed for business: a wool suit, expertly tailored, and high-heeled leather pumps. Her hair was streaked blond and carefully styled, her face heavily made up. Did she look attractive, or ridiculous? Ridiculous, Gwen decided, her cheeks burning. Like a little girl playing dress up. But was her perception accurate, or clouded by her own insecurities? Did other people see the woman as she did?

Gwen laid aside her newspaper and stood. *Hi there*, she rehearsed. *Where on earth did you find those shoes?* But at that moment a pack of teenage boys blocked her path, huge gumchewing boys in matching track suits, a sports team traveling to or from a game. Noisily they commandeered a group of chairs. Gwen felt suddenly timid. Years of savage teasing had left her with a lifelong terror of such hooligans. A tiny woman was conspicuous enough, a lightning rod for derision. Two of them together would make an irresistible target.

Gwen sat again and hid behind the sports page. When she lowered it a few minutes later, the woman was gone.

At that moment—a weak, self-pitying moment—she had considered calling her mother. Now the feeling returned to her in a wave. Gwen looked down at the Pleasures patio, the giddy strangers bobbing in the pool like dumplings in soup.

There was a commotion in the hallway, a jingling of keys; then Miracle Zamora burst into the room. "Gwen?" She came out to the terrace and leaned in the doorway. "Hey there! Great dinner, huh?" Then she noticed the tray on the glass-topped table, Gwen's half-eaten turkey sandwich, ordered from room service. "What, you didn't go?"

"I wasn't in the mood," said Gwen.

"I know what you mean. When I saw that pig with the head still on it"—she grimaced as if in pain. "I mean, Jesus. They could have taken the head off." She bent to unbuckle her highheeled sandals. "These shoes are killing me. Look." She extended a bare foot, the toenails painted scarlet. An angry blister had opened on the sole, another at the heel.

"Ouch," said Gwen.

"I always forget how big this place is. Last night I went down to the nude spa with that guy Brian. Have you been yet? It's behind the tennis courts, on the other side of the bridge. Like, two miles away. I don't walk that much in a month."

Gwen smiled.

"I'm heading over there now, once I find my flip-flops. Want to come?"

"Maybe later," said Gwen.

"God, I ate too much." Miracle stepped into the room, bent and rummaged through her suitcase. Her yellow thong underwear was visible above the waistband of her skirt. "I've been dieting for this place for a month, and I gain it all back the first night." She slipped on plastic sandals decorated with yellow daisies, then kicked them off. "My calves look like telephone poles. I need heels."

"You'll be naked in ten minutes. What's the difference?"

"Oh, no," Miracle said seriously. "They let you wear shoes." She slipped her room key into her pocketbook. "You're sure you don't want to come?"

"Maybe I'll see you over there," said Gwen.

"Okay." Miracle eyed Gwen's half-eaten sandwich. "Are you going to eat that pickle?"

"Take it."

"They have negative calories," Miracle said, chewing. "Less than zero."

"How is that possible?"

"They do something to your metabolism," said Miracle. "It's true. I looked it up."

Gwen listened to her go, the click of high heels fading gradually down the hallway. It seemed that she and Miracle had known each other a long time. Not since childhood—the screened sleeping porch at the Captain's House—had Gwen shared a bedroom, and she was stunned by the intimacy of it: the strange underpants on the floor, the sodden bikini top hung over the towel bar to dry. After only two days, she knew things about this near stranger that made her seem closer than family. No McKotch would speak so candidly of her digestion, her allergies, the vagaries of her menstrual cycle. The top of Miracle's dresser resembled a pharmacy shelf. She'd invited Gwen to try her lotions and hangover remedies, her vitamins, suntan oil, and pineapple-scented shampoo. Miracle was prone to hives and urinary-tract infections; she took birth-control pills to keep her skin clear. In one way or another, she was always talking about her body. It was the kind of conversation Gwen's mother frowned upon, and that Gwen herself avoided instinctively.

On that subject she had nothing, nothing to say.

They waited at the end of the pier, a group of nine, in swim trunks and T-shirts, bikinis and flip-flops. Gwen counted three couples—two young and American, one middle aged and German—and two teenage girls, deeply suntanned. Most had rented dive gear; except for Gwen, only the Germans had brought their own. They were tall and lean and blond, with look-alike short haircuts and identical wire-rimmed glasses. Their gear was well used and expensive. The woman wore an elaborate dive computer strapped to her wrist.

"Jesus, where are they?" one of the girls complained. "I mean, was there a *reason* I got out of bed at eight in the morning?"

Gwen glanced at her watch. The dive boat was twenty minutes late. Waves lapped the dock in a strange pattern, coming in from the west. The wake of a jet ski, or maybe a boat. She listened intently. A low rumble in the distance, growing louder. "Here it comes," she said to no one in particular.

Eight heads turned toward the horizon. A small boat with an outboard motor was approaching the pier. A red dive flag flew at its helm. The letters *2STE* had been stenciled across its stern.

"Well, what's he waiting for?" said a short, beefy man with a crew cut.

"It's pretty rough," Gwen said, surprising herself. In her real life she never spoke to strangers. "He can't come straight in with this current. He needs to approach from the side."

Crew Cut frowned. "Well, he needs a bigger motor then."

Gwen glanced pointedly at the water. The *2STE*'s wake had generated some powerful waves. Fifty yards away, at the Pleasures beach, disgusted swimmers were retreating to shore. A larger motor would have meant a virtual tidal wave.

The Germans regarded Gwen with interest. "You are a sailor?" the husband asked.

"Not really," said Gwen. "I just like boats."

Finally the boat motored up to the pier. From the bridge the captain gave them a wave. A boy stood at the bow, brown and shirtless. "Hello!" he called, waving. "Are you ready to dive?"

"We were ready half an hour ago," Crew Cut muttered under his breath.

The divers crowded onto the boat. "Watch your step," said the boy, extending a hand to one of the girls. "It's a bit slippery in here."

Gwen hefted her air tank to her shoulder.

"Can I help with that?" the boy asked. He was her height, and skinny. He might have been twelve years old.

"No, thanks," she said. "I've got it."

The perimeter of the boat was lined with benches; the divers arranged themselves there in pairs. The captain cut the engine and stood. He was shirtless, his skin cocoa brown, his head shaved nearly bald. His arms were knotted with muscle. A silver medal hung from a chain around his neck.

"Welcome to the *Toussainte*," he said. His voice was low and musical, with a distinctive accent. "I am Rico, your dive master. You have met my nephew, Alistair.

"Today we'll be diving near what is known as the Blue Wall, on the leeward side of the island. It is a beautiful dive with a moderate current and an incredible variety of marine life. It takes normally half an hour to get out there, perhaps longer today since the sea is rough. But first some business. I need to see your dive cards."

The divers reached into backpacks and wallets. Gwen fished hers out of a back pocket and handed it over. Captain Rico looked closely at her photo, then back at her.

"Your hair was darker then," he said.

She nodded, embarrassed. For a brief time, in graduate school, she'd dyed her hair sable brown, her mother's color.

"I like it better red," he said, handing back the card. He moved on to the girls.

"Just a second," said one, a busty brunette with a spider tattooed at her ankle. She slid a finger into the back pocket of her shorts and squirmed. "I can't get it out," she said. "I guess they're a little tight."

A burst of laughter from her friend, a broad-shouldered blonde. She reminded Gwen of the field-hockey girls she'd known at Wellesley. *Same phenotype*, her father would say.

Finally the brunette offered her card. Gwen gave it a quick glance. It was the temporary kind all the resorts offered: for a few hundred dollars, a lifeguard took you to the pool, showed you how to connect your regulator and weight your belt, and just like that you were certified to dive.

"Amanda," said Captain Rico. "You have been diving before?"

"Sort of," she said. "Only, you know, in a pool."

He rubbed the dark stubble at the crown of his head. "No problem," he said smoothly. He turned to face the group. "You will each choose a dive buddy whom you must keep in sight at all times. I will be Amanda's dive buddy. So she has nothing to worry about. I am an excellent buddy. The best!"

Amanda's blond friend looked pained. "What about me?"

Captain Rico glanced around the circle. "Who does not have a buddy?" And, when Gwen raised her hand: "See? There is your buddy."

Gwen ignored the girl's frown. Her brother Billy was an excellent diving partner, adventurous and capable, but she didn't mind diving with strangers. She was confident in her skills.

"Any other questions?" Captain Rico asked.

"How deep is the water?" said Amanda.

"Fifty feet. Give or take."

Amanda's eyes widened. "I'm not a great swimmer," she said, fiddling with her dive belt.

"Don't worry." He laid a hand on her shoulder. "I'll make sure you're okay."

Oh, brother, Gwen thought. The guy was shameless—but, she had to admit, very handsome, with his muscled shoulders, his musical voice. She noticed the sign, then, hanging at the stern: TIPS WELCOME. Handsome Captain Rico made his living by charming people, women especially.

Your hair was darker then. I like it better red.

Even me, she thought.

THEY DROPPED anchor a half mile from the reef. One by one the divers slid into the water. Rico and Amanda first, followed by the Germans. Gwen lowered herself into the water, clear and shockingly warm. She took a moment to adjust to the sounds: the hollow gasp of her regulated breathing, the loud beating of her heart. She watched her dive buddy—Courtney, the field-hockey girl—plunge into the water. There was an explosion of tiny bubbles, a loud sunlit rush.

Gwen swam toward the girl. Through the dive mask her eyes were wide with terror. Gwen laid a hand on her shoulder and gave her the okay sign. Courtney nodded and signed okay in return. Gwen pointed in the direction of the reef and Courtney began flailing toward it, the classic beginner's mistake. She was a strong swimmer, but panicky. *Slow down*, Gwen wanted to tell her. *Keep your arms still.*

It was one of the frustrations of diving: the desperate urge to communicate, the helplessness of being without speech. On dry land, where conversation was easy, Gwen maneuvered to avoid it. Underwater, its very impossibility made her eager to speak. That, and the practical considerations: if the girl continued her thrashing, she'd use up her air supply in twenty minutes.

Gwen swam up beside her and rapped on her own tank until the girl made eye contact. She pointed to herself, then pulled her arms in close to her sides, as though she were wearing a straitjacket. Miraculously, Courtney seemed to understand. She pulled her arms in tight and swam a little, powered only by a flutter kick.

If only life were like this, Gwen thought. Underwater, with a regulator in her mouth, she had no problem making herself understood.

Together they swam toward the reef. The water was deeper here, the white bottom more distant; Courtney's pink bikini had lost its color, washed out, like everything else, to a moody shade of green. Fan grass waved lazily with the current. A school of bright cichlids engulfed them. Courtney turned toward Gwen, her head cocked; the regulator made it impossible to laugh or gasp or smile. Instead Courtney clapped her hands together, a languid, wavy applause.

At the edge of the reef Gwen touched Courtney's shoulder, and pointed down. The ocean floor gave way here, sloping sharply downward; from where they hovered, the drop was probably a thousand feet. There were no words to express the shock, the sudden vertigo—and then, the profound feeling of safety. Floating above the chasm, buoyant and perfectly balanced, was as close as you could come to flying. Gwen had experienced it dozens of times, but still the feeling overwhelmed her. She was gliding like a spirit who'd escaped its container. She had no body. It was the freest feeling she had ever known.

ON DECK Alistair had laid a buffet of cut melon and pineapple. Gwen peeled off her fins and unbuckled her BC, then rinsed them in the tubs of fresh water the boy had set out.

"That was awesome," Courtney told Gwen. "You're an awesome diver. I had a great time." She turned to her friend Amanda, wrapped in a green Pleasures towel, teeth chattering. "We swam right into a bunch of striped fish. It freaked me out at first. I never would have done that by myself." She turned back to Gwen. "Sorry I flaked out at the beginning. I don't know what happened."

"It happens to everyone," said Gwen.

"Maybe, but—I'm on the swim team? At Duke? It's not like I'm afraid of the water."

"Shut up," said Amanda.

"Oh, chill out. You know what I mean. Did you go down at all?"

"A little," said Amanda. "But I got water in my mask. It was really scary. I made him bring me up."

"That sucks," said Courtney. "They should definitely refund your money. It's not like you saw anything."

Gwen could have pointed out the sign at the helm—NO RE-FUNDS—but didn't. The girls seemed to have forgotten she was there. On dry land, the natural order had been restored.

THE SUN was blazing as the *Toussainte* roared up to the pier.

"Thank you, everybody," said Captain Rico as he helped the divers, wet and sunburned, off the boat. Amanda handed him a slip of paper as she passed. He smiled but said nothing, just tucked the paper into his pocket.

Her room number, Gwen thought. Of course: it was probably a regular occurrence. How many pretty, scared divers did Rico comfort in a week, a month, a year? No wonder the man was always smiling.

She hefted her tank to her shoulder and headed for the pier. "Wait," said Rico, touching her shoulder. "Are you in a hurry?"

"Um, no," she mumbled.

"Please. Sit down a minute." He called to Alistair, who was tying the boat to the pier: "Tomorrow I come at eight o'clock sharp. *Me fais pas attendre.* This time you will be ready. Yes?"

"Yes," the boy called.

Rico turned to Gwen. "I want to thank you for your help today. I saw you with that girl. You were very patient with her."

Gwen flushed. "She was just nervous. She did fine."

"The other one was barely able to swim. She had no business doing scuba." Again he rubbed the stubble on his head. It seemed to be a habitual gesture. "The resorts, they are totally irresponsible. But they are very powerful on the island. They do what they want. It's surprising nobody has been killed yet. Anyway." He smiled disarmingly. "You saved my skin today. Often there is one diver who needs extra help. Normally there are not two."

"I didn't mind," Gwen said, smiling in spite of herself.

"The Blue Wall is an extraordinary dive. It isn't fair that you spent all your time looking after that poor girl. That's my job, not yours. So I owe something to you." He paused. "Have you ever been diving at night?"

"No," Gwen said.

"It's a beautiful thing. You see different fishes, langoustines, all the nocturne animals. It's like the second shift coming to work." He looked up at the sky, vivid blue, a faint, chalky moon hanging in the distance. "See? The moon will be full tonight, perfect conditions. Will you come with me?"

Gwen hesitated.

"This question is an easy one. You say, Yes, Rico, I would love to come."

"Yes, Rico," said Gwen, her heart hammering. "I would love to come."

SHE RETURNED to the pier at just before sunset, empty handed. No need to bring dive gear, Rico had told her; Alistair's would fit her fine.

They motored away from the pier. A stiff wind lifted her hair. Calypso music tinkled in the distance—the same musicians, probably, as the night before, in their dark trousers and white shirts. She glanced back at the shore, the resort ablaze with lights. Pleasure's own second shift—the crowded hot tubs, the swim-up blackjack—had just begun.

They traveled half a mile before Rico cut the engine. A strange current passed through her, an exhilarating terror. Alone at sea, at night, with a total stranger. It dawned on her that nobody in the world knew where she was.

They dropped anchor just before sunset. Rico raised the dive flag as Gwen got into her gear. Alistair's BC fit her snugly, but would loosen up underwater. Silently Rico lifted the air tank to her back. His silence surprised and pleased her. She had always disliked conversation before diving. Her brother Billy, sensing this, had always left her in peace.

"I'll carry the floodlight. Just stay close to me." Rico showed Gwen a smaller flashlight. "This is your marker light." He attached it to the plastic D ring on her BC, just below her breast.

They stepped off together. Gwen blinked, her eyes adjusting to the dimness. She could discern the darting outlines of triggerfish diving downward, settling into the coral. Rico pointed to a sleeping parrot fish wrapped in its jellied blanket. In the distance a sleek shape lurked: a reef shark skirting the coral, hunting its prey.

They drifted on, passing other travelers. A jaunty seahorse floated overhead. An octopus parachuted through. Gwen watched in amazement the tiny crabs emerging from their holes. *The second shift coming to work.*

Up ahead Rico waited. He had trained his light on a flat rock. *What is he doing?* Gwen wondered. A moment later a black shape swooped in out of nowhere, and her heart leaped. The manta ray was big as a barn door and quick as a bat. The floodlight had attracted plankton; now the rays were coming in to feed.

Suddenly Rico stopped short. He shone the light upward. A school of fish—an immense cone of grouper—swam toward the surface. Gwen held her breath: a spawning rise. She stayed perfectly still, feeling Rico's nearness, her own breathing, all the life surrounding them, the two of them suspended in this grainy and fertile bath.

Rico touched her shoulder. The water was speckled with dinoflagellates, tiny particles of iridescent green. Sparks flew.

WHO WAS he? Where had he come from? On deck, wrapped head to toe in an immense beach towel, drinking wine from a plastic tumbler, Gwen asked these questions.

Rico came from the south side of the island, across the Calliope Mountains, a hundred kilometers away from the posh resorts of the north side. He was raised in a small village called Le Verdier, where his grandmother Toussainte Victoire farmed a small plot of land with her deaf son, Nestor. Her older sons had been killed fighting for the British. The men of St. Raphael, in no other sense British, were British enough to be killed in the war. Rico's mother was Toussainte's youngest, the child of her middle age. She had run away at sixteen to the city of Pointe Mathilde. "It was a rich city at that moment, and full of foreigners," Rico explained. "They came for the beau kseet."

"Beau kseet?" Gwen repeated.

"It is used to make aluminum. For years the British took our beau kseet and gave us nothing for it—one shilling per ton."

"You aren't crazy about the British," said Gwen.

"How can that be," said Rico, "when I am British myself?" His father was a Londoner; he'd stayed several months at the Victoria Hotel, where Rico's mother worked as a chambermaid. When she discovered her pregnancy, he had already gone back to England, leaving no phone number, no address. Rico's mother returned to the village to give birth.

She disappeared soon after, and it was Toussainte Victoire who'd raised Rico in her tiny house. She had been born a slave. The British had outlawed this practice, but the plantation owners paid no attention. Toussainte's father, a cane cutter, was paid nothing and was not allowed to leave. "To me that is a slave," Rico said.

An act of God had won his ancestors their freedom. One Sunday morning, after belching steam for many years, Montagne-Marie blew wide open, burying the plantation in molten rock and engulfing the church of Marie des Anges, where the plantation owner and his family had gone to pray. That morning Rico's great-grandparents had gone fishing; they watched the explosion from a kilometer offshore, from the mahogany-trunk canoe his great-grandfather had made. As they watched, his wife had gone into labor. Shrouded in smoke from the *volcan*, Toussainte Victoire was born.

The plantation destroyed, Toussainte's father moved his family six kilometers inland. He grew breadfruit and yams for a man called Thibault, who let them keep enough to feed themselves.

After her parents died Toussainte continued to farm the land. Her plot was bordered by fig and mango trees, which she had planted herself. Fruit trees were rare in the village; they would not grow in its poor soil, thin and ashy from Montagne-Marie. Only Toussainte Victoire could make them flourish. The village women wondered why. The land she farmed was no different from their own, the soil so meager that even breadfruit was difficult to grow. Toussainte, born as the volcan erupted; a fierce, tiny woman with reddish hair—"like you," Rico said. Her son's deafness had saved him from the war; if he had been born normal, his mother would now be alone. All this was considered evidence of sorcery. The villagers kept their distance. All except for Toussainte's sister-in-law, Mignonne Dollet, who every few days appeared at her front door, demanding her share of Toussainte's fruit. If she had been a stranger (Rico was insistent on this point), his grandmother would have given her an armload, but her whole life she'd had nothing but grief from Mignonne Dollet, who'd convinced her brother Toussainte was beneath him. Too ugly. Too black.

When she refused to hand over the fruit, Mignonne was *furieuse*. And the next day Thibault drove up in his wagon. He had been told about the fruit.

To his surprise Toussainte had a basketful waiting, and handed it over graciously. But later that day, enjoying a ripe mango on his porch, Thibault had collapsed to the floor clutching his chest. The half-eaten mango had rolled to the ground where it was soon covered with ants. Thibault's wife refused to touch it. "Let them have it, the dirty thing," she said. "At least we will be rid of our ants."

Gwen frowned. "I don't get it."

"A cardiac," said Rico. "He suffered a fatal cardiac."

She regarded him with amusement. "The fruit gave him a heart attack?"

"Yes, the fruit. What else could it be?"

Gwen laughed. "My brother is a cardiologist. He could give you ten reasons."

"If he were a cardiologist in the Caribbean," said Rico, "he would know of such things."

The wind kicked up. Gwen adjusted the beach towel, shivering a little. "What happened to your grandmother? Is she still living?"

"Oh yes. She is always living." Rico looked at Gwen. "You look cold. Come here."

He said it simply, naturally, as though they had known each other for years.

Gwen rose. Her body felt loose and warm. Rico parted his legs and she sat between them, as a child might. She leaned back against his chest. His skin surprised hers with its warmth. She hadn't been so close to another human being in ten years. And probably never would be again.

"What's that?" said Rico. "Just now. Something made you shiver."

He wrapped an arm around her rib cage and reached around to hand her the cup of wine. They sat this way for a moment, or several years, who could tell? Gwen drained the cup.

"It's getting late," he said finally. "I should get you back to land. Come." He squeezed her shoulder and got to his feet.

Don't go, she thought.

Touch me, she thought.

It was as if he had heard her. He lowered his mouth to her neck. A liquid thrill ran through her, from his lips downward. It spread over her chest and dropped clean through her stomach, pooling sweetly between her legs. She wished for cover, the safety of darkness. This full-mooned night she could not hide herself.

Thrill and fear wrestled inside her. They tore at each other like two dogs fighting.

He slid the strap of her swimsuit over her shoulder.

What are you doing? she asked, or maybe she only thought it.

Your bathing suit is wet, he said, or didn't. *That is why you are cold.*

Gwen saw the logic in this.

He slipped the suit from her shoulders, down to her waist. The cool breeze thrilled her skin. She looked down at herself, the white skin of her belly, her small spreading breasts.

She turned to face him.

chapter 5

Halfway through a wet April, Massachusetts went to war.

The morning had been cool and foggy. A damp rain soaked the town green. Down the road, in Lexington, eight militiamen had fallen beneath a cloud of musket smoke. Then the murderous column of British regulars had arrived in Concord, looking for weapons. The local militia had stockpiled cannon and muskets, which the regulars had been ordered to destroy.

In Concord the colonists were ready. Had been readying for months, in fact, gathering supplies—a dozen cords of wood, six hundred bales of straw; a hundred and forty portable toilets, discreetly placed in strategic locations around Minuteman National Park. Troops had been mobilized and bivouacked—at the Best Western on Route 2A, the Comfort Inn in Woburn. By hand and machine, uniforms had been sewn.

Properly outfitted, the soldiers massed around North Bridge. The minutemen were stationed on the far side, over the Concord River; three companies of his majesty's troops held the low ground. The regulars had uncovered, and burned, small stockpiles of weapons. The British had come to set fire to the town! The order was given, the muskets loaded. As it did every wet April, the American Revolution began.

Paulette stood in her assigned spot, shivering despite the two wool petticoats she wore beneath her cloak. She hadn't missed a Battle Road in years; it was her third time as a costumed interpreter, and still as the first shot rang out, a thrill ran through her. Long ago, back when schoolchildren still memorized poetry, young Paulette Drew had learned the words to Emerson's "Concord Hymn." They returned to her like a prayer:

Here once the embattled farmers stood /
And fired the shot heard round the world.

She waited for her cue to speak. Some of the other interpreters gave the same address year after year, but Paulette was not complacent. Every year she made an effort to add something new. It wasn't easy to do. The battle at North Bridge had lasted only a few minutes. Just one colonist and one British soldier had been killed. Only later, when colonists from the bridge met up with another group of minutemen at Meriam's Corner, did the real fighting begin.

A bit nervously, she deliverered her remarks. Later, after she'd finished, she was approached by a man in leather breeches. *You're Paulette. I've been working next door for Barbara Marsh. She says you need help with your kitchen floor.*

Now, ten months later, she remembered everything about that moment: the blond man handsome in his uniform, his serious gaze, the surprising gravity of his voice. She recalled it as she sat drinking weak coffee in the town library, waiting for the rest of the committee to arrive. Waiting, if she were to be honest, for Gil Pyle, who must surely be back from Florida. She kept her eyes on the door, waiting. Then, just as the meeting started, she felt a hand on her shoulder

"Hi there," Pyle whispered. "Do you have a minute afterward? I need to talk to you."

The meeting seemed to go on forever. Minutes were read. Selectmen got up to speak. Paulette watched Gil Pyle from across the room, her view partially obscured by another of the reenactors, an aged gent named Harry Good. Perhaps it was fortunate that she couldn't see Pyle's face, that she was spared the embarrassment of meeting his eyes. From this vantage point she saw only his left shoulder, his plaid shirt rolled up to the elbow, his forearm tanned from the Florida sun.

Finally the meeting ended. Pyle made his way across the room.

Paulette rehearsed a greeting in her head. *How lovely to see you. How was your trip?* He would offer his hand to shake, and she would take it in both of hers. It seemed appropriate. They hadn't seen each other in five and a half months.

Head ducked, he approached her. His face was deeply tanned, white around the eyes from wearing sunglasses. The beard was gone, but he seemed to be growing a new one. She imagined touching the stubble at his chin.

"Listen," he said. "I'm kind of in a hurry, but I wanted to let you know that I haven't forgotten. I have a couple of jobs lined up. I should be able to pay you back in three weeks. Four at the most."

She blinked, taken aback. Money? He wanted to talk about money?

"That's fine," she said in a low voice. She'd spotted Barbara Marsh a few feet away, refilling her Styrofoam coffee cup. The woman could hear like a dog. "Not to worry. Four weeks is fine."

An awkward pause.

"Are you driving back to New Hampshire tonight?" she asked. "To your brother's house?"

"Providence, actually. I've got a friend there." He nodded to someone over Paulette's shoulder. She turned to see a girl, a young woman, coming toward them.

"All set?" the girl said to Pyle. She was short legged and a little heavy through the thighs, or maybe it was the way she was dressed: as Pyle was, in faded jeans and a plaid shirt. But her face was lovely, her skin radiant, her hair long and wavy and streaked by the sun.

Paulette thought, *She is half my age.*

"Oh, hey," Pyle called to her. "This is someone you should meet. Paulette, this is my friend Melissa."

AFTER THE MEETING Paulette drove around town, feeling restless. The loan had been her own idea. Pyle hadn't asked for it, or expected it. It seemed now that she had ruined everything, though this possibility hadn't occurred to her that afternoon last fall, when Gil

Pyle was gathering up his tools. She'd been driven by fear and need, her desperation to have him back.

Florida will be lovely this time of year, she'd said, remembering with a sudden pang October in Palm Beach, the cool mornings, the blinding sun. Her father had died in the fall.

I haven't spent a winter in New Hampshire in ten years. I'm not sure I could handle it anymore. He chuckled. *I might never come back.*

He must have sensed her alarm. Briefly he touched her shoulder.

I'm kidding. There's nothing down there worth fixing. Plenty of work, but nothing interesting. He glanced around the dining room, the hallway. He gave the door frame a smack, like the shoulder of an old friend. *I'll miss this place.*

Paulette thought, I will miss you.

When do you come back? she asked, busying herself with a plant at the window.

March, usually. But this year I don't know. Depends on how fast I can dig myself out.

Paulette looked at him quizzically.

I'm behind on child support. It's tough on Sharon. I'd love to give it to her on schedule, like a regular citizen, but I don't get paid that way. I'll tell you, I'm getting too old to live like this. Week to week, eating what I kill.

Pyle scratched at his beard, a gesture she disliked. The beard itself had come to annoy her. One summer night she had wakened from a dream, Gil Pyle shirtless at her bathroom sink, his face lathered, herself drawing a razor slowly across it. The dream was vivid, oddly arousing. The razor had floated like a feather over his skin.

My truck is on its last legs, he said. *I might make it down there, but I'm pretty sure the old wreck won't make it back.*

He took the toolbox outside and loaded it into the truck. When he returned, Paulette asked, *What does a truck cost?*

Ten grand. Eight for a fixer-upper. Pyle shrugged. *If I work like a dog all winter, I might be able to swing it.*

Well, you can't miss the battle, she said. *Who would play Gilbert? It would compromise the integrity of the whole event. Harry Good would have a fit.*

Pyle laughed.

Because I care about preserving the heritage of New England, I insist that you buy a new truck. I'll lend you the money. You can pay me back in the spring.

He stared at her. *Are you crazy? You'd lend money to a deadbeat like me?*

You're not, she said softly. *Don't say that.*

He looked away. *No job, no known address. Face it, I'm a flight risk. Aren't you afraid I'll skip town and you'll never see your money again?* His tone was teasing, but his face was flushed. He would not meet her eyes.

No, she said simply. *I'm not.*

She took her purse from the divan and opened her checkbook. *I'll see you in the spring, then.*

She handed him the check, and finally he looked at her. To her astonishment his eyes were full.

He bent and kissed her cheek.

A T   H O M E , after the meeting, she fixed a simple supper, tea and toast. She thought of Gil Pyle in the truck she had bought him, driving back to Providence with Melissa. The windows down, Melissa's long hair blowing in the breeze.

He had asked Paulette, once, why she and Frank had divorced. *Gwen's condition*, she said reflexively. *It was too much for him.*

Pyle seemed unconvinced.

I suppose there was more to it, she admitted when he pressed her. *Frank always had a roving eye.*

Was it just his eye that roved?

I don't know. I tried to find out, she admitted. *I still don't know for sure.* She was revealing too much of herself, but couldn't stop. There was an odd pleasure in confessing, a silent release.

My first wife was like that. I was faithful, but she never believed me. I gave up trying to convince her. That's no way to live.

Did you love her? she asked. *Your ex-wife.*

At the beginning, he said. *But love is like any other material. You can only lean on it so hard, for so long. Sooner or later it's going to give.*

• • •

A WOMAN is her body.

That night, after her bath, Paulette did a thing she hadn't done in years. She stood before the mirror and looked at herself. Her smooth shoulders, the delicate bones of her forearms and calves—these were still recognizably Paulette, the person she'd always been. But her flat belly was striated with pale wavy lines. Her breasts, once merely small, now looked deflated. Her pubic hair was mostly gray. Her thighs were very lean, but the skin was textured like crepe paper. Wrinkles? Did thighs wrinkle?

Dear God.

Clothed, she could face the world. But nobody had seen her naked in years. She remembered with a pang the way Frank used to undress her, the hungry way he'd looked at her. *Keep the lights on. Let me see you.* After the divorce, with Donald Large, she'd been more reserved. She was forty then, and already self-conscious. His words had reassured her, a steady stream of sweet compliments that soothed like a gentle rain. And there was this: his own body was far from perfect. Perhaps that's why she'd chosen him in the first place.

They'd met at an antiques show in Hartford, Connecticut. Both had arrived early, before the doors opened. Donald offered her espresso from his thermos, his breath steaming in the cold. He was twenty years older, but still handsome. She learned that he lived alone, widowed and childless, in an antiques-filled house in Cos Cob. From the outset they were inseparable. Thinking of him she remembered the clear blue skies of autumn, long drives on Sunday afternoons. On pleasant fall days they drove deep into Vermont and New Hampshire, browsing, sometimes buying. They traveled in Donald's van, outfitted with built-in shelving to accommodate their purchases. Always Paulette took the wheel. Unlike her ex-husband, Donald considered her a fine driver. He did not bark instructions or clutch the dashboard or tap insistently with his right foot, as if hitting an invisible brake. Instead he napped or read to her, poetry or essays, the editorial page of the newspaper. They spent long days at the shows, tireless in their enthusiasm.

Afterward they retired to a lovely country inn, to nap before dinner, to read or daydream or simply talk. It had struck Paulette, then, that this was the marriage her younger self had wanted. Donald was soft-spoken and thoughtful, loving and refined. He dressed wonderfully— corduroy trousers and beautiful sweaters, soft leather shoes he bought each summer in Italy. He petted and praised her, and never criticized; he cherished her exactly as she was. He loved her for more than her body. How sad, how cruelly funny that she'd met him now, when her older self had different needs.

At first they made love occasionally, and later not at all. She'd been shocked to discover, a year into their relationship, that he'd had two heart attacks, that he injected insulin twice a day. If he'd told her these things at the beginning, would she still have fallen in love with him? He'd asked her this once near the end, as she drove him to the hospital for dialysis. *Of course, dear,* she said softly. He had deceived her, and now he wanted reassurance that she hadn't minded. She had no choice but to give it. He was a sick man.

Would she have fallen in love with him anyway?

Paulette had no idea. He hadn't given her a chance to find out.

Now the thrill of undressing for a man was lost to her forever. She allowed herself to imagine it, a young man like Gil Pyle caressing her withered breasts. Why on earth would he want to? And even if he did, how could she bear to be seen in this condition?

In that moment the truth dawned on her. No one would ever touch her again.

To live another twenty or thirty years untouched and unloved: it seemed impossible that this was what nature intended. Her whole life Paulette had believed in a natural order, nature a loving mother, wise and provident. Yet aging and childbearing were natural processes. There was no escaping it: her ruined body was nature's work.

Nature was not kind.

She realized, of course, that not every life unfolded as hers had. Couples could grow old together. Paulette remembered Frank as he'd looked on Christmas Eve, his eyes hooded, his red hair dusted pink. Age hadn't spared him either. But Paulette had known him young and handsome, his athlete's shoulders, the square cut of his jaw. In her mind the two pictures blended together. The result was something infinitely kinder than what a stranger saw.

Paulette thought of Rand and Barbara Marsh, Wall and Tricia James: couples her own age, couples who'd endured. After so many years, did these husbands and wives still look at each other, still want each other? Perhaps *that* was what nature intended. No woman of fifty-six should have to undress for a new lover. She should be spared that anguish.

There was nothing wrong with nature's plan. It was Frank and Paulette who had failed.

Late fall, a raw November. A steady rain soaks the dormant lawns of Newton, Massachusetts, where Scotty and his sister have been taken, as they are every Sunday, to visit their grandparents. They have kissed Mamie, answered the usual adult questions about classes and teachers. Now they are watching televison.

(Where is Billy in all of this? He is often missing from Scott's recollections of childhood. Was his brother often elsewhere? Or did Scott's memory simply edit him out?)

Scotty and Gwen are planted in front of the old Philco, a heavy cabinet model. Their grandparents are the only people alive who still have black and white. The set is kept in what Mamie calls the sitting room, a small second-floor bedroom at the rear of the house. The TV is hidden away like an unmentionable relative—blinded by syphilis, crippled by some shameful defect. Papa and Mamie were of a generation that found television extraneous. It had arrived in their middle age, and they were unwilling to reorder their lives around it. The parlor had so many other uses—bridge, reading, drinking. A television would simply have gotten in the way.

That Sunday afternoon, Scotty lies stretched out on the uncomfortable old sofa, what Mamie calls the divan. Gwen sprawls on the floor, close enough to change the channel when they get bored. The TV has rabbit-ear antennae and receives four channels, five on a good day. This is not a good day.

The choices are few and grainy. A cooking show, a football game, an old man preaching a sermon. Sunday movies are ancient and nearly always boring, soldiers or cowboys or detectives wearing hats. Once in a while they find a monster terrorizing Japanese people. Mothra is Scotty's favorite.

They stumble upon a movie already in progress. A blond girl lies sleeping, satiny sheets pulled demurely to her chin. Her lips are dark; a marceled wave dips over one eye. A stranger approaches her bedside, a man swathed in a black cape. Like the girl, he wears red lipstick. He creeps closer. The actress is a blond ingenue, her name relegated to obscurity. Bela Lugosi bends toward her. With a great flourish he buries his face in her neck.

At that moment, in his grandparents' sitting room—threadbare oriental rug, doilies on every flat surface—Scott experiences his first little-boy boner. (That such a thing is possible at eight—Ian's age—will later astonish him.) He feels an odd euphoria, a lifting and a lofting. He is not aware of wanting anything. He wouldn't know what to want.

"This is boring," says Gwen, reaching to change the channel.

"No!" Scotty springs from the couch and pounces on his sister. At eight he is already bigger, but she is quick and feisty. She wriggles furiously, her white throat arching.

"Get off me, you little freak!"

He does not break the skin, but still he bites in earnest. The next day a purplish mark appears like a smudge on her skin.

Darling, what happened? their mother asks at breakfast.

Nothing, Gwen says with what will become her trademark opacity. Her flat tone discourages further questions. His sister is not a crybaby, a trait Scotty honors. Gwen can keep a secret.

It is the beginning of his career as a biter. Around boys he is reasonably well-behaved. It is girls who provoke him. At Pilgrims Country Day no third-grade girl is safe, though some are safer than others: Carolyn Underwood, with her eczema; Madeleine Hopewell, whose fingers are always in her nose. His teacher Miss Terry tries to contain him, which only aggravates the problem. Miss Terry is young and pretty; her behind jiggles when she writes on the chalkboard. The jiggling, her blond hair, her pale blushing skin that reminds him, mysteriously, of strawberries. All this agitates him.

Many years later, summoned to a bright classroom at Walker Elementary School, he remembered the jiggling behind of Miss Terry, how he would have given anything to bite her neck. His son's teacher, Ms. Lister (they were all Ms. now) would prompt no such impulse. She was a pale, doughy young woman who managed to look both overfed and undernourished. Her lank hair, pulled back with a barrette, seemed to be thinning. There was a crusty white residue at the corners of her mouth. On a good-looking woman this might seem sexual. On Meredith Lister it suggested toothpaste, or a vitamin deficiency.

Listerine, he thought. *Listeria.* Yet compared to the classrooms of his childhood, Ms. Lister's looked quite aseptic. At Pilgrims the rooms had been drafty, the wood floors creaky. Each classroom had its own cloakroom, a word that had delighted him. He would have loved, like a studious young Dracula, to go to school in a cloak.

"Thank you for coming," said Ms. Lister, shaking his hand and Penny's. Meeting in the classroom was an indignity that seemed calculated: the shamed parents squeezed into desks sized for eight-year-olds. Penny was able to pull this off with a modicum of grace, her deerlike legs pliable from daily yoga; but Scott hadn't touched his toes in ten years. Even as a high school athlete he'd never been limber. Now—at six feet, one-ninety—he had nowhere to put his limbs, no conceivable way of extricating himself when the ordeal finally came to a close.

"This visit is long overdue," she said. "My fault. Ian has had behavioral problems since September, but I've been so swamped I haven't had time for conferences. We have a new principal this year, and with all the standardized testing—"

"Say no more," Scott said warmly. "I understand. I'm an educator myself."

She looked at him with grateful eyes. "So you know, then. Where do you teach?"

"At Ruxton."

"Oh." Her smile faded. "That's private, right? I mean, sort of."

Sort of.

"And you do lots of testing," she added.

"Exactly," Scott said smoothly. "So I understand how disruptive that can be."

He had her. She was overworked, underpaid and starved for appreciation, a condition Scott knew all too well. A little empathy, a little appreciation from parents would go a long way toward softening her attitude. Suspending an eight-year-old was disproportionately harsh, the act of a desperate woman. Yet it was an impulse Scott understood. On a daily basis, he experienced such desperation himself.

"Great," said Penny. "But the thing is, Ian's really upset. He feels like a little criminal. I don't know what to do with him." She paused. "Just coming here today, you know? You wanted to see both of us, which I understand, but where is Ian supposed to go? We had to get a sitter, and you have no idea—"

"Honey." Scott shot her a warning look. Their difficulties with babysitters—none, to date, had agreed to a return engagement—would do nothing to help Ian's case. If Penny would keep quiet and let him handle it, they'd be home in ten minutes.

Ms. Lister folded her hands. "I'm sorry to inconvenience you, Mrs. McKotch, but I don't think you understand. We're not talking about normal misbehavior. Ian is showing symptoms of a much larger problem."

She paused a moment to let this sink in.

"But he's *trying*," Penny insisted, as though she hadn't heard. "He's at the computer all evening. I make him show me his homework every night before he goes to bed. And he's *amazing* on the computer. You should see the way he clicks around. He knows more than I do."

Please shut up, Scott thought. He saw them both clearly through Ms. Lister's eyes: the father clueless and disengaged, an affable bullshitter. The mother whining and defensive, raising a misunderstood genius. He and Penny were the kind of parents teachers hated. The kind he himself hated.

"Maybe so," said Ms. Lister. "But I never *see* this homework. He manages to misplace it somewhere between home and class." She counted on her fingers: "Ian is easily distracted. Disorganized. He shows poor impulse control. Stop me if any of this sounds familiar."

"All of it," Scott said with feeling. "All of it sounds familiar."

Penny shot him a fierce look.

"I thought so," said Ms. Lister.

"Wait a minute. I have no idea what you're talking about," said Penny.

The teacher leaned forward in her chair. "I think Ian should be evaluated for attention deficit disorder. And perhaps depression and anxiety as well."

Scott blinked. *He's eight*, he thought.

"Ian's always been a happy boy," said Penny, responding to the word *depression*. Scott had learned long ago not to overload her; she processed ideas one at a time. Whether she was stupid or simply very focused was a question that plagued him. After all these years he still wasn't sure.

"Maybe he's depressed because you keep throwing him out of class," Penny said. "He's so embarrassed. He won't say so, but I can tell. "

"If that's true, I'm sorry," said Ms. Lister. "Ian can be very sweet, when he wants to be."

This was true. Scott thought of his son as he'd been the night before, fast asleep in front of the television; the boy clinging to his shoulders as Scott carried him to bed.

"When he acts up, it's because he's frustrated," said Penny. "He's having a hard time with math. I think he needs extra help."

Ms. Lister nodded manically. "Exactly. That's exactly what I'm saying: extra help. But I have twenty-four other children to consider. There's a limit to what I can do." Her fingernails, Scott noticed, were bitten to the quick. He felt a rush of sympathy. Charged with a class of twenty-five Ians, he would chew his fingers bloody.

"Do you have any suggestions?" he asked.

Ms. Lister turned to him. "These are common issues, as I'm sure you know. Parents deal with them in a variety of ways. Medication is one option—"

"Forget it," Penny said. "No way is Ian taking drugs. No way."

The teacher raised her hands, as if in self-defense. "That's your call, of course. No one can decide that for you. I will say, though, that until Ian is evaluated, I can't have him back in my classroom."

"You're kicking him out?" said Penny. "It's a public school. You can't just throw him out."

"True," Miss Lister agreed. "But this situation has gone on long enough that we need to look at other options. A special-needs class-room, for example."

"Ian's not retarded," said Penny.

Just, Scott thought. *Shut. Up.*

Ms. Lister glanced at her watch. "All I'm saying is that Ian may need more help, or a different kind of help, than *any* public school can offer." She took a brochure from her desk drawer and handed it to Penny. Scott leaned close to take a look, nearly capsizing his desk.

"Whoops," said Ms. Lister, reaching out to steady him. "Fairhope is an independent school in Fairfield County. An old classmate of mine teaches there. They've gotten incredible results with kids like Ian. If you're dead set against medicating, it's something to consider."

Penny handed Scott the brochure. The photos reminded him of Pearse: the stone buildings, the grassy lawns and towering trees. He turned it over, scanning downward. The information he sought was in tiny print at the bottom of the page. More zeroes than he would have thought possible.

"Good luck to you," said Ms. Lister, rising. "I wish you and Ian all the best."

They drove home in silence, Penny at the wheel. It was a pecu-liarity of their marriage Scott couldn't account for: anytime they were in a car together, Penny always drove. This marked them different from every other couple he knew. What it meant, he had no idea. He was the sexual instigator, and the breadwinner. Not a very successful one, it was true; but what bread they had, Scott had won.

Penny's silence was damp and heavy; he sensed a storm approach-ing. Scott waited, his senses heightened. After ten years of marriage he was like an old geezer who ached from humidity, who felt the weather in his bones.

"I can't believe you," she said at last.

Scott felt his muscles relax, a palpable easing of tension. Like the punishments of his boyhood, fights with Penny were never as bad as waiting for them.

"You sold Ian down the river. You just agreed with everything she said. Is that how you defend your son?"

"Defend him from what, Pen? Getting an education? A teacher who's concerned and wants to help?"

"She wants to put him on *drugs,* Scotty. You call that help?"

He took a deep breath. "Ian's in trouble. He can't get through a school day without freaking out. And the tantrums, the bullying. You told me yourself that Nathaniel Moss won't play with him anymore."

"Nathaniel is a spoiled brat."

Stay on target, he told himself. "I agree: Nathaniel is spoiled. But what about the way Ian torments Sabrina? The hitting, the hair pulling—" He paused. "The biting."

"I give him time-outs," said Penny.

"I know: you're doing everything you can. But how bad does it have to get before we admit it isn't working? That we need professional help?"

"You sound just like Ms. Lister," said Penny.

"Well, maybe she's right. It was pretty decent of her to spend half an hour talking to us. After the day she puts in, she wants to go home and mix herself a good stiff drink. Not sit in the classroom with two hostile parents."

"Hostile? When was I hostile?" Penny ran a red light, narrowly missing another minivan coming from the opposite direction. The schools had just let out; at this hour Quinnebaug Highway was like a bumper-car ride, with Plymouth Voyagers standing in for rubberized cars.

"He's always been a happy boy," Scott mimicked. *"Maybe he's depressed because you kicked him out of class.* Was that necessary, Pen? How is she supposed to take us seriously after a comment like that?"

"Take us *seriously*?" She looked at him in wonderment. "I don't care if she takes us seriously. Why do you care what she thinks?" She hit the brake. "That's what this is about for you. What it's always about. *What will people think?*"

"What?" He stared at her, genuinely baffled. It was the conversational equivalent of a squealing U-turn in rush-hour traffic.

"You're ashamed of us," said Penny. "Of Ian, and me, and us."

Not this again, he thought. Ever since they'd moved to Connecticut, it had been a recurrent theme in their arguments. As near as Scott could figure, the charges stemmed from two incidents in the winter of 1995:

1. While shopping for a new couch at an off-price furniture outlet called Rooms Unlimited, Penny had screamed at Sabrina and Ian to stop jumping on the demo mattresses, in a voice that made several heads turn. When Scott had asked her, in a calm, well-modulated voice, to stop cawing like a fishwife, she had stormed out of the store.

2. The evening of the Ruxton faculty holiday gathering, Penny had emerged from their bedroom in a dress cut down to her navel, revealing a third of each breast; they had swollen to the size of grapefruits during her second pregnancy and had never returned to their original dimensions. When Scott wondered aloud if a skirt and sweater wouldn't be more appropriate, she had told him to go fuck himself. He had gone to the party alone.

"I couldn't believe the way you sucked up to her," Penny said now. *"I know how it is. I'm an educator too."*

He winced at her gruff imitation of his voice, aware, on some level, that he had mocked her first. The dull churlishness of their fights depressed and mortified him. He felt strongly that marital spats should display some *esprit*: some brittle cleverness, some Edward Albee-like theatricality. His parents had fought brilliantly, though his mother had often resorted to tears in the end. Penny, luckily, was not a crier; but neither did she engage in clever repartee. Together they sounded like children on a playground.

"I was trying to show some empathy," he said. "Sow a little good-will. It was working too until you opened your mouth."

"It was *working*?" She spat out the word like a knot of phlegm. "What do you mean, 'working'? She wants to put our son on *drugs*!"

"Since when are you so righteous about drugs?"

He had her there. The early years of their marriage had been an out-and-out potfest. Recently, out of concern for Scott's urine—Ruxton teachers were subject to random drug testing—she had instituted a strict zero-tolerance policy in the house, but they were both prone to lapses.

"Scotty, we're talking about *Ritalin*. That's gnarly stuff."

With the reverence of a former surfer, Penny reserved the term *gnarly* for the truly atrocious: ritual killings, self-immolations and child torture, the lurid subject matter of *Faces of Evil*, a tabloid TV show she watched every evening while preparing dinner.

"You may be right," he allowed. "But it won't kill us to do a little research. We're not doctors, Pen. Let me call my brother."

"Billy?" Again the van swerved. "Billy barely knows Ian."

Please God, Scott thought, *get us home in one piece.*

"Well, he saw what happened at Christmas."

"Please. Don't get me started on Christmas. Your mother and that freezing-cold house. She makes the poor kid sit at the table for hours on end. And all that fussy food! You can't expect kids to behave like adults. She doesn't know the first thing about children."

Scott regarded her with amusement. "Well, she raised three of them."

"Oh, please. Don't tell me you and Billy and Gwen sat at the table for an *hour* every night!"

"That's just it, Pen. We *did*. I don't know how we felt about it, or if we even gave it any thought. It's just what we *did*." As he said this, he remembered a time his mother had stormed away from the dinner table in frustration and refused to return. *You deal with it, Frank. I've had them all day.* The exact nature of his infraction, Scott had forgotten, but he was sure, from the guilt curdling his stomach, that the misbehavior was not Billy's or Gwen's. It was his.

"We weren't perfect, of course," he added. "But that's not the point. What matters now is Ian, and what we can do for him."

"A different teacher, for starters. This one doesn't know what she's doing. And she obviously has it in for him."

"I don't think that's true," he said. "And anyway, I doubt we have that option, unless we want him in special ed."

"No!" The van swerved, finally, into Canterbury Lane. "Those kids get *tortured*, Scotty. My stepbrother Benji—" Her voice broke. To his astonishment, two fat tears rolled down her cheeks.

"Easy." Tentatively he touched her shoulder, trying to remember if she was premenstrual. "Benji? In Idaho?"

She pulled into the driveway and engaged the brake. Finally he relaxed his grip on the door handle.

"He wasn't retarded, Scotty. He was actually very smart. He just had some trouble reading, and he was very shy." She spoke softly now, just above a whisper. "My asshole stepfather let them put him in special ed, and oh my God, you wouldn't believe what the other kids put him through. Finally he couldn't take it anymore, and he ran away." She sniffed loudly. "I'm dead serious. He ran away to California. He never came back."

"Okay," Scott said, stroking her shoulder. "No special ed. We'll figure out something else. I promise."

THAT EVENING, at the basement computer, Scott clicked through Web sites, avoiding those plastered with drug advertisements: *Meds by Mail. Ritalin and Adderall. PharmCanada. Rock-Bottom Prices.* Finally he found what he was looking for, a sober list of diagnostic criteria. There were two types of attention deficit disorder—inattentive and hyperactive-impulsive. Scott scrolled down the page and read:

1. Inattention
often does not seem to listen when spoken to directly

Just then he became aware of a banging on the ceiling above his head. "Honey!" Penny shouted from upstairs. "I've been calling you for five minutes."

"Jesus, what?"

"The garbage disposal is still making that noise. I thought you fixed it."

"I did," he said. "I will." He stared at the screen.

often does not follow through on instructions and fails to finish schoolwork, chores, or duties in the workplace

"You said that last week," Penny crowed.

"I know, I know. I have to buy a part."

often loses things necessary for tasks or activities (e.g., school assignments, books)

"Honey, you already bought it. It's sitting on top of the refrigerator."

"Oh," said Scott. "Good. I've been looking for that fucker all week."

"Great, but Scotty?"

"Can you leave me alone for five minutes?" he yelled. "We talked about this, remember? No more shouting up and down the stairs."

often has difficulties sustaining attention in tasks or play activities

No answer from above. He returned his attention to the screen, but the letters had begun to swim before his eyes. He skimmed to the bottom of the page. Wow, he thought. This list is long.

Scott sat back in his chair, ready to admit defeat, when a line of text caught his attention. Helpfully, it had been underlined in red.

<u>Signs of ADHD may persist into adulthood. This is particularly true when there is a family history of the condition.</u>

Scott blinked. The realization hit him like a physical blow. He was aware of a pounding headache beginning at his temple, a rhythmic thumping, as though some creature trapped in his skull were trying to escape.

Quickly he signed off the computer. The CompuCom USA logo appeared on the screen. A helpful banner informed him, *YOUR US-AGE IS 61 MINUTES.*

Shit, he thought. They were on an hourly billing plan, and the first hour was free. If he'd clicked just a minute faster his session would have cost nothing.

He clicked on a tab marked BILLING. Another helpful banner informed him: *YOUR USAGE THIS MONTH IS 7,920 MINUTES.*

He did some quick math. By his calculation, someone had been using the account, on average, six hours a day. He sprang from his chair.

"Penny!" he roared.

She appeared at the top of the stairs. "I thought we weren't yelling anymore."

He ignored this. "Have the kids been using our CompuCom account?"

A wary look crossed her face. "Why? What's the matter?"

"I just looked at our monthly usage. Someone's been on this computer, like, six hours a day. What did I say about keeping them out of my office? Isn't this why we got them a computer in the first place?"

Penny ran a hand through her hair. "Chill out, will you? It's a mistake. I'll call CompuCom tomorrow and straighten it out."

"Where's Ian? Let me talk to Ian."

"No way," said Penny. "Not until you calm down."

She slammed the door. It made a hollow sound, like the clap of a horse's hooves.

Scott returned to his desk and riffled through a tattered little notebook until he found his brother's phone number. As he dialed, he watched the digits appear on the liquid crystal display of his cordless phone.

Who had invented such a thing? And how the fuck could you liquefy a crystal?

His father would know. His father would explain it for two hours straight, thinking Scott really wanted to know.

Scott didn't really want to know.

The last four digits of Billy's number were 5151. The display showed SISI. Penny would love that. She'd insisted for years—to Scott's irritation—that his brother was gay.

He hung up quickly. Then, just for laughs, he punched in his office number at Ruxton, which spelled nothing. He turned the phone upside down. The digits still spelled nothing.

He hung up the phone.

The list of diagnostic criteria had made him acutely aware of the movement of his own thoughts, scattering like buckshot. His mind had always worked this way. He'd assumed everyone's did, but how could that be true? People like his father spent lifetimes concentrating on dry, abstract, complex material. Years ago, at Pearse, Scott's classmate "Jens" Jensen had tutored him in chemistry, physics, and calculus, all the subjects Scott hated **(avoids tasks that require sustained mental effort).** He'd watched, mystified, as Jens pored over a complicated problem, his pale brow furrowed in concentration. At the time Scott had chalked it up to cultural difference. Jens was from—Norway? Denmark? Some cold northern latitude where it was always dark and people stayed indoors solving equations.

He knew at the time that Jens had saved his bacon. Now he saw that, in a larger sense, the Jenses of the world were saving *everybody's* bacon. That if every brain worked the way Scott's did, there would *be* no science or higher math, the kind used to design tall buildings and bridges and airplanes that didn't fall out of the sky. People would live in huts and wear animal skins, or become crummy English teachers who hadn't read a fraction of the books they should have. Who'd only recently, in the last three years, read the ones they assigned to their students.

His whole life he'd concocted explanations for his failure to achieve. His parents' divorce was a favorite. His brother Billy had a stable home life until he left for Pearse; Scott, given the same send-off, would likewise have torn up the lacrosse field, gotten into Princeton, graduated with honors. When Frank encouraged Billy's interest in science, let him spend entire days in the Holy of Holies, his lab at MIT, Scott's jealousy had nearly choked him. *I'll take you too someday*, Frank had promised when Scott threw a grand mal tantrum. But by the time Scott was old enough, his father was long gone. And of course, there was Gwen: Frank and Paulette had been so busy squabbling over her medical problems that they'd let Scott flounder; if they'd paid more attention, he would have stayed on course. He saw, now, that none of this was true. If his parents had stayed married, if Gwen had been normal, he would still have been a dud.

This condition, if he had it, would explain the way his life had turned out, a fact that both depressed and comforted him. His derelict academic history. The long series of disastrous decisions that had landed him at Ruxton **(impairment in occupational functioning).** He was a mediocre teacher, a bad actor in a cynical parody of a prep school. A balding thirty-year-old man flattened by marriage, with a daughter who laughed at him and a son who—

Jesus.

A son who would turn out exactly like him.

He picked up the phone. Even his brother's telephone rang differently. Billy's ring sounded expensive—low and melodious, a throaty mechanical purr. Scott had noticed, in making local calls, that phones in Gatwick rang with an annoying falsetto chirp. Was the local phone company to blame? His long-distance carrier? Was it a mechanism inside his own telephone, or the one he was calling?

He shook his head to clear it.

Billy answered on the second ring. It took him a moment to recognize Scott's voice. Well, no wonder. Scott hadn't phoned his brother in years.

If Billy realized this, he gave no indication. "What's up?" he asked easily, as though they spoke every day.

Scott pictured him settling into a sleek modern sofa, expensively leather covered. He'd never seen Billy's apartment, but his mother had described it in abundant detail, a fact that drove Penny crazy. He felt a stab of envy for his brother, single on a Friday night. Free to chat up strange women in bars or, even better (this was a symptom of Scott's descent into middle age), simply to be left in peace.

At Billy's, soft jazz played in the background. There was no other ambient noise. On Scott's end, television vibrated the ceiling. Loud running in a southerly direction, from the kitchen to Ian's room.

"Listen, I want to run something by you," said Scott. "What do you know about Ritalin?"

"The hyperactivity drug?"

"Yeah. Ian's teacher wants us to put him on it."

"Have you discussed it with your pediatrician?"

"We did," Scott lied. "I want a second opinion."

A pause. "Scotty, I'd like to help, but you know I'm not a pediatrician. And even if I were, I haven't actually seen him."

"You saw him at Christmas."

"I haven't seen him *clinically*. It would be irresponsible for me to give you a medical opinion based on what you tell me over the phone." He sounded less like a brother than a doctor worried about a malpractice suit. *Good Christ*, Scott thought. *What a SISI.*

"Jesus, Bill. I'm not going to sue you."

Billy sighed. "All right. Fine. This behavior—the hyperactivity, the aggression, the stuttering—"

"Whoa, wait a minute. Ian *stutters*?"

"Um, yeah," said Billy. "When he gets excited. You haven't noticed?"

"Oh, that," Scott lied again. "Yeah. Sure."

"So tell me: when did you first—"

"Bill, even as a baby he was tougher than Sabrina. Wouldn't sleep through the night. That kind of thing. But he's a boy, you know? I thought it was just the difference between boys and girls. Sabrina was a dream by comparison, Bill. A total dream."

"Let me finish, will you?" said Billy **(blurts out answers before questions are completed).** "The onset of symptoms. Was it before age seven?"

Scott recalled the endless drive from California to Connecticut, a week of sleeping in roadside motels, the four of them crammed into a single cruddy room. The Golf stifling hot, Ian and Sabrina kicking each other viciously in the backseat. Ian had been five then, a scream-ing terror. With the same intensity he'd brought to teenage sexual fantasies, Scott had daydreamed of leaving his entire family by the side of the road.

"Yes," he said. "Definitely before seven."

"That's significant," said Billy. "It's consistent with ADHD."

The water pump kicked in explosively, rattling the plywood wall. Scott ignored this, though he was **easily distracted by extraneous stimuli.**

He pressed on.

"Look, don't tell Mom this. Any of it, actually. But especially this part: Penny has a sister who's schizophrenic. Could that have anything to do with it?" Years ago, when he and Penny were living in Eureka, they'd made a weekend dope run to Portland and spent a night on her sister's floor. JoAnn had been heavily medicated then, a bloated, silent version of Penny, her hair hacked into a spiky helmet. It seemed to Scott that she'd cut it herself. (In a fit of self-hatred. With a machete.) She had scared the hell out of him.

"No," Billy said. "Although, you know, it's an interesting ques-tion. There appears to be some genetic basis for schizophrenia. And there is comorbidity with ADHD."

Scott let this slide past him, like a taxi with its light off. He had stopped listening at the word *no*.

"Back to the drug," he said. "Penny says there are side effects."

"Weight loss, sleep disturbances." Billy paused. "On the other hand, certain questions arise with any drug you're prescribing. You have to weigh the risks of the therapy against the consequences of leaving the problem untreated. He's in what, first grade?"

"Third."

"How's he doing in school?"

"Shitty," said Scott. "They're ready to kick him out. That's why I'm calling."

"From public school? I didn't know they could do that."

"If he doesn't go on Ritalin, they're going to put him in special ed." Scott hesitated. "Look, you saw him at Christmas. Based on that, if he were your kid, would you do it?"

A long pause.

"He did seem agitated at Christmas," Billy admitted. "I think Mom was concerned."

Concerned. Drewspeak for *ready to hurl the little monster out an open window.*

"I know he's a handful," Scott said lamely. "Mom isn't used to that."

Billy chuckled. "She raised you, didn't she?"

Scott felt a knot of resentment in his throat. Reluctantly he swallowed. Billy was five years older; he would remember, if anyone would. And who else was there to ask?

"Was I like that?" he demanded. "Like Ian?"

Again the chuckle. "Are you kidding me? You just about landed her in McLean. The way you and Gwen used to pound on each other—" He broke off. "Hey, have you heard the news?"

"What?" said Scott.

"Are you sitting down? Gwen has a boyfriend."

"You're shitting me."

"Some guy she met on her dive trip. And Mom is freaking out. All hell is breaking loose."

That Sunday morning Paulette ate breakfast in her nightgown. This was something she did just once a year, when her old friend Tricia James came from Philadelphia to visit. In Tricia's honor she had brewed a pot of coffee, though her second cup had made her jangly. (She had switched to chamomile tea at menopause.) With Tricia, coffee and nightclothes were a tradition, an unconscious reenactment of their roommate days at Wellesley, where they'd guzzled coffee and spent a great deal of time in their pajamas. Paulette and Tricia had not forgotten. They would always remember the girls they had been.

We're closer than sisters, they liked to say, and in Paulette's case it was certainly true. Her actual sister had moved to New Mexico ten years ago—to take advantage of the spectacular light, she said; to mix her own paints with desert sand. Martine lived in a house with two other woman artists, and Paulette had never been invited to visit. They spoke twice a year, on their birthdays, and every Christmas Martine sent her a painting. Paulette knew from their brother that Martine had once again succeeded, that her paintings hung in a gallery in New York and sold for thousands of dollars. That *Martine* hadn't told her this wounded her deeply. Paulette loved nothing more than celebrating accomplishments (those of her family, of course, since she had never accomplished anything herself). In her mind, this was what accomplishments were *for*.

Tricia James was of the same mind. This shared belief mortared their friendship. For three days Paulette had allowed Tricia to praise

Billy, Gwen, and Scott. She responded with kind words about Hadley, Patrick, and Eleanor. This was the way she and Tricia had always operated. To prattle on about their own children would have been gauche.

At Wellesley their classmates had been struck by their resemblance. Though one was blond, the other dark, they had similar features and identical petite figures. Frank had once remarked, to Paulette's horror, that she and Tricia would feel exactly the same in the dark.

She had never repeated this to Tricia.

They both enjoyed telling the story of how they'd met: how they'd glimpsed each other in the dining room wearing identical sealskin skirts, butter yellow cashmere sweaters, kitten-heel pumps, and Hermès scarves. Showing up in identical dresses would have been embarrassing, but putting together the same entire *outfit* down to shoes and scarves, was simply delightful. Paulette Drew and Tricia Boone, strangers to each other, had both burst out laughing. They were nineteen, and filled with identical feelings: hilarity, recognition, joy.

For a time it seemed they would put together whole identical lives. Both left school to marry. Like Frank, Walter James was handsome, charming, virile; and for a brief, delicious time Paulette and Tricia had both been courted. In Frank's old jalopy—Frank and Paulette in the front seat, Wall and Tricia in back—both girls had been kissed. They had fallen completely and hopelessly and simultaneously in love.

Both had three children, though Tricia's had come at closer intervals. Pregnancy had not agreed with her, and her attitude had been soldierly; she was determined to get it over with. And here was where their paths diverged, because Tricia, with her live-in nanny, could *afford* to get it over with. Tricia had married a man with earning potential, a man interested in making money.

Recently, while having her hair colored, Paulette had flipped through a magazine and read a fascinating statistic, that the tallest men in the workforce earned the highest salaries. Lulled by the hum of the dryer, she'd thought of the unusually tall Walter James. While Frank spent endless years in school, Wall had worked as an investment banker at Goodman

Schering; back when Paulette and Frank were still living in dilapidated graduate-student housing, Wall had built Tricia a house in Bryn Mawr. On a tight budget, with a workaholic husband, Paulette had raised her children singlehandedly; she'd hinted to her parents that help would be welcome, but her father was only formerly wealthy, while Tricia's remained so to this day. Paulette had watched from a distance as Tricia lived the life of a prosperous young wife and mother—the life Paulette had expected to lead, almost certainly *would* have led, if Frank hadn't appeared one night at a Wellesley mixer and hijacked her wagon for good.

Now, their children grown, the two friends saw each regularly. Each spring Tricia came to Concord for a weekend. In the fall Paulette spent a weekend in Bryn Mawr. These visits began with a hug and a kiss, a quick assessment and readjustment. In Paulette's mind Tricia was still a young woman, but those first moments reminded her otherwise. More than any other person in the world, Tricia reminded Paulette of her own aging. *You look wonderful*, they told each other, and in a way it was true. They were both slender, beautifully dressed, carefully coiffed. They cared for their bodies like museum treasures, precious artifacts saved behind glass. But they were nearer sixty than fifty, and no amount of maintenance could change that.

It was the oldest friends who mattered most. With each passing year, Paulette realized this more deeply. She thought of her brother Roy, retired to Arizona, to golf with other men who were also—she loathed the expression—*senior citizens*. Roy had arrived in Phoenix with an entire life behind him, a career, a marriage; to his new friends he'd always been old. Not so with Paulette and Tricia. Strangers might mistake Paulette for an old woman, but Tricia knew that the years had changed her very little, that she was much the same person she'd been at twenty: her stubborn hopefulness, her bottomless capacity for disappointment, qualities that came braided together like a hank of hair. This was Paulette's basic nature—*my foolishness*, she called it—and she hadn't outgrown it as her mother had predicted she would. Like everything else, maturity had disappointed Paulette. She believed there ought to be some benefit to the grotesque business of aging, some thin compensation for all it took away. She waited for wisdom, but wisdom did not come. On the downslope of her life she wanted the same things she'd always wanted, with undiminished intensity; and suffered just as profoundly when those things did not appear.

Because Tricia understood this, Paulette still needed her, still cherished their time together despite the inevitable comparisons between Tricia's life and her own. Tricia's children were healthy, her marriage intact. Though whether Wall, who'd once grabbed Paulette's rear end as they danced at a friend's wedding, had been 100 percent faithful, Paulette had her doubts. (Did Tricia trust him? Was this the reason she was still married after all these years, while Paulette was alone?)

In between the museum and the Ibsen play, the lunches and the shopping, a conversation was taking place, a conversation centering, always, on husbands and children. Given recent events—three days of anxious brooding, fear, and stifled rage—Paulette would have preferred to avoid these subjects entirely; but with Tricia that wasn't possible. Their friendship was too old, its customs too entrenched.

A packet of photographs lay on the table between them. *Show and tell*, Tricia had announced as she took it from her pocketbook. They had sorted through the photos together, Paulette making appropriate noises of amusement, appreciation and delight. Tricia's daughters were lovely, blond like their mother; they hadn't been attractive children, but in adulthood had come into their own. In one photo Tricia stood arm in arm with Hadley and Eleanor; it was immediately apparent where the girls had gotten their good looks, and where Tricia's had gone. Paulette wondered how Tricia could stand it. Would she, in Tricia's position, have envied her beautiful daughters? Was some weak part of her grateful to be spared the sort of humiliating Christmas photos Tricia submitted to, the pain of fading as her daughters blossomed? Was she glad that Gwen had not grown up?

I am not a generous person, she thought,

More photos. Tricia's daughters each had two children. Patrick and his wife, both attorneys, had none. Tricia found this vexing, though she'd been a good girl and held her tongue. "I can't imagine what they're waiting for," she'd confided to Paulette. "Claire is thirty-four, the same age as Patrick. The same age as Gwen."

Paulette studied the photo. Patrick looked paunchy and bloated; he had lost his beautiful curly hair. *Poor Patrick*, Paulette thought. She'd always had warm feelings toward the boy. She would never forget his kindness in taking Gwen to the dance.

Because Tricia expected it, she went to the parlor and took her lone Christmas photo from a drawer in the highboy; she still hadn't gotten around to buying a frame. In it, the family stood around the Douglas fir, Paulette at the center, her handsome sons on either side. In the foreground stood Ian, Sabrina, and Gwen.

Billy, Scott, and Sabrina photographed beautifully; to the others, the camera was less kind. Gwen looked rumpled and stocky in her hideous sweatshirt; in the glare of the flashbulb her face was very pale, with no lips or eyebrows. *(Lipstick!* Paulette thought.) Ian's shirt was decorated with stains. And Paulette simply looked old.

"Oh, how precious," Tricia said dutifully. "I assume Scott's wife took it?"

"She's the best photographer in the family," said Paulette.

"Apparently so. She's never in the picture." Tricia held the photo at arm's length, squinting; like Paulette she was too vain to wear her glasses. "Scotty's little girl is going to be a beauty." She didn't say, but surely noticed, that Sabrina was now as tall as her aunt Gwen.

"She's a lovely girl," Paulette agreed.

"So fair. Like her mother?"

"Yes," said Paulette. "Penny is fair skinned."

"I can't believe how handsome Billy is. Honestly, what's the matter with girls today? I can't believe no one's reeled him in yet." Tricia studied the photo. Finally she reached for her pocketbook and took out her glasses.

"Oh, my heavens," she exclaimed. "It *is* Scott!"

"Well, of course," said Paulette, puzzled. "Who else would it be?"

"Oh, this is remarkable. I wasn't going to say anything, because it seemed so silly. I was sure I was mistaken." Tricia removed her glasses. "As I was driving here, I had the strangest experience. Somewhere in Connecticut, I saw Scotty on a billboard."

Paulette frowned.

"It was advertising some type of school, I believe. At first I thought, Tricia, you've lost it completely. You're seeing things. But, darling, I was right! It was your Scott."

Paulette shook her head as if to clear it. Too much caffeine, too many photos, the intense effort not to think what she'd been thinking all weekend. And what was this nonsense about a billboard? She felt pressure behind her eyes, a migraine building. To her horror she was near tears.

"What's the matter, darling? Have I upset you?" Tricia reached across the table for Paulette's hand. "What is it? What's wrong?"

Paulette grasped Tricia's hand, more tightly than she intended. "Tricia, I have to tell someone, and you're my oldest friend. Something terrible has happened to Gwen."

THE PHONE had rung on Friday morning, while Paulette was paying the housecleaner—a new girl who also did the Marshes' next door. Guadelupe was a pretty brown-skinned girl who spoke five words of English, so the transaction was slow going. Yet her price was reasonable, and she did an impeccable job.

Paulette rushed for the telephone. She was of the generation that couldn't simply let it ring, as her children exhorted her to do. Billy had long pestered her to buy an answering machine, but Paulette found the idea unappealing. She couldn't bear the sound of her recorded voice.

"Billy, what's the matter?" she asked immediately. Her son was a creature of habit; they spoke in the evening at six o'clock precisely. He had never, in her memory, called on a weekday morning.

"Relax," said Billy, who did not, himself, sound very relaxed. "Everything is fine."

"I'm in a bit of a hurry," she explained. "Tricia is coming this weekend, and the cupboard is bare."

"Okay then. We can talk another time." He sounded relieved to be rid of her, as though she'd kept him on the phone for hours. As though *she* had called *him*.

"Billy, you sound edgy. What's going on?"

"I spoke with Gwen last night. She sends her love."

"That's nice, dear." Paulette glanced at her watch. "How was her vacation?"

"Well, that's just the thing, Mother. She was supposed to come home a week ago. But she's still down there."

"Is she all right?" Paulette felt her heart rush. Already her mind was racing: she could leave immediately for the airport. She might be able to catch Tricia before she left Philadelphia. If not, she could leave a note at the Marshes'. Tricia would have to understand.

"She's fine," said Billy. "In fact, she sounded happy. Apparently she met somebody on the island." He paused, as if aware of the import of what he was about to say. "Mother, Gwen has a boyfriend."

The details, what few he knew, made no sense at all. They had met on a boat of some sort. They went scuba diving together. The young man's name was Rico.

Absurdly, Paulette thought of Guadelupe the housecleaner, the recent ordeal of writing the girl a check.

"Heavens," she said inanely. "I suppose she does speak Spanish."

Rico wasn't Spanish, Billy explained; he had some sort of French surname. He lived on the island, apparently. On St. Raphael.

Later, driving back from the market, she pondered what Billy had said. She tried to picture this Rico, with no success. She knew nothing, not the first thing, about the sort of people who lived on St. Raphael.

As always, when confronted with the unfamiliar, she consulted World Book.

She had bought the set long ago, early in her marriage, from a handsome salesman who rang the doorbell of their apartment in Cambridge. Frank had called the purchase extravagant, the books worthless, but all these years later Paulette still found them invaluable. True, they were thirty-five years old; but to Paulette this seemed a minor point. The parts of the world she cared about hadn't changed all that much.

ST. RAPHAEL One of the Leeward Islands of the eastern Caribbean. Discovered by the explorer Sir Francis Drake, it was first colonized by the British in 1693, and later taken under French control (1782–1790). The sugar trade was temporarily suspended in 1800 by a mass suicide of sugar-growing slaves. Sugar production ended finally in 1910 when the eruption of the volcano Montagne-Marie wiped out nearly all the plantations on the island's southern coast. Presently the principal economic activity is bauxite mining. Its capital is Pointe Mathilde.

Next to the entry were two postage-stamp-size photos. Palm trees laden with coconuts. A smiling brown-skinned man holding a bunch of bananas.

Paulette put down the book.

Heavens, she thought. Is this Rico black?

Like a traveler expecting a train, she waited for this thought to affect her, some additional rush of shock or distress. Curiously, the train didn't come. Her body was already on high alert—heart hammering, heat masking her face and throat and chest. Just now further alarm was impossible. The volume was turned as high as it would go.

And in fact, when she thought about it—once every twenty years or so—she considered black men handsome. She was thinking primarily of Harry Belafonte, and of that young man who reported the sports scores on the local news.

She returned to World Book.

ST. RAPHAEL AT A GLANCE

POPULATION: 72,500
CAPITAL: Pointe Mathilde
GOVERNMENT: Protectorate (United Kingdom)
LANGUAGE: English (official), French patois
RELIGION: Various
INDUSTRY: Agriculture (sugar, bananas), mining (bauxite)
MONETARY UNIT: Caribbean dollar

She laid down the book. She had rarely been disappointed by the World Book, but aside from the possibility that Rico might be black, this entry hadn't told her anything she needed to know. His blackness, or possible blackness, was like a disorderly room in a burning build-ing, hardly worth fretting about. There were more urgent questions she needed to have answered. Such as: Was this Rico a serious person? Did he have a profession, a stable way of making a living? Or was he a criminal, an opportunist who preyed on American tourists? Did he see in Gwen—tiny, vulnerable Gwen—an easy mark?

Had they had sexual relations? From movies and television she knew that this was an expected part of dating, that girls much younger than Gwen made love easily, casually, with young men they were not yet, and might never be, in love with; that the young men expected this, and that the whole arrangement was pleasing to all concerned. Contrary to what Frank had sometimes said, Paulette was not a prude. She had enjoyed the physical side of marriage, and missed it when it ended. (Missed it, to her surprise, a great deal.) On the surface, anyway, this new kind of dating seemed sensible, simpler, and more straightforward than the elaborate gavotte they'd danced in her day. At the same time, it struck her as unbalanced. Paulette believed, at her core, that women were different from men, that they risked a great deal in love and wanted things in return—devotion, fi-delity—that men did not always want to give them. While the things men wanted from women were simpler, and could be gotten nowa-days with almost no effort.

It seemed to her a very pleasant time to be a man, and a hazard-ous, unfairly difficult time to be a woman.

And Gwen was no ordinary woman. Life had taught Paulette hard lessons about how men loved, the meaningless, ephemeral attri-butes they found attractive. When she was young and beautiful, Frank had loved her. His faithlessness—in thought if not in deed—had co-incided with her own aging. Gil Pyle—she couldn't think of him without wincing—was no different: he had chosen beauty, as any man would. And Gwen—it was beastly to say it, disloyal and cruel, but Gwen was not beautiful. Could any man see past the surface to what was dear in her? It was tempting to believe that such men ex-isted. But Paulette did not, could not. Her own experience made faith impossible.

Did this Rico care for her daughter? Did he love her for herself, her odd, difficult, uniqueness? Or were there other, darker reasons for his interest in her?

PREGNANT WOMEN dreamed. Asleep, tossing fitfully, they gave birth to birds and flowers and fantastical creatures. Paulette remembered one dream in particular, in which she'd expelled a whiskered catfish with a mouthful of tiny teeth. She had dreamed vividly through all three pregnancies, but especially the second; she'd been most anxious, most unwell, while carrying Gwen. Then the baby was born a month premature—a serious business in those days—and she did not sleep for a week. Finally the scare passed; her baby girl emerged from the incubator. Gwen was fine, just fine.

Paulette believed this for a long time, right up until the moment Frank forced her to see otherwise. Then she was simply livid. It wasn't rational—she knew it even then—but she couldn't shake the feeling that Frank, with his tests and scientific journals, his relentless hunger for bad news when even their family doctor wasn't worried, had brought on Gwen's condition all by himself.

The tests done, Paulette stayed angry. What was the point of all this knowledge if the condition couldn't be treated? Frank had been adamant about starting growth hormone, but it was Paulette who'd taken Gwen for the injections, soothed her fears for days beforehand; Paulette who'd comforted her later when the shots had no effect.

At such moments Frank, as always, was in the lab.

Paulette was no scientist, only a mother. And as a mother she wondered what exactly they'd accomplished by assigning a label to their daughter. They'd made a small but healthy and happy child feel like a curiosity, a medical freak.

It was Frank who'd insisted on *classifying* Gwen. This struck Paulette as cruel, unforgivably so. And she would not be a party to it. Even to her own family she had dissembled: *Oh, she's fine, Daddy. Just small for her age.* To her parents, to Anne and Martine, she had lied without compunction. Knowing the cruelty of children, she'd made sure Billy and Scott kept quiet too. *Don't say anything to your cousins. It's nobody's business but ours.*

She wondered, later, if this had been the right impulse. Yes, she'd wanted to protect Gwen from any stigma; yes, she had the child's welfare at heart. But there was more to it, just as there was more to Turner's syndrome than simply being short. The other aspects of the condition—the sexual aspects—had mortified her. Was she to tell her father, her brother, that Gwen would never go through puberty? Nothing in her entire life had prepared her for such a conversation. In the Drew family, nobody went through puberty. Such matters were not discussed.

Mortally embarrassed, she had avoided the whole subject. The family could see for themselves what was happening to Gwen, or not happening. Cowardly, perhaps; but it had seemed to Paulette the best course. And even now, more than twenty years later, she couldn't say with certainty that she'd been wrong.

THAT EVENING she telephoned Billy, something she hadn't done in years; mindful of her long-distance bills, he insisted on phoning her himself. Annoyingly, Billy's recorded voice answered the phone. Paulette did not speak to recordings, on principle, but this time she made an exception. "Billy, this is your mother," she said, a bit self-consciously. "It is *critical*"—Frank's word; why had she used that word?—"that I speak with you. I need your help." She was surprised when, a moment later, her telephone rang.

"Darling," she told him, "I'm worried to death about your sister."

"Mom, take it easy."

"Take it *easy*? I'm surprised at you, Billy. You and Gwen have always been so close. Aren't you at all concerned?"

Billy hesitated. "Yeah, sure. But it's her life, Mom. There's nothing we can do about it."

"Of course there is! You could go down there and have a talk with her."

"I already talked to her on the phone, and she sounded fine. Anyway, I don't think she'd appreciate me rushing down there."

It took Paulette a moment to comprehend this. "You mean you won't go?"

"It's a terrible idea, Mom. Trust me on this."

"Billy, I don't know why you're being so stubborn! Your sister could be in danger."

"There's no reason to think that," Billy said calmly. "If this guy were a total creep, I'm sure Gwen wouldn't get involved with him."

"But how would she *know*, Billy? Your sister is very inexperienced."

"Is she?"

"Well, of course!" Did he know something she didn't? "Why? You don't think so?"

Billy sighed. "I really have no idea, Mom. Gwen never talks about that stuff."

Paulette tried a different tack. "Well, we don't know the first thing about this young man. Doesn't that bother you?"

"A little," he admitted. "Maybe you should talk to her yourself. The next time I hear from her, I'll tell her to give you a call."

"Darling, don't be silly. You know she never listens to a word I say."

Billy did not disagree with this.

"Mom, I'd leave it alone if I were you. She's thirty-four years old. She's entitled to make her own mistakes. And maybe—" He broke off.

"Maybe what?" she said, utterly perplexed. She'd always been able to count on Billy. It was inconceivable that he'd refuse to help.

"It's a weird situation, I know. But maybe he makes her happy."

Happy.

Long after she'd hung up the phone, Paulette tasted this word. She had always wished for Gwen to meet someone—an anthropologist perhaps, or an archaeologist. (They weren't the same thing, though Paulette couldn't recall what the difference was.) He and Gwen would fall in love. It would be clear at a glance what had drawn them together (their common love of anthropology, or archaeology). The young man's motives could be trusted because they would make *sense*. Gwen would marry and adopt children or, like many women these days, live contentedly without. With each passing year, this scenario seemed increasingly unlikely; but Paulette continued to hope.

Yet now a young man *had* appeared, and she was filled with dread. Her daughter was in love, possibly for the first time. Paulette had learned long ago—and had been reminded again recently—that there was no more vulnerable state. A woman in love would part with anything. Comfort, security, dignity; her own plans for the future. And when love raced off to Providence in the new truck she'd bought him, she would stand at the curb waving good-bye.

Frank climbed the stairs to an outdoor platform in the far end of Brookline, along a sleepy spur of the Green Line. He had left his Saab at the dealership; he would catch the inbound train to Park Street, where he would change trains to Kendall Square. The whole business would eat up most of his morning. He glanced at his watch. The Green Line trains were notoriously slow, and today he had no time to waste.

Back at the lab his docket was full. A presentation this afternoon, the Genetics in Medicine lecture series at Harvard. Afterward he'd drive straight to the airport. He was scheduled to speak early the next morning at Stanford. With publication looming, his life had grown hectic. Cristina had submitted just after New Year's, and the enthusiasm at *Science* was palpable: almost immediately, the paper went out for review. The reviewers, whoever they were (Frank had his theories), made a few minor suggestions, and Cristina had done the revisions in record time. In a mere three weeks, the paper would be in print—the fastest publication of Frank's career. Waiting was a kind of sweet torture, not unlike the first weeks of courtship, the runway leading up to sex. Daily, hourly, he thought of the apoptosis labs at Baylor and Chicago, the lingering danger of being scooped. With the paper in print, his lab would have a clear title to Cristina's findings. There would be more speaking engagements, interviews with the press. For the first time in ten years—since the heady days of XNR—Frank McKotch would have the world's ear.

And then.

In just a month the Academy would announce this year's nominees. Frank had been hopeful in the past, but this year he was dead certain. His moment had arrived.

Until then, he was cagey. The trick was to talk about the research, to generate excitement, without giving away too much. *I'm like a tired old stripper,* he grumbled happily to Margit. *Take off the gloves, the stockings. Keep the pasties on.* He'd prepared two versions of the same spiel: a quick forty minutes for Harvard, a longer, more detailed (but still oblique) talk for the meeting at Stanford. Frank was a natural public speaker, relaxed and confident; but he knew better than to show up underprepared. He'd planned to spend this crucial morning reviewing his notes. Instead he'd squandered it on errands. The Saab's inspection sticker would expire while he was in California, leading to even more headaches when he returned. His colleagues had wives to look after such details: the unending, time-consuming maintenance, the hidden costs of owning a car, a house, a body. That fall he'd caught a cold that developed into bronchitis; hacking and aching, he'd driven himself to the emergency room. At such moments he felt deeply his aloneness. In these ways and others, life was more complicated for a man on his own.

He glanced around. A small crowd had gathered under the shelter. A cold rain beat its Plexiglass roof. In the distance was a well-funded public high school, new and gleaming, overlooking athletic fields. It was the kind of school Frank's children might have attended if Paulette had not insisted on Pearse, where *all the Drew men* were bound to go. That Billy and Scott were not Drew men but McKotch men was a point he never bothered to articulate. His surname was a joke, an alias, a sore reminder of his father's disgrace. If anything, it was the brand of failure. Certainly it had never done a thing for Frank.

He stared out at the football field, unchalked, useless, a soggy, undifferentiated expanse of dying brown. The snow had melted; rainwater pooled in the end zones, reflecting the dull gray sky. Melancholy came upon him in a wave. For most of his life he'd evaded it with sprints and deft pivots, like the gifted quarterback he'd once been. Now, with old age looming, his fancy moves had abandoned him.

He'd believed, always, that success was the cure, that a major find in the lab would melt his despair. And now, after ten years of frustration, he had a major publication in *Science*. In a month the Academy would announce its new members, an honor that again seemed within reach. So why did he feel exhausted and hopeless? His appetite was off, his sex drive nonexistent. When the alarm rang at five each morning, he could scarcely drag himself out of bed.

A train approached, horn sounding, the airy chuff of brakes. Frank stepped aboard and grabbed a strap. The train was crowded, the last wave of the morning commute. He studied the passengers with interest. They wore hip, casual clothes, carried laptop computers or backpacks. Most were middle aged, or nearly so, yet dressed like students. Fully half were female. Frank wondered what sort of work they did.

He'd have expected a different crowd this far out in Brookline, which was almost the suburbs: young married men, a few yarmulkes maybe, everyone in business attire. Years ago this would have been the case. But times had changed: people were more reflective, now, about what was called *settling down*. Frank himself had settled down at twenty-four, willingly, cheerfully, with no thought to how much settling was actually involved. In those days only misfits stayed single past thirty, mamas' boys and sad sacks who couldn't get themselves a girl. He'd been a young husband and father when the world began to change. He had scoffed at the hippies, with their beards and ponytails; but all these years later, he could see the appeal of bumming around California or Europe, taking earth's pleasures like healthy young animals, innocent and vital and strong. If he'd been born just a few years later, Frank McKotch might have joined them. Instead he had married, studied, sweated away his best years in the bright lights of the laboratory. Now he was aging rapidly, shuffling toward sixty. And he was still in the lab.

He was thinking such thoughts when the train slowed at a crossing. He glanced out the window and saw a girl riding a bicycle, wearing a long black skirt. The bike was battered and heavy, an old-fashioned model with a low-slung crossbar, a *woman's frame*. As a youngster he'd found such bikes confounding. A boy, after all, carried the pendulous genitals, the fragile packet prone to accidental blows, the mildest of which could drop him like timber. It seemed wrong that Frank was expected to straddle the crossbar, while girls—their nether parts so well hidden that studying them would become his life's work—got the special low-slung frame.

He'd begun his life's work on a girl who rode just such a bike, a farm girl named Elizabeth Wilmer. Her father owned three hundred acres on the other side of the forest, where coal country gave way to dairy land. Unlike the miners, who were mostly Catholic, the farmers were German Protestants. Every Wednesday and Sunday, the Wilmers walked to services in the next town, at a small white frame church called Living Waters. The denomination—considered extreme even in God-crazy Pennsylvania—demanded tithes and summer Bible camp and full-immersion baptisms, plus austere dress for women and girls. Lizzy Wilmer's dresses buttoned to her chin and hung to midcalf; her lank dark hair lay flat as a bedsheet down her back. Yet despite her prim appearance, Lizzy could hit a ball farther than Blaise Klezek. Frank would never forget the sight of her running the bases, hair and long skirts flying, as though she might go airborne. He and Blaise and Lizzy played ball all spring and summer. In the winter they rode sleds and built tunnels in the snow, Lizzy in long skirts always, her bare legs pink with cold.

One winter day Lizzy had crept up behind Frank in the woods, as he stood at a tree to urinate. He was eleven then, Lizzy twelve. *Can I watch?* she asked, shocking him. No girl had seen that part of him before. *Write your name*, she whispered, hands at his waist, and he did, or started to. The F and r were nearly legible, the hot piss melting the crusty snow.

I ran out, he said, embarrassed, but Lizzy only laughed.

Watch this, she said.

He gaped in amazement as she tugged beneath her skirt and dropped her white underpants to the ground. She stepped out of them and raised her skirt to her waist, then crouched slightly, her legs parted. Her face was clenched in concentration, the tip of her tongue caught between her teeth.

She drew the letters large and wide, crab-walking to make the

base of the L, stopping the stream expertly to make a fresh start with
the I. She paused a moment before beginning the last letter—laughing, her hips swiveling, ending with an exuberant whoop, like the
finale of a burlesque act. The Z was soft and rounded, as Lizzy herself
was not yet. Not that Frank could see her, really, with all the fabric she
held bundled about her hips. That came months later, on the muddy
spring ground, not far from the spot where Lizzy had pissed.

She was an old woman now with a dozen grandchildren. Jesus,
how life worked.

Years had passed, and there was no rewinding them. Frank would
never be young again. He had never cared about money; he'd always
known that time was the only wealth that mattered. He'd spent all his
on a single purchase: his career as scientist. It was the only thing he'd
ever truly wanted. Foolish, foolish, this creeping regret.

BRISKLY HE jogged up the stairs to his office. Betsy Baird looked
up from her desk.

"You're my watchdog," he told her. "I need half an hour to review my notes. Make sure I'm not disturbed."

"Frank, just to let you know—"

"I'm serious, Betsy. Half an hour. And don't worry about lunch.
I'll grab something at Harvard."

He charged down the hallway to his office and stopped short. In
the chair opposite his desk sat his ex-wife, Paulette.

"*There* you are," she said irritably. "I've been sitting here half the
morning. Frank, have you been *running*?"

"No, no." He paused to catch his breath. "What are you doing
here?"

She eyed him balefully. "I've been trying to reach you for days.
Truly, I don't see the point of these machines if you never listen to the
messages."

He blinked, flustered. She wore a slim skirt. He eyed her shapely
legs, crossed at the knee. He closed the door.

"This is a surprise," he said, slipping behind his desk. "Is everything okay?" He noticed, then, the high color in her cheeks. Her right foot, in its high-heeled pump, quivered rhythmically, as though itching to kick him. "You're upset."

"*Upset?* Yes, Frank, I am extremely upset. Have you heard from Gwen?"

"Gwen?" He blinked. "Why, no, not since Christmas. I thought she was on vacation."

"She was." Paulette paused. "As a matter of fact, she's *still* on vacation. I'm not sure when, or if, she's coming back."

He listened in amazement as she told him the story.

"Wow," he said finally.

"Wow?" Paulette looked at him as though he'd belched or farted. "That's all you've got to say? *Wow?*"

"What were you hoping for?" Family crisis notwithstanding, he was due at Harvard in twenty-five minutes, and hadn't so much as glanced at his notes. Paulette had never been any good at getting to the point.

"What I'd *like* is for you to get involved, for once. Gwen has always respected your judgment. Heavens, it's been fifteen years since she's listened to anything *I* had to say."

"Well, I suppose I could call her," he said.

"*Call her?* I'm afraid that's not going to do it. Somebody needs to go down there and meet this young man. Find out what sort of person he is."

"Go down there? *Now?*" He stared at her in disbelief. "Look, I know you're concerned, but frankly you couldn't have picked a worse time. We have a major paper coming out in a few weeks, and that means—" He glanced surreptitiously at the clock. "Now, for instance. I'm due at Harvard in twenty minutes. I have a talk to give, and then a plane to catch."

"You're saying no."

"I'm saying I can't. There's no way I can leave."

She sighed wearily. "I should have expected this."

"Paulette, I'm sorry," he said, reaching under his desk for his briefcase. "I wouldn't do this if it weren't extremely important. But I really do have to go."

chapter 6

What he'd lacked his whole life—Scott understood this now—was a mission.

He'd been slow to grasp this truth, despite the fact that everybody who'd ever known him—parents, girlfriends, teachers at Pilgrims and Pearse and Stirling—had pointed it out. Even Penny, who'd drifted through life waitressing and running cash registers, who'd let him keen for years the miseries of teaching *Great Expectations* to subliterate sophomores, had recently interrupted him: *Fine, Scotty. But what do you want to do?*

For his thirtieth birthday she had given him, without irony, a book called *What Color Is Your Parachute?*

At Concord High, where he'd touched down briefly after being booted out of Pearse, he'd spent a morning filling in hundreds of tiny ovals with a number 2 pencil, affirming that he preferred skiing to basketball, bowling to crosswords, rock and roll to jazz or folk. Based on such answers, a computer in Madison, Wisconsin, concluded that he'd make a fine soldier, fireman, or manufacturing floor supervisor.

He did not share these insights with his parents.

Only now, sitting in the first-class cabin of a Boeing 747 heading southward, did he experience the exhilaration that came from having a true mission. He was a man transformed. He drained his champagne glass, wolfed down the complimentary Brie and strawberries. His mother had paid for a seat in coach, but a flirty gate agent had upgraded him with a sly smile. Such a thing had never happened to him before, and Scott took it as a harbinger of good fortune to come.

He sat staring out the window, his hand folded inside *Great Expectations,* which he'd recently assigned to his juniors. Scott hadn't yet read the final two chapters; but he understood, now, that this wasn't due to laziness; he was hampered by a medical condition. He put Dickens aside and took a flashy paperback from his rucksack. It was *Man of Action,* by Dashiell Blodgett, a brash Australian who'd climbed Everest and K2 (where he'd lost a toe to frostbite) and now stalked, with his camera, the most dangerous big game in the world, in a wildly popular cable television program aired around the globe. *Man of Action* was a narrative of Blodgett's adventures—ice climbing and cave diving, traveling the perimeter of Africa by motorcycle. Really, though, it was a meditation on man's true nature, his need for risk and conquest. *Today's man,* Blodgett wrote, *lives in a state of full-body impotence. He's been castrated by comfort. The softness of modern life has ruined him.*

Hear, hear, Scott thought.

Blodgett had cowritten the book with his wife, Pepper, a stunning blonde who accompanied him on his adventures. A photo of the two occupied the entire back cover. In it Blodgett squatted in some rugged rocky landscape, holding open the jaws of a crocodile, his sleeves rolled back to expose his beefy forearms. Pepper leaned over him, grasping his shoulders, her breasts crushed against his back, her long blond hair brushing his neck. Blodgett grinned triumphantly, the very picture of masculine conquest.

Scott had bought the book a week before, on a Saturday afternoon, shortly after receiving his orders. That morning he had borrowed Penny's van—the Golf was ailing—and set off at first light, his nerves twinkling with adrenaline and exhaustion. He'd been up late with Penny discussing strategy. *Just be direct,* Penny had advised. *She's his grandmother, for Christ's sake. It can't hurt to ask.*

He thought, It sure as shit can.

He thought, Sister, you have no idea.

Cowed, craven, he had hoped to make the mortifying request by phone. *Mom, you've always been so concerned with the kids' education* (she had, after all, given them books for Christmas). *And Fairhope is a wonderful school. I knew you'd want to help.*

He held the words ready in his mouth—like some hated food, liver or Brussels sprouts, turning to an acrid poo on his tongue. But his mother had cut him off. She was glad he'd called; there was a matter they needed to discuss. Could he come to Concord that Saturday? *We'll have a chat,* she said. *Just the two of us.*

He'd rolled into Horsham Road at eight in the morning and sat in the familiar kitchen, eating a plate of eggs Benedict. The kitchen, its sounds and smells, brought back memories long forgotten, the summers home from Pearse, when he dragged his lazy teenage carcass out of bed each morning to find his favorite breakfast in the works. His father and Billy were gone by then, and it was Paulette who'd greeted him at the train station like a returning hero and cooked his favorite dinner, prime rib and Yorkshire pudding, to welcome him home. She'd asked a hundred questions about his friends and classes and listened in rapt attention to the lies he told. She'd had hopes for him then. Her confidence was a burden, not heavy but unwieldy, like a huge empty box he'd have to carry until he could fill it. All these years later, the box teemed with failures, regrets heavy as hammers. He was staggering under its weight.

He ate slowly, savoring the breakfast, dreading the conversation that would follow. Finally Paulette took his empty plate, and he could hang fire no longer. *You always taught us the value of education,* he began, consciously including his siblings; Billy, especially, was a saint you could invoke when praying for favors. *And now there's a situation with Ian—*

She raised a hand as if to stop him. The gesture was startling. His mother never talked with her hands.

The boy needs help; I can see that. Simple as weather, an obvious fact. *But first things first, dear. Your sister is in serious trouble.*

It took him a moment to understand. His whole life his mother had buried him in blessings, done for him until he was, truly, done for. Now, for the first time, she needed something from him.

Not from his father, or Billy. From him.

The notion staggered him. The men of his family were titans, endowed with vital powers. His father the wizard, an alchemist curing cancer; Billy the gentleman scholar, effortlessly superior with his movie-star smile. What was left for Scott to be? His father was a genius. His brother was a prince.

In his mother's kitchen it all came clear.

Like a dream he recalled an earlier, more hopeful vision of himself. When he squealed out of Stirling College in that Pontiac Sunbird he'd imagined himself a rebel and a wanderer, rugged and fearless, living by his wits. He had longed to travel, to see the rough parts of the world. But along the way he faltered. His early life had been too easeful. He couldn't—could anybody?—claw his way out of snug Concord. Then he thought of Warren Marsh, who'd grown up next door, graduated Williams and joined the Peace Corps, the path he himself should have taken.

Another missed opportunity. Toss it, if you can lift it, into the box of regrets.

So like Columbus dispatched by the queen of Spain, he received his commission, and drove back to Gatwick with a check in his pocket: twenty thousand dollars, the otherworldly cost of fourth-grade tuition at Fairhope. In return he would do what was asked of him, and go down in his family's history as the bold savior of his sister. Even his father would have to be impressed.

No problem, Scott told Paulette. *Don't worry, Mom. I'll take care of it.* He was overcome with gratitude, humbled by her faith

He settled into his first-class seat. The plane was packed with students in Trinity and Wesleyan sweatshirts. A few of the boys seemed drunk already, red faced and jubilant, cranked up for a week of joyful parent-financed depravity in Lauderdale or Daytona. In their dumb happiness they reminded Scott of dogs, panting with the confidence that came from never having failed at anything. Gratefully he watched the girls, their glossed lips, their thighs in snug blue jeans, glad they drew breath in the world. Years of teaching high school had inoculated him, mostly, against the charms of the young, though he backslid briefly each September when he cast his prettiest students in riotous

daydreams. These fantasies lasted a few days, a week at the outside; and
ended as soon he heard the girls speak.

He understood, now, that only one woman could move him, a
woman halfway around the world, who'd dispensed with the miseries
of Kosovo and was now braving the war-torn deserts of the Sudan.
Last week, galvanized by his upcoming adventure, he'd typed out a
brisk message on his office computer. Then, with a single click of the
mouse, he'd inserted himself boldly into the universe of Jane Frayne.

He had received an automatic response: Jane was traveling in the
Sudan and unreachable by e-mail. She would return to New York in
April or May or June, and would respond to messages then.

Fair enough, Scott thought.

AT THE airport in Pointe Mathilde, he took a taxi to the Mistral Inn,
where his mother's travel agent had booked him a room. Scott would
have preferred to find his own lodgings, in the pleasingly random
manner he and Penny had employed years ago, bedding down in the
upper rooms of back-street cantinas, on the porches of near strangers,
in sleeping bags by the side of the road. But the inn was small and
charming, on a side street behind the Place de la Capitale; and he had
no time to scrounge around looking for a hotel.

The proprietor's daughter, a shy black girl his daughter's age, led
Scott to a sunny upstairs room where a warm breeze riffled the lace
curtains. The high bed looked plump and inviting. He kicked off his
shoes and stretched out. The room overlooked a rear courtyard, lushly
planted with flowering bushes and lemon trees. Those, at least, Scott
could identify; they'd bloomed all over his old neighborhood in San
Bernardino, in every yard except his own. NO LAWN MAINTE-
NANCE, they'd been promised by the ad in the *Sun*; and this turned
out to be true: the square lot, enclosed by a chain-link fence, had
been paved over with concrete. In the front yard two trees had been
spared. The squat palms were long dead, teeming with roaches; but the
landlord, a dark, wizened man named Guzman, refused to cut them
down.

Scott still dreamed feverishly of that house, the pea-colored carpeting, the tiny windows barricaded with air conditioners that periodically overloaded the third-world electrical wiring. The first time it happened, Guzman showed up to shake his head in disapproval, a cigarette hanging out of his mouth. When Penny explained the problem in Spanish, Guzman continued to disapprove, shaking his speckled bald head.

Thinking of this, Scott remembered he had a wife back in Connecticut. He picked up the bedside phone and dialed his own number; he had promised her a call. If the situation were reversed—his wife spending spring break on an island, himself stuck at home with the kids—he would have been torqued; but Penny had been excited for him. *Scotty, an adventure!* she'd said, the reckless girl who'd loved camping in the desert, climbing in the Sierra, diving the depths of Crater Lake, her naked body bathed in starlight. He had taken her from those wild places and locked her in a tract house in the suburbs.

The line was busy; he hung up the phone and unpacked his rucksack, a relic of earlier travels. Inside was a manila envelope, a stack of quizzes he would not grade. He tossed his few possessions—extra shirt, socks, and underwear—into bureau drawers. From a side pocket he took his razor and toothbrush. Then he felt a strange lump at the bottom of the bag. Recognition lit inside him, the briefest flicker. He unzipped an inside pocket and felt around inside it, for the tiny hole his younger self had cut. He withdrew a tiny Saran-wrapped package and a narrow wooden cylinder the size of a shell casing. It was his old friend, Smoky Joe.

He'd bought the pipe a lifetime ago, at a head shop in La Jolla. The hollow tip was sized to hold a single, tightly packed hit of weed. He'd found it useful in emergencies: stuck in freeway traffic, or on breaks at the cavernous publisher's warehouse where he'd once worked, loading bundles of magazines onto pallets that were to be moved, for no apparent reason, to another part of the building. Mostly, though, he'd used the pipe for skimming. Stealing. From the person who loved him most.

At the beginning, he and Penny had split their pot evenly. For a time the arrangement worked seamlessly. They smoked only when they were together—they were nearly always together—and their appetites were perfectly matched. Later, when they were both working, they'd smoke a bowl on the terrace after dinner; but while Penny would be satisfied for the rest of the evening, an hour later Scott was ready for more. One night he moved to roll himself something extra, a dessert joint, remembering how his mother used to fill the dinner plates: heaping portions for his brawny father, more delicate ones for herself.

Baby, I'm not ready, Penny protested.

I know, said Scott, *but I am.*

Thus began the Dope Wars of 1987, a period of internal conflict that tested the newly formed alliance of Scott and Penny and tore it nearly asunder. For a magical spring and summer, they had pooled their resources: Scott's leftover tuition money, the proceeds from selling Penny's VW bus, which got eight miles to the gallon and broke down twice as often as Scott's Sunbird. Paychecks from the surf shop, the warehouse, various convenience stores; Penny's share of tip jars at lunch counters and snack bars and coffee shops. Who earned what was never clear, and didn't matter. Rent was paid, gas and food bought. Whatever remained, they spent on pot. Penny had lived this way for years, with a discipline Scott admired. Without it he'd have piddled away his paycheck on beer and cigarettes and barroom pool, pleasant nonessentials he scarcely missed. Under Penny's system they could get high every day, twice a day. And for a long time that was enough.

He'd heard for years that weed was nonaddictive, and he'd found this to be true. He could live without the high. But what he needed, truly *needed*, was the looseness pot afforded, the relaxed improv, the shuffle and dance. Smoking, he could glide through life's humiliating scut work, the night foreman's insults, the flat-out exhausted dread he felt at the end of the day and sometimes at the beginning, when he contemplated the endless bouncing bus ride—Penny was delivering pizzas and needed the Sunbird—the numberless mountains of pallets to be loaded, the mindless grind of machinery, the bundled magazines that came and came. He remembered with a creeping bitterness his

Kap Sig buddies at Stirling, those dullards; the whole priceless bags they'd smoked away for dim-witted amusement, the obscene giggling pleasure of staring at Cheech and Chong movies and falling asleep on the floor. For Scott weed was no longer a diversion, but a necessity, the only thing that made work tolerable. And if, at the end of a back-breaking, soul-killing shift, he needed a few more tokes than his girlfriend did, why should he deny himself?

He would remember the fight forever, their first and ugliest. Eleven contentious years later, he couldn't recall a more savage bloodletting, a more searing wound.

I'm bigger than you are, he began. *Half a joint knocks you out, but I can barely feel it.*

To which she had responded: *You're bigger than you used to be.*

It was a surprise blow, stunning in its cruelty. He had fattened on meatball subs and fast food, cheap workingman's lunches. His face was round and puffy, a moony Elvis in his declining days.

You're smaller, he shot back, which was also true. *I can't find your tits in the dark.*

The rest of the fight was too painful to remember, though its denouement—him sleeping on the wet grass after she'd locked him out of the house—would stay with him forever. They were twenty years old, new to love's expansions and contractions, its fissures and failures. How it could leave you broke and busted on the neighbor's lawn, weeping and seeing stars.

HE RETURNED Smoky Joe to the rucksack and headed out into the broad sunshine, toward the Place de la Capitale—far, far away from Gatwick, where an onion snow was falling on his mean little house. The Place was triangle shaped, like a New England town green; it was fronted on one side by the white stucco capitol building with its arched porticoes. Standing there, the sun warm through his shirt, Scott felt thawed back to life.

He crossed the square in the direction the innkeeper had pointed, heading, he hoped, toward the beach. The air was redolent of diesel.

A dearth of stoplights kept traffic at a standstill; taxicabs idled at intersections, clogging the winding streets. A slow parade wound through the sidewalks, tourists complaining of new-shoe blisters. Scott stared at the damp armpits of their bright new cruise wear, the shopping bags brushing their winter-white thighs. He stepped around the pedestrians, mumbling to himself. The complexity of his mission overwhelmed him. He had come to this crowded island looking for a girl, a small, silent girl who did not attract attention, who moved invisibly through crowds. A very stubborn girl who, in all likelihood, did not wish to be found. His mother had provided scant details: a guy named Rico, something about scuba diving. Other information that might have been useful—the name of Gwen's hotel, for example—Paulette simply didn't have. *Ask Billy*, she said, but pride had prevented him from doing this. The mission was Scott's, not his brother's. He would figure it out himself.

The road curved sharply. On the horizon Marengo Bay appeared, gleaming silver. Scott blinked. For a moment an office building seemed perched upon it—gleaming white, larger than the capitol building.

"What's that?" Scott asked the woman ahead of him, a sturdy grandmother in pink slacks. Though portly, she was surprisingly quick. It was like chasing a car in first gear.

"That's our ship," she said proudly, as though she'd had a hand in building it. "The Star of the North."

Now the road sloped sharply downward, as though collecting this human runoff into a giant basin. The crowd flowed faster, flat feet smacking the pavement. In a final grab for tourist dollars, the street signage became more insistent. CLEARANCE! NO DUTY! CHEAP, CHEAP, CHEAP! American flags slapped the blue sky. Scott looked around, a little frantically. He felt as though he were running with the bulls at Pamplona, slow geriatric bulls with aching hooves. Still, stopping seemed dangerous. The woman behind him had already stepped twice on his sandal.

"Hey, mister," said a voice at his elbow, a black boy of about twelve. "What you looking for?"

"The beach," said Scott.

"These people, they going to the ship. You come this way."

The boy headed down a narrow side street. Scott, hand on his wallet, followed behind. He was alert to scams, having fallen for most of them in Mexico years ago. But this boy was well dressed; he had not pulled at Scott's sleeve, or seemed insistent. Even now, he didn't look back or slow his pace. He seemed not to care whether Scott followed or not.

They passed fortune-tellers, a couple of barbecue joints. The air smelled of roasting meat. Scott felt his stomach squeeze. The airline Brie sat inside it like a lump of chewing gum, dense and indigestible. He would have to eat something, and soon.

He followed the boy down another block. The street grew narrower, the faces blacker. On one corner was a small café, three tables on a rickety porch, the sort of plastic chairs sold in American drugstores for five bucks apiece. Neon signs glowed in the windows: CORONA, CARIB, RED STRIPE. From the rafters hung a homemade banner, the clumsy block letters of a dot matrix printer. Scott squinted to make out the words: AMBROSIA CAFÉ.

Across from the café the boy stopped, stepped backward into a doorway. He produced a plastic bag from his pocket.

Scott blinked. Was the word *STONER* tattooed across his forehead? Was it so easy to pick him out of a crowd? "No thanks," he said, glancing over his shoulder.

"You sure? It come by boat from Jamaica. Top stuff." The kid offered the bag. "Here. Smell."

Scott leaned forward. Somewhere deep in his memory this thought lurked: *They can't arrest me until I touch the bag.* Was this still true? Had it ever been? He didn't know.

The pot smelled incredible, moist and skunky. "Nice, right?" the boy asked.

He named a price that was good, but not too good, slightly more than Scott had paid in Mexico seven years ago. Quickly he calculated. The boy seemed calm and relaxed; the few drinkers at the café paid them no mind. This door frame, Scott realized, was the boy's storefront, like a lemonade stand overlooking the street.

"Smells great," he admitted. "But I can't today. I'm working."

"You come back later," the boy said coolly, looking away, as if showing even this little enthusiasm had compromised him.

"Maybe," Scott said.

He walked on. On the other side of the street he noted two boys in wet swim trunks. *Beach*, he thought. *They're coming from the beach.*

He quickened his pace, still thinking of the pot, green as lawn parings. He tried to recall another time he'd been offered weed of this quality—of any quality—and refused it.

There had never been such a time.

The beach was the most crowded he'd ever seen, a strip of sand no wider than a suburban driveway. A checkerboard of colorful towels lay across it. Scott glanced in both directions. He was the only white man on the beach.

He picked a direction and set off walking. Reggae poured out of an enormous boom box, the kind he'd owned at Pearse fifteen years ago. A leaning plywood stand sold pork sandwiches and Red Stripe. A hundred children, by his estimate, squealed in the surf.

He stepped up to the sandwich stand and bought a Red Stripe. "I'm looking for a guy named Rico," he told the man who made his change. "He takes people scuba diving."

The man looked at him like he'd lost his mind.

"You lost, man. There's no scuba from this beach."

"Well, where do people go scuba diving?"

He pointed to the direction Scott had come from, the cattle chute leading to the cruise terminal. "Look for the red flag, man. Dem can take you scuba diving."

"I don't want to *go* diving," Scott explained. "I'm looking for a dive operator. One guy in particular. His name is Rico."

"Rico," the man repeated. He broke into a wide grin, shaking his head in disbelief. "You looking for a guy named Rico."

Scott nodded, taking a long pull on his beer.

"My name is Rico," the man said, laughing. "My little boy named Rico. On this beach I can find you twenty Ricos. You can talk to all of them."

A horn sounded in the distance, so loud Scott's molars throbbed. "Your Rico," the man shouted. "He a black guy or a white guy?"

"I don't know," Scott shouted back.

He retraced his steps along the narrow side road, stopping to buy a tourist map of the island. At the Ambrosia Café he bought a second Red Stripe and sat at a table on the porch—aware, in a deeper, more honest part of his brain, that he was waiting for the boy to return, the proud little businessman with his fragrant bag of weed.

Waiting, he unfolded the map and stared at it, trying to get his bearings. He'd never been any good with maps. The island was larger than he'd imagined, and he was on the wrong side of it. Most of the beaches, according to his map, were on the north side.

"Excuse me," he said to the man who swiped a damp rag across his table. "Do you know where I can rent a car?"

"At the airport, man." He was Scott's age and very black, his head wrapped in a colorful scarf. "But it gonna be close now. Saturday night, you know? That type of business, it close at five."

This was news to Scott, but the man said it with such assurance that there was no doubt.

"I can take you to the airport Monday," the man said, seeing his angle. "My brother has a car."

"Not tomorrow?" said Scott.

The man shook his head. "Sunday. Everything close."

Scott thought, *This is not possible.* "Well, I need to get to the north side of the island tomorrow."

"Take a taxi," the man suggested.

"I guess," said Scott. "But I'll need the car for a while. Maybe all day."

The man pondered. "You come back here in the morning. Nine o'clock. My brother be back from church then. He can take you for a ride."

BACK IN his room Scott felt fretful, restless. He had waited at the café for two hours, but the boy hadn't returned. Dejected, he stretched out on the bed and dialed his brother's number. A strange male voice answered the phone.

"Um, sorry," said Scott. "I think I have a wrong number. I'm trying to reach Bill McKotch."

"Billy's out for a run." The voice was soft and cultivated, with a British accent. "May I tell him who called?"

Scott felt strongly that only women should have British accents.

"This is his brother. Can you leave him a message, please? It's kind of urgent." He paused. "I need to know the name of our sister's hotel in St. Raphael."

"Gwen's hotel? She isn't staying there any longer."

It was an annoying voice, Scott decided, effete and snotty. *Who the fuck are you?* Scott thought. *And why do you know my sister's name?*

"Just give him the message, okay?"

"Fine," said the Brit, and hung up the phone.

What did they call them over there? Wankers? Peckers? *Asshole,* Scott thought—though whether he meant the Brit, his brother, or himself was impossible to say.

He took his rucksack from under the bed and reached inside the lining. The packet contained a single cannabis bud, slightly grayish but otherwise perfect. Scott sniffed it intently, recalling the mossy smell of the boy's brilliant green contraband. His own elderly stash had no smell whatsoever, but it was all he had.

Later—stoned, sunburned, too exhausted to shower, he stripped naked and crawled into bed. He was a thousand miles from home, and he missed his wife.

It was the first time in ten years he'd spent a night without her. Last time he'd crept out of bed at dawn, careful not to wake her. He took an early flight from Los Angeles to Logan where, recalling those school vacations, his mother had met him in the old Volvo. But this was no joyous homecoming. He had called Paulette late one night, drunk and high and desperate. He hadn't spoken to his mother in two years. Still she wired him the money for a ticket.

He landed in Boston in the middle of a snowstorm, sober and shivering; he'd sold all his winter clothes. Paulette met him at the gate, looking old and tired. He could see at a glance the pain he had caused her. It was in the fierce way she clasped him, her hungry eyes examining his face.

I'm sorry, he thought.

It was nearly the only thought he would have that weekend. Paulette took him home to Concord, where he showered and ate, then slept for two days straight. Finally he sat at the kitchen table and told his mother everything.

Oh, not everything. He omitted some loose nights, some scrapes and misfires, a dope squabble involving an ex-con named Duane Farley, ending when Scott pinned the guy to the ground and held Farley's own knife to the guy's throat. He did not mention the four joints discovered in his rucksack at the Mexican border, disaster averted when Penny disappeared with the border agent for ten minutes and came back smiling. *You're a free man*, she said.

Apart from these events, and others like them, he told his mother everything. He finished with words that would haunt him forever. *I want to come home.*

He met her eyes then, which were brimming with a feeling he couldn't name.

When is the child due? she asked.

Six weeks, he said.

He had asked permission to leave his wife and child—not yet a wife, not yet a child, but alarmingly close on both counts. His mother had listened, wearing a look very like sickness. Then silently shook her head.

No.

"Hi, Pen," he told the machine.

He had burrowed into the mound of pillows, hugging one—a hard frilly cylinder the size of a football—to his chest.

"I tried you before but the line was busy. I'm here on the island and wow, it's gorgeous. But then this massive cruise ship—you wouldn't believe the size of it—"

He was surprised when the beep came. Had he already used up the tape?

"Hi," his wife said. "Did you find Gwen?"

"Baby!" Joy flooded him. "I can't believe you're there! Why didn't you pick up?"

"I was in the bathtub." She sounded distracted, a little breathless. "I had to run for the phone."

"Oh, wow." He paused a moment to contemplate this, Penny naked in the living room, the moist flesh of her belly, the droop and swing of her now-generous breasts.

"I love your tits," he swore, his voice breaking with grief at the way he'd once insulted them. He was nearly sick with remorse.

"What's the matter with you? Scotty, are you high?"

Well, that was marriage. Through a staticky connection, over a thousand miles, she could hear cannabis in his voice. She had seen him stoned hundreds of times. For years she'd scarcely seen him another way.

"A little," he admitted. "Pen, I found something in my rucksack. Remember Smoky Joe?"

"Oh, Jesus. Hang on a minute." To his surprise the line went silent. Their new cordless phone came equipped with a HOLD button. Penny used it when her sister called late at night on a manic rant, oblivious to the time difference. She had never used the HOLD button on him.

For no reason, he remembered that she was still naked.

"Sorry," she said when she returned. "This place is a pigsty. I can't find anything. Your brother called awhile ago. He left a message." There was a sourness in her voice that made her sound older, much older, than the naked girl in his head.

"Billy," he said. "Yeah, I called him. Some snotty British guy answered the phone."

"'Gwen's hotel was Pleasures,'" Penny read.

"Excellent!" said Scott. "Did he say anything else?"

"I didn't talk to him. Sabrina answered."

"Pleasures," Scott repeated. "Okay, good. Hey, I'm sorry I smoked. I love you, Pen."

"Me too," she said—to which part, he wasn't sure. "Listen, I have to run. Let's hope Ruxton doesn't make you piss in a jar."

"Where are you going?" He glanced at the bedside clock. It was nine thirty on a Saturday evening. Where could she possibly have to go?

Penny sighed. "Sabrina is sick, and I can't get Ian to bed for love or money. You may be stoned on a Caribbean island, but we're right where you left us."

She hung up the phone.

THE NEXT morning Scott arrived at the Ambrosia Café at five minutes to nine, so that a stranger's brother could drive him somewhere, beat him senseless, and rob him blind. That he'd hatched this plan while sober was a distressing thought.

He took a seat on the porch and waited. Two little girls in white dresses raced down the sidewalk, veils tracing behind them like vapor trails. He thought of his daughter's First Communion, the spring after they'd moved to Gatwick; how profoundly it had moved him, Sabrina like a tiny bride in her dress and veil. Her hair was redder then, and she bore a startling resemblance to his sister at that age. Scott had a clear mental picture of Gwen at seven, thanks to a framed photo that still hung in his mother's parlor. It had been taken the morning of Gwen's First Communion, before everything went awry in their lives. His parents stood arm in arm, smiling. In front the three children in Sunday clothes, Billy, Scott, and—still normal then, still innocent—lovely red-haired Gwen.

Gwen. For the first time it dawned on him that she could be in actual danger, kidnapped, held hostage. That he could be walking into a dangerous situation, for which he was—face it—tragically ill equipped. Now, for instance. Getting into a car with a total stranger who'd want to be paid for his trouble. How much? Scott hadn't even asked.

"Hey, man," said a voice. "My brother say you need a ride."

Scott looked up. Standing in the door of the café was the little businessman, the kid with the fragrant bag of weed.

"Yeah," said Scott. "That's me."

"Come on. I got a car in the back."

"You're not old enough to drive."

"I'm eighteen, man."

"Bullshit," said Scott.

"Okay, sixteen."

"Fourteen, tops."

The boy laughed. "Thirteen, but it doesn't matter. On Saint Raphael you got a car, you allowed to drive."

Scott doubted this was true. "This is a terrible idea," he said.

The boy shrugged elaborately. "You don't want to come with me, you don't come. But you want a taxi for the whole day, it cost you two hundred dollars. If you can find one. It's Sunday, man."

"How much do you want?"

"Fifty," said the boy. "Less maybe, if we do some other business."

Scott pondered this. He was persuaded by the boy's logic. And by the memory of his emerald weed, its haunting skunky smell.

"Let's go," he said.

They sped across the island in the boy's Plymouth Reliant, its bench seats covered in wooden beads that vibrated Scott's sacrum in a way that was not unpleasant. It was late morning, the sun nearly overhead. They stopped briefly in the parking lot of a barbecue joint, where Scott purchased a quarter ounce of weed. An eighth would have been plenty, but the boy, whose name was Gabriel, seemed disappointed. He'd been hoping for a bigger sale. He brightened visibly when Scott twisted up a joint.

"What, you not going to share?" he asked, outraged.

"You're just a kid," said Scott.

The boy laughed. "I been smoking this shit since I was six."

Afterward the morning took on some jingle. The sun burned. The sky blued. Scott rolled back his sleeves and stretched his arm out the window. He hadn't done a wake-and-bake in years. Penny claimed that it polluted the whole day—Penny who thought nothing of firing up the television at dawn, fouling her clean sleepy brain.

As they drove he explained his mission. "No problem," Gabriel answered—brisk and professional, like a concierge at an upscale hotel.

They crossed over what seemed an immense mountain, the cheesy little engine huffing mightily. Scott remembered his father laughing at these wrecks, Lee Iacocca's K Cars, back in the eighties: the bargain-basement parts used interchangeably on sedans, convertibles, and coupes, the square bodies designed, it seemed, by an unimaginative child asked to draw a car.

"How old is this piece of shit?" Scott asked.

"Same as me," Gabriel said.

"How many miles?"

"Whatever I say. Look," he said, pointing to the odometer, which read 514.

A moment later they were whizzing down the mountain. Scott leaned back and closed his eyes, recalling the Speed Racer cartoons of his childhood, the car that could swim and leap and fly.

"We coming to the big resorts." Gabriel gave a low whistle. "Fancy, man. You not going to believe it. You can't see them from the autoroute." He pointed to a turnoff, marked by a stucco archway, a jauntily painted sign that read SUNSET POINT. And, in smaller letter: GUESTS ONLY. PRIVATE ACCESS.

Scott frowned. "I don't think that's it." Shit, he thought. He'd been so shaken by his conversation with Penny, so moved and humbled, that he'd forgotten the name of the hotel.

"You don't *think*? You not sure?"

"I can't remember the name exactly."

They passed another a second turnoff, then a third. BREEZES RESORT. CALYPSO BREEZE. BIMINI BEACH CLUB. MONTEGO CAY.

"They all sound the same," Scott said.

"Come on, man." Gabriel seemed to be losing patience, so they pulled onto a dirt access road and smoked another joint.

"Listen, man," the boy said, his equilibrium restored. "We running out of resorts. We got one more up ahead"—he pointed—"and that's it."

They approached another turnoff, another flowering hedge, another stucco wall. The sign said WELCOME TO PLEASURES.

"That's it," said Scott.

They turned. Halfway up the drive was a booth manned by a uniformed attendant. At the sight of the K Car he shook his head and frowned. Scott motioned for Gabriel to roll down his window. "Hey there," said Scott.

"Are you a guest here?" The man was brown skinned and built like a linebacker. His calves looked stuffed with softballs. His thighs were cased in bright green shorts.

"Um, not exactly. I'm trying to find my sister." He glanced over the guard's shoulder, as though Gwen might appear from behind him. "If I could just talk to someone at the front desk. Reservations, or whatever."

"There's a phone number for that," the man said.

Scott nodded energetically. "Okay, good. But since I'm already here—"

"I can't let you in," the man said. "You're not a guest."

"What about visitors? Surely you allow visitors?"

"This is private property. If you don't get that thing out of here, I have to call security."

Gabriel threw the car into reverse and backed up squealing. They veered onto the autoroute.

"Motherfucker," he said. To Scott's surprise he seemed truly rattled.

"He was just doing his job," said Scott.

"No, man." Gabriel turned his head and spat savagely out the window. "He's light skin. He take one look at my black face and treat me like shit. That's how it work on this island. You light skin, you a Frenchman. You dark skin, they treat you like shit."

Scott blinked. If asked, he'd have described them both as black. The world seemed suddenly more complicated than he'd ever imagined. He'd had this feeling before, at the birth of his daughter, or watching "Jens" Jensen solve a calculus equation. It was a crushing awareness of his own idiocy, all that he would never understand, or even see.

They turned back to the service road where they'd smoked the joint, and settled on a plan. Gabriel would wait in the car. Scott would approach Pleasures on foot.

Scott checked his reflection in the rearview. His eyes were red and heavy lidded, his hair wild from the wind. He ran a hand through his hair and set out walking.

Half a mile later, he found a break in the hedge and shimmied through it, the branches scratching his arms. He felt buoyed by this small success. Before him stretched a manicured lawn. He crossed it with an easy stride, as though he belonged here, a carefree tourist on vacation. He heard squeals and laughter in the distance, the thwack of a volleyball. The sounds of leisure, of wealthy white people—he thought of Gabriel in the hot car overlooking a power plant—enjoying themselves in the sun.

He headed in the direction of the sounds, following a path through a grove of mangrove trees. He stopped a moment to admire them, their trunks long and swanlike, the arching necks of primeval creatures half buried in the earth. He was grateful for the momentary coolness, the soft sandy path beneath his feet.

Ahead was a sunny patio, paved in flagstones. Scott stopped short.

Everybody was naked.

Naked people stretched out on chaise lounges, bubbled in the hot tub, tiptoed barefoot across the hot flagstones. Naked breasts wobbled invitingly. Dicks and scrotums danced and dangled. A naked girl careened down the water slide, bouncing and squealing. In the vast swimming pool naked volleyball was under way.

It appeared to be naked lunchtime. A waitress in a green bikini served sandwiches to naked diners. The chairs, Scott noted, were thoughtfully padded. The prudent had laid napkins across their laps.

A hostess approached him. Like the waitress she seemed overdressed in her green bikini. The three triangles of Lycra looked as incongruous as a parka.

"I'm sorry," she said with a smile. "This patio is for nude guests only. You can leave your clothes in the locker room"—she pointed to a white stucco building behind her—"or dine on the main patio, if you prefer."

It struck him as very funny, the businesslike way she'd asked him to shuck his pants.

Scott smiled stupidly, grateful for the dark glasses that hid his roving eyes. "Actually, I'm a little lost. I'm looking for the reservations desk."

"The main building is right up that path," she said, pointing. "And please come back later." (Or was it *come buck naked*?) "We serve lunch until three."

He turned and headed through another grove of mangroves, blinking. His mind had stalled, the gears jammed at the sight of so many bodies, the ripples and nipples and hairy flesh. When the machine finally restarted, a stunning thought occurred to him: his sister had stayed at a nude resort. The idea was so mind boggling, so completely at odds with his notion of Gwen's character, that he wondered if he had the wrong hotel. Again the feeling overwhelmed him: his instincts were worthless, his perceptions skewed. The trees themselves seemed suspect. Nothing was as it seemed.

Pot could make you paranoid. He'd heard this for years, from so many different people that there had to be some truth to it. Scott, who'd smoked more weed than most people on earth, had dismissed this as user error, a hidden psychic weakness in the smoker himself. Cannabis was not to blame, any more than you could blame a car if you drove it into a wall. Yet now, for the first time, he felt frozen with paranoia. A disastrous development for a man on a mission.

He scolded himself to stay focused. To stop looking at those freaky trees.

He found the main building, took a deep breath and approached the front desk. It seemed rude not to remove his sunglasses, rude but necessary. Who knew what paranoid gleam flickered in his eyes?

"Excuse me," Scott said pleasantly, in the voice he assumed on such occasions. It was a deep, courtly voice, manly and charming. His father's voice. "I'm looking for my sister, who was a guest here recently. Can you tell me if she's still staying here?"

The pretty desk clerk regarded him quizzically. "I'm sorry. I can't reveal any information about our guests."

"Of course," he said smoothly. "But this is a family emergency, and I need to find her. Her name is Gwen McKotch." He took his driver's license from his wallet and laid it on the desk. "See?" he said, pointing to his name. "I'm her brother. Scott McKotch."

The girl looked worried. "Wow," she said. "I hope it's nothing serious. But Pleasures has a strict privacy policy. I'm not allowed to tell you anything."

"Not even if she's staying here? If she's ever stayed here?"

The girl smiled sadly. "My manager is off for the weekend, but he'll be here tomorrow morning. If it's really an emergency, maybe he can help you then."

"*Tomorrow?*" Scott repeated. In twenty-four hours he would be on a plane to Connecticut.

At that moment, a plump middle-aged couple crossed the lobby, sunburned and wet haired. The man was carrying two heavy tanks.

Scuba tanks.

Scott jogged across the marble floor. "Excuse me," he called in his Frank voice. "Are you going scuba diving?"

"We just got back," the woman said.

"Well, can you tell me the name of the—instructor, I guess? The guy who took you out."

The two looked at each other, frowning.

"I can't recall," the man said in an English accent. Another English accent! This seemed ominously significant. Scott's paranoia flared. Deliberately he tamped it down.

"I'm drawing a blank," the woman said.

"There were several of us." The man glanced behind him. "The others should be coming any minute. We were the first ones off the boat."

Scott headed toward the door, nearly colliding with two middle-aged blondes showing freckled cleavage. The women toted vinyl duffels. A pair of blue rubber fins poked from one of the bags.

Scott repeated his question slowly, in his most resonant Frank voice.

The women looked at each other and grinned broadly. "Rico!" they shrieked in unison, and dissolved into giddy laughter.

His heart kicked up. "Can you tell me where to find him?"

The taller blonde pointed. "The dock is that way."

Outside Scott broke into a run. He raced across a wide lawn toward a sign marked BEACH ACCESS, then clattered down a boardwalk toward another sign: BOAT RAMP. In the distance he saw a motorboat, spanking white, roar away from the dock. A brown-skinned man, shirtless, coiled a rope around his elbow.

At the helm, her red hair flaming, was his sister, Gwen.

"YOU SERIOUS, man? You find this guy, and you don't even talk to him?"

Gabriel spoke slowly, incredulously, though he didn't look especially surprised. He didn't look especially awake. Scott had found the car, to his immense relief, just where he'd left it, on the sandy access road overlooking the power plant.

"I tried." He had run to the end of the dock waving his arms, shouting Gwen's name, then Rico's, at the top of his voice. They hadn't heard him over the roaring engine, but everyone else had—including two green-suited security guards who'd escorted him off the property and dumped him at the gate.

He sat a moment pondering. He would meet this Rico; in noble, masculine fashion he would take the measure of the man. He tested the feel of the words in his mouth: *What are your intentions regarding my sister?* Then again, he wasn't sure the answer mattered. The goal was to bring Gwen home safely, to *put an end to this foolishness*, as his mother said. Paulette, after all, had financed this mission, and only one outcome would satisfy her.

Define success at the outset, Dashiell Blodgett counseled. *Set your compass, then keep moving.*

Tomorrow morning he would return to Pleasures and wait at the boat ramp—all day, if necessary—until Gwen and Rico reappeared. He had memorized the letters stenciled at the helm of the boat: 2STE. Recent experience had proven his memory unreliable. Before he twisted up another joint—which he needed to do, immediately—he was going to write it down.

"Gabriel," he said. "Buddy. Do you have something I can write with?"

Gabriel opened one baleful eye, like a sleeping cat unhappily disturbed.

"Pen and paper," Scott said.

Gabriel reached beneath his seat for a notebook and ballpoint pen. He flipped through the book—the pages filled with neat columns of figures—and tore out a clean sheet.

"What are all those numbers?" Scott asked.

"What you think?"

Scott wrote down 2STE, folded the paper and slipped it into his pocket. "All right. Let's have a smoke."

He reached under his own seat and felt around for the plastic bag. Nothing. He turned to Gabriel, whose heavy eyelids were fluttering.

"You're kidding me," he said. "You smoked the whole bag?"

"You were gone a long time, man."

"How long? An hour? Two?" A long walk each way, the mangroves and naked people, the front desk and the boat ramp. It hadn't occurred to him, then, that he'd left Gabriel alone with his stash.

"There's a little left," said Gabriel, taking the bag from his pocket. "We can roll one more."

"That was a *quarter*, man. You smoked a quarter in two hours?"

"We smoked two joints before," Gabriel reminded him.

"But still." Scott had had this conversation a hundred times, in cars and back alleys, dorm rooms at Pearse and Stirling, shitty apartments in La Jolla and Portland and Oakland and San Berdoo. He had lived most of his adult life in a pot-based economy—which, as it turned out, was not so different from the other kind. In their attention to price and quality, their obsessive tracking of profit and inventory, potheads were not so different from Carter Rook and his Wall Street friends, the most fervent capitalists Scott knew.

"Okay. Fine." Scott took the bag from Gabriel and set to work rolling. He managed to scrape together two joints, the second composed of a disemboweled Marlboro from Gabriel's pack and the ganja dust at the bottom of the bag. Scott slipped the joints into the bag and returned it to its place beneath the seat.

"You don't want to smoke?"

"Later." Scott got out of the car and circled around to the driver's side. "Move over," he said, taking the keys. "I'm driving."

Surprisingly Gabriel did not protest. They headed back over the mountain, Scott at the wheel, Gabriel offering occasional directions. They wove through the back streets of Pointe Mathilde and parked behind the Ambrosia Café.

"You owe me fifty dollars," said Gabriel.

"You smoked fifty dollars," said Scott. "Come on. I'll buy you dinner."

On the front porch of the Ambrosia they ordered two steak-frites, a Fanta for Gabriel, a Red Stripe for Scott. Revived by the sugar, Gabriel looked alert and bright eyed. He waved and called out to acquaintances in the street.

"*Salut, mon pote!*" he called to a boy on a bicycle wheeling swiftly down the street. The boy braked, turned, broke into a smile. He was a handsome kid, smaller than Gabriel. He leaned his bike against the porch rail and came to shake Gabriel's hand.

"Where you been, man?" said Gabriel.

"Working," said the boy. "All day on that fucking boat. Pretty soon I be black as you."

"I'm working too, man. Driving for him." Gabriel pointed a thumb at Scott. "He looking for some guy. Dude ran off with my man's sister."

"He takes people diving," said Scott. "Some guy named Rico."

"*Rico?*" Gabriel turned to look at Scott. A moment later he dissolved into stoned laughter. "Shit, man. How come you didn't tell me his name Rico?"

"What's so funny?" Scott demanded.

"My friend, here. He *work* for a guy name Rico."

The other boy grinned.

"I don't believe you," said Scott.

"It's true." The boy lowered his voice. "What, you got a problem with Rico?"

"No problem. I don't even know him. I'm just trying to find my sister."

The boy eyed him, considering. "You give me fifty dollars, I take you to her."

"Bullshit," said Scott.

"Your sister name Gwen. A little redhead girl."

"How the fuck do you know that?" Scott gaped. "Where is she? I want to see her."

"You got fifty dollars?"

"Whoa, whoa. Hold on a second." Scott glanced at Gabriel, the thirteen-year-old drug dealer who'd smoked up all his pot. "You know this guy?"

"Relax, man." Gabriel clapped Scott's shoulder. "You in good hands. This my great friend Alistair."

THEY SPED through the night in the Plymouth Reliant, Scott McKotch and two thirteen-year-old drug dealers, down the winding mountain roads of an island Scott still couldn't find on a map. The strangeness of the situation struck him moment by moment, but oddly, he was not panicked. He had a full belly, two joints for later. The boys, though clever, were little and skinny. Scott had a hundred pounds on either of them. If necessary he could break them both in half.

He had never felt better in his life.

They followed the autoroute westward, in the opposite direction from that morning, then turned onto a narrow road that hugged the coastline. For once Scott was paying attention. For once he knew exactly where he was.

The road ended in a sandy clearing, where a few old cars and motorcycles were parked. "There's the boat ramp," Alistair said, pointing. "Rico's slip is number four."

Scott got out of the car and started down the walkway, glancing over his shoulder at the boys in the car. The orange sun hung low in the sky. Gabriel gave a little salute, and Scott returned it, suspecting—correctly—that he would never see the boy again.

He headed down a shaky aluminum ramp pitched at a steep incline. It clanged loudly with each step. He recognized the boat immediately. Rico, naked to the waist, sat on a kind of plastic locker, writing on a clipboard. *What is he writing?* Scott wondered. *And doesn't he own a shirt?*

"Excuse me," Scott called. "Are you Rico?" Only then did he realize he didn't know the man's last name.

The guy looked up from his clipboard. "Who wants to know?"

"Is Gwen McKotch on this boat? I'm her brother. I want to talk to her."

"Billy?" Rico grinned broadly. "Come on up, man. This is a marvelous surprise. Gwen's at the bathhouse taking a shower. She'll be thrilled."

Scott clambered up the ladder onto the deck. "Hi. Thanks. Except I'm not Billy. I'm the other brother, Scott."

"Scott," Rico repeated. "I didn't know she had another brother."

The words hit him like a cold wind. "Oh. Well. I was away for a while," he said idiotically. "We didn't see each other very often."

They stood there a long moment staring at each other. The words Scott had rehearsed—*What are your intentions regarding my sister?*—were too lame-brained to be spoken aloud. Rico's eyes bristled with alertness. He looked to be in his thirties and was built like a bantam weight boxer, lean and powerful; his muscles seemed to twitch beneath his skin. Scott thought, absurdly, of Dashiell Blodgett, the half-wit who'd lost a toe on K2 and now wrote books about it. Screw Blodgett. This was what a man of action looked like.

They stood staring at each other. Scott would tell the story later with some embellishment: the tension in the air, the fierce and possibly fatal contest of masculine will that would surely have ensued if Gwen hadn't, at that moment, come clanging down the ramp. She stopped short, shading her eyes. "Scotty? Is that you?"

Immediately Rico relaxed; his bulging muscles ceased to twitch. He broke into an affable grin. "Scott," he said, offering his hand. "Forgive me. Welcome to our home."

Gwen scrambled up the ladder. "Wow. God." She was flushed, a little breathless. A man's white T-shirt hung nearly to her knees. Her hair, slightly damp, hung in loose waves to her chin. She looks pretty, Scott thought. He couldn't have been more astonished if she'd walked on her hands.

"What are you doing here?" She sat on the plastic locker and ran a comb through her hair.

"I came to see you." He turned to Rico. "Buddy, can you give us a minute?"

Rico glanced uncertainly at Gwen.

"It's all right," said Gwen. "He's my little brother."

Rico bent and kissed her, his hand lingering protectively on her shoulder. "Call if you need me. I won't go far."

Scott waited until Rico had descended the ladder. He sat on a canvas deck chair across from Gwen.

"God, Scotty, what are you doing here?"

"What do you think? I wanted to make sure you're okay."

She gave an exasperated sigh. "I'm okay, I'm okay! For God's sake, I've always been okay."

"Well, Mom's out of her mind. You had to expect that when you just disappeared."

"*I* disappeared?"

"Well, you didn't tell her where you were going."

"Spare me," said Gwen. "Aren't you the one who ran away to California and didn't call for two years?"

"That's not the same," he said. "She doesn't worry about me like she does about you."

"Are you joking? She practically had a nervous breakdown," said Gwen. "Seriously. I thought she was going to end up in McLean. Dad and Billy were gone, and I was stuck in Concord for two years babysitting her." She stopped. "You get the idea. My point is, I can still call her once a month like always. Whether I call from here or Pittsburgh isn't anybody's business. Honestly, I don't see the problem." She clamped her mouth shut, then, the familiar Gwen-like set of her jaw. Until that moment she had seemed a stranger. Here, finally, was a Gwen he recognized.

"Well, what about this guy?" he asked, changing tactics. "This Rico. You have to admit it's pretty sudden."

"Sudden? Scotty, I'm thirty-four years old." She cocked her head. "Think about it. You get to run away and get married, and Billy goes to New York and falls in love. Why am I the only one who's not allowed to have a life?"

Billy's in love? Scott thought, but there was no time to process this information. Gwen, silent for twenty years, wouldn't stop talking. It was as though she'd been saving up words her whole life.

Scott looked around him then, really looked. The boat wasn't new, but handsome and well maintained, the deck spanking clean. A small table had been unfolded, Murphy bed style, from the port side. On it were a bottle of wine, half a loaf of French bread and a bowl of cut fruit.

"I interrupted your dinner," he said.

"Oh, no. That's left over from breakfast. There's a terrific bakery in town. Rico goes every morning. He eats bread all day long. He could live on bread." She smiled then, fondly, a little amused. She had a beautiful smile.

"So you live here," he said, checking his facts. "On the boat?"

"For now. It's a little cramped for two. We're looking for a bigger boat."

"What do you do for money?" As he said it, he feared the question would offend her, but Gwen seemed not to mind.

"We run dive excursions. It's Rico's business. He's been doing it for years."

Scott pondered this. He knew plenty of successful people—too goddamn many, in fact. But none of them—his father, Billy, his Drew or Broussard cousins, not even Carter Rook—owned an actual business.

"What about your job?" he asked.

"I quit. I spent eight years of my life cataloging fossils. I was turning into one myself." Gwen paused. "I still have to go back there and deal with my apartment. Have a tag sale, maybe. I don't have much stuff."

"Are you going to get married?"

"We're talking about it," she said, suddenly shy. "I don't care one way or the other, but Rico's old fashioned. He doesn't want to live in sin. And get this: he's Catholic! Mom would love that."

Scott smiled. He had run out of questions. He wanted only to sit awhile and look at her, his little big sister, happy at last.

"I should have done this a long time ago," she said. "Like you did. I'm sorry for what I said before, about you going to California. You were the brave one, Scotty. I was proud of you."

Jesus: Gwen, proud of him, when in all the years he was gone he'd scarcely given her a thought. When he remembered her at all, he thought of Gwen as Billy's sister, his lieutenant and disciple, whose outs and runs counted; as one more thing Billy had that he did not. All that time, she had also been his?

"What do I tell Mom?" he asked.

Gwen sighed. "I don't know. Tell her I'm happy. Tell her I'm impossible and stubborn. Just tell her you tried."

That night, after Gwen had driven him back to his hotel, after he'd rested and showered and smoked a joint, he dialed his mother's number.

"Dear, where are you? Goodness, it's late. When the phone rang I nearly had a coronary."

"Sorry, Mom." He glanced at the clock: eleven thirty. What an endless fucking day.

"Well, did you find her? Is she all right?"

"Easy, Mom." He wanted to take his time telling her, to savor his victory. Against tall odds he had found his sister, really found her. Gwen, who'd been lost not for months, but—to Scott anyway—for many years.

"I saw her and she's fine. She's great, actually. She's living on a houseboat"—he forgave himself this slight exaggeration—"with a guy she met on vacation. He's—let me tell you, Mom. He's a pretty impressive guy."

Dead silence from the other end of the line. Scott pressed on.

"He grew up on the island—grew up pretty poor, from the sound of it. But he's done well for himself. He's got a decent boat—not like Uncle Roy's, but not bad. And he's got this business running scuba-diving trips for the big resorts down here—there's a lot of money in tourism, Mom, a *lot* of money to be made if you know what you're doing. And this Rico does. He's a smart guy, good looking, very"—he searched for the right word—"dynamic."

A long pause on the other end.

"On a boat," his mother said. "Gwen is living on a boat."

"That part's a little unusual," he admitted, "but listen." And he described how it felt to sit on deck late in the afternoon, watching the sun drop into Candlewick Bay, a spectacle of such stirring beauty it made you believe in God. He talked about the sunset, the bread and wine and flowers on the table, the gentle rocking of the boat in its slip, waiting all the while for something from his mother's end, some murmur of interest or comprehension or hey, maybe a word of thanks. At some danger to himself he'd done what no one else in his family could do. He had found his sister. He'd gotten to the bottom of things.

"She's going to stay there?" his mother said.

"That's the plan, Mom. They run the business together. In fact, when I first saw her they'd just dropped off a bunch of people at this very *elegant*—his mother loved that word—resort.

Silence.

"Rico's Catholic," he added. "Did I tell you he's Catholic?"

Finally his mother began to laugh. "Oh, that's delightful."

"You're still there," said Scott.

"Yes, I'm here. I don't understand any of this."

"It's pretty simple, actually. Gwen loves this guy, and he loves her."

"For heaven's sake, I don't mean *that*," she said, her voice crackling with impatience. "There's no mystery to *that*. What I don't understand, what I will never in my life understand, is what on earth is the matter with *you*." She paused. "I didn't send you all the way down there to watch the sunset with your sister. I sent you to bring her home."

"I know," said Scott. "But the thing is, she's happy. If you could just see her—she's like a different person."

His mother sighed. "I'm sure she is, dear. But what happens six months from now, a year from now, when he's gotten what he wants from her?"

Scott frowned. Sex? Was she talking about sex?

"Think, darling. They get married, he gets American citizenship—"

(Rico's old fashioned. He doesn't want to live in sin.)

"—takes all her money—"

"Gwen has money?"

She made an impatient noise. "I'm certain she has every penny Daddy left her, and then some. And for a person like this Rico, an ambitious person from a poor background, don't you think that would be enticing? Cash to put into his business. To buy—heavens, I don't know what. Equipment of some sort. Another boat."

(It's a little cramped for two. We're looking for a bigger one.)

Shit, Scott thought.

"If this Rico is so impressive, as you say, don't you think he's had a great many women to choose from?"

He thought of the two blondes in the lobby at Pleasures, spilling out of bikini tops. *Rico!* they'd shrieked, giggling like schoolgirls.

"So why would he choose to take up with your sister? I'll tell you why." His mother paused. "Many women might have a love affair with such a person, but very few would toss their lives into the air like a deck of cards and give him everything he wants. It takes a particular kind of woman to fall for a character like this. A lonely and vulnerable and inexperienced young woman. And your Rico found his mark."

Scott hugged a pillow to his chest. An iron fist squeezed his stomach. Had Rico conned him too? His earlier paranoia returned in a wave. He had shown up at the dock stoned and ready to weep over the magnificence of the sunset, and Rico had read the situation immediately. Every word he'd spoken had maximized his advantage *(I didn't know Gwen had another brother)*. Had made Scott feel insignificant and small.

"Sooner or later this Rico will show his true colors," his mother said. "People always do. And it will be terrible for Gwen, just terrible. I was hoping to spare her that."

Scott thought of Gwen on the boat, the sun setting behind her, turning her hair to fire. *You were the brave one, Scotty. I was proud of you.* His new love for his sister flamed alongside the old one—the dumb, ancient one that had always been there.

"I love her too, Mom," he said. "I did my best."

His mother sighed. "I suppose you did."

For long after they'd said their good-byes he sat with his back to the door. He had underestimated his opponent. His sister was in serious danger; he could not, would not, leave her at Rico's mercy. His mother's plan had failed, but Scott had a few ideas of his own. His flight back to Connecticut could be changed. There was still time.

Scott rose early the next morning, shaved, and showered. When the bank opened he was waiting at the door. A pretty teller directed him to a cash machine, where his Quinnebaug Trust card worked as promptly as it did at home. He selected "Savings," an account he and Penny never touched, with good reason: until recently its balance had hovered around eighteen dollars. Scott waited, holding his breath. Seeing that his mother's check had cleared, he enjoyed a celebratory moment. Then came a harsh rebuke. *YOUR DAILY WITHDRAWAL LIMIT IS $500,* he was informed in stern capitals.

He approached the comely teller, who seemed moved by his plight.

"You go and talk to the manager," she crooned. Her voice was low and soothing, as though comforting a cranky child. "He can do a wire transfer. Don' worry. This happen all the time."

An hour later he hailed a taxi, acutely aware of the envelope inside his jacket, bulging with Caribbean dollars, heavy against his heart. Unused to carrying anything of value, he felt vulnerable, an easy mark for thieves and hooligans. Noble sentiments filled him, a rush of solidarity with his sister, with victims everywhere. That anyone should take advantage of Gwen outraged him.

The taxi took him to the entrance of the marina. The driver parked and waited. Scott glanced nervously at his watch. Was he too late? Gwen had always loved sleeping in, but Rico had the look of an early riser. It was hard to imagine him sleeping at all.

I can always come back tomorrow, Scott told himself. He would come back as often as necessary, until the deed was done.

He glanced idly into the rearview mirror and swiped at his hair, wishing he had worn his hat. In that moment Rico appeared in white shorts and T-shirt, striding briskly toward the dock, a wrapped baguette tucked under his arm. His very promptness gave Scott a chill. It was as though the guy had been waiting for him.

He got out of the cab and slammed the door. "Rico," he called, in a voice totally unlike his father's. It was the gruff, thuglike grunt he'd employed in his younger years, mostly when buying drugs.

Rico looked up. In his white getup he looked like the handsome tennis instructors, suave and suntanned, who strutted around his mother's club making wealthy women swoon.

Gigolo, Scott thought.

He crossed the parking lot at an easy jog, sweating inside his heavy jacket.

"Gwen is still sleeping," Rico told him.

"That's all right," said Scott. "I came to see you."

Given enough time, the creature revealed himself. The drunkard drank, the bandit stole. He could hide his true nature, but not easily and not for long. In his darkest parts he did not wish to. Perversely, irresistibly, he ached to show himself, naked beneath the grubby raincoat. In all his darkness, he wanted to be known.

Again Scott felt the weight in his jacket. He said, "I've got a business proposal for you."

chapter 7

The sun rises over St. Raphael. Gwen wakes first, roused by the slow rocking of the boat, the regular breathing of the water beneath. The same motion that lulls her to sleep can also waken her from it. This is a mystery, one of many lately revealed to her. Another miracle she will never understand.

She turns toward the man sleeping beside her, and sees him. This is no small thing. For years she woke in a blur, fumbled for eyeglasses on the bedside table. Now she sees with humming clarity. From the moment she opens her eyes, the world offers itself without equivocation, without distortion. The dark smudge of morning beard, the strong bones of his face. His bare skin draws her; it seems to have its own life, separate from the rest of him. Before Rico is awake, Gwen steals these moments with this other part of him, this radiant welcoming skin.

You are so small, he murmurs as he curls around her. *I love how you are small.*

And because he does, she has begun to love this about herself. She is small enough to be lost at the center of a man, every part of her touching him, enrobed completely in his skin. Rico was gentle at first, sensing her discomfort. He loved her with his hands, his hot breath, his mouth. Now the magic pills make all things possible. He moves behind her and inside her, the same wavy rhythm. Wordlessly he lifts and turns her, arranges her above or beneath or beside him. His sureness enraptures her. He seems to know her body in ways that Gwen, who's lived inside it forever, is only just learning.

Her body has changed. Her stomach is flat now, her arms muscled. Living on a boat is work. More and more, she forgets to worry
about how she looks. In town, around the marina, she is recognized.
This does not distress her. She feels important, worthy of notice. Gwen
and Rico walk everywhere together; always he keeps a hand on her.
Your little woman, the locals say, a title that pleases her. She would always
be little, but now she was a woman. She would always be little, but
now she was his.

She watches him rise from the bed, hears him in the galley making coffee. He will walk to town for morning bread, and Gwen will
fall into a deeper sleep than is possible with him beside her, the distraction of his skin. She sleeps the trusting sleep of a child, knowing
he will return.

She sleeps less than she used to. Then, which is not so long ago,
she hibernated through the long Pittsburgh winter, waiting for the
earth to turn, for life to begin. She is living now, not waiting. Now
there is a boat to pilot, a business to run, divers to outfit and guide and
watch unobtrusively but vigilantly, to save from their own ignorance
and panic. Gwen excels at this unseen watching. She has always known
how to be invisible.

With the divers Rico is not invisible. He is a star. The women
jockey for his attention. They appear in shorts, in thongs, squeezed
into bikini tops. Gwen hides in oversize T-shirts. The voice inside her
is small but insistent. Several times a day it asks: *Why choose me? Why
love me?*

The women are beautiful and willing. Every few days, one will
slip him a room key—white women always, Germans or French,
Americans or Swedes. The first time she saw this, Gwen was angry.
The second time made her cry. Rico touched her face and spoke to
her softly. *It's not important. People are lonely. Have confidence in me.* They
don't speak of it again, even when the women return a second time,
a third; when Rico takes them diving at night. In a week Gwen sees
them two or three times. Then, never again.

It is the *never again* that matters.

The night dives are lucrative, and the business is their future.

Have confidence in me.

In five days she will return to Pittsburgh, but only briefly, to sign papers and pack boxes. She has already quit her job—a meaningless task, dispatched by phone—but she will stop by the Stott to take flowers to Heidi Kozak, the friend who waited out her silence, who sent her to St. Raphael.

Her savings she will put into the business. She has quite a lot of money, more than anyone knows. Papa left her a little something. Invested aggressively for ten years, a little something becomes a considerable something. Alone among the Drew grandchildren, Gwen knows how to save.

I can't take your money, Rico said, but Gwen insisted. In the end he was convinced. They need a new boat, and Gwen has enough for a large down payment. Debt makes Rico anxious. He has never made monthly payments on anything. It is Gwen's turn to reassure him: *Don't worry. The money will come.*

They work hard together. Six days a week they run dive excursions—from Pleasures and Bimini Bay, the largest of the resorts. In the morning, and again in the afternoon, they host divers; in the evening a little supper, the never-ending repairs on the boat. Every few days Gwen drives Rico's truck to the market, to buy provisions—fruit, bottled water—for the divers, and flowers and wine for themselves.

The aged truck is full of surprises. One evening as Gwen drives away from the marina, the glove compartment springs ajar. She slams it shut, and again the door falls open. Inside is a pair of sunglasses, a tube of her sunscreen, the notebook where Rico records his mileage. And a bulging manila envelope.

She doesn't hesitate, has no reason to. She and Rico sleep in a compartment eight feet square. They prepare dinner side by side, close enough to hear each other breathe.

Thoughtlessly, guiltlessly, Gwen opens the envelope. The East Caribbean bills show birds and fish and mountains, a young queen of England, her neck ringed with jewels.

The bills are all hundreds. Quickly Gwen counts. There are five thick stacks, and one thinner one. Five hundred and forty bills.

She has never been good at arithmetic, but this conversion has become automatic. Keeping books for the business, she does it many times each day.

Fifty-four thousand Caribbean dollars equals twenty thousand American dollars.

Overhead a seagull screams.

WHERE WOULD Rico get twenty thousand dollars? For a day, two days, Gwen broods on this question. They have discussed the future, the best way to pool their assets. Rico has no savings account, no investments—at least, none he'd admitted to. She has access to his checkbook, the ledger he keeps for the business. No large sums have been recorded—recently or ever, as far as Gwen can tell. So where did the cash come from? Had it simply fallen from the sky?

There is one evil possibility. In St. Raphael drug smuggling is rampant. Every month or two inspectors descend on the marina, searching for contraband. Just recently they'd searched a boat two slips over, a massive power yacht called *Island Girl*. Her owner was a white man of indeterminate nationality, a—friend? acquaintance?—of Rico's. The marina gossips said he made trips to Jamaica. *Island Girl* was impounded, her owner taken away in handcuffs.

The man was arrested a week ago. Ten days at the most.

Is Rico involved with drugs? The very thought is a betrayal. Gwen is appalled by her suspicions, rendered mute by shame.

Unable to speak, she watches and waits. She believed them cemented together. Now she begins to see the gaps, the places where the seal is bubbled.

Have confidence in me.

For two days she monitors the glove compartment, to make sure the money is still there. On the third day she takes the envelope and hides it in her purple backpack, crammed into a corner of the V berth.

That evening Rico returns from town looking sweaty, panicked. His distress is obvious. But if she weren't looking for it, would she have seen it? Exactly how blind has she become?

"Everything okay?" she asks. Her voice is clear and innocent. She is horrified by her ability to dissemble, and strangely proud.

Rico squeezes her shoulder, his smile so disarming that her heart breaks a little. *What am I doing?* she wonders.

She will realize later that this is the wrong question. Better: *What have I already done?*

ANOTHER DAY passes. They dock at Pleasures to pick up a crew of divers. Gwen watches Rico help them onto the boat. His welcome speech—the same one he always delivers—sounds false and facile, a hollow performance. *He is an actor,* she thinks. His easy banter with the divers, his warm smile: none of this is genuine. She sees him with new eyes.

That night she feigns sleep when he reaches for her. She lies awake a long time listening to him breathe.

Finally, the morning she is to leave for Pittsburgh, she takes her backpack from the V berth and sets about packing. She removes the manila envelope and places it at the center of the bed. Rico is expecting to drive her to the airport. "Gwen, are you ready?" he calls from on deck.

She zips shut the backpack. Her dive gear is already packed. The purple duffel waits, in plain view, on deck. Hasn't Rico noticed? His little woman is ready to go.

The moment is painless; she will ache later. She has always known that she would lose him. Now that the loss is nearly behind her, she feels a curious relief.

He comes down into the hold. She keeps her back to him, gives him a moment to notice the envelope on the bed. Her heart is racing. She doesn't say a word, doesn't meet his eyes.

Finally he touches her shoulder, and she turns to look at him. *I was going to clean out my bank account,* she thinks. *All my savings. The money Papa left me. I was going to buy us a boat.* She says none of this. For the first time in months, Gwen adopts the Silence. She waits for him to speak.

"You found it," he says finally.

She thinks, *Apparently so.*

"Why didn't you ask me about it?"

She thinks, *Why didn't you tell me? Why should I have to ask?*

"It's a lot of money," says Rico.

She thinks, *Where did you get twenty thousand dollars? Are you selling drugs?*

"You are angry," he says.

She thinks, *You used me, and I let you. You would have taken me for everything I have. Yes, genius. I am angry.*

He stares at her, mystified. "Gwen, say something." His voice breaks a little, and this is the thing that unglues her.

"You weren't going to tell me," she says finally, choking on the words.

"I couldn't. It's complicated."

She thinks, *I'm so stupid. I thought you loved me.* And then: *My mother was right.*

Outside a horn sounds.

"That's my taxi." Gwen hoists the backpack to her shoulder. "I have to go."

As a child in Pennsylvania, Frank McKotch had seen a boy trapped inside the trunk of a tree.

This happened in springtime, the year he and Blaise Klezek were ten. Blaise was his best friend, nearly a brother—Frank's own brothers, nine and twelve years older, had never been much good to him. It was late March, damp and leafless, the first sunny day after a week of soaking rain. The boys spent the morning in church, the interminable hymning and incensing of Palm Sunday. They sat through chicken dinners in uncomfortable clothing. Finally, gratefully, they roared into the forest with Indian whoops, a great stream of pent-up boyhood rushing to escape.

They lived on a hill scored with rows of company houses; behind the hill were acres of dense poplar, oak, and beech. In buck and doe season these woods were off-limits—some years before, a boy had died there, hit by a hunter's stray bullet—but in springtime the boys owned the forest. The stream was alive with frogs, water skippers, small snakes that wriggled but didn't bite. The oaks—their low, spreading branches—made easy climbing. The poplars were less accommodating, stretching indifferently, magnificently toward the sky.

For a long time the boys had eyed a certain tree, a mighty poplar sitting atop a ridge, the tallest tree for half a mile. The poplar's bark was crenellated and silvery, its trunk wide as a barrel. Its branches were unreachable, but close beside it was a tall beech to which someone had nailed crude scraps of two-by-fours, spaced like the rungs of a ladder. Midway up the beech was a wooden platform, a hunter's look-out. Standing on the platform, a boy might reach across to the lowest branch of the poplar.

It was Frank who pointed this out, Blaise who shinned up the makeshift ladder. But when he reached the platform, he hesitated.

"Can you reach it?" Frank called.

"I don't know," said Blaise. "It's farther than it looks."

Frank held his breath as Blaise reached and swung into the poplar's bottom branch. After that it looked easy. Blaise crabbed toward the poplar's trunk, where the branches were thicker. He reached up to a higher branch, and then a higher one. For a gasping moment he lost his footing. Quickly he righted himself.

"Slippery," he called.

"Careful," said Frank.

"I can see the schoolyard," Blaise said. "I can see the Twelve!"

"Are you sure?" The tipple of Mine Twelve, nearly a mile away, was the tallest structure in town.

By now Blaise was twenty feet off the ground. "It's wet," he shouted. A moment later he let out a tremendous yell. Then he was simply gone.

"Blaise?" Frank circled the tree, craning his neck, but there was no trace of his friend. It was as if a passing angel had snatched him in midair.

He heard another shout that seemed far away. Then, Blaise's voice, curiously muffled: "It's hollow! I'm in the tree!"

Frank rushed to the trunk. The sound seemed to come from above his head. "Are you okay?" he shouted.

Another muffled cry.

"I can't hear you," Frank shouted.

"My leg," Blaise said, louder this time. "I hurt my leg."

"Can you see anything?" said Frank.

"It's dark." Blaise's voice sounded choked.

"I'm going to go get my dad," Frank said into the tree.

"No!" Blaise shouted, so loudly that the bark vibrated next to Frank's cheek. "Don't go!"

"I can't reach you," said Frank. "My dad has a ladder." The only way in, as far as he could see, was the way Blaise had gone, through a soft rotted spot in the trunk, maybe twenty feet up. Frank saw, now, that the spot was blackened. The tree had been struck by lightning. It had died from the inside out.

"I'll be right back," he called.

He ran furiously to his house, and came back with his father and Blaise's; when their rope and ladder proved too short, Frank raced across town to the firehouse. When Blaise was finally extricated two hours later—leg broken, shoulder dislocated, face and hands scraped raw—he seemed stunned and disoriented, still bewildered by the fall.

Frank hadn't thought of Blaise Klezek in a long time—he'd died ten years back in a drunk-driving accident—but the episode came back to him vividly in the spring of 1998, as he walked the streets of Cambridge muttering to himself. His mind, ever the athlete, raced like a star rebounder between two hoops. One, Cristina Spiliotes. Two, Blaise in his narrow prison: stunned, immobile, with no window to the outside. It was a prison nature had made; by following his instincts, Blaise had fallen in. Reaching for the next branch was a boy's imperative. Boy took what tree offered. He did this because he could. What pulled the boy down was likewise a force of nature. The laws of the universe bent for no one.

Humans had mass. Humans fell.

FRANK FELL to earth on a Monday morning. He returned from an early meeting at Protogenix to find Betsy Baird on the phone.

"Frank, where have you been? I've been calling all over town looking for you. Steve Upstairs wants to see you. As soon as possible, he says."

Upstairs, Frank knocked at the door of the corner office, where Zeichner was eating his lunch. He was white haired now, short and pugnacious, with a low, swollen belly. He resembled an army cook or perhaps a baker, rather than a geneticist who'd won the Nobel Prize.

"Frank, I'm glad you're here. Have a seat." Zeichner pushed away his sandwich and licked his fingers. "I don't have a lot of time, so I'll cut right to it. We have a situation on our hands. It concerns one of your postdocs." He folded his hands. "Cristina Spiliotes."

"Cristina," Frank repeated.

"Talk to me about the paper, Frank."

Immediately Frank felt the winds change. Like many athletes, he fed on adversity, consequence. Crisis fired his blood. He did a quick inventory of his body, inhaled courage, shored up the reserve.

"Well, as you know, it's been accepted at *Science*," he said cautiously. "Scheduled for the first week in April."

Zeichner closed his eyes a moment. He looked slightly ill. "That's what I thought. Frank, if you're aware of any irregularities in the data, now is the time to tell me."

"Irregularities," he repeated slowly. "What are you talking about?"

Zeichner paged through the paper on his desk. "This." He handed Frank the paper. A line diagram had been Xed out in red ink, a fine line the color of blood.

"The tail blot?" Frank frowned. "What's the problem? It shows clearly that she got the knockout. It's there in black and white."

"So it is," Zeichner said.

"What exactly are you suggesting?" Frank paused. "Steve, she showed me the gel from the tail blot. I *saw* it."

"I would hope so."

"I mean, I scrutinized it. Many times. There was nothing wrong with that gel."

Zeichner met his gaze. "Listen, I don't doubt that she showed you *a* gel, and I'm sure it looked fine. But that DNA didn't come from the tail. She lied, Frank."

Frank blinked, not comprehending.

"She did the tail blot," Zeichner continued. "She just didn't like the results. That gel showed that she didn't get the knockout, so she faked it. This gel"—his fat finger stabbed viciously at the page—"didn't come from the tail blot. It came from the stem cells."

Frank's mind raced. Was it possible?

"This is crazy," he said. "She's a bright girl, Steve. I haven't seen a postdoc this promising in years." As he said it, Frank realized it was true. "Who's making these allegations?"

Zeichner watched him levelly. "Another of your other postdocs came to me this morning. Apparently he was in the lab meeting last fall, when the girl presented the blot from the stem cells. And when he saw a copy of the paper, the tail blot looked familiar. He'd seen it before. She recycled the stem-cell blot; only this time she said it came from the tail." He paused. "She lied, Frank."

"But then—" Frank's mind raced. If Cristina hadn't gotten the knockout—if XIAP *had* been functioning—her deception wouldn't have ended there. The transgenic mice who appeared resistant to tumors—what accounted for their good health?

"She faked the animal data?" he said softly.

Zeichner shrugged. "Frank, you know as well as I do: there are a million ways she could have massaged those numbers."

Frank stared at the floor. It was true, of course. *Any* animal data was vulnerable to statistical manipulation; only a scientist's integrity stood in the way. And if Cristina were devious enough—desperate enough—to lie about the knockout, why stop there? Three cohorts of transgenic mice, three cohorts of control mice: six sets of numbers, the tumors counted and measured with tiny calipers. By leaving out the sickest mice, and underreporting tumor size in the others—a few millimeters here or there—she could have exaggerated the differences between the two groups. It would have been shockingly easy to do.

"Who says so?" Frank demanded. "One of *mine*?"

"Martin Keohane."

Frank blinked. Martin had worked in his lab for nearly four years, the organizer of the famous birthday roast. Frank had attended Martin's wedding and the baptism of his son.

"*Martin?* You're joking." *This isn't happening,* he thought. "This makes no sense. For God's sake, why wouldn't he come to me first?"

"I wondered that myself." Zeichner leaned forward in his chair. "Frank, I have to ask: is there some reason why your postdoc would think you couldn't address this problem fairly?"

"What are you getting at?"

"Look, I don't know anything about your relationship with this girl, and I'm not asking. I really, *really* don't want to know. You're both adults, and the institute has no policy on extracurricular relationships between colleagues. Although in this case—" He paused. "Look, Frank. There's a hierarchy here. If your relationship with her, whatever it might be, clouds your judgment, if you can't oversee her research as rigorously as you would any other postdoc's, if things start slipping through the cracks—" His voice trailed off. "Then we have a problem."

Frank opened and closed his fists. He realized he'd lost feeling in his hands.

"Steve, I'm only going to say this once. My relationship with this girl has been perfectly proper. Perfectly," he added for emphasis. "Has anybody *talked* with her, for God's sake? Heard her side of it?"

"Not yet." Zeichner glanced at his watch. "That's up to you. But by five o'clock I want her work off the bench. Get her reagents out of the freezer. I'd see to it personally, if I were you. It's all evidence, Frank. We'll need it for the internal review."

FRANK HURRIED down the stairs, taking them two at a time. *Pull the paper*, he thought frantically. *We've got to pull the paper.* He loomed over Betsy Baird's desk. "Have you seen Cristina?" he demanded, more harshly than he'd intended.

"Noooo." She looked at him quizzically. "Is something wrong?"

"If you see her, tell her I want to talk to her," he barked.

In his office he stared into space a moment, collecting himself. There was only one person he could imagine calling in such a crisis. A scientist whose ethics had never been questioned, who played the game better than anyone he knew. The past was irrelevant now; the present crisis was all that mattered.

He picked up the phone and dialed Neil Windsor.

He'd been on the phone half an hour when he heard the click of high heels in the corridor. Through the glass pane of his office door, he saw Cristina walking down the hall.

"I've got to go," he told Neil. "That's her now."

"Don't lose your temper," Neil cautioned. "Just get a look at her notebook. That's all you need to do."

"Thanks, buddy. I'll let you know how it goes."

He hung up the phone and hurried down the hall. Cristina had gone into the lab, a Styrofoam takeout tray in her hand. She turned, startled.

"Frank, you scared me!" Her eyes scanned his face. "Is something wrong?"

"You could say that." Firmly he closed the door. "Have a seat."

She pulled out a lab stool and sat, staring up at him. She didn't *look* guilty. She looked utterly mystified.

"I talked with Steve Zeichner this morning," he said. "It seems we have a problem."

She cocked her head quizzically.

"He's been looking at your data. Our data. The tail blots."

She frowned.

"Cristina, is there anything you want to tell me?"

A shadow passed across her face, or maybe he imagined it. "What do you mean?"

He nodded. "All right, then. I need to see your notebook."

Cristina did not move.

"Well?" he barked.

She looked up at him, her eyes wide. Six months ago the look would have melted him. Now he felt only rage.

"Cristina," he said through his teeth. "SHOW ME THOSE GELS."

She bowed her head. For the first time he noticed a glint of silver in her hair.

"I'm sorry," she said softly.

"You did this?" He stared at her, horrified. "For Christ's sake, you falsified data?" If she hadn't succeeded in knocking out the gene, the mice would have been riddled with tumors. Her paper—*their* paper—had lied outright.

"Do you understand the magnitude of this? Your career, your reputation. My career, for God's sake! The future of this lab. Do you have any idea what you've done?"

He waited, his cheeks flaming.

"Say something! Just *tell me why.*"

She raised her head. "I was certain I'd gotten the knockout. I don't know what went wrong." She hesitated. "If I could just try again—"

He stared at her, his cheeks flaming.

"But there was *no time*! Frank, you wanted to submit immediately, and I didn't want to disappoint you. I was afraid you'd change your mind."

"You're not suggesting I encouraged this." He stopped, breathed, chose his words carefully. "I admit, I was eager to submit the paper. But a fraudulent paper? Are you out of your mind?"

"But you said it was ready! No reason to drag our feet, you said. You didn't want to get mired in the details."

"Nonsense," he snapped. "When did I say that?"

"Christmas Eve! You left a message on my answering machine. You said the paper was ready to go. You wanted to get it out the door."

He remembered then: Christmas Eve in Cambridge, a lonely old drunk in bedroom slippers, holding forth.

"That's exactly what you said," Cristina insisted. "I can prove it. I have the tape."

Cornered, he got angry. Loudly, unapologetically angry. "Oh, come off it! You knew full well those comments were off-the-cuff. It was Christmas Eve, for God's sake! That hardly qualifies as a final review."

She met his eyes. "I've made a terrible mistake; I know that. I'm not making excuses. But you did ask me why, so I'll tell you." Her voice faltered. "I felt for a long time that things had gone bad between us. You were so supportive of my work at first, so encouraging. But then something changed."

Frank watched her soberly. Shame burned his cheeks.

"You were different with Guei and Martin; I could see that. I felt that I had disappointed you somehow. And I wanted to make you proud of me."

Billy and Gwen sat in the grass near the reservoir, eating greasy takeout from a Chinese place on Eighty-sixth Street. It was a Sunday afternoon in April, unseasonably warm, the air spongy and odorous, the first teasing hint of summer. Women wore sandals and flowered dresses. A steady parade of wheeled people—cyclists, skaters, infants in strollers—rolled in and out of the park.

As they ate, Billy caught himself watching her. His sister a constant in his life, comforting, reliable. Unchanged since childhood, or so it seemed: wearing the same clothes, listening to the same music—Supertramp, the Allman Brothers—on vinyl, of course. Now Gwen, at long last, had changed. Her hair had grown nearly to her shoulders. Her ears pierced twice, seven of her fingers decorated with silver rings. He noticed that she had pretty hands.

"So Scott just showed up there? You must have been floored." Billy popped half a wonton into his mouth, already feeling queasy with guilt. He rarely ate fried food, and certainly not a week before a race; but the dumplings were Gwen's favorite. She'd shown up at his apartment the night before, her eyes red from crying. Billy hadn't seen her cry since she was a little girl. In this condition, he couldn't refuse her anything.

"Maybe I shouldn't be telling you this," he said, "but Mom called me about a month ago in a panic. She wanted me to fly down there and bring you back."

"You're kidding me."

"You're surprised?"

"No, I guess not. Mind if I finish this?" Gwen held up the carton of fried rice. "It makes sense that she asked you first. I mean, why would she have picked Scott?"

Billy chuckled. "Last resort, I guess."

"He was stoned out of his mind when he showed up."

"That figures," Billy said. "Then what? He tried to talk you into leaving?"

"For about a minute. Then he sort of forgot about it." Gwen shrugged. "We sat on deck and watched the sunset. Then I drove him back to his hotel."

"But it worked," Billy said, puzzled. "I mean, here you are."

"It had nothing to do with Scott." Gwen's eyes began to well. "I just came to my senses, is all. New subject, please."

And as always when they were together, they spoke of childhood. Lying in the grass, rubbing his bloated stomach, Billy told Gwen about the time Paulette took him into Cambridge to spy on his father.

It was a morning in September, his first week in the eighth grade. Paulette had kept him home from school, a thing she'd never done before; they dropped Scotty and Gwen at Pilgrims, then drove into town. To this day he wasn't sure why she'd taken him along, what possessed her to include him in their jazzy adult gaming. Maybe she'd merely needed a witness, someone to share in her triumph when she caught Frank in a lie.

Billy hadn't understood, at first, where they were going. Then they made the turn into Cambridge and he recognized the square buildings of MIT where, that summer, his father had taken him to spend a day in the lab. That other day had begun brightly, with orange juice and muffins in a university cafeteria. Then his father had walked him through the lab, pointing out the different equipment, letting him look through the microscopes. Finally he left Billy in a corner with some scientific journals—to browse through, it seemed, as though he were waiting for the dentist—and started banging away at a typewriter, the bell ringing periodically as he came to the end of a line. At first Billy waited patiently, staring at the old Seth Thomas clock—the humming sweep of the seconds, the caffeinated jump of the minutes. Later he waited impatiently, fidgeting in his chair. It didn't matter which he did. His father never looked up from his report.

Finally his father's secretary, a blond girl named Betsy, walked past the open door and saw him sitting there. She took him into a cramped room filled with filing cabinets. The radio was playing, which surprised him. At home he listened whenever possible, but he'd always thought adults didn't like music. This seemed to be true of all the adults he knew.

Stacks of manila folders were piled on the desk, the cabinets, the floor. The papers had been moved from some other office and Betsy was supposed to file them. She asked if Billy would help.

Sure, he said, happy to do something besides stare at the clock, yet nervous, because Betsy had very long hair and wore fruity perfume and smiled at him when she spoke.

She showed him the code written on each file, a long string of letters and numbers, corresponding to labels on the cabinet drawers. They worked back-to-back, their bodies nearly touching, Betsy's perfume filling the tiny room.

They worked that way minutes or hours, who could tell, until a particular song came on the radio. Billy recognized the opening bars immediately. The song was "Billy Don't Be a Hero."

He knew all the words, of course—if you were a kid in those days and your name was Billy and you listened to the radio ten hours a day, you couldn't *not* know the words. It was a silly song he secretly liked, a girl pleading with some Billy who was going to enlist and get his head blown off unless he came to his senses and married her. Listening, he marveled at how stupid this other Billy was. Of course it was the girl he identified with, the girl who had the passion and the good sense, who was clearly in the right.

It's your song! Betsy squealed. She upped the volume and, with a goofy expression on her face, stared into his eyes and sang the song to him, her pretty girl voice stronger on the high notes. It was a moment he would always remember, Betsy in her short skirt and dangling earrings, holding an imaginary microphone to her pink glossy lips. Betsy's shoulders bobbing to the music, a spoofy anguish in her voice that filled him with delight.

And so there he was a few months later in his mother's station wagon, circling the building where his father worked. Billy spotted Frank's new car, a dark green convertible, parked on the street. His mother parked illegally, blocking a fire hydrant, and left the engine idling. Billy looked at the gas gauge. Like everybody, he was obsessed with gas then, the intrigue of filling the tank on even or odd days, depending on the license number.

We're wasting gas, he almost told his mother, but didn't. He sensed that something important was about to happen.

They sat there a long time, until Frank came out of the building with Betsy. A breeze played with her long hair. She laughed as his father spoke. Billy watched his mother. Her lips were white; she had chewed away her lipstick. Round red splotches were on both her cheeks, like a clown's makeup.

There's a cafeteria in that building, he said. *Dad took me there once. They're going to eat lunch.* That's not bad, he wanted to add, but didn't. They're just eating lunch. He was old enough to grasp the basics, the reason for his mother's pain.

"Did Dad see you?" Gwen asked.

"Nope. We drove back to Concord and I remember Mom was very quiet. I wanted to turn on the radio and she said no, if she didn't concentrate she was going to crash the car. Then we got home and she made me a sandwich." Billy paused. "But here's the weird part. The very next morning she *did* crash the car. Not the station wagon. Dad's convertible. The Saab 97. Remember this?"

"Sure," said Gwen. "It was the day before my birthday. She went to the bakery to get me a cake."

"Yeah. I don't know why she took his car, though. It was a stick shift, which she hated. I remember how mad she was when he bought it, this car she could barely drive. Remember?"

"I remember when she wrecked the car," Gwen said slowly. "Dad was bullshit. But the other thing? The spying?" She frowned. "I thought they were happy then. Before—" She stopped.

Before the doctors, before the Turner's. Before I ruined everything. Billy thought for a second that she might say it. But she was Gwen, and did not.

"They always had problems," he said. *It wasn't you,* he wanted to add, but didn't. *It wasn't your fault.*

That evening, waving at the back of Gwen's taxi, which had been joined by so many others that he might have been waving at the wrong one, Billy wondered why he'd told the story at all. He hadn't thought of that day in years. It was true: his parents' marriage had been rocky all along. Yet when anyone asked what had caused the divorce—Sri, Matthew Stone, the few friends close enough to ask personal questions—he found himself telling a very different story. *My dad couldn't handle Gwen's condition. After she was diagnosed, he was out of there like a shot.* That was his mother's version of events, and Billy realized—on some level, had realized all along—that it wasn't entirely true. For one thing, Frank had hung on for nearly a year after Gwen's diagnosis, the marital bloodshed escalating until Billy, for one, had been relieved to see him go.

Why are you so tough on Dad? Gwen often asked him. It was Frank, after all, who'd gotten her properly diagnosed, who'd pursued what were then cutting-edge treatments for Turner's. No father could have been more concerned, more involved. Yet in Billy's eyes, Frank's few virtues didn't cancel out his many failings. The damage he had done.

Better than anyone else, Billy knew how Paulette had suffered. All through the divorce he'd been her confidant. *Your father is leaving us. Abandoning your poor sister. Honestly, it's more than I can bear.* Her tears had frightened him, the sheer force of her rage. Each time he waited silently for the storm to pass, ashamed of his helplessness, his inability to comfort her. He felt obligated to blame his father. It was a sign of loyalty, one his mother seemed to require. At fourteen, fifteen, he had dreaded school vacations: the ongoing drama of shuttling Gwen to doctors, the bitter parental arguments that preceded and followed. How gratefully he'd returned to Pearse, finally free of both his parents. Free, even, of Gwen. Back then it had seemed safer and wiser to keep them all at a distance. In this way, the System had begun.

He crossed the avenue and climbed the stairs to his apartment, feeling suddenly exhausted. Not by the easy eight he'd run yesterday—his training was in the tapering phase—or by his sister's company, but by his own. All weekend he'd worried—grimly, relentlessly—whether he was saying the right things, whether he'd done enough to help. Sri, if he'd been there, would have seen him fretting, his thoughts spinning like laundry in the washer. *You're doing fine*, Sri would have told him, and Billy would have believed him. Sri was no expert on Gwen —since Billy's accident they'd had no contact beyond pleasantries on the phone—but he was an expert on Billy. *You've got to stop improving*, Sri had once told him. *You're so busy trying to do everything better that you're missing your whole life. Stop. Stop.*

And it helped. When Billy worried—about his patients, his tricky IT bands that acted up a week before a race, an impending visit with his neurotic family—Sri's face was a silent reminder: stop, stop.

Billy made a quick tour of the apartment—cleaning, straightening—and headed into the kitchen. He scrubbed down and began chopping—carrots, celery, scallions, ginger. Sri would be home in two hours, and Billy intended to surprise him with dinner, something he rarely did. He wasn't a bad cook—you didn't live alone for ten years without learning to flip an omelet—but most of his old repertoire was now off-limits. His arteries were nearing forty, and he couldn't spike his blood with sat fat the way he once had. He had learned to love the freshness of Sri's cooking, the way you could detect the delicate flavors of foods you didn't think had any: rice, lettuce, milk. *This would be delicious the old way*, Sri sometimes said wistfully as he sampled a dish. His grandmother had cooked with ghee, a notion Billy found appalling.

It's better this way, he told Sri. *We'll live forever.*

What he meant, but didn't say: I want to grow old with you.

Even thinking the words had unleashed a tide of feeling in him; he didn't trust himself to speak. His love for Sri ambushed him at odd moments. Last week, when their clean laundry was delivered, he'd spent a long moment placing Sri's things in his bureau, profoundly moved by the neat stacks of folded jeans and T-shirts, the soft piles of his lover's clothes.

He'd recalled that feeling as he watched Sri packing, the rough, angry way he'd stuffed clothes into his overnight bag, oblivious to the care that had gone into folding them, the young Chinese girl creasing them with delicate hands.

It's just for a couple of days, Billy had said. And then, disingenuously: *I'm worried about her. I have to make sure she's okay.*

Sri had silenced him with a look. They both knew this wasn't the point. By all means, take care of your sister, the look said. But why must you kick me to the curb?

They'd parted without kissing good-bye. "I'll call you," Sri said over his shoulder.

But he hadn't called.

For two days Billy had distracted himself with Gwen's problems. Now his anxiety returned in a wave. Nursing his sister through heart-break was taxing enough, strange and awkward and worrying enough. Would she confide in him? Expect wise counsel? Dear God, was she going to cry? The presence of his boyfriend would have heaped on more strangeness. Yet Gwen had seemed surprised by his absence. "Where's Sri?" she'd asked the moment she walked through the door.

It was true, what Sri often said: he was terrified of change.

He was thinking such thoughts when the telephone rang.

"Hey," he said breathlessly.

"Billy?" His mother sounded puzzled. "Dear, I can't believe you answer the phone that way."

"Sorry," he said, flustered. "I was in the middle of something."

"Well, don't keep me in suspense. How did it go with your sister? I've been so concerned about her."

Here we go, Billy thought. His own fault: he had told Paulette that Gwen would be visiting. He had brought this on himself.

He settled into the sofa. "She seemed a little—stunned, I guess."

"Did she tell you anything? Of course I'm delighted to have her back, but I'd love to know what happened. What changed her mind?"

Rico wasn't the person I thought he was, Gwen had explained.

"She didn't say much. They had a fight, I guess."

"How did she look?"

"Different," he said thoughtfully. Walking to the diner Saturday morning, they had passed a hip hair salon, and for a moment he'd considered dragging Gwen inside—her hair was long enough, finally, that a stylist would have something to work with. But he had stopped himself. The gesture would have been far too gay.

"Darling, that's not very helpful. Can you at least tell me what she was wearing?"

Typical Paulette.

"The usual," Billy said.

"Oh, dear." She paused. "And what about work? Can she get her job back?"

"She doesn't want to." She'd sooner work the drive-through window at a burger joint, she told Billy, than go back to the Stott. *Maybe I'll finish my dissertation*, she said without enthusiasm. *I haven't figured it out yet.*

Billy heard a strange whirring at the other end of the line. "What is that noise?"

"A saw, I believe. Your brother is in the backyard cutting some wood."

"Scott?"

"Yes, dear. He's been here all weekend, working. I can't tell you what a relief it is, to have something done about the porch."

"Scott?" Billy repeated.

"He's doing a magnificent job. I didn't realize how complicated it was to do an authentic period restoration. Your brother has done quite a lot of research."

Billy frowned. His brother doing anything constructive—hell, anything not patently *de*structive—was hard to imagine.

"That's great, Mom," he said, eyeing the clock. "Tell him I said hi."

More whirring, followed by a shrieking.

"Tell him yourself, if you like. He's eager to talk with you."

Oh, Jesus, Billy thought. He waited.

"Hey, Bill," Scott huffed, sniffling. "Mom said you saw Gwen."

"She was here for the weekend." He was struck by the oddness of the situation: his brother was in Concord with their mother, and Billy himself was not. Except for his grudging holiday visits, wife and rug rats in tow, Scott hadn't visited in Concord in years.

"What happened, man?" Scott demanded. "That dirtbag kicked her out?"

"Um, no," Billy said, a little confused. "She left him, apparently."

"*She* did." Scott's tone was skeptical, as though he knew otherwise. As though Billy had gotten it all wrong. "O-*Kay*. Why would she do that?"

"I'm not sure." Billy hesitated. "I got the impression that he was up to something—illegal, maybe. And Gwen caught wind of it."

"No shit," said Scott. "What exactly did she say?"

"'He wasn't the person I thought he was.' Something like that." Billy paused. "You met the guy. Could he have been some kind of criminal? A drug dealer maybe?"

"That's an interesting question," Scott said expansively, as though warming up for an oration on the subject. There was something oddly familiar in his tone—a self-importance, a leisurely appreciation of the sound of his own voice. For a moment he sounded just like their father. "He was definitely nervous. You should have seen the look on his face when I showed up out of the blue. He was shitting his pants. Of course he was on good behavior with me. The brother from the States. But there was something slippery about him. A little too smooth, if you know what I mean. A drug dealer?" He paused as if weighing the matter. "Yeah, it's possible. Wouldn't surprise me a bit."

Thank you for your expert opinion, Billy thought.

"Anyway, all's well that ends well," said Scott.

Billy thought of Gwen as she'd looked when she'd appeared on his doorstep, her eyes swollen, as though she'd spent the whole flight from Pittsburgh crying like a child. No, not a child: the sorrow had remodeled her face in ways that seemed permanent. As though, like a war widow, she'd been crying for months or years.

"What are you doing there, anyway?" Billy asked. "Fixing Mom's porch?"

Scott laughed, a low, hearty chuckle. "I wish it were so simple. The porch is beyond repair. I'm starting from scratch here, Bill, and given the historical value of the house, I want to get it exactly right. It matters, you know? I mean, for the National Register of Historic Places—"

"The house is on the register?"

"No, but it should be. Josiah Hobhouse and all. I'm looking into nominating it. But one thing at a time, you know? Anyway, long story short—"

Too late for that, Billy thought.

"I met this carpenter the other day—he knows Mom, actually—and he does nothing but historic restorations, on the Vineyard mostly. He's walking me through the whole process, which materials to use—"

"That's great, Scotty. Listen, I have to run. I have something on the stove."

"You're cooking?" Scott whistled. "Say no more. She must be something."

"Must be," Billy agreed. "Good luck with everything, and give Mother a kiss from me."

He hung up the phone, aware that he hadn't said a proper good-bye to his mother, a delicate extrication that usually took ten minutes or more. He felt a little relieved, a little lost.

In the kitchen he resumed chopping. His whole life his brother had seemed so much *younger*—a toddler in diapers when Billy started Little League, a pot-smoking delinquent when Billy was busting his ass in med school. Then Scott came back from California with a wife and kids, and suddenly Billy had felt old. For the first time in years, he found himself imagining the life he might have had with Lauren McGregor, or someone like her. It was nothing he pined for. Family life, that grimy jumble: tiring and chaotic on a good day; on a bad one, a nerve-shearing slice of hell. Watching his kid brother wrangle two children of his own, Billy had suffered a series of realizations. That his own choices—like Scotty's, like Gwen's—were binding. That like a grave illness, adulthood had befallen all three of them. That fortuitously or not, their courses in life had been set, the only lives they were going to get.

SRI ARRIVED at seven, ever prompt. "What's all this?" he said, peering into the kitchen.

"Dinner." Billy leaned in to kiss him. "I thought I'd feed you, for once."

"I can't stay."

Billy noticed, then, that he wasn't carrying his overnight bag.

"Why not?" he asked, though he already knew. Had known it, in some way, all weekend: his stomach, his nerves, the jangle and hum.

"It's better this way," said Sri.

"How?" Billy's voice cracked, surprising him. "How is it better?"

Sri sat on the edge of the couch, but did not settle in. He moved differently in the apartment, as though he were a visitor. As though he had already gone.

"I made a mistake," Billy began haltingly. "Asking you to leave. I missed you constantly. Gwen would have loved to see you."

"So it's not Gwen," Sri said softly. "It's you."

"It's complicated with Gwen. It always has been." How to explain his weird protectiveness, the fact that, until a car accident knocked him unconscious, his sister had never met a single one of his friends? His impulse, always, was to hide her, to shield her from embarrassing questions. He hadn't spoken to his cousin Mimi in years; she'd taken up permanent residence on his shit list for inquiring about Gwen's health. At fifteen he'd started the only fist fight of his life, over a stupid joke: Warren Marsh, the twerp next door, calling Gwen his *leetle seester* in a Peter Sellers accent, a high squeaky voice.

"I've been doing it forever," Billy said. "Keeping things separate. My parents separate from my friends. Gwen separate from everything. It's just the way my family is."

"So you're not ashamed of me," said Sri.

"Of course not," Billy lied, knowing that he was, in fact, ashamed of everything: of Sri, of Gwen, and of himself. That he was globally ashamed.

"It's hard to explain," he said slowly. "If I had a girlfriend, I wouldn't tell my mother that either. And she would never ask. She wouldn't lean across the dinner table and ask, Billy, are you dating someone? The whole subject is off-limits. Because if she asked me that question, she would have to ask Gwen."

"So your whole family is in the closet," said Sri.

"So to speak." Billy agreed.

"How is Gwen?"

"Heartbroken." *Like me*, Billy thought. *We are both heartbroken.*

He would realize later that he should have said it. The latest on a long list of things he should have said.

I love you. Don't leave me.

Mother, I'm

Dad, I'm

Lauren, I'm

Yes, I am.

"Your family is not simple," Sri said. "Mine isn't either, I suppose—what's left of it. But they're very far away. And I've been gone so long that I no longer care what they think."

"I don't care either," Billy said, too quickly. "My family. I don't care what they think." As he said it he heard how absurd it was. The biggest lie—among many—he'd told in his life.

"I'm tired of being temporary," said Sri. "We've been a temporary couple for four years. If it were up to you, we'd be one for the rest of our lives." He frowned. "It's as if you're waiting for something to change. You like to believe you can still change your mind."

"But I hate change. You say that all the time."

"Yes. But you like the illusion that change is possible. That's the thing you can't give up."

"Listen to me," Billy said. "It can be different. I can—"

"—change." Sri smiled broadly, as though Billy had said something extraordinarily funny. He pressed a fist to his eye. He seemed delighted and furious and ready to weep.

chapter 8

S cott had become an early riser. His whole life he had cursed the alarm clock, but now something inside him had shifted. He made a game of creeping silently out of bed, careful not to wake Penny. There was a plush satisfaction in landing at Ruxton at sunrise, a full hour before Rick O'Kane. Unlocking the door to his office, eyeing the plastic toys decorating Jordan's desk, he felt a calm mastery of his time and surroundings. Dashiell Blodgett: *Conquer your environment before it conquers you.*

He didn't waste these precious early hours grading papers. Mornings were for his own projects. He had borrowed from the library a half dozen books on building and architecture: *Residences of Olde New England, Maintaining Your Historic Home.* Fueled by coffee—he picked up a Styrofoam bucket each morning at Dunkin' Donuts—he pored over them tirelessly. The porch completed, he'd identified several other projects at his mother's house that needed his attention. The west-facing windows should have been replaced years ago; no wonder the house was drafty. A bedroom ceiling showed water damage. The roof had been replaced a few years back, but apparently not soon enough.

He committed his plans to a small grubby notebook: sketches, notes, shopping lists for Builder's Depot. Often, as he planned, he called the mobile phone of Gil Pyle, a carpenter his mother knew. On his way to an early job in Newton or Wellesley or Newport, Pyle would greet him curtly—"Hey, shithead"—as though they were the oldest of friends. This, Scott realized, was half the reason he called. Pyle would listen to the details of Scott's plan and offer a few curt suggestions: use number twelve, not ten; give the stuff a full day to dry; check out the salvage yard in Dorchester, they got windows coming out the ass. Things the books didn't tell you, tricks that only builders knew. Pyle shared this information freely, expecting nothing in return. *Your mother's been good to me*, he said. *I owe her big time. Anything you need, man. Just ask.*

That his mother knew such a person continued to amaze him. *Battle Road, dear*, she said when Scott asked where they'd met. As a kid Scott had found the battle reenactment hilarious, grown men dressing up in costumes to charge and salute and fire muskets. Now that he knew Gil Pyle, he saw it differently. He wished, secretly, that he could do it himself.

He was surprised to discover that Pyle knew quite a bit about him. *I hear you spent some time in Cali*, he said once when they were unloading his truck. *I rode my bike out there when I was a kid. Landed myself in the hospital with heat exhaustion.* Pyle knew that Billy was a cardiologist in New York; he knew how Scott's parents had met and even, he implied, why they'd divorced. Most improbably, Pyle knew—and this was so astonishing that Scott nearly dropped a hundred pounds of lumber on his foot—everything about Gwen.

Even within the family, his sister's condition had always been top secret. *Don't tell Mamie your sister is at the doctor's.* Without ever having asked why, he'd understood the importance of keeping quiet. That his mother had discussed Gwen with a stranger, a man who banged nails for a living and dressed up once a year in breeches, was stupefying. Gil Pyle had spent whole summers on the Cape and islands; he'd done clapboards for a Kennedy, floors for a Kennedy ex-wife. He'd built a gazebo for an aged actress in Edgartown, an open-air theater for a rock-star couple who liked to perform in their own backyard. If pressed, Pyle would serve up details—both rock stars kept a stable of beautiful lovers; the old actress answered her door each morning in full starlet makeup, each day a different wig. The stories ended always with the same refrain: *She's a nice lady when you get to know her. He's a decent guy.* About his own life Pyle was equally forthcoming. He had a daughter in college, an ex-wife in Maine, and an old girlfriend in Florida, the mother of his two young sons. He had spent six years in the army; there were stories about German girls and others, Belgian and French, he'd met on leave. Scott thought of his father's threat, years ago, when he was flunking out of Stirling: *Another semester like that, and the army can have you. I wish them luck.* It seemed, now, that Frank's idea had been a good one. It might have been the making of him. Scott could have, like Gil Pyle, seen the world. He might have become a man. Instead he'd wasted his parents' money in one school after another and was no better for it, an indentured servant who'd even sold his own likeness. Day after day he drove past the billboard on Route 11, unconsciously averting his eyes. Ruxton was his Siberia, a prison of humiliations. Only now, empty at sunrise, smelling of floor cleaner and the janitor's weary ministrations, did the place offer him any peace.

LATER, AFTER teaching his first-period class, he returned to his office and found the red message light flickering on his phone.

Hi, Hon. Ian's school called again. They need his fall tuition tomorrow. They were really bitchy about it too. So don't forget, okay?

Ian's tuition.

He hadn't forgotten about it, not remotely. The phrase "twenty thousand dollars" came to mind approximately three times per hour. The number *twenty thousand* haunted his dreams. His dream self wandered the towering aisles of Builder's Depot panicked and perspiring. He needed twenty thousand nails, or twenty thousand gallons of primer. This dream recurred two, three times a week, supplanting his usual Stirling dream, the flashback of academic panic. Scott lived in dread. Someday soon Penny—and perhaps even his mother—would discover what he'd done. As in the past, his dread paralyzed him. He hadn't yet progressed to planning, for example, how he would break the news to his wife. *The money's gone. Ian can't go to Fairhope.*

The bell rang loudly, startling him. He had another class to teach. He took a stack of weekly quizzes from his desk drawer and shoved them into his briefcase.

"McKotch." Rick O'Kane stood in the doorway in a pale, expensive-looking suit. His tan had deepened. He looked like a million bucks.

"Slow down, fella." O'Kane sat in the chair opposite Scott's desk, hiking up his trousers to preserve their crease. "What's your rush?"

"I have class this period," said Scott.

"You don't, actually. I got Mary Fahey to cover for you." He reached into his jacket and produced a long envelope.

Scott stared at him dumbly.

"You have been selected for drug testing," O'Kane recited. "This selection is random and, as you will recall, a condition of your employment."

Scott felt suddenly light-headed. His mind raced, trying to calculate how many weeks had passed since his trip to St. Raphael. "When?" he asked.

"Now." O'Kane handed him the envelope. "You're to report immediately to the testing center on Quinnebaug Highway. Standard procedure, McKotch."

Scott frowned. For his last drug test, he'd driven to a medical complex near the hospital. "Not the other place?"

"We use a different company now. The address is in the packet." O'Kane rose. "It's a ten-minute drive from here. Go directly to the testing site. Don't stop for doughnuts," he said, eyeing Scott's Styrofoam cup. "If you haven't reported in half an hour, they'll call me. Have a nice day." He watched Scott levelly. He seemed to be waiting for something.

"Then what?" said Scott.

"I'll have your results in twenty-four hours. Oh, and don't worry about your classes," O'Kane said over his shoulder. "You're covered for the rest of the day."

DASHIELL BLODGETT was right about one thing: ineptly, perhaps unconsciously, you forged your own destiny. Fate was a child's fingerpainting, a macaroni hut, a drunken calypso song improvised in the shower. Even in that final moment, as O'Kane handed him the packet, Scott could have talked his way out of it. He had a cold, a backache, a toothache; he was taking cough syrup, decongestants, massive doses of ibuprofen, which might skew the results of the test. Jordan Funk had pulled this very stunt a year before, a move Scott had reluctantly admired.

Nice strategy, he'd whispered to Jordan later.

I really do have a cold. I don't do drugs, Jordan insisted, so primly that Scott knew he was lying. Yet O'Kane had fallen for his story, or pretended to. He might have done the same for Scott, if Scott had even tried.

Why hadn't he tried?

Idling in traffic on Quinnebaug Highway he saw the truth clearly, elegant in its plainness. He didn't *want* to keep his job. Ruxton had been misery from the beginning. As a boy he'd been a surly, reluctant,and underachieving student. Now he was a surly, reluctant, and underachieving teacher. School had been the great torment of his life, the scene of all his shames and rages. He was an adult now, free to choose where and how to spend his precious years on earth. And where had he chosen to spend them?

In school.

He had never wanted to be a teacher. Marooned in California, with a baby he hadn't planned and a woman he wasn't sure he loved, he'd wanted to be a kid again. His mother had dashed this hope. *Finish your degree*, she'd begged him. *Let me help.* Cal State San Bernardino had accepted his credits, the courses he'd selected more or less randomly his three semesters at Stirling: History of the Fertile Crescent, Introduction to Psychology, Shakespeare on Film. He'd been high when he chose these courses, which amounted to exactly nothing. General Studies was the only degree within his reach. He tacked on an extra semester to get his teaching certificate (what else could he do with a degree in general studies? become a general?) and a few months later Scott was standing in front of a classroom.

He had jumped at the chance to teach at Ruxton, imagining Ruxton would be just like Pearse. He was desperate then, delusional, a stoned amnesiac who'd forgotten that Pearse had been a jail to him. At fourteen he'd felt exiled there, sent up the river for poor table manners and teasing his sister. A convicted serial biter, banished from his family, doing hard time.

Jesus, he'd hated Pearse.

As Ian would hate Fairhope.

This revelation so startled him that he nearly veered off the highway.

The money wasn't the point. Suddenly it didn't matter that he'd handed twenty thousand dollars to a near stranger, that Ian's tuition check, when Penny wrote it, would bounce into another galaxy. *Ian's not going to Fairhope*, Scott would tell her. *He's not a criminal. We're not sending him away.*

He saw instantly the rightness of this decision. Penny might require convincing, but she would come to see it too. With righteous conviction he pulled into the parking lot of QuineMed Testing associates.

Oh, and guess what, he thought. *I pissed into a jar this morning. And tomorrow I'm going to lose my job.*

THE HOUSE looked dead at ten in the morning. Scott got out of the car, breathing deeply. His shirt smelled of formaldehyde, an odor he'd acquired in the offices of QuineMed. His experience there had been less humiliating than he expected. For his last drug test, a male nurse had followed him into the restroom and stood outside the stall, ear cupped, no doubt, to hear his piss fall into the sample cup. QuineMed's operation was lackadaisical by comparison. Scott had watched another testee take his sample cup into the washroom. The nurse on duty seemed not to notice that the guy wore a battered Carhartt jacket too heavy for the balmy weather, voluminous enough to hide ten containers of clean urine. Scott wondered, briefly, if O'Kane had chosen this slapdash outfit for a reason. If he expected the guilty to cheat; if he was, in fact, inviting deception. Scott could have beaten the test with minimal effort, if only he'd wanted to.

The garage was open, Penny's van parked inside, as though rest-
ing from the ordeal of getting the kids to school.

"Penny," he called, stepping into the living room. "Pen, I need to
talk to you."

He glanced around the room. The usual disorder: junk mail, the
random sneaker, the Diet Coke can on the coffee table. (Penny drank
several cases a week.) The smell of toast hung in the air. All this was
normal, perfectly usual. Yet something seemed very wrong.

He realized it then: someone had turned off the television.

"Honey?" he called, slightly alarmed. He headed down the hall
toward the bedrooms, rubbing at his stubbly chin. *Pen, I have something
to tell you*, he practiced. *Don't worry. Everything will be okay.*

Their bedroom door was open, the bed unmade. The bathroom,
Ian's room: both were empty. Only Sabrina's door was closed.

"Penny?" He pushed open Sabrina's door and stopped short. On
the pink carpet, his wife sat on the floor in her underwear, her back
against the bed. Beside her, his arm around her shoulders, was a blond-
haired man in head-to-toe denim: jeans, vest, shirt. They did not stand.
They cowered like misbehaving children.

"What the hell?" he said, his heart hammering.

"Scotty." She got to her feet, looking stricken. She wore bikini
panties and the bra he liked.

"Who the fuck is this?'

The man got up slowly. He was bigger than Scott, but oddly
graceful.

"This is Benji," Penny said.

"Benji," Scott repeated.

"From Idaho," Penny said. "Benji, my brother."

Life prepared you for certain calamities. With practice, it was
possible to condition oneself for loss, abandonment, failures of every
stripe. Scott had been arrested and insulted, suspended and fired and
put on probation, cold-cocked and sucker-punched and kicked in
the groin. His sanguine nature had been beaten out of him; from
Concord to Pearse to Stirling to California, he'd left a sticky trail.
He'd believed himself inoculated against disappointment, readier

than most to meet the maimed gaze of ruin. He believed this right up to the moment when Penny told him she was in love with her brother.

"Stepbrother," she corrected, flushing mightily. The flush reminded Scott of a time years ago, sleeping beside her on a secluded beach in Baja, stoned on new love. They had awakened with wicked sunburns, their bodies filled with strange heat.

"I was going to tell you," said his wife in the sheer panties that hid nothing. "Soon. I just didn't know how."

Scott was familiar with this problem.

"How did this happen?" he asked calmly, as though he and Penny were chatting over coffee. He was showing polite interest in his wife's activities, the useful errands that filled her day. He did not look at the guy, the denim presence behind her. Under no circumstances would Scott meet his eyes.

"I was in a chat room one day, and Benji found me. My screen-name is PennyCherry," she explained. "And he thought, you know, how many could there be?"

Scott nodded thoughtfully, grasping too late the value of the patriarchal tradition, why for centuries women had taken their husbands' names. To guard their virtue in online chat rooms. To keep away horny long-lost stepbrothers, lovelorn since childhood, lying in wait.

"So he found you," Scott said encouragingly. Sunlight bled through his daughter's pink curtains. He felt as though he'd wandered into a lung.

"Yeah. And we started chatting, and then the phone. Then last month he came out here."

"Last *month*?"

"When you were on the island," she said. "How long ago was that?"

"Twenty-four days," said Scott, who'd recently done the arithmetic. He remembered calling her from the Mistral Inn, the breathless way she'd answered the phone. Naked, he'd pictured her; dripping from her bath.

"And you hadn't seen him since—how long? Since you were

kids?" Scott enjoyed pretending Benji wasn't in the room with them. He understood that it was the last fun he would ever have.

"Twelve years, I guess. Not since that camping trip in Yellowstone. Remember?"

Blood rushed him, then, roaring like the ocean, a hot tidal wave of blood. With a heroic expenditure of will he looked at the guy, the ghostly presence in the corner. The ghost who'd been there all through his marriage. Benji tall and lean like a cowboy, a young Henry Fonda, his long face brown from the sun.

"You were there?" Scott said.

Benji nodded. He had pushed back his denim sleeves, showing his paisley tattoos. Scott felt a stab of recognition, shrill and alarming, like a siren in the distance.

"You were . . . together then?"

"We were trying not to be," Penny said, with the flush that now seemed permanent. "And then I met you."

Scott nodded thoughtfully, as though he understood.

"And we lost touch for a long time. It was hard for him, you know? Me getting married. And then the kids."

Jesus, the kids.

"Tell me the kids don't know."

Penny looked away. "It was kind of an accident. Sabrina came home early one day. I didn't have a choice."

Scott looked around the room, at his daughter's pink girlhood, the piles of toys she'd already outgrown. In this room, surrounded by dolls and stuffed animals, his wife and Benji had undressed each other.

Penny seemed to read his mind. "Not in our room," she said softly.

It was a measure of Scott's desolation that he felt grateful for this.

"Benji's great with Ian," she added. "They went camping last weekend in the Whites. Ian had a blast."

Scott felt his pulse in his ears. "You let him take *Ian*? Where the fuck was I?"

"Concord."

"Overnight?" Scott said, nearly shouting. "You let him take Ian *overnight?*"

"Well, he *is* Ian's uncle," she pointed out, without a whiff of irony.

Someday this conversation will be over, Scott reflected calmly. *The next thing that's going to happen will begin to happen.* The thought comforted him like lightning, cracking open a humid day in summer. He was desperate to leave this room, the walls papered with pop stars, the pubescent boys who leered at his sleeping daughter, seeing what they should not see. His life would continue along its lurching path, but a part of him would stay here forever. Himself, his wife, and her lover facing off for all eternity, in the pink and girlish chaos of Sabrina's room.

The list came out the third week in April, just after the annual meeting. For two days Grohl's most eminent scientists had been absent from the corridors: Steve Upstairs; Ira Babish, the computational biologist; Malcolm John Liddy, whom a sarcastic postdoc had nicknamed *Dr. Genome*. Frank regarded these men as equals; how galling, then, that they were off discussing the most important scientific issues of the day while he was left behind to babysit his mournful staff. Since Cristina's departure, a pall had settled over the lab. The door to the postdocs' office was always closed. Martin Keohane came and went in silence, like a dour young priest.

It was a Thursday afternoon when Betsy Baird knocked gently at Frank's office window. He knew by her gentleness that the news was bad.

"The list is up," she said. All day she'd been monitoring the Academy's Web site.

Still he looked at her with hope.

"I'm sorry," she said.

At lunchtime he slipped out through the back door, like the Garbo of Grohl. He drove across the bridge for a late lunch, in no mood to run into colleagues in Kendall Square. Afterward, feeling too feeble to climb six flights of stairs, he got into the elevator and found himself shoulder to shoulder with the other Steve—the immunologist Steve Palumbo, also known as Steve Downstairs.

"Frank." Palumbo clapped him hard on the back. "I just heard."

He was a sturdy, compact guy with intense dark eyes and an unruly mop of hair, always wet from the shower. Palumbo spent mornings and lunchtimes running or sculling; for a couple of years back in the '80s, he and Frank had played weekly racquetball. Scientifically speaking, Palumbo was a lightweight; but Frank had a healthy respect for physical prowess. Grohl was run by moribund old turds. In any sort of physical contest—push-ups, arm wrestling—only he and Palumbo would be able to hold their own.

"Man, it's got to hurt," said Palumbo. "Coming so close. Maybe I should be grateful they don't know who the hell I am."

"Ah, but you're just a youngster," said Frank, in his new role of doddering has-been. As he said it, he realized that Palumbo was nearing fifty. Wifeless, childless, he seemed inoculated against aging. The guy spent every spare moment watching sports or playing them. His interests mirrored the average twelve-year-old boy's.

"Well, I wouldn't want to be that guy when you find him," said Palumbo. Then, seeing Frank's look: "You didn't know? You made the final list. Somebody challenged you."

Frank stared in disbelief. The Academy spent months winnowing down the list of nominees. Hundreds of eminent scientists were considered and rejected. The final list—men and women so distinguished that any one might be a future Nobel laureate—was voted on by the entire membership, and usually passed without a hitch. Only once, in Frank's long memory, had a nomination been challenged.

"I heard it from my old mentor as USF. He was there, Frank. Said it was like a bomb went off in the room."

"Someone *challenged* me?" said Frank. "You're sure?"

The elevator arrived at the top floor; Frank had forgotten to press the button marked 4. Now he hit the Doors Close button. "Well, who was it, for Christ's sake?"

"No clue," said Steve.

On what grounds? Frank nearly asked, but stopped himself. This wasn't a conversation he wanted to have with Palumbo. With anyone at Grohl. Here, especially, on the top floor of the institute, ten yards from the office of Steve Upstairs.

"You don't know either?" Steve gave a low whistle. "I figured it was some kind of personal thing. Someone with a grudge against you."

Frank's mind raced. In thirty-five years he'd racked up some rivalries—didn't everybody? But until now there was nobody he'd have called an enemy.

"I'll tell you one thing," he said. "I'm going to find out."

After work he met Margit at their usual haunt, a Thai restaurant on Mass Ave. Her hair looked freshly mown and had been dyed a deep burgundy, a rich color not found in nature, at least not on women's heads. She wore new eyeglasses, small rectangular frames that matched her hair, her lipstick, the silk scarf draped across her shoulders. She had gone to great effort to achieve—not beauty, exactly, but an organized sort of handsomeness.

They ordered their usual appetizer, a double plate of chicken satay; but Frank's guts were in a knot. His hasty lunch, a lobster roll slick with mayonnaise, sat heavy in his stomach, right where his gullet had dumped it. He couldn't eat a thing.

"My God," she'd said as he approached the table. "What happened to you?"

He told her the story in five sentences, barely stopping for a breath.

"You know the reason, of course," she said, her eyes downcast. "That business with Cristina. It was bound to get out that you pulled the paper. Somebody probably figured out why."

Frank nodded, recalling the way Margit had reacted when he'd first told her the news, her reproachful silence eloquent beyond words. In general she was not easily shocked. He remembered, a few years back, a particularly juicy cycle of Grohl gossip: an emeritus professor busted in a cathouse in the Combat Zone; a male postdoc stopped for speeding in bustier, pumps, and wig. When Margit heard that story from Betsy Baird—who saw all, heard all—she reacted with a kind of amused tolerance: *I too drive faster in high heels. There is less weight on the accelerator. It is natural to overcompensate.* But when it came to scientific integrity, she was a moralist of the first order. When it came to science, Margit was a prude.

"You were the PI on the paper," she said. "What else could it be?"

"Sure," Frank said. "But it was an internal matter, and Grohl had every reason to keep it quiet. Even Steve Palumbo didn't know anything about it. So who could it have been?"

"Frank." She took his hand in both of hers. "This is a terrible injustice, and I understand why you are upset. But in the end, does it really matter who challenged you? Regardless of who it was, the outcome is the same."

"Trust me," he said through clenched teeth. "It matters."

"Well, let's think, then. There is the staff in your lab. And anybody else they might have told."

Frank's mind raced. Morale had been so bad recently that any of the staff might have grumbled about the situation.

"And Cristina," said Margit. "Don't forget Cristina."

"I haven't." He'd heard from Betsy Baird that the girl had returned to Greece. "But I can't imagine she'd have much to say on the matter."

"Well, the editors at *Science* know about it," Margit added. "And possibly the reviewers."

Frank nodded. He had no idea who'd reviewed the paper—the process was confidential, in theory, but it was sometimes possible to find out. Driving home, he came up with a handful of likely names, half of them affiliated with Harvard or MIT He knew them all in a distant way, from conferences and colloquia. But that was all.

I figured it was a personal thing, Steve Palumbo had said. *Someone with a grudge against you.*

Frank parked in front of the house, his stomach squeezing. A cold sweat trickled down his back. Jesus, what was the matter with him? He was unused to heartburn, backaches, rashes. He hadn't been sick to his stomach in twenty years.

Inside he stripped naked and crawled into bed, pulling the covers around him. The days were getting longer; the last dusky light peeped through the blinds. He had left a window open, and a cool breeze rattled the shade. He thought of Cristina Spiliotes and her falsified data, the lame-brained hoax that had kept him out of the Academy, cast aspersions on the career he'd worked a lifetime to build. Stupid, stupid: the idiocy of it boggled the mind. Yet in a perverse way, didn't the artlessness of her deception argue in her favor? She was no huckster. She'd dissembled like a novice, a girl who'd never told a lie in her life.

He ought to have seen it, and in a sense he had: he'd understood all along that the paper wasn't ready, that Cristina, exhilarated by her early results, dazzled by the prospect of publication, had rushed to the finish line. For a kid like Cristina, a paper in *Science* would have been a career-making event. Even for a veteran like Frank, it was no small achievement. He hadn't had a publication that significant in several years.

So the girl had cheated; she had lied about her results. Frank, with all his past accomplishments, had survived the fracas: withdrawing the paper, the displeasure of Steve Upstairs. The stain on his reputation would be temporary. And hadn't Cristina paid for her skullduggery? Now that the whole debacle was over and done with, why couldn't he let it rest?

The deception had been Cristina's responsibility. But Cristina herself—there was no escaping this fact—had been *his*. There was a reason the system functioned as it did, a reason postdocs toiled under more senior scientists: to be counseled and guided, fostered and trained. Frank thought uneasily of the weekly meetings he'd canceled, always with a good excuse: he was needed at Protogenix; he had a grant proposal due. But wasn't the real reason something darker? That he wanted her and couldn't have her. Like a petulant child, he had withheld his attention, punished her for not desiring him.

Of course, the rest of his team had been aware of his lunacy. It was a lesson Frank had learned early on: there were no secrets in a lab. Had Betsy Baird cackled over his folly—with Guei, or Ursula the lab tech? And Martin Keohane, who'd once idolized him: What must he think of Frank now? The camaraderie of his team, their respect and affection, the warm collegiality he had always fostered—he realized, now, how much those things meant. He had sacrificed all this, and more, to an adolescent crush.

I'm an old fool, he thought.

He rolled onto his side, clutching his stomach. Somewhere in the distance a baby was crying. A baby in Cambridge: odds were good that somewhere in the vicinity of Kendall Square, its father was in the lab.

Frank tried to imagine where his own children were at that moment. He knew so little of their adult lives that this was difficult to do. He pictured Billy wining and dining a beautiful woman; Scott reading to his own children, whose names were Sabrina and Ian and who were . . . six and eight? Seven and nine?

Truly, he didn't know.

And what about Gwen?

He recalled, suddenly, the day Paulette had appeared in his office, frantic about Gwen and the new boyfriend, needing his comfort, his counsel, his help. A month ago? Longer? Before the pulling of the paper, the firing of Cristina. The implosion of his reputation, his career, his hopes for the future. In that time he hadn't given a thought to his daughter. He'd had a few other things on his mind.

He picked up the phone.

"Frank?" Paulette sounded surprised—flat-out amazed, in fact—to hear his voice.

"Paulette, hi."

"You sound terrible."

"Something is wrong with my stomach."

"What did you eat?"

He hadn't phoned her in years, yet it felt natural to describe the churning miseries of his digestive tract, to curse the treacherous lobster roll curdling his stomach, to be scolded for the lapse in judgment that had put him in such straits.

"Sorry for whining. That's not why I called," he said, though this wasn't entirely true. "I wanted to get an update on Gwen."

"Oh, Frank, wonderful news. She's back in Pittsburgh. Scott went down to Saint Raphael and talked some sense into her."

"Scott talked sense into her? Impossible. Who talked sense into Scott?"

"You're terrible." The chuckle in her voice gratified him. He had always enjoyed making her laugh. "Honestly, I have no idea what he said to her, but she seems to have done an about-face."

"*Gwen?*" said Frank. "Gwen has never changed her mind about anything."

"Will wonders never cease."

Frank learned, then, that his grandchildren were eight and ten years old, that besides rescuing his sister, Scott had singlehandedly rebuilt Paulette's front porch. That he'd done a wonderful job.

"How's Billy?" he asked.

She hesitated. "It's the strangest thing. I haven't heard from him in nearly two weeks. And he didn't sound at all well when we last spoke. He said something about taking a vacation."

"A vacation?" he repeated, mystified. Frank did not vacate. Neither, as far as he knew, did his hardworking son.

Paulette sighed. "There must be a girlfriend."

Frank lay there listening, his gut seizing. Her voice in his ear affected him strangely. For a moment he felt her next to him, close enough to touch. He squeezed his eyes shut to preserve the illusion. *Don't go*, he thought.

He listened to her talk about the children they'd raised, engaged in activities so unlikely that she might have been speaking of strangers. He had formed, long ago, certain ideas about Billy, Gwen, and Scott; each was a known compound that behaved in predictable ways. This awareness had freed him from worrying about them unnecessarily. There was no need to fret about their futures, to contemplate the ways he had failed them. In spite of his negligence they had turned out—not perfectly, exactly, but they had turned out nonetheless. They were grown, completed; they had achieved their final states. He wondered, now, if any of this were true.

His stomach lurched.

"Frank, are you listening? I asked you a question."

"I'm sorry. My stomach is killing me."

"Peppermint tea, dear."

He smiled. Through all three pregnancies he'd brought home pounds of the stuff from Harnett's in Cambridge. The *dear* was unconscious, a habit that had survived the wreckage of their marriage, like a charred treasure found after a fire. Frank knew it was unconscious. Still it moved him.

"I asked you if you'd heard from Neil. He's in town, you know."

"Windsor?" He sat up in bed, ready to hurl. "I didn't know you kept in touch."

"Oh, he calls once in a blue moon. On my birthday. That sort of thing."

Frank frowned. Paulette's birthday was in . . . September? Or was that Gwen's?

"We're having lunch tomorrow, as a matter of fact. At the Harvest." She paused. "Frank, where on earth can I park at that hour without a Harvard sticker? Honestly, I have no idea."

He named a side street off Mass Ave, another south of the square. His GI tract thrummed like a cement mixer. An eruption of one kind or another seemed imminent.

"Paulette," he said. "I have to go."

THE PAST IS always with us.

He had fallen hard for Paulette, immediately and completely. She was a child at nineteen—Frank saw that instantly—but the child could sail and play the piano and ride horseback, skills he was too much of a rube even to wish to possess. She had traveled through England and Scotland and Spain and Italy; he would learn on their honeymoon that she spoke French like a native. She had a memory for names and faces; charming strangers was her gift. Men, especially, were enchanted by her attention. Frank knew exactly how they felt. From the beginning he'd believed she hung on his every word, that she'd remember them for the rest of her life and quote them in his eulogy, weeping prettily, wearing a stunning hat.

Neil had seemed startled when Frank asked her out.

Really, fella? I wouldn't have said she was your type.

They're all my type, he'd joked, a little insulted. Neil's tone suggested Paulette was out of his league. She was, of course, but who was

Windsor to say so? Frank was accustomed to his deference in all matters romantic. Neil the humble disciple, desperate for guidance; Frank the oracle, a role he'd come to enjoy.

It was obvious to him that Neil was jealous. He'd known Paulette first, and Frank had taken her out from under his nose. Frank understood this and didn't care. More than that: he took pleasure in Neil's resentment, accepted it as his due. He saw Paulette every weekend, phoned her nightly from his and Neil's apartment, not caring what his buddy overheard. His flirtations with half a dozen Radcliffe girls withered from neglect. He returned from dates to Neil's questions—those probing, scientifically curious questions—and answered them in rich detail. Paulette was a virgin, but playful; she would let him touch her anywhere, passive in his arms. Frank had encountered such females before and knew how to handle them. With the right approach, her resistance could be overcome.

Neil let him blather on this way until he began to feel ridiculous.

Well, then what? Neil asked finally. *Say she gives in. You're her first. What happens when someone else catches your eye?*

The question startled him. Tapeworm had always applauded his conquests.

That won't happen. Frank knew it a moment before he said it: *I'm going to marry her.*

Their wedding at Holy Cross Cathedral seemed to him a scene from a movie, a complicated pageant to which he'd been invited as an afterthought, a last-minute guest. Neil was his best man, the only familiar face in the crowd. He produced the ring at the crucial moment; at the reception he danced dutifully with the bride. Neil was a stand-up guy, a gentleman, Frank's closest friend since Blaise Klezek, the surrogate brother of his childhood. He believed this for years, right up until the bloody final month of his marriage, when Paulette savaged him with the truth.

They'd been arguing over Gwen, fights that had become habitual. *We should have her hearing rechecked,* Frank said. *It's been nearly a year. I want to make sure there's no change.*

It seemed to him a reasonable request. Hearing abnormalities were common in Turner girls. Paulette knew this as well as he did. But to his astonishment, his wife had exploded. As usual, there was no predicting what would set her off.

Her hearing is fine! Don't you think I'd notice if she weren't hearing properly? And then, her usual refrain: *Why are you always looking for trouble? Why can't you let anything be okay?*

Finally she'd exhausted his patience.

For Christ's sake, Paulette! I just want to know what we're dealing with. That's the difference between you and me. You hide your head in the sand. I want to know the truth.

It was this phrase that had set her off. *Oh, really?* she said, with a smile that made him nervous. *I beg to differ. There's plenty you don't want to know. You've never shown much scientific curiosity when it came to* me.

And what was that supposed to mean?

You weren't my first, she said. *Neil was. He loved me.*

If she had made a lifelong study of his neurology, she couldn't have placed the hit better. Traffic halted along his neural pathways. A flood of hostile chemicals bathed his brain. She watched him intently as she said it, her eyes blazing. God knew how long she'd been waiting. Through every late return, missed dinner, forgotten anniversary; every time he'd insulted her brother or disparaged her father or ogled a waitress in a restaurant, she must have held the words in her mouth, savoring them, waiting for the optimal time.

His face burned; blood pulsed in his hands. *Windsor*, he said.

She nodded once, resolutely.

And in that moment, Paulette freed him. Their marriage was a sack of miseries he'd thought never to escape. She was insecure and jealous, vain and neurotic. Unmoved by logic, she judged him guilty of offenses he committed only in dreams. For years this had been their unhappy baseline, an unfortunate set of givens that Frank had accepted completely—so blind, so foolish was his love for her. He had watched her fail their daughter in critical ways, crippled by her own shame. For months their marriage had dangled by a thread. Now Paulette—he saw this clearly—had handed him a knife.

Frank slashed the thread.

He had never cared about marrying a virgin. A woman's past didn't trouble him; before they'd met, Paulette could have serviced the entire Harvard crew for all he cared. But she had given herself to only two men, and this implied a similarity between them. In her eyes, he and Neil Windsor were peers, equals. Not merely interchangeable; they had, in fact, *been interchanged*. It was a notion Frank could not tolerate. For years he'd watched Windsor soar—the top-drawer publications, the big finds. Envy gnawed at him. What had saved him, always, had been Paulette—the one achievement Windsor couldn't top, the ultimate prize.

THE HARVEST was crowded at lunchtime, beards and tweeds, wool skirts and pearls, a few decent suits—the business school—and students on good behavior, their parents picking up the check. At the bar Frank saw Otto Mueller from the med school and gave a cursory wave. Normally he'd have stopped to chat, poke around a bit—Mueller was on the SAB of Protein Therapeutics and loose lipped when he'd had a few. Not today, though. Not today.

He spotted them at a table near the window, his wife and Neil Windsor, Paulette in a cream-colored suit, like a midlife bride. He watched her a moment, the sun catching her necklace. It was the sort of delicate jewelry she'd always favored, a plain gold chain fine as a nerve. She hadn't seen him, and it felt luxurious to watch her unobserved. Her face lit at something Neil said and the smile cut Frank like a scalpel, in its precision nearly painless, but not quite.

He approached the table. Paulette noticed him over Windsor's shoulder. "Frank! What are you doing here?" She looked puzzled, a little alarmed.

"Look at what the cat dragged in." Windsor stood, beaming, and shook Frank's hand. "Pull up a chair."

Frank eyed him levelly.

"What's the matter?" said Windsor. "You look like hell."

"He hasn't been feeling well," Paulette explained.

Because he felt like it, Frank bent and kissed her, his lips grazing her cheek. He had not touched her in twenty years. She still wore the perfume whose name he couldn't remember, though over the years he'd bought her bottles of it. It smelled like nothing in nature, no flower he recognized. It smelled only like Paulette, a thought that nearly reduced him to tears.

Frank noticed the leather folder at Windsor's elbow. He had paid the check, of course. As though he and Paulette were on a date.

"I'm sorry to run, Frank, but I have an appointment downtown." Paulette glanced at her watch. "Hair," she explained.

Windsor rose. "Dear girl, it was a pleasure to see you," he said, taking her in his arms.

Their embrace was brief, socially appropriate. There was no reason for Frank to burn. No longer any marriage or family, any friendship or youth or love or innocence, any honor or sentiment left to justify it. There was no reason to stand quickly, knocking back the flimsy chair, and chuck Neil Windsor on the shoulder, with the false friendliness of an angry bully. But Frank did this anyway, and Jesus, did it feel good.

Heads turned in their direction. Frank, smiling, bent to retrieve the overturned chair. "Bring my friend a cup of coffee," he told the waiter. "Sit," he told Windsor. "Let's catch up."

Paulette eyed him nervously. "Frank, is everything all right?"

"Right as rain, dear." He reached for her hand and pressed it briefly to his face. "You run along now. I'm going to have a visit with our friend Neil."

He watched her go, her slender legs, the swell of her hips. "She still looks good," he told Windsor, who'd obediently taken a seat. "Don't you think she looks good?"

"Frank, what's the matter with you? Are you drunk?" Windsor looked concerned, his brow furrowed.

"Jesus, listen to you. You're like an old woman." Frank smiled. "How was the meeting?"

"The Academy?" Windsor patted his sparse hair, as if making sure it was still there. "Well, it was eventful. As I'm sure you've heard."

"Why'd you do it?" Frank's heart pounded slowly, the final spasms of a dying thing. With his last strength he would reach across the table and break Windsor's arm.

"Do what?" Windsor looked stricken. "My God, Frank. You think I challenged you?"

"Can we admit that we've always been competitive? The publications, tenure, Progen." He paused. "Paulette."

"Paulette," said Windsor, as if the rest didn't matter. As, in fact, it didn't. "What about her?"

"Oh, come off it," Frank said. "Don't bullshit me. *I know.*" He felt swollen with outrage. He had carried it for years, a sturdy mass lodged in his innards, actively growing. Over the years it had invaded his *muscularis mucosae*, his *submucosa*, his *muscularis propria*. The malignancy was stage B, he judged. Infiltrating, but without metastasis.

Windsor blinked twice, rapidly. "She told you? When?"

"A long time ago."

"Oy. Thank you," he told the waiter, who'd appeared with coffee. "So all these years—Frank, I'm speechless. Why didn't you say something?"

Frank stared ahead, avoiding Windsor's eyes. He focused very deliberately on the life moving around them, the diners chewing and swallowing, the scrape of cutlery, the waiters serving drinks. "Why didn't *I*? Jesus, Weisberg. You were my best man. My best friend. *You* should have told *me*, at the very beginning. But you never said a word."

"My God, what should I have said?" Windsor lowered his voice. "I loved her; I was crazy about her. Would you really have wanted to know that? And what did any of it matter, if she didn't love me back?"

"She didn't," Frank repeated, in the interests of clarity. Of getting the facts straight.

"No. Look, amigo: it was forty years ago. We're all old now and neither one of us has her. The End."

Frank nodded. The End, the End.

Windsor stirred his coffee. "Now this other business. The Academy. You really think I did that? Knifed you in the back?"

Frank stared at him, doubt prickling his skin. "You knew the whole story. The postdoc, the phony data. I spilled my guts to you. And Grohl has kept a lid on it; nobody else has any idea. So if you didn't challenge me, who did?"

Windsor sipped his coffee. "Know a guy named Alan Manning?"

Frank frowned, trying to place the name.

"Well, he knows plenty about you. The data, and the girl who got suspended. He implied that she was a scapegoat."

Frank blinked. "He said I falsified data?"

"No, not exactly. Just that you were probably aware of it, or should have been. And I'm here to tell you, my friend: *you should have been.*"

"She must have told him," Frank said slowly. "Manning was her mentor at Baylor. I hired her away from him."

"Seems like he took it personally."

"She has that effect on men."

Windsor smiled crookedly. "Don't tell me. I don't want to know."

"Nothing happened," Frank said, profoundly ashamed—of how little he understood of the world's workings, of the fierce conviction with which he could be wrong.

"Don't say anything to Paulette," he added. "About the girl. She would misunderstand."

"Believe me, that is not a conversation I want to have." Windsor rose. "This has been fun, Frank, but I have a plane to catch."

"I'm sorry," said Frank. "I shouldn't have accused you. I had no right."

"You have no idea." Windsor grinned. "I'm the idiot who nominated you."

Frank covered his eyes with his hand.

"I'm a new member. I'm supposed to sit there quietly, behave myself, raise my hand when I want to take a piss. Instead I go out on a limb and nominate a schmuck like you."

"Goddamn," Frank said. "This looks bad for you."

Windsor shrugged. "What are they going to do? It's like being on the Supreme Court: they can't unload me. Like I can't unload you."

chapter 9

For most of her life, Paulette had loved Sundays. As a little girl she'd walked to the corner store with her father early in the morning, to get the newspapers before church. For some reason her brother and sister were excluded from this ritual, and for Paulette this was half the pleasure. Her father bought the Sunday *Globe* and, every week, a lottery ticket. The ticket was a secret between them. Paulette was to tell no one, especially not her mother, a promise she had never broken. Later they drove to Concord for Sunday dinner at Grandmother Drew's, a crowd at the adult table: Aunt Doro and Aunt Tess and their husbands, Paulette's parents and grandmother, her maiden aunt Grace. And, at what was called the young people's table, were Roy and Martine and Paulette, their cousins Trudy and Peter and Gabby and Abigail and Dick.

As a young bride she'd found Sundays glorious. To her initial displeasure, Frank refused to attend mass with her, but this had its compensations. Sunday was the one morning of the week when he would linger in bed instead of springing up at dawn and racing to the lab. He would make love to her early, before she was quite awake, and fall back to sleep afterward clutching her, a lover's embrace. For this she would miss a year of Sunday masses, and did. Billy—she was sure of this—had been conceived on such a morning. She'd been accused, by her mother and Martine, of favoring her eldest, and Paulette supposed it was true. Billy was her Sunday baby. Of all her children, he had been conceived in the greatest love.

Later, her marriage ended, her children gone, it was on Sundays that Paulette most felt her aloneness. In the Sunday *Globe* she read about a massive antiques show in southern Maine, two hours' drive away. The long drive had been a selling point, a way to fill the empty hours. The size of the show overwhelmed her, the crowd and commotion, the hundreds of vendors showing their wares. The buyers were men and women of all ages: some expensively dressed, others down and out. Most, like her, were alone. That year she went to shows in Framingham and Brattleboro and Derry and Hartford, in Bristol, Rhode Island; in Katonah, New York. She bought copies of Kovels' and Warman's, studied photographs and price lists. When she learned about the Mount Washington Glass Company, based in New Bedford, a bell of recognition sounded inside her. New Bedford! Clarence Hubbard Drew! In a real way these plates and vases seemed connected to the Drews, to the family she'd once had. Her husband and children had deserted her, but her ancestors weren't going anywhere.

She made her first purchase, the Mount Washington biscuit jar, at a price she now knew to be exorbitant. She'd suspected this at the time, but found herself unable to bargain with the seller. In a year haggling would become second nature to her, but at the time she'd been too embarrassed to speak. Her family had never discussed the price of anything. It was Donald Large who'd taught her to speak up, to ask for what she wanted, to admit wanting of any kind. Who had lovingly provided for her future; who in a real way looked after her still.

Bless Donald. He had left her better than he'd found her, in every possible way.

Since his death, more lonely Sundays. Drinking her tea, she scanned the paper. Recently she'd developed an interest in politics. For years she'd had virtually no idea who was running the country; since the Kennedy assassinations she'd found the whole business too painful to contemplate. Now she followed obsessively the career of Madeleine Albright, who'd been in Martine's class at Wellesley: ambassador to the United Nations, the first female secretary of state. Reading about these achievements, Paulette felt keenly her own wasted potential. At Wellesley she'd studied French and art history, planning to graduate with both majors. Then she'd met Frank, and hadn't graduated at all.

Now she cherished her tenuous connection to Madeleine Albright, who was not merely an eminent diplomat but also elegant and feminine. How different from awkward Janet Reno, the spinster attorney general, who seemed not to own a lipstick. Reno with her boyish haircut, her unflattering baggy suits, her flat, matter-of-fact voice.

My heavens, Paulette thought.

The attorney general was much older and more than a foot taller, but in other respects the resemblance was uncanny. She was an aged, lanky version of Gwen.

Like Gwen, Janet Reno refused to present herself in the way women were expected to. She was not feminine. To Paulette that word had always seemed complimentary, like *romantic* or *decorative*; though in actual fact, none of those words was necessarily positive. To Paulette *feminine* meant something very specific—a womanly appearance, not just dressing and hairstyling but a way of walking and speaking, of moving through the world. But why, exactly, were these things important? What was the actual point?

The point was to attract men.

And once a man had been secured, to marry and have children. Mothers too were feminine: as a matter of reflex they smiled at babies, their own and other people's, and cajoled them in a sweet singsong voice. That voice was useful for soothing and encouraging children; but Paulette was struck by how many women of her own age, their families grown and gone, still spoke in these dulcet tones. Increasingly, she found this irritating. If a woman had no children to soothe and encourage, why should she go through life simpering like a nursemaid? And if she had no interest in attracting a man—which, increasingly, seemed a wise attitude to adopt—why *should* she wear lipstick? Undoubtedly Janet Reno had more pressing concerns than her hairstyle. And so—the thought struck Paulette like a gust of wind—so, perhaps, did Gwen. She thought back to those frustrating Christmas Eve suppers, her daughter's monologues about her job at the Stott. Consumed with anthropology or archaeology, Gwen had tried to share what was most important in her life. Paulette had only pretended to listen.

I am changing, she thought.

She turned her attention to the *Globe*. The local section covered yesterday's Battle Road reenactment in exhaustive detail. For the first time in eleven years, Paulette had not attended; she'd handed over her interpreter duties to Harry Good's wife. *I'll be visiting my sister in New Mexico*, she'd lied. A few weeks before, an envelope had appeared in her mailbox: no postage, delivered by hand. Inside was a postal money order for four hundred dollars, and a scrawled note: *It's not much, but it's a start. Thanks for everything. Best, Gil.* Now Paulette couldn't bear the thought of seeing him in uniform, firing the musket of John Hawes Gilbert. She didn't want to see him at all.

Imagine her surprise, then, to glance out her kitchen window last week and find him standing in her own backyard, chatting easily with her son Scott. A shiny new truck was parked next door at the Marshes', where something—a floor? a bathroom?—was being replaced. She'd listened dizzily at the open window, but they had talked only of carpentry. He hadn't even spoken her name.

Later Scott had questioned her eagerly: How did she know Gil Pyle? Did she realize the man was a genius?

Apparently he's a fine carpenter, she said mildly. *Where is he living these days? With his family in New Hampshire?*

Nah, said Scott. *With his girlfriend. In Providence, I think.*

She'd understood, then, that whatever had passed between them—or hadn't; perhaps she'd imagined the whole thing—had come to a close. She and Gil Pyle would never be lovers, or even friends; to him she was merely a creditor. The money she'd lent him—Donald's money!—would come back to her slowly. Each time he made a payment, her heart would ache. Under these circumstances it was absurd to look out the window ten times a day, to see if his truck (*her* truck? *their* truck?) was parked next door.

She was past the age of love. Her fascination with Gil Pyle had been its last flowering; she saw this now, in sadness and in relief. It seemed suddenly idiotic that this one small part of life should be the focus of so much weeping and gnashing. For a few years men and women flattered and chased and pined for each other; then the rest of life stretched ahead of them, to fill with whatever else the world contained. Which was, when you thought about it, quite a lot. So how to account for all the novels and operas, the plays and poetry and pop songs on the radio: was love really so fascinating, so consuming, that nothing else was worth singing about?

Perhaps it was. But Paulette, finally, had had her fill. It was time to think about something else.

She turned to the classifieds and scanned the ads, looking for estate sales. With Donald she'd made great finds at such sales—her Roseville jardinière, a few pieces of Rookwood, a full set of Scroddleware in near-mint condition, having spent its life in a stranger's china closet. But without him she found the sales disheartening, whole houses turned inside out and opened to strangers, families dispersed or died out or simply uninterested in the boxes of framed photographs: unsmiling children, sepia toned, dressed like tiny adults. These photographs unsettled her profoundly, the children gazing somberly at the camera as if foreseeing a bleak future. Children who were dead now, or ancient or dying, abandoned to nursing homes. Sorting through the photos, she'd been overwhelmed by a feeling she couldn't name, the realization that these lives, now extinguished, had once been as real as her own, as passionate and confused and pained. Like all young people, she'd once harbored the unconscious conviction that the world had begun the day she was born. Time had disabused her of this notion. It was, she supposed, the fundamental difference between youth and age.

She was about to set aside the classifieds when she spotted the ad.

LAST-MINUTE SUMMER RENTAL. LARGE HISTORIC HOUSE IN TRURO, SECLUDED, SLEEPS 16! SLEEPING PORCH, OCEAN VIEWS, MANY EXTRAS. CALL NOW!

It couldn't be. But there, astonishingly, was the address: *1 NECK ROAD.*

She phoned the agent and placed a deposit.

You don't want to see it? he asked, stunned at his easy good fortune.

Not necessary, Paulette said. *I'm familiar with the house.*

This settled, she called the children. For the first time ever, she called Gwen first. As the phone rang she imagined walking with her daughter along Mamie's Beach, deep in conversation. She would listen, really listen, to whatever Gwen wished to tell her. She would learn about anthropology or archaeology; she would accept her daughter exactly as she was. Seeing this, Gwen would open up to her. There would be no more strained silences between them. They would have much to discuss. Not just the Ricos of the world, or the Gil Pyles, but the world full stop.

Paulette waited, but Gwen was not at home; she was out doing whatever people did on a Sunday morning in Pittsburgh. Finally a recording answered.

"I can't wait to see you," Paulette said, feeling only slightly foolish at saying this to a machine.

She phoned her sons. Scott, naturally, was free all summer. Billy did not answer; Paulette supposed that he was on call. It seemed to her that he was always working. Of her children, only Billy was truly ambitious. In that way, only Billy resembled his father.

His father.

She hadn't quite recovered from the shock of seeing Frank at the Harvest. The intent way he'd looked at her, the queer urgency in his voice. He had seemed slightly unhinged. She'd been flabbergasted when he pressed her hand to his face—an inexplicable gesture, more intimate than a kiss. And how strangely he'd behaved with Neil! The two men's friendship had always confounded her—the competitiveness, the animosity barely concealed. How unlike her friendship with Tricia James, for example. Paulette considered this. Well, perhaps not so different.

She had called Tricia immediately after she rented the house, bursting with enthusiasm, unable to contain herself. "Darling, that's wonderful!" Tricia crooned. "How many are you expecting?"

"Why, just the children," said Paulette. "And Scott's family, of course."

"Not Gwen's boyfriend?"

"I didn't tell you? That's over and done with." Paulette said this lightly, trying to recall what had possessed her to confide that particular bit of news to Tricia in the first place. "Gwen came to her senses. She's back in Pittsburgh now. All is well."

How relieved Tricia was to hear this! How concerned she'd been, positively beside herself with worry.

"And what about Billy?" she asked. "Will he be bringing someone?"

"He isn't dating at the moment," said Paulette.

"Well, you ought to invite him to bring a guest. He may have a girlfriend he isn't telling you about." Tricia paused. "And what about Frank? Surely he'd like to spend some time with the children."

"Heavens, no," Paulette said. "What an outlandish thought."

Hanging up the phone, she'd felt the beginnings of a headache at her left temple. Lately Tricia seemed to have that effect on her. The last time they'd spoken, Paulette had been hit with a full-blown migraine. Swallowing aspirin, she considered canceling her autumn visit to Philadelphia. Perhaps this year she and Tricia would take a break.

F rom the safety of his bed, Billy watched the Boston Marathon on television. Two hours had passed since the firing of the gun, the elite men blasting off from Hopkinton. Soon the front-runners would be turning the corner onto Boylston Street, the Hancock Tower coming into view.

He would never run Boston.

Billy glimpsed his reflection in the bedroom mirror. He looked haggard. His sleep had been troubled lately, interrupted by savage dreams. He was chased by armed assailants, beautiful boys with guns, knives, clubs. That the boys were attractive made the visions more terrifying. He woke exhausted.

He hadn't left the apartment in eight days.

First he had taken a week's vacation. His partners grumbled about the short notice, but both owed him favors. Every summer Billy worked like a dog while Matt escaped to the Hamptons. And when Lucia had gone into labor prematurely, it was Billy who'd covered her emergencies—missing the 1995 Boston Marathon, a fact he'd never let her forget.

When the week was up, he left two voice mails: one for Lucia, alluding to vague health problems; another for Geri the receptionist, instructing her to reschedule his patients.

This accomplished, he stopped answering the phone.

He glanced again at the television. Six times, now, he'd trained for Boston; six times, for various reasons, he had choked. The groin pull, a bad case of mono; the chronic exhaustion of residency. A car accident, whiplash and broken ribs. A life accident, whiplash and broken hearts. Year after year, he ran New York with no trouble. So why did Boston continually elude him?

Last night he'd lain awake plagued by this question. Finally, exhausted but wide eyed, he had called Jeremy.

He's sleeping, you barbarian, Nathan said irritably. *Jesus, what time is it?*

It was two-thirty in the morning. But: Boston.

Maybe, Nathan said, *you don't want to go home.*

Billy's time in the apartment had not been idle. He had spaces to fill, closets to rearrange, to disguise the vacancies left by Srikanth's things. They each owned a large volume of clothing; a lengthy, complicated, shockingly expensive renovation had turned the three-bedroom condo into a two bedroom with large walk-in closets. Sri had emptied his on a Tuesday. Billy came home from work to find the mirrored door open, the racks bare. Closing the door he heard a faint rustling. On the back of the door, hanging from a brass hook, was a suit covered in silky dry cleaner's plastic. It was the sand-colored linen Sri had been wearing the day they met.

Had Sri forgotten it, or left it on purpose? Did he want Billy to keep it? Or hail a cab and race across town to return it?

A person could lose his mind wondering.

To distract himself, Billy undertook a massive reorganizing. With Sri gone, his own woolens would have room to breathe. His silks and linens could summer in Sri's old closet, like suntanned Drews at the Cape. He was thinking this very thought when his mother phoned. This was only briefly surprising. For as long as he could remember, he and Paulette had thought alike.

When the phone rang he glanced at the clock—11:30 on the dot, Gwen's usual time. He hadn't heard from his sister in two weeks, not since her visit to New York. A fact he hadn't registered until this very moment.

"Red Leader," he barked into the phone. "How the hell are you?"

A long, mystified pause.

"Billy?" his mother said. "Heavens, what's the matter with you?"

"Mother, sorry." Of course: it was a Monday, not a Sunday. The days had begun to blend together, a bad sign. "I thought you were Gwen. I haven't heard from her in a while."

"That's odd. Neither have I. But the last time we spoke she sounded fine." Paulette paused. "In fact, she was planning to meet with someone at the university about finishing her thesis. Her adviser is retired now, which apparently complicates matters. Billy, it makes me sick to think about it. How silly of her to have given up when she did. A year away from a PhD. Can you imagine?"

Billy closed his eyes. *Not this*, he thought. *Not now.* He hadn't the strength to help his mother bemoan Gwen's life choices. He thought of Sri's linen suit still hanging in the closet. He felt as though he had a lover waiting in the next room.

"Anyway," Paulette said, "your sister is fine, considering. I'm just glad to have her back in civilization, after all that business. That young man."

Billy thought of Gwen's red-rimmed eyes, her quavering voice. The shock of seeing her in tears, the first time in twenty years.

"I think she misses him," he said, swiping at his eyes.

"You sound congested. Is this why you're home on a Monday? I was certain I'd get that terrible machine."

"I feel lousy," he admitted.

"I tried you all day yesterday. I was starting to worry. Darling, the most remarkable thing happened. I was glancing at the Sunday paper, and you'll never guess what I found. The Captain's House! The new owners are renting it out." The house was available, as luck would have it, the third week in June—the week of Paulette's birthday.

"Only a week," she said apologetically. "I asked for more, but they're booked for the rest of the summer. I suppose beggars can't be choosers."

She had already mailed in the deposit. Billy allowed her to tell him this, her voice rising with excitement.

"That sounds great, Mother," he said, when he could bear it no longer. "Let me check my schedule and get back to you."

There was a chilly silence.

"Check your *schedule*? Billy, you can't be serious. For once I'd like the whole family to be together on my birthday. That hasn't happened in *years*." She hesitated. "Of course, you're welcome to bring a guest."

A guest?

Billy nearly dropped the phone.

"Mother," he said, more gently. "Things are complicated just now." He paused a moment, not trusting his voice. "It's hard for me to think about next week. Never mind next month."

"But it's summertime!" his mother said. "You have to take a vacation sooner or later. You can't work every single minute. No wonder you're ill."

I am desperately ill, he thought. *I've had a heart attack. I've been attacked by my heart.*

"People don't stop having heart attacks in the summer," he said instead.

He could tell by her silence that he'd said something terribly wrong. *I'm sorry, I'm sorry*, he thought. But what did she expect, calling at this particular moment, when his own life had frayed to a single quivering thread?

He stared at the television. He had missed the finish. A commentator was interviewing the lean Kenyan who'd crossed the line first.

Billy thought, *I will never run that race.*

"Darling, what's the matter with you? Are you upset with me for some reason?" She paused. "For heaven's sake, this isn't about Gwen?"

"She loved him," he said, surprised by his own vehemence. "He made her happy. She's a grown woman, you know. I know you don't think of her that way, but she is."

He took a deep breath.

"You've always tried so hard to protect her. But maybe that wasn't what she needed. Sending Scott down there to f— to mess things up—it wasn't right, Mother. It wasn't fair to Gwen."

For a long time the line was silent.

"Billy," his mother said softly. "Is everything all right?"

G wen climbed the stairs to her apartment, laden with bags of groceries. She turned the key in the lock. She had been home just over two weeks, and the emptiness of the place still startled her, the blank corners where plants had once lived. Her first day back she'd hauled out a dozen corpses—amaryllis and ferns, ivy and ficus, clay and china pots packed with hard earth and dead leaves. The sole survivor, an ailing cactus, she placed squarely on the kitchen table. The cactus was grayish and gnarled. Round lumps grew on it like polyps. *I hate this thing*, Gwen thought each morning as she sat down to breakfast. But perversely, spitefully, she kept it alive.

Now she set her groceries on the kitchen counter. Mrs. Uncapher's television was audible through the floorboards. *Like sands through the hourglass, so are the days of our lives.* The steady drone comforted her. It made her feel less alone.

The morning's errands had depressed her. First, the university, a meeting with the new chairman of the anthropology department. The news was not good. After ten years, many of Gwen's credits had expired. She would have to reapply to the PhD program. If she was accepted— if!—she'd have to make up the credits she'd lost. Then there was the matter of her thesis, whose exact subject she remembered only dimly. The very word, *thesis*, had unleashed in her a wave of antipathy, an old panic. She'd been unable to write it ten years ago, when she still believed it mattered. In her current state of mind, failure seemed inevitable.

The meeting ended, she'd wandered the campus. Her bright months in St. Raphael seemed as distant as childhood. The world was this gray Pittsburgh sky, this cold rain falling in sheets. It seemed, now, that she'd always expected to return. This life was correct, her logical destiny. The wild, random joy of her time with Rico had been a mere detour. An error had occurred, a crazy glitch in the system, an arbitrary pairing too improbable to last. Gwen understood, now, that she'd been waiting for him to betray her. In the end he had done so, though not in the way she'd expected. The brazen tourists with their room keys: he had never succumbed to their charms. At least, not as far as she knew.

She watched the students scuttle between buildings, laden with backpacks, and tried to imagine herself among them. At nineteen, twenty, she'd felt like an outsider. At thirty-four she would feel like a freak.

Head down, zipped into her ugly purple slicker, she walked the streets of Oakland, past the bar where she'd once kissed Eric Farmer, tipsy on Stott Golden Ale. At the next corner she ducked into Fast-Cuts, empty at that hour. "Where've you been?" asked her usual stylist. "Your hair is so *long.*"

Gwen ignored the question. "I need a haircut."

"Are you sure? It's so pretty this way."

"Take it off," Gwen said.

Now, shorn, she stared at herself in her bathroom mirror. This face, this body that Rico had loved, or pretended to. The stubby arms, now covered with freckles; the short neck, the nipples spaced wide on her flat chest. She recalled a night in March when they'd delivered a group of divers back to Pleasures, then motored around to the far side of the island and dropped anchor. The pink sun sliding low in the sky. *Let's swim,* Rico said, dropping his shorts. Whenever possible he swam naked. His lean buttocks were as brown as his back. To his eternal amusement, Gwen persisted in wearing a swimsuit. *What are you hiding?* he often teased her. *I've seen more of you than you have. I've seen everything there is to see.*

Which, of course, was true.

What had possessed her, that night, to peel off her swimsuit? She was aware of him watching her. It was not yet dark. Rico applauded as she dove into the surf. They swam together a long time, darting at each other like cichlids: the charged rush and run of marine life, the watery dance. Had she really done this? Was Gwen McKotch capable of such a thing?

In the Caribbean she had met two astonishing people, Rico and herself.

She was sitting in her kitchen, poring over the classified section of the *Post-Gazette*, when the telephone rang. For an instant her heart leaped. Ridiculous, of course. Rico didn't have her phone number, and wouldn't know how to get it. There was no way he could possibly find her.

Still hoping, she picked up the phone.

"Darling, there you are! I've been trying to reach you for two days. Is everything all right?"

Gwen hadn't cried all day, a major accomplishment. Suddenly she felt her eyes fill. Her mother's concern and tenderness. Her mother's voice.

"Um, no. Not really." Gwen broke off, not trusting her voice. "Mom, I miss him," she said softly—Gwen who did not say such things.

"Oh, sweetheart. I know you do." Paulette sighed. "Love is such dangerous business. I'm just glad you're back, and safe. Promise me you'll never run off that way again."

"I won't," said Gwen.

"I'm not going to interrogate you about what happened. You don't have to tell me anything you don't want to."

"Mom, thank you," said Gwen, oddly touched. How unlike her mother to show such restraint.

"I can't bear the thought of you being disappointed. If that young man couldn't treat you properly, he didn't deserve you. That's all I'm going to say on the matter." Paulette seemed to hesitate. "I know it's no consolation, but I do have some good news. How would you feel about coming to the Cape this summer?" The Captain's House, she explained. For Paulette's birthday. She had just spoken to Billy. He and Scott would be there.

"Stay the whole week," Paulette urged. "It will be wonderful to have you close."

"I will," said Gwen. As before, as always, she had no other plans.

Y ou left him?"

They were sitting in a Mexican restaurant on the North Side, a few blocks from the Stott. Heidi Kozak was still in work clothes. She had a new hairstyle she called the Rachel, inspired by the star of a television show.

"I don't get it. A few weeks ago you were so happy I couldn't stand you. Seriously. I'd get off the phone and think, enough with these local yokels. I need an island guy." Heidi drank deeply from her margarita glass. "God, these are good. We need a whole pitcher. Now: What the hell happened?"

"He lied," Gwen said. Then, flushing mightily, she told Heidi about the envelope in Rico's glove compartment, how she'd placed it on the bed the morning she left.

Heidi looked utterly perplexed. "Let me get this straight. You didn't even *ask* him where he got it?"

"No," Gwen said. "Honestly, it doesn't matter. He could have robbed a bank for all I care."

Heidi frowned. "Then what's the problem?"

"The problem is that he's a liar. He said he was broke, and I believed him." The words came out in a rush. "I was going to fly up here and sell my car. Empty out my bank account. The money my grandfather left me. I was going to put *every cent I had* into that business. And Rico would have let me." Gwen stopped for a breath. "He was using me. He only wanted my money."

Heidi poured half her margarita into Gwen's empty glass.

"I thought he loved me. Isn't that ridiculous? I feel like such an idiot."

"Are you sure?"

Gwen nodded. To her horror she felt her eyes tear.

"Well, fuck him, then. You're better off without him."

"That's what my mother says. Not in those exact words, of course." Gwen grinned feebly.

"Your mother? She must be loving this." Heidi gave the Rachel a fluff. "It's exactly what she wanted, isn't it? You back in Pittsburgh. Rico out of the picture for good."

Gwen hesitated. "Sure. I guess so. But she means well. Billy, Scott—they were all worried."

"Oh, right: Scott." Heidi signaled the waitress with two fingers: two more margaritas. "I still can't believe he showed up there."

"It was bizarre," Gwen agreed.

"Interesting . . ." Heidi's voice trailed off.

"What?"

"Don't you think the timing is weird? Your brother shows up out of the blue, and—a week later? two weeks?—Rico has twenty thousand dollars."

Gwen drained her glass, licked the salt from her lips. "What are you saying? That *Scott* gave him the money?" She frowned. "Why would he do that?"

"How would I know? But you have to admit, the timing is freaky."

Gwen shrugged. "Anyway, Scott doesn't have twenty thousand dollars lying around. Trust me. I'm surprised he could afford a plane ticket."

"Well, what about your mother? Didn't she have some rich old boyfriend who died? No offense, but it sounds like she might have some spare change." Heidi covered her mouth with her hand. "Oops. I shouldn't have said that. My point is, somehow or other, your mother got exactly what she wanted. Am I wrong?"

Gwen blinked, and remembered.

I'm just glad you're back, and safe.

It will be wonderful to have you close.

Promise me you'll never run off that way again.

"No," Gwen said slowly. "You're not wrong."

chapter 10

C*ape Cod is the bared and bended arm of Massachusetts.*
    Creeping along the highway, at the frustrating speed of fifteen miles an hour, Paulette remembered the verse. The traffic was even denser than she remembered. No longer a small knot of cars approaching the Sagamore Bridge, the jam now extended for miles in both directions. It was Saturday, changeover day on the Cape: a flood of weekly tenants passing over the bridge to take possession of their cottages; an equal volume headed in the opposite direction, heading home to the Empire State, the Constitution State, or north to truculent New Hampshire (which had given the world Gil Pyle) to Live Free or Die.

We're tenants now, Paulette thought. This had occurred to her a month ago, when she wrote the crushingly large check to the rental agent; but the realization had been fleeting. Now, sitting in changeover traffic on Route 6, she felt its full force.

The backseat she'd packed full of picnic gear and beach towels. In the past they'd kept such items at the Captain's House, ready for whomever might need them: the cousin who turned up without warning, the unexpected guests. In her attic Paulette had found two old wooden tennis racquets, a badminton set, an inflatable raft somebody—Gwen or Billy—had used as a child. In a dusty corner was a bag of golf clubs. (Martine's? Why would she have Martine's clubs in Concord?) Feeling foolish, Paulette had lugged these items, minus the clubs, out to the station wagon. Of her children only Billy was a golfer.

She hoped he'd remember to bring his own clubs.

She thought of the dozen bags of groceries in the hot trunk of the car, and worried about the perishables. Extra eggs for Billy (he ate only the whites, so an omelet used up half a carton), Canadian bacon for Scott's eggs Benedict. Strawberry ice cream for Gwen, who devoured it by the pint, or used to. Did she still eat ice cream? For years Paulette had seen her only at Christmas. Of Gwen's adult habits and tastes, she had no idea.

She had a great deal to learn.

In addition to the towels and tennis rackets, she'd packed two books Gwen had given her, in different years, as Christmas gifts: one a paperback thriller, the other a hefty tome involving women and wolves. For years they'd sat unread on a shelf. Now Paulette was determined to read them, to understand why Gwen had chosen these books for her. Who was this daughter she'd raised? This scuba diver, this anthropologist (or archaeologist), who was brave or foolish or passionate enough to run away to a tropical island and fall in love with a total stranger: Who was this independent, secretive, impulsive young woman? Paulette was looking for clues. For years, struggling to raise the daughter she'd *expected* to have, she had failed to see the one she'd gotten. But it wasn't too late. The week at the Cape stretched ahead of them. There was plenty of time.

At long last, she reached the turnoff. The cool shade of the No Name Road soothed her like a poultice. She felt herself in sympathetic company, the tall trees for whom twenty-two years was a trifle. *I'm back,* she told them. *I'm back.*

On the No Name Road Frank had taught her to drive. It was early March, the house still closed for the season. They'd driven down from Boston on a false spring day: hot sunshine, an evening chill, an early dark. Paulette had made a decision she'd confided to no one, not even Tricia Boone. She and Frank would become lovers in the Captain's House. But first, the driving. That afternoon, coasting down the No Name Road, he had surrendered the wheel of his old Chevy. *Gently now. Let out the clutch.* Each time, for emphasis, he had touched her. This was more distracting than helpful, the warmth and weight of his hand on her thigh.

She rolled down her window. A seagull squawked in the distance. The air smelled of sweet ocean, a special thing. As a little girl she'd identified a half dozen ways the sea could smell, briny or fishy or sandy or green. A few times each summer, for reasons she couldn't explain, the breeze smelled of molasses, dark and sweet.

She was remembering the six ocean smells when a remarkable thing happened. A car whizzed past her, a convertible with its top down, a bald man at the wheel. A moment later a second car followed, a Range Rover with a kayak strapped to its roof.

Cars on the No Name Road!

Who *were* these people?

Then, as the road curved, she saw the houses. Two of them, built close together, high on the ridge. The places were immense, twice as large as the Captain's House. Their brand-new clapboards glowed yellow in the afternoon sun.

TO HER relief the lane had not been paved. Paulette parked in front. The familiar dry rasp of tires on gravel filled her with pleasure. Oh yes, she thought, closing her eyes. I'm here.

She got out of the car, taking an armload of groceries. It would take several trips to unload the rest. Had it always been such a chore to unpack the car? No, it hadn't. Not with a sister, three children, and occasionally even a husband to help.

She stood there a moment, staring at the front of the house, the three diamond-shaped windows above the entryway. Roy, Martine, and Paulette.

Billy, Scott, and Gwen.

The key was under the doormat, as the leasing agent had promised. Paulette turned it in the lock.

Her heart fluttered.

As she stepped over the threshold of the Captain's House, as she set down her groceries and rushed from room to room, as she took inventory of each rug and curtain and stick of furniture, inhaling deeply each closet and hallway, checking the smell against the unarticulated but remarkably specific memory deep in her limbic brain, there was one person in the world who'd predicted what emotion would flush her cheeks and tremble her hands, one person who'd prefigured her steps precisely from front door to kitchen to Cook's Corner, up the staircase to Fanny's Room and the Whistling Room and finally the sleeping porch of her girlhood, where she would drop to her knees beside a bed and kneel there a long while as if praying.

This premonition—immediate, acute, dead accurate and profoundly discomfiting—had gripped Billy the moment his mother invited him to Truro. He'd felt ill-equipped to assist at Paulette's upcoming nervous breakdown. He was barely managing his own.

THE HOUSE had changed.

Paulette had expected this, of course. Before the sale her brother had plundered anything he imagined valuable: an antique spittoon in the entryway, a couple of amateurish watercolors (Roy had no eye for art) hanging in the stairwell. Everything else he'd sold along with the house. The place had always been furnished with odds and ends, comfortable castoffs: worn sofas, low and square, in the sitting room; faded canvas rugs terminally encrusted with sand. Naturally the new owners, a Portuguese couple from Rhode Island, would make adjustments. Still, she was shocked by the new furniture, overstuffed sofas and chairs in a bright nautical stripe. They seemed much too large for the room.

Upstairs the situation was more dire. In all four bedrooms— the Captain's Quarters, the Lilac Room, the Whistling Room, and Fanny's—the wood floors had been covered with carpet, the sturdy synthetic kind found in public buildings and roadside motels, chosen by people who wouldn't have to live with it. Paulette knelt in the corner of the Lilac Room and examined the edge of the carpet, firmly tacked to the floor. Professionally installed: the Medeiroses had gone to some expense.

It was there, kneeling in the corner of the Lilac Room, that she made a more troubling discovery. The sign had been removed from the door.

She crossed the hall to Fanny's Room. Its door had been repainted, the nail hole filled. The same had been done to the Captain's Quarters, the Sleeping Porch, and the Whistling Room.

All the signs were gone.

Paulette stretched out on the bed in the Whistling Room and cried as she hadn't in years, not even during her divorce. She had forgotten how pleasurable crying could be. She cried for Roy and Martine, and poor Anne; for her dead parents; for Grandmother Drew and Aunt Grace and Tess and Doro; for Fanny Porter, whose room had been decommissioned and poorly carpeted and now resembled an overdecorated suite at a grubby bed-and-breakfast. She cried for generations of Drews and their summer friends, the sandaled guests who'd watched the sunset from their terrace. The lumpen tribe who'd surrendered the Cape to all takers, who had themselves scattered to unfortunate places like Taos and Tucson. Foolishly, carelessly, they'd let go of everything that mattered, including each other. They'd forgotten the life that had been.

Paulette cried this way for several minutes, until she began to feel rather silly. She had never known Fanny Porter, after all; the woman wasn't a relative, just a schoolmate who'd latched on to Grandmother Drew at Wellesley and come to the Cape summer after summer until the whole family had doubtless gotten sick of her.

It was a bit shameless, when you thought about it.

So forget Fanny Porter. And—it came to her in a wave—forget Roy and Martine. Her brother was the bandit who'd sold the house in the first place. And Martine—why pretend otherwise?—had always been a pill. The others Paulette could legitimately cry over. She'd been fond of her aunts and grandmother, and of course her poor parents.

Though her father, if he were alive, would be ninety-seven years old, hardly in any shape to climb the stairs to the Captain's Quarters. He would be moldering in a nursing home somewhere.

Which would probably have similar carpeting.

Paulette laughed at this thought, long enough that laughter too began to feel strange. It wasn't good to be left alone too long with one's own emotions; it wasn't healthy or attractive. She wished Gwen would arrive.

At that moment she heard a car turn down the lane, its tires crunching the gravel.

She rose, smoothed her hair, examined her face in the small wood-framed mirror. Here was another reason adults shouldn't indulge in tears. Her children had looked beautiful after crying, their soft cheeks rinsed clean and hopeful, their delicate skins flushed like fruit. On adults, especially aged adults, the effects were less fetching. She looked as though she'd been taking chemotherapy.

There was a knock at the front door. A male voice called, "Hello!"

She hurried downstairs. The rooms had grown dark; someone less familiar with the layout would have taken a nasty fall on the stairs. She flicked on a light.

"Frank," she said.

He stood on the front step, a bouquet of daisies—*daisies?*—in one hand.

"Honey, what's the matter?" He looked alarmed, which puzzled her. Then she remembered that her eyelids were swollen like blisters.

What are you doing here? she could have said. *Who told you we'd be here?*

"They took down the signs," she said instead.

He threw open the door and took her in his arms.

It wasn't precisely what she wanted. Her years of wanting him— his touch, his presence, his sorrow for the pain he'd caused—were long past. Even as a young man, strong and vital, he'd been unable to give her what she needed. Now he seemed tired and diminished, while her needs had only expanded, grown dense and gnarled, like the roots of an ancient tree. Yet here he was, as large and vividly out of place as the new striped sofas. The screen door was open, insects swarming the overhead light. But she had learned this much: you took life where you met it, even in an open doorway. You took it, and held on.

They were clutching each other like this, rather embarrassingly, when another car rolled into the driveway and crunched to a halt.

"Who on earth is that?" Paulette murmured, stepping back from him, thinking of a time her mother had caught them kissing in this very spot. Of course Frank wouldn't remember such a thing. For this she was grateful.

"Dad?" Scott got out of the car. "What are you doing here?"

"Hello, dear!" Paulette approached the car. Her granddaughter was sitting in the passenger seat. Penny and Ian were nowhere to be seen.

"Where is everybody?" she asked.

"That's a long story," said Scott.

THEY ATE dinner on the terrace, the four of them. The refrigerator was full of breakfast food, the ingredients for a frittata. Sabrina proved surprisingly helpful in the kitchen. She seemed delighted when Paulette showed her how to mix a simple vinaigrette. "I didn't know you could *make* this," she said, rather cryptically. Her hair was honey colored, neatly braided; she didn't slouch the way so many girls seemed to. Both Scott and Penny had terrible posture. Who had taught Sabrina to stand up straight?

Paulette glanced out the window. Scott and Frank were sitting on the porch, deep in conversation. Scott was speaking, his father nodding in agreement. This surprised her. With Frank it was usually the other way around.

How very strange, to see him sitting on the terrace as though he'd never left, as though it were his rightful place. Why on earth had he come? Last month on the phone she had sensed his loneliness, his hunger for information about the children. He hadn't spoken to any of them since Christmas.

Who, then, had told him about the trip to the Cape?

Among other things, his arrival complicated the sleeping arrangements. She'd planned to give Billy the Captain's Quarters, but when Frank had placed his jacket there, she hadn't demurred. It was a violation of protocol—*certainly* he was no longer head of the household—but she remembered, would never forget, how he'd always wanted to sleep in that room. She could put Billy in the Lilac Room, but then where would Gwen sleep? On the porch with Sabrina? Paulette, herself, adored the sleeping porch, but Gwen might find the suggestion insulting, as though Paulette were treating her like a little girl.

Leave it to Frank, she thought, to cause problems between her and Gwen.

"I didn't know Grandpa was coming," Sabrina said.

Paulette looked up, startled. The child had read her thoughts, something Billy used to do.

"I didn't either," she admitted. "I suppose he wanted to see your dad, and Uncle Billy and Aunt Gwen. And you, of course."

"And you," Sabrina added.

Paulette did not respond to this.

"My mom has a boyfriend," Sabrina said.

Paulette, cracking eggs for the frittata, dropped a yolk on the floor.

"Ian likes him, but I don't. He never talks, and he has tattoos. I *hate* tattoos," she added, as though this were the central issue. "Especially on guys."

"You've *met* this person?" said Paulette.

"A couple of times. He took us to play minigolf, which I don't like *at all*." She was a child of strong convictions. "And he was there once when I came home from school."

"Does your father know about this?" Paulette asked, her voice trembling a little.

"He does now. I think they're getting a divorce. I wasn't supposed to tell you. Is this okay?" Sabrina asked, showing her the salad.

"It looks wonderful," said Paulette, impulsively kissing her. "Darling, you're a wonder. I'm so glad you're here."

They carried the plates out to the terrace, where Scott was mixing drinks; somebody—he or Frank—had stocked the bar. After some protest Paulette let him make her a weak gin and tonic.

"Be careful with that stuff, missy," Frank said, smiling slyly. "Scott, did I ever tell you about the time your mother tried to drink a martini?"

Paulette flushed. "Frank, for heaven's sake."

"We were at some joint in Philly with Wall and Tricia James. I had to carry her to the car."

"Grandma!" Sabrina said, laughing.

"It was terribly embarrassing," Paulette said, flushing. "I felt so sophisticated drinking from that beautiful glass. Then dinner was over, and I realized that I couldn't stand."

"We made quite an exit," said Frank.

Paulette joined in the laughter. It was oddly pleasurable to be laughed at. Her family—a part of it, anyway—was together at the Captain's House. Tomorrow Gwen and Billy would arrive, and her birthday would be complete. Except for Ian, of course. In principle she wanted to see her grandson, though in actual fact she was a bit relieved. Perhaps by next summer he'd have outgrown his obstreperous stage.

Penny she did not miss in the least.

She watched Scott across the table. He looked tired, which was not surprising. He was losing hair and weight; he seemed to be caving in on himself. For years she had wished him free of that dreadful girl, but she'd never considered the pain this might cause him. Certainly she had not wished for this.

Scott woke to the smell of breakfast. A cool breeze riffled the striped curtains in the Whistling Room. Had the windows whistled last night? He'd been too plastered to notice. After his mother and Sabrina went to bed, he and the old man had stayed up for hours, knocking back G and Ts on the terrace.

Had this really happened? Had he stayed up half the night getting loaded with his father?

He sat up in bed holding his head. Frank had taken over as bartender, and offered him another and another and another. Though he hadn't needed much convincing. Given recent events, he felt entitled.

All at once he remembered the mess he'd left back in Gatwick. Since her revelation Penny had seemed strangely calm and contented, as though a vexing problem had been solved. She was cheerful and pleasant. She showed a renewed—perhaps unprecedented—interest in housekeeping: vacuuming behind the furniture, cooking actual dinners instead of picking up a bucket of chicken from the supermarket deli. Most astonishingly, she stopped watching television. Scott slept in the basement under a comforter that smelled of mushrooms, but he woke to a clean, quiet house. In many respects, his domestic life was much improved. Had Penny discovered the secret to successful marriage? Was it as simple as having an affair with your brother?

She had ceased, abruptly, to nag him. For years they'd played a kind of tug-of-war. Now Penny had simply dropped the rope. She moseyed through the day in a trance of contentment, a quiet bovine happiness that reminded Scott of their pot-smoking days, Penny slow and sweet and infinitely accepting, asking no more of life than what was immediately before her. Nothing could shake her composure.

Well, almost nothing.

One night after the kids were in bed, lulled by her apparent calm, Scott made an admission. For years Penny had been his confessor. Over the years she'd absolved him of a thousand failures, had listened, posed questions, doled out penance. After each clownish pratfall, he'd found comfort in her. Now, despite her recent betrayal, he needed her more than ever. His guilt was a parasite, feeding on his blood. He could rationalize blowing Ian's tuition money—boarding school would have been a mistake anyway, or so Scott had convinced himself. It was his sister's face that haunted him, Gwen in St. Raphael: her dreamy smile, her radiant happiness. When he thought of what he had destroyed, he was nearly sick.

"You did *what*?" Penny said.

"The twenty thousand dollars. I gave it to Gwen's boyfriend. I bribed him, Pen. To leave my sister alone."

"Jesus, Scotty!" She looked at him in openmouthed horror. "Why the fuck would you do something like that?" Then her brow cleared. "Of course. I get it. You wanted to score points with your mother. And if you had to ruin Gwen's life—well, no big deal."

After his disclosure a pall settled over the household. Penny would not absolve him; she wouldn't even meet his eyes. His wife—who'd been boinking, who *continued to boink* her stepbrother—found Scott's actions repugnant. Gnarly, even. And in his heart, he had to agree.

His other disgraces seemed tame by comparison. The day after his drug test, he'd arrived at Ruxton to find his desk already emptied, its contents packed into sturdy corrugated boxes. Jordan Funk got up from his desk, his face somber.

O'Kane left this for you. He handed Scott a sealed envelope.

Scott stuffed it into his pocket.

You idiot, Jordan said, shaking his head. *You should have told me you were getting p-piss-tested. I could have, you know, helped you out.*

He helped Scott carry the boxes out to his car, his girlish arms trembling with the strain. When the car was loaded, Jordan stood back, arms crossed.

I guess that's it, said Scott.

This is such bullshit. Jordan's face was flushed, his eyes blazing. Scott had seen a similar look on Ian's face, just before he flew into a sobbing rage that would send blocks or Power Rangers flying. Jesus Christ, Scott thought. Is he going to cry?

Thanks for the hand, said Scott. *You saved me an extra trip.*

There was an awkward pause.

What are you going to do? Jordan asked.

Scott shrugged. *I know a guy who does carpentry in Massachusetts. He needs a helper for the summer.*

Again Jordan looked ready to cry.

Hey, it's not so bad, Scott said, thumping Jordan's skinny shoulder. *I kind of like it.*

Jordan looked unconvinced. Scott watched him as he drove away, his arm raised in a limp wave.

He remembered, now, describing the scene to his father: Jordan standing at the curb, Aaron Savitz's Beamer pulling into the parking lot, the fat fuck recognizing him just in time to flip him the bird. Frank had laughed at this, manly gin-fueled laughter. Now, sitting in bed with a raging hangover, Scott marveled at this fact. He couldn't recall the last time, any time, he'd made his father laugh.

He'd been stunned, last night, to find his parents on the porch of the Captain's House, in what could have been either a friendly hug or a passionate clinch. Scott wasn't sure which would have surprised him more. He'd noticed, then, the new Saab convertible parked at the end of the driveway. *Dad's Nobel Prize.* In that moment a feeling had gripped him, half forgotten from childhood. He wanted to rush his father, head down like a billy goat; to charge and pummel and wrestle him to the ground, not in anger but in the purest delight. His father had returned.

And then it hit him: *Ian. This is how Ian feels.*

Now, lying in bed in the Whistling Room, he thought of all the times, exhausted and fed up and demoralized by his day at Ruxton, he

had pushed his son away. *I can do better,* he thought. He had no interest in climbing mountains like that ass Dashiell Blodgett; he would
not cure cancer or become wealthy or save anybody's life. But with
Penny's help, he had made two entire people, something neither Gwen
nor Billy had managed. He was Ian and Sabrina's father. Perhaps this
was mission enough.

It had cut him when, at the last minute, Ian refused to come to
the Cape. *He wants to go climbing,* Penny had explained. *You know how
he gets.* Ian was an obsessive kid; a few times a year he chose a new
object for his fixation—the skateboard, the Power Rangers—and pursued it with alarming enthusiasm. Now that his uncle Benji had introduced him to rock climbing, they would be inseparable all summer, or
at least for a few weeks.

What can I do? Penny shouted over the neighbor's lawn mower.
She was standing barefoot in the driveway, watching Scott pack the
Golf. *Just go, and have a good time with Sabrina. Ian will snap out of it even-
tually. You know he loves you, Scotty. This is just a phase he's going through.*

And what about you? Scott slammed shut his hatchback. *Is Uncle
Benji a phase for you too?*

Penny ignored his sarcastic tone. *We belong together.*

Are you kidding? Next door the mower stopped; Scott lowered his
voice. *He's your stepbrother, for God's sake.*

He's my best friend.

Scott flinched, thinking how, in the early days, Penny had called
him "my partner in crime." Now Benji was her best friend. It was the
cruelest thing she'd ever said.

*He thinks I'm smart, Scotty. He likes the way I dress. He doesn't care if
I watch TV. You still don't get it,* she said, seeing his blank look. *He loves
me exactly the way I am.*

I love you! Scott exploded. *Eleven years, Pen! You don't think I love
you? Are you*—he nearly said "retarded." *Are you crazy?*

Penny sighed. *Yes, fine, crazy. And I can't cook and I don't read the
newspaper and I like the wrong things and say the wrong things and I have no
idea why you ever wanted me in the first place and if I hadn't gotten pregnant
you'd have bailed ten years ago. Am I right?* She didn't expect an answer;

she was only pausing for breath. *I'd be some girl you picked up out West when you were young and stupid. You wouldn't even remember my name.*

Scott opened his mouth to speak.

I guess you love me, she said, *but, you know, why? I'm not a Drew. I didn't go to Pearse. I can't talk to your mother.*

My mother? Scott blinked. *Jesus, Penny. For the hundredth time: my family doesn't hate you.*

Maybe not, she allowed. *Maybe they just don't understand why you married me. I don't blame them. For a long time, I didn't get it either.*

Scott stared at her, his heart loud. He and Penny had never been known for subtlety. It seemed strangely appropriate that the final aching moments of their marriage happened in the front yard, with a UPS truck idling in the street.

You think you're a loser, and I make you feel better. You need somebody to look down on. That's why you're always lecturing me. It makes you feel smart.

Scott flushed. After eleven years of listening to him pontificate, Penny had finally schooled him.

Benji makes me feel good. And you, basically, make me feel like shit.

The lawn mower resumed.

Penny, no. He felt suddenly shaky, flooded with panic. *That's not right. I never meant to* — He groped for words. *I need you, Pen. Don't leave me.*

Penny was not a crier. Her clear blue eyes were perfectly dry.

Don't worry, Scotty, she said. *You'll be just fine.*

SCOTT DRESSED and went downstairs.

"Well, good morning! It is still morning, isn't it?' His mother kissed his cheek, took a swipe at his uncombed hair.

"Have a seat, son." His father had already been to town, picked up the *Globe* and the *Times*. He sat at the table parsing them into piles: front page, national, local, arts. Sabrina sat beside him braiding friendship bracelets, breakfast half eaten on her plate.

"Coffee?" Scott asked.

His father chuckled. "I've had a whole pot, myself. Didn't much help."

"Where is everybody?" He'd resolved to talk to Gwen alone, at the first opportunity. To grovel, if necessary, for her forgiveness. He had no dignity left to lose.

"Billy should be here any moment. As for your sister, I have no idea. The last I heard she was planning to rent a car at the airport. I expect her later today." Paulette handed him a glass of orange juice. "Darling, do you remember this?"

"My lobster glass!"

"I saved it," she explained. Years ago, before the house was put on the market, she and Martine had sorted through the old china closet. The mismatched dishes weren't worth keeping, but she'd made a point of nabbing the children's favorite drinking glasses: Scott's lobster, Gwen's CrisCraft. "I'm afraid I couldn't remember which one Billy liked," she admitted. "A lighthouse maybe? Or was it a fish of some sort?"

This made it even better.

After his eggs Benedict, his grilled tomatoes, Scott lingered at the breakfast table, glancing through the papers. To his astonishment his parents did not interrogate him about work. Penny's name was not mentioned. Instead they reminisced about summers past—the time his uncle Roy capsized the *Mamie Broussard*; the time Martine's boyfriend, given his own room for propriety's sake, fell down the stairs and broke an ankle while sneaking out of hers. Stories Scott had forgotten, or hadn't been told in the first place—the one about Martine's boyfriend had been deemed too risqué. As the youngest he'd been a victim of censorship, sent to bed hours before the other cousins, when the sky was barely dark. He'd been keenly aware of the vacation life buzzing around him, the teenage and adult Drew life from which he was excluded: movies at the open air in Wellfleet, midnight sails, barbecues on the front lawn, the house swollen with guests. *I'm missing everything*, he often complained at bedtime. *Be patient*, his mother admonished him. *Your turn will come*. But by the time Scott was a teenager the house had been sold, the family dissolved. His father and brother and sister, the Drew aunts and uncles and cousins, were all gone.

He recalled, now, that feeling of injury, outrage at the injustice. What a relief to sit with his parents as pleasant adults, lingering over coffee, not stewing over the myriad ways he'd disappointed them, the shamed certainty that he would never be enough. He tried to remember the last time they'd sat this way, himself and Paulette and Frank, laughing, remembering. Never, he realized. This had not happened in all his life.

Childhood was over. What a fucking relief.

At that moment his mother froze. "Did you hear that?" she cried, springing out of her chair. "Billy is here!"

She hurried out the front door, patting her hair, Frank quick on her heels. Scott sat a moment, staring into his empty lobster glass. He rose heavily and followed them out to the porch, just in time to see the car roll up the lane.

Scott glanced at his Golf parked in the shade, the dented side panel, the rust spreading up from the undercarriage like an aggressive cancer. *Go ahead, asshole*, Scott thought, eyeing Billy's gleaming Mercedes. *Park next to me.*

"There's somebody with him," said Frank.

The car stopped. Billy stepped out of the car. Then his passenger, a dark-skinned man in pale linen trousers.

Paulette shaded her eyes. "Who on earth is that?"

The two approached the porch. Then Billy stopped short.

"Dad," he said.

"Hello, son." Frank stepped forward, thumping Billy's shoulder. Paulette leaned in for a kiss. Billy seemed momentarily confused, like a wealthy tourist mobbed by gypsies in port.

"Mom, Dad," he said, disengaging himself. "This is my partner, Srikanth."

The dark-skinned man offered his hand.

For three days Billy had rehearsed the words in his head. *Mom, there's somebody special I'd like you to meet. This is my partner, Srikanth.*

He'd agonized over *special*, which made Sri sound retarded. And *partner*, which sounded so businesslike. But he detested the word *boyfriend*—he was not a teenager. And *lover* made him want to run screaming into the street.

Of course, *partner* was open to misinterpretation. For Billy this was part of its appeal. His mother was welcome to misinterpret the relationship, if she wished to. What mattered was the saying. Billy would say the words, and Sri would hear them. His family could think what they liked.

Sri asked him one last time, as they turned off the highway to the No Name Road: "Are you sure you want to do this?"

"Of course," Billy said.

But a moment later he saw the Prize parked in the driveway. Then the screen door flew open and *both* his parents were waiting on the porch.

"What is he doing here?" Billy said.

He felt, but ignored, a sudden urge to hang a U-turn in the driveway, to test the Mercedes's vaunted acceleration by flooring it back to Manhattan.

It was too late to change his mind.

He said the words he'd rehearsed, and waited. After a stunned moment, his father had shaken Sri's hand.

How ironic, how unsettling, how flat-out astonishing that it was Frank who saved the day, who sent Paulette down to the beach with Sabrina and a very strong Bloody Mary, who asked Sri a series of polite, then interested, then rabidly fascinated questions about his work.

Jesus, his father. Standing in the doorway to the kitchen, Billy watched the scene unfolding in the living room. His father sat opposite Sri on the hideous new couch *(stripes?)*, in rapt attention. Sri's eloquence on the subject of gene-expression patterns seemed to have eclipsed the fact that he had sodomized Frank's son. A casual observer would have said that Frank was in denial, but Billy knew that the truth was more exotic. He'd understood for years that something was wrong with his father, some basic human quality missing. (The way he'd treated Paulette. Remember? The way he'd treated Gwen.) Now, suddenly, Frank's odd detachment looked for all the world like virtue. The old man was not incapable of love. He simply reserved his love for the natural world, the subtle mysteries that governed it. It was a type of love that did not lead to happy marriages, or successful parenting; yet it was a sublime thing, beyond the capacity of most humans: to love what had nothing to do with oneself.

And yet.

Watching his father nodding, smiling, laughing in hearty approval, Billy remembered the wretched Thanksgiving Lauren McGregor had suffered in Concord, his father's warmth and welcome, the intuitive way he had put her at ease. Now he offered Sri the same kindness.

His father was kind.

BILLY DIDN'T get loaded in the afternoon, not normally. Not ever. But he was in Truro; he was an adult now; and at the Captain's House, adults drank. Cocktails at five, earlier on weekends. Those golden summers of his childhood: it had somehow never occurred to him that his grandfather and Mamie and Roy and Martine, probably even his mother, had spent them half in the bag. How else, really, could you spend an entire summer with your family? There was wisdom in the old ways, he reflected, improvising a second pitcher of Bloodies. A different sort of System.

He took the pitcher out to the front porch, where his brother was waiting. It was a spot where nobody ever sat because it offered only a view of the road. For Billy this was its appeal. He liked having his car in plain sight, his keys jangling in his pocket. There was comfort in knowing he could get behind the wheel at any moment and roar down the No Name Road, heading toward the highway.

"What's Dad doing here?" he asked Scott.

"He was here when I pulled in last night. He and Mom were on the porch." Scott hesitated. "They might have been kissing."

"Mom and Dad?" Billy flinched. On a day when it seemed nothing could shock him, this did. "Are you sure?"

"No," Scott admitted. "And they seem totally normal together. Which itself is abnormal." He held out his empty glass.

"Where did he sleep?" Billy demanded.

"Captain's Quarters. Mom slept in Fanny's Room."

Billy filled their glasses. He waited for Scott to speak. When he could wait no longer, he took a long gulp of his Bloody Mary. He was about to discuss his sex life with his brother. Some distant, sober part of him was stunned and horrified.

"Seriously, man," he said finally. "All these years, you never had a clue?"

"Nope," said Scott.

"How is that possible?"

Scott shrugged. "You had girlfriends. Lauren."

Lauren?

"That was fifteen years ago," Billy said, a bit testily. "I haven't had a girlfriend since Reagan was president. That didn't throw up any red flags?"

"Shit. I didn't realize it was that long ago." Scott reached into his pocket for a pack of Camels.

"You are *not,*" Billy said firmly. "Don't even think about lighting a cigarette." He could scarcely breathe as it was.

The whole situation was breathtaking. He was dazzled by his

brother's self-absorption, his unapologetic thoughtlessness. For twenty years Billy had agonized, monitored his behavior, censored every conversation. Packing for family gatherings *(is this shirt too gay?)* had triggered cluster headaches. How misguided, how laughable to think that anybody was paying attention. He could have preened around the Christmas tree in a feather boa for all his brother would have noticed. You'd think Scotty was running General Motors or brokering peace in the Middle East, he was so preoccupied with his own affairs. But being a fuckup took focus, Billy realized. You couldn't make such a royal mess of your life simply by letting things happen. You had to work at it.

"Penny knew," said Scott. "She always said you were gay. It used to piss me off."

"Penny?" In a family of bright people, Billy would have tagged his sister-in-law as the dullard. Yet only she had seen the obvious.

"Where *is* Penny?" he asked. Until now he hadn't noticed her absence.

"She didn't come." Scott drank long from his glass. "She's leaving me. She's having an affair with her stepbrother."

How to respond to a revelation of this type? Billy stared for a long moment at the ground.

"Quality," he said finally.

He allowed Scott to tell him the whole story: the stepfamily in Idaho, the chat room, finding the two of them in Sabrina's bedroom. Somewhere in the middle—the camping in Yellowstone, the paisley tattoos—Scott scrabbled in his pocket for a cigarette. This time Billy didn't say a word.

He listened. He forced himself to take it all in, the myriad ragged, deeply unsettling details. This was his brother's life, the little brother his System had kept him from knowing. He understood, then, that the System had outlived its usefulness. For years it had served as a kind of container, a way of organizing his love and anger and weird loyalty, his unpredictable and overpowering tenderness for the four people who had always known him, his mother and father and Scotty and Gwen.

• • •

AT MAMIE'S Beach the tide was going out. The lowest of the clouds had parted, revealing a white disk of sun.

Paulette and Sabrina made a slow tour, stopping to pick up a perfect shell, a bit of colored glass. Paulette walked slowly, pleasantly wobbly from the strong drink. Sabrina ran ahead, gleefully barefoot in the soft sand. For no good reason Paulette missed her sister. Martine had loved whizzing along the shoreline in her kayak. As a girl she'd pored over the framed nautical map hanging in the entryway of the house. *There's Pamet Harbor!* she would exclaim, pointing. *Mamie's Beach. Full-Moon Cove.*

How do you know? Paulette demanded, to which Martine simply shrugged.

You just look, and figure it out.

Paulette had tried this, but the correspondences eluded her. The formations on the map looked nothing like the sandy beaches and inlets she saw before her. In her mind they were entirely different things.

They had spoken two days ago, in honor of Paulette's birthday. Martine, as always, had asked after the children, and for the first time in years, Paulette had confided in her sister. *Billy's so distant lately. He's always in a hurry. I'm lucky if he calls once a week.* Martine—Paulette ought to have expected this—had been inadequately sympathetic. *Cut him some slack, will you? You're not his only concern. You have no idea what else is going on in his life.* Paulette wondered, now, if Martine knew something she hadn't. Yet as far as she knew, Billy hadn't spoken with his aunt in years.

Martine had always been smarter about these things, more worldly, more sophisticated. Years ago, when Gwen and Billy were babies, Martine had shown up at the Captain's House with a friend from New York, an art director—whatever that was—at the agency where she worked. His name was Anthony—pronounced in the British way, with a hard T—a good-looking man with sandy hair cut long in the front, so that he was always brushing it from his eyes. They had all assumed Anthony was Martine's boyfriend; but it was Paulette he followed around the house while Martine sailed or golfed, Paulette he joined at the piano in the afternoon while the children were napping. He seemed smitten with her, a startling development. Exhausted by her last pregnancy, she felt worn and homely. No one had been smitten with her in ages. She wished Frank were there to see it. (Though, being Frank, he probably wouldn't have noticed. He had always been immune to jealousy. Further evidence that he had never loved her enough.)

Martine, to her surprise, was not upset by Anthony's defection. *I'm glad you two had fun,* she told Paulette after they dropped him at the ferry terminal. Then, seeing Paulette's confusion: *For God's sake, he's not my boyfriend. He's queer, you know.* Anthony was, to Paulette's knowledge, the first homosexual she'd ever met. Martine knew a great many, apparently, in New York; she was the first person of Paulette's acquaintance to use the word *gay.* Had she known about Billy all along? Probably, Paulette realized. Billy hadn't needed to tell her. Martine had simply looked, and figured it out.

Why didn't I see it? Paulette marveled. *Heavens, what is the matter with me?*

She glanced at her watch and wondered if Gwen had arrived.

CLIMBING THE stairs to the porch, Paulette heard male voices inside. She was shocked to see Frank and Srikanth holding forth on the sofa. In her ruminations about Billy and Martine, she had forgotten about them both. Frank was speaking; she listened a moment and picked out two words, *transgenic* and *mutation.* Enough to convince her that nothing significant was being discussed.

Billy's friend was handsome. She took note of his elegant profile, the delicate arch of his eyebrows, his long and graceful hands. For years Billy had been her yardstick for male beauty, the standard to which she held all men—the very young ones in magazine advertisements, the toothy actors on television—usually to their detriment. But this Srikanth had the most beautiful skin she had ever seen on a *person,* male or female. His dark curly hair was glossy as mink.

He seemed to sense her gaze. He looked up from his conversation and met her eyes. When Paulette smiled, he smiled back, dazzling her. He was, she realized, even handsomer than Billy. She was undeniably drunk, yet she felt confident in her perceptions.

He was possibly the handsomest man in the world.

This should not have mattered, of course. But to Paulette, it made the situation comprehensible. Her son was a homosexual, but who could blame him? The world would be rife with homosexuals if more men looked like Srikanth.

"My mother is in love with you," Billy said.

They were lying in the dark in the Bunk House, Sri in the top bunk, Billy down below, having refused the double bed in the Lilac Room. He was relieved beyond words to have the day behind him. He had no regrets. Yet he was unprepared to sleep with Srikanth in the Lilac Room with Paulette to one side of them, Frank to the other. He would likely never be prepared for that.

"She was staring at you all through dinner. It was embarrassing."

"I think she was a little drunk," said Sri.

"She was tanked. We all were. Welcome to the family." Billy reached for the glass of water he'd placed beside the bed. "I'm going to be puffy tomorrow."

"I'll still love you," said Sri.

"You say that now."

Above them the floor creaked. Movement in the Captain's Quarters.

"My father is on the loose," said Billy. "He's coming down here to show you his grant application."

Sri chuckled.

"You think I'm joking," Billy said.

Frank lay awake a long time, thinking. He remembered a night long ago, driving back from Nantasket Beach with two girls and Neil Windsor. The night he had misread the situation entirely, convinced that Windsor was gay.

With his own son he had made the same mistake, in reverse.

A hundred times he'd questioned Billy about girlfriends. The answers were uniformly evasive. Always Billy's reticence had stung him: Why wouldn't the kid *talk* to him? Had he been that negligent a father? All these years later, was Billy still angry about the divorce?

Once again he had misinterpreted the data. The truth had taken him by surprise, but he was too seasoned a scientist to panic at unexpected results. This outcome defied quick interpretations—it would take Frank the rest of his life to make sense of it—but it was certainly more favorable than the one he'd predicted. Billy, though gay, did not hate him. Frank still had his son.

The bedside clock ticked loudly. On a normal Sunday night he'd be asleep by now, the better to spring awake at dawn and get an early start in the lab. Instead he lay in a strange bed in a place he'd never expected to be. The big bed in the Captain's Quarters. Truro, Cape Cod, Massachusetts, New England, USA.

For a dozen summers, more, he'd made grudging trips to this house—muttering and grumbling, keenly aware of all he was missing back in Cambridge. Which was . . . what?

A few long days—among thousands—spent in the lab.

Back then he'd made the trip to please Paulette. Now she no longer wanted him in Truro. And he no longer wanted to be anywhere else. Was this old age, then: the end of all wanting? In April he'd celebrated—the wrong word—his sixtieth birthday. Whatever he'd desired from life had been gotten, or not; his wishes satisfied, or not. His wants—Paulette's too—were exhausted. It was their children's turn to want. Billy wanted . . . whatever he wanted. (Best not think too much about that.) Scott wanted his freedom. And then, Gwen.

Daddy, please do this for me. Billy isn't answering his phone. There's nobody else I can ask.

Rolling out of bed, Frank groped for his shirt and trousers. The floor creaked. Years ago, before they were married, he and Paulette had been assigned to separate rooms. At night they'd crept around the house as her parents slept. Frank and Paulette in love: cursing the noisy stairs, and wanting. Always privacy had eluded them. It seemed, then, that Drew relatives were around every corner—Roy and Anne on the lawn, chain-smoking and already squabbling; Aunt Doro and the other one whose name Frank could never remember, their tipsy laughter rising from the terrace. Now the house felt empty, and to his surprise this saddened him. For years he had fled the family—his own and Paulette's alike. Now, for the first time, he wanted them close.

There now. There was still something left to want.

He tiptoed down the hall, past Scott's closed door, and refilled his water glass at the bathroom sink. He peered out onto the sleeping porch: five empty twin beds, the sixth occupied by Sabrina. She looked tiny under the coverlet, and somehow forlorn, like a girl stood up at her slumber party. To his amusement, the thought made him misty. Jesus, was this his future? A weeping grandpa.

A crack of light showed beneath the door of Fanny's Room. Paulette had always liked to read in bed. At the door he paused.

The last time, yes. The summer of the bicentennial was the last time he and Paulette had shared this room. Time was no ghost; it had weight and smell and substance. Fit you like lead boots, it did. And yet those years could go in an instant. You could find yourself knocking at that same door.

"Paulette?" he whispered. "Are you still awake?"

"Frank? Is that you?"

He opened the door just in time to see her hide reading glasses beneath the coverlet. She sat up in bed, her back braced by pillows. She looked astonished to see him.

"I'm glad you're awake," he said.

"I don't sleep well anymore. Frank, what is it? Is something wrong?" The night had turned chilly; she wore a cardigan sweater over her nightgown. "I can't imagine what's keeping Gwen."

He sat at the edge of the bed. "I need to talk to you."

Paulette closed her eyes. "Not about Billy, please."

"You're upset," he said.

"Not at all. It's his own business, as far as I'm concerned. Honestly, I can't imagine what possessed him to tell us in the first place." She rubbed gingerly at her temples. "Please. Let's not discuss it."

"Fair enough." He handed her the glass of water. "Drink this. You're going to have a hangover tomorrow."

She took the glass.

"Actually, there's something else I need to tell you. It's why I drove down here in the first place. I didn't mean to horn in on your vacation." He hesitated. "It's about Gwen."

Paulette frowned.

"She called the other night and asked me to tell you—" He broke off. "Honey, Gwen isn't coming."

She stared at him wide eyed.

"She went back to the island. Apparently she's patched things up with the guy."

Paulette listened in silence as he told her everything he knew.

"But *why?*" she said when he'd finished. "Why couldn't she tell me herself?" Her voice startled him, husky with anguish. It was a voice he'd never heard before.

"I don't know," Frank admitted. "I begged her to, but she was adamant. She wouldn't say why." He reached for her hand, this woman he'd made his life with. Paulette who hadn't changed and wouldn't, perhaps couldn't; who had loved their daughter so imperfectly. Who had so imperfectly loved him.

"Paulette, I'm sorry. I know how important this was. You wanted the whole family together, and now everything—"

"Stay with me," she said.

prognosis

Winter comes late to St. Raphael. The November sun sets early. The big ships return to the harbor. The resorts, empty during storm season, begin to fill.

At Thanksgiving, at Christmas, the tourists appear like refugees. They are escaping the holiday, the anguished pilgrimage to the family stake. Instead they fly southward, moneyed travelers with seasonal depression, ashamed of their pale winter hides. Gwen is glad to see them, and not just for the dollars and euros they charge to their credit cards. She greets them kindly, with a warmth she'd never suspected she possessed. To her they are survivors of natural disasters. Her impulse is to offer cots and blankets, to bandage wounds.

There was a time, not long ago, when she wouldn't talk to strangers. That time seems remote now. Like a dream remembered, it haunts her for a moment, then quickly seems like nonsense.

Where did you come from? she asks them all. *Are you here for the holidays?* The two questions are enough. Travelers are lonely. They hunger to discuss themselves, to remember who they are.

It is Gwen who mans the storefront, a trim stucco building on the Quai des Marins, Gwen in her Steelers T-shirts, her reassuring Americanness. She does not often, these days, pilot the boat. The new one is large and cumbersome, difficult to maneuver. The boys, Alistair and Gabriel, handle it expertly; so she is content to stay landlocked, to hand out tanks and equipment and take calls from the cruise lines. The cruisers keep the dive shop in business. They show up without so much as a snorkel, and Gwen outfits them from top to bottom. Masks and fins; a hundred brand-new regulators; BCs hanging on wheeled racks, in bright shades of yellow and green. The equipment had cost a small fortune. Rico had been reluctant to make the investment, to take on any more debt.

We have to, Gwen told him. The cruise lines would deal only with full-service shops, able to equip boatloads of divers. And the cruise lines were their ticket to freedom, independence from the greedy resorts, which made huge profits on dive excursions and paid the outfitters a slim 20 percent.

At first Rico had balked. Gear for a hundred would cost more than the 2STE. But Gwen persisted, and finally he listened. Two years later, the loan was nearly paid.

In large matters she is adamant. In small ones—the daily schedule, the hirings and firings—she lets him have his way. The boy Gabriel is a friend of Alistair's, another delinquent Rico is determined to save. Gabriel is prompt and responsible, a better sailor than Alistair. Gwen thinks of them sometimes, the three boys on the boat. Her husband, despite his posturing, is less man than boy. Gwen still notices the comely tourists, the flirty divers in their bikinis. Undoubtedly Rico notices them too. But there are no more dive excursions at night.

She has been married three years, and she chooses to trust him. The other road is her mother's, ending in heartbreak. A road she chooses not to travel.

Rico is her family now, Rico and Alistair and Gabriel. The two boys are her children, the only ones she will ever have, or need. Her other family she thinks of rarely. They have receded for her, like buildings on a distant shore. She phones Billy once a month, sends occasional e-mails to her father. In this way, she learns that Penny has decamped for Idaho, leaving the kids with Scott. That—is it possible?—Frank has sold his house in Cambridge and moved back to Concord.

The earth has tipped on its axis.

To these revelations Gwen does not respond. At first she pretended her silence was unintentional. The move to St. Raphael, the buying of the dive shop: she was preoccupied with other things. Then her life settled, and still she remained silent. It was better that way.

She could not forget what her family had done. The truth had come clear to her in a single moment, at the Mexican restaurant with Heidi Kozak. Scott had given the money to Rico. The money and the plan—the cruel, insulting, breathtakingly devious idea—had come from her mother.

That night she'd dialed Rico's number. *My brother gave you the money. He paid you to leave me. Why didn't you tell me?*

If my brother had done such a thing, he said, *I wouldn't want to know.*

Were you? She stopped, started again, knowing that the rest of her life hung on his answer. *Were you going to leave me?*

Never, he swore. *You left me. I would never leave you.*

But you took the money.

You don't know what it is to be poor, he said. *How could you possibly know?*

I T W A S astounding what a person could forgive, if she wanted to.

This: Rico had taken money from her family.

And this: Scott had engineered this betrayal.

And this: Gwen herself had allowed it all to happen. She had run away in silence, ready to believe the worst.

She forgave Rico. There was no other choice. She refused to surrender the life that was possible. Anger and shame were no match for love.

Forgiving herself was more difficult. Compassion did not come easily to her. Kindness toward her former self, the Gwen who'd flown to St. Raphael, innocent as a sparrow. She had been ill equipped for love. Nothing in her life had prepared her for it. It pained her, now, to recall those first months on the 2STE: the frantic way she'd adored Rico, her creeping doubt and fear. She was a grown woman, yet she'd loved him desperately, as a young girl would. Her first love: two bodies conjoined, sharing a heart. Now Rico is her husband, and she loves him differently. She maintains a heart of her own.

She's so little. She needs time to catch up.

Finally, finally, Gwen had caught up.

FORGIVING SCOTT took longer. Pride wouldn't let her hear his apologies. His letters she sent back unopened. She refused to answer the phone when he called. Finally, in desperation, he had sent a telegram:

I SUCK. I HOPE YOU FORGIVE ME.
I LOVE YOU. SCOTTY. P.S. DON'T BLAME MOM.

In the end his Scottness had melted her. *You do suck*, she wrote in an e-mail. *You also bite. I love you too.*

She ignored the telegram's last line.

Gwen had learned that forgiveness was elastic. Forgiving Rico, and later Scott, had been a stretch. But never in this life could she forgive Paulette. The very thought of her mother nearly snapped the band.

For months, a year, she was sick with rage. Mysteriously, it was marriage that cured her: saying the vows had unblocked a drain, and in that moment her anger seeped away. Now her mother is with her always, a curious development. Years ago, after Mamie died, Gwen had thought of her grandmother constantly, as she hadn't when Mamie was alive. And now that Paulette is lost to her, Gwen remembers her mother with great tenderness. It is perhaps a feature of Gwen's condition, or perhaps her own personal strangeness, that she finds it much, much easier to love a person who is dead.

She no longer wonders what is normal, whether she feels correctly. It is impossible to say. Her whole life she's known that her condition is untreatable. Now she understands that it *requires* no treatment. The difference is vast; you could fit a whole life in the gulf between. And so she has.

FOR A long time, then, her life seemed finished—not ended but polished and sealed, like a piece of furniture, as though it had achieved its final form. The hot summer, slow and quiet. In September, on Gwen's birthday, she and Rico celebrated their second wedding anniversary. That night Hurricane Cleo swept across the Caribbean, battering St. Lucia. Gwen and Rico boarded the shop windows. This time at least, St. Raphael was spared.

A week later she was sitting behind the counter, poring over *Smithsonian* magazine, when Gabriel rushed into the shop.

"Turn on the radio!" he cried. "Some crazy shit happening in New York."

The radio was tuned to a local reggae station. *Stir it up. Little darling, stir it up.* Gwen turned the dial. Static. More reggae. More static.

"This fucking island, man," Gabriel fumed. "It's like we living on the moon."

"What happened?" said Gwen.

"A plane flew into a building."

"That's all?" New York seemed as distant as China, or Pluto, or heaven. Still she locked the store and followed Gabriel across town. At the Ambrosia Café a crowd had gathered around the television. Gwen stared. The gaping hole in the tower, the rising cloud of smoke.

Billy, she thought.

The last time she'd visited, she took a cab directly to his office. Together they'd strolled across the Brooklyn Bridge and back. A chilly spring evening, the sun setting early. In the towers every window was lit, a thousand panes of fluorescent light.

All day long she tried to phone him, cursing the recorded voice— *All circuits are busy. Please try again later*—that foiled her attempts. And that night, gripped with panic, she did what she'd sworn not to. She dialed her mother's house in Concord. The number floated like a buoy to the surface of her memory, the first telephone number she had ever learned.

A deep voice answered the phone.

Daddy?

A tide of feeling hit her, a tropical storm.

Billy's here, he said. *They got out of the city. It took them all day, but they got out.*

And she was passed from brother to brother; to Ian and Sabrina and Srikanth; then to a refugee she didn't know, Scott's girlfriend Jane. Was passed, finally, to her mother. And here Gwen lay flat on the deck, her home rocking beneath her, and stared up at the glittering sky.

They talked a long while. Gwen thought about the signal that made this possible, that bounced her voice into space and down to the house in Concord, mighty and infinitely small.

author's note

For various kinds of help and support, I am grateful to:
The MacDowell Colony, the Ucross Foundation, the Eastern Frontier Society, the Bogliasco Foundation, and the Hawthornden International Retreat for Writers

Dr. Elizabeth McCauley and Dr. John Brauman

Karen Reed

Dan Pope and Thomas O'Malley

Claire Wachtel, Dorian Karchmar, Jonathan Burnham, and Michael Morrison

Dr. Michael Cardone